Commendations

for

The Reason of Fools

Thank you for the honor, the privilege, and the pleasure of reading The Reason of Fools. I enjoyed it on several levels. The title struck me first. I felt it was sort of "no nonsense," seemingly meaningful, and not gimmicky. It gave me no clue as to the subject matter, and I was so pleasantly surprised that it encompasses an era in my life that gave me some familiarity with the times and places of many of the chapters in your book–a really sobering but satisfying feeling.

I found myself constantly comparing where I was on the dates of your chapters. Near the middle of the book, I found that I had flown on at least a few of the missions on the dates referenced. I was a combat fighter pilot, flying P-51 Mustangs with the 99th Fighter Squadron, 332nd Fighter Group, known as the Red Tails and as the Tuskegee Airmen.

It is apparent that you did a huge amount of research, and your organizational skills are superb. I was more than surprised to note the town of Erding, Germany mentioned. Erding is not a well-known town, but it was the town where I was shot down by antiaircraft fire while strafing on April 15, 1945. I was a guest in Erding's jail and I was a prisoner at Stalag VIIA in Mooseburg until liberated by General Patton's 14th Armored Division.

You do your craft well, and I enjoyed the book immensely. It was captivating reading and insightful writing on the vagaries of the vicissitudes of life.

Thurston L. Gaines, Jr., M.D., FACS, Tuskegee Airman (Murrieta, CA)

∞ ∞ ∞ ∞ ∞ ∞ ∞ ∞

A must read for those who love history, romance, and an unlikely outcome all based upon a real story.

Roger Ogden, Former President & Managing Director, NBC Europe
Former President & CEO, Gannett Broadcasting

∞ ∞ ∞ ∞ ∞ ∞ ∞ ∞

This book presents characters who are alive. It is suffused with emotion. The capacity for presenting human beings who sound so real is not so frequent.

Pierre Ferrand, Refugee from Nazi Germany; International Banker
Author, *A Question of Allegiance*; Book Reviewer (Association for
Psychological Approach by Isabel Myers of Myers-Briggs)

∞ ∞ ∞ ∞ ∞ ∞ ∞ ∞

This is one of the best things I've ever read. Dodie is incredibly talented and thoughtful and real.

Duane Davis, Professor Emeritus of Philosophy and Religion
Author, *Light in Dark Places* (Jasper, GA)

∞ ∞ ∞ ∞ ∞ ∞ ∞ ∞

In The Reason of Fools, author Dodie Cantrell-Bickley takes a fresh perspective on World War II that could only be told by her. The historical data that emerged from her own family story provide a compelling tale with rich characters and intriguing plot lines. The dual storylines tell of racial tension and inequality continents apart, and yet we find the similarities and parallels between the characters ripe for comparison.

Cantrell-Bickley has successfully combined two narratives, each a full-bodied historically accurate tale, and found a way to make them intersect. The Reason of Fools is the perfect selection for book club discussion. I am eagerly awaiting its sequel!

Kelly Deushane, Avid Reader/Bent Creek Book Club (Alpharetta, GA)

∞ ∞ ∞ ∞ ∞ ∞ ∞

The Reason of Fools is terrific! I was enthralled as the stories of Lilo and Bud developed. I loved the parallelism and the flashbacks within certain narratives. The drama that built as the two characters slowly made their way to a meeting was gripping.

Your imagery and use of language are outstanding. I've been to Dachau—in 1969 February in the cold and snow, and it has always haunted me. Your description of the U.S. troops entering the camp is very moving.

This is really a remarkable story.

David Fleming, Former Senior Legal Counsel, Gannett Co., Inc.

The Reason of Fools

The Reason of Fools

A Novel Based on a True Story

by

Dodie Cantrell-Bickley

Regeneration Writers Press

Macon, Georgia

2012

Published in 2012 by
Regeneration Writers Press, LLC
1191 Adams Street
Macon, GA 31201-1507

www.regenerationpress.com
editor@regenerationpress.com

ISBN 978-0-9843747-5-5   0-9843747-5-5

Dodie Cantrell-Bickley, Author
Margaret Eskew, Publishing Editor
Jerome Gratigny, Technical Editor
Kelly Jones, Design Editor
Order *The Reason of Fools*
from
www.regenerationpress.com
or
www.amazon.com
or
Regeneration Writers Press, LLC
1191 Adams Street
Macon, GA 31201-1507

DEDICATION

The Reason of Fools
is dedicated
to the two people
who above all others
made this work possible:

My Mother,
Liselotte R. Cantrell,
who inspired this book,

&

My Husband,
Randy Bickley,
who refused to let her story
die with her.

ACKNOWLEDGMENTS

When I first began my research for this novel, I had no idea that's what I was doing. I was either on a quest to satisfy my curiosity about my mother or helping a reporter research an idea for a news story. Once I learned the information or passed it along, I had no reason to keep my notes. As a result, while I would love to share the name of every person who contributed to this work over the past twenty-five years, that's not possible. Instead, I have to settle for thanking the numerous African American WW II veterans–from both the Army and, what was in the 1940s, the Army Air Corps, as well as a Russian tanker–all of whom took the time to share their stories with me. Studying the works included in the selected bibliography helped me understand and put into context what I had learned from talking with the men whose sacrifices forever changed their lives–and ours. I owe these veterans and authors my deepest thanks.

I thank the National Archives, Washington, D.C. for permission to use the following photographs on the cover of *The Reason of Fools:*

Front Cover Photo: National Archives, "Pictures of African Americans during World War II," Lt. Gen. George S. Patton, U.S. Third Army commander, pins the Silver Star on Private Ernest A. Jenkins of New York City for his conspicuous gallantry in the liberation of Chateaudun, France. October 13, 1944. 208-FS-3489-2. (African_americans_ wwii_017.jpg)

Back Cover Photo: National Archives, "Easter morning, T/5 William E. Thomas ... and Pfc. Joseph Jackson ... will roll specially prepared eggs on Hitler's lawn." March 10, 1945. 1st Lt. John D. Moore. 111-SC-202330. (african_americans_wwii_021.jpg)

I would also like to express my profound gratitude to the people listed below who played the most important roles in bringing this book to life.

To my husband **Randy Bickley** who doesn't say much–but like the old E. F. Hutton commercials, when Randy speaks, I listen. Okay, maybe only when he said, "Write your book–I don't want you worrying about anything else." "Thank you" doesn't begin to cover it.

To my daughter **Kristina**, whose extraordinary bond with her grandmother lives on–as I see my mother live on in her.

To my bonus daughter **Hope**, who knew just what to say about the earlier drafts of this book and how to say it.

To my brother **Mike Cantrell**, who may think he didn't rate a character name in the book. Mike, it is only because you are too much of a character in your own right. Don't go all cry-baby on me when I tell you how much I appreciate your belief in this novel. You invested your time, your considerable wit and intellect, and your military expertise in pointing out every single flaw you found in this book. Thought you'd find more of them, didn't you? Ha, ha!

To my brother **Bud Cantrell**, who I hope recognizes a bit of himself in the book. It all started when you punched William for hurting the turtle. Before you read a word, you told me how great it was. Thank you for your faith in me, Buddy.

To **Laura Moore**, who understands that it is a compliment for me to give her a dishtowel monogrammed with the mantra of her life: "Here in the South we don't hide crazy. We parade it on the porch and give it a cocktail." Without your brand of crazy, Laura, this novel would never have made it to press. Cheers to you!

To **Joe Duraes**, one of the first people to read the early manuscript. Joe called me from a subway train in New York to tell me he loved it and was laughing his *** off. At that time I'd never met Joe. For a Georgia girl, getting a call from a publicist who worked for an NYC publishing company was a big deal. Thanks for believing from the start, Joe.

To **Gisela Böhle Deason**, my mother's best friend and, after Mom died, one of mine. When I found my mother's hidden love letters, it was Gisela who found a translator and then spent every Saturday morning with me for months working with her. Gisela, thank you for crying with me when those letters brought me to tears, and for inspiring laughter in me with your stories about my mom.

To **Angela Taylor**, a woman who has her own compelling story about her escape from the Russians during World War II. For so many, many Saturdays she welcomed me and Gisela into her home, plied us with fresh coffee, and then pored over the faded love letters to bring them to life for me. She would accept no monetary payment. Angela, you have my undying gratitude.

To **Dr. Thurston Gaines**, a WW II aviator in the squadron known as the Tuskegee Airmen. Dr. Gaines wrote me a lovely letter after reading the first draft of this book. I cannot express how honored I am that a true American hero who lived through the challenges described in this novel told me the book was authentic and asked if he could pass it on to others. Dr. Gaines, it would be my privilege to provide as many copies as you would like for that purpose.

To **Theresa Collington**, the Empress of Online, who after reading the book said she was going to commit all of her magical powers to "Bringin' on the Buzz" about *The Reason of Fools*. Theresa, I know your magic is old-fashioned hard work but with your crown, key words, and fairy dust you do make it look so magical. I am deeply grateful.

I owe special thanks to **Erith Collinsworth**, who gets the first copy of *The Reason of Fools*. Erith, you know why, and I promise you'll get the first copy of the sequel, too.

To **Jerome Gratigny** who understood the vision for the cover . . . and wouldn't stop until it was fully achieved.

There are so many others who listened to me–who pushed me, but most of all who believed in *The Reason of Fools*. It's very difficult not to name each of you, but there is one person without whom this book would never have come to fruition. **Dr. Margaret Eskew** called me out of the blue one hot day in Jacksonville. She had spent her weekend reading my book. Before I knew it, I had a publisher and not just any publisher–finally one who didn't demand that I sacrifice one story line for the other. What do you think are the odds of finding a publisher who did her doctoral work on Hitler, speaks fluent German, and spent most of her academic career teaching at Historically Black Colleges and Universities? I'm thinking–meant to be.

--Dodie Cantrell-Bickley

"Prejudice is the reason of fools." --Voltaire

FOREWORD

During the process of writing this book, I would occasionally attempt to explain its contents to people. They would invariably ask, "Oh, so it's a story about your mother's life?" No, this is not solely the story of my mother's life. Yes, it is based on true stories of her life and her coming of age in Germany during the Nazi terror. This book is the product of the very little my mother revealed about her life, the stories her mother shared with me, nearly thirty years of research, and a hidden cache of letters to my mother from two World War II German soldiers. I found the letters only after my mother's death in 2006. Translations of excerpts from them are included in this novel.

There is much, however, that I could not learn–most of it because there were no witnesses to events that had to be hidden, or those involved would have faced severe consequences. Ultimately, this book is the result of my search to find out who my mother really was and why she seemed so different from the mothers of my friends.

In this book you will also learn about a real-life World War II unit called the 761st Black Panthers, the first African American tank battalion. While my imagination added a few characters and conversations to the battalion's experiences, the names of their leaders, the words of General Patton to these troops upon their arrival in Europe, and the stories of several of the battalion's true heroes, including a soldier named Ruben Rivers and world-renowned baseball player Jackie Robinson, are authentic.

I have done my best to make certain that the information in this novel is as accurate as possible. Some names, details,

15

and physical descriptions were changed to protect the privacy and sensitivity of those intimately involved and their families, but the basic narrative is true. The reality is that my studies coupled with my imagination have had to fill in the blanks. The characters, other than those expressly acknowledged, are fictional. Their names were selected randomly and their resemblance to real persons, living or dead, is purely coincidental.

I believe that memorializing and passing on the individual stories of our shared human history are vital to the continued evolution of a civilized world. I hope that some of what I learned and have passed on to you in this novel will result in your having a few of those "Wow, I didn't know that!" moments. As an avid reader myself, though, my most fervent hope is that you enjoy *The Reason of Fools*.

INTRODUCTION

Wet, half-frozen, miserable, and stinking, Bud set off to
the front of the line. The first hail of machine-gun fire erupted so
quickly he barely had time to flag down his men and dive into
a ditch beside the road. C.T. fired the first strike from his tank
against the machine-gun nest hidden somewhere beyond the
low-hanging gray snow clouds, but not before another barrage
blew a hole in the muck that passed for a road, less than twenty
feet from Bud. With his mouth open, Bud half walked, half
ran, trying not to inhale the stench of the bombed and broken
sewer mains. The vile smell mingled with the semi-sweet odor
of putrefaction from the dead cows and horses dotting the land,
their bloating bodies reeking of rot.

Bud spotted two of his men lying in a freezing mud-filled
ditch, their rifles aimed at the unseen enemy. For a split second
he savored the pride he felt as he noted the calm and deliberate
way both soldiers aimed at the hill. The two were the youngest
men in Bud's unit. Men? They were boys. Even though Willie
Jefferson and Jedediah Leonard had claimed to be eighteen, Bud
had his doubts. He didn't doubt their devotion to him though, or
to their country.

"Leonard! Jefferson! Come over here and man the
big gun. I'll send some help back to you." The boys stood,
shouldered their weapons, and after glancing up the road, bent
low and ran to obey Bud's command. A hail of bullets, so close
they ricocheted splinters of icy mud into the soldiers' faces,
raced ahead of the pair. Just as Leonard sprinted to safety behind
the howitzer, Bud loosed a silent scream as he saw Jefferson's
frightened but determined face transform into a grotesque
blossom of crimson gore. The boy's knees buckled as he threw
up his hands to where his face had been just seconds before. In
one motion his body pitched forward into a shallow grave of
muddy tank tracks.

17

The dog tags–Bud had to get Jefferson's dog tags. The boy had no face. Who would recognize him in death? Bud slumped to a low crouch and began running toward Jefferson when a torch of heat seared his shoulder driving him into the mud. As the pain radiated down his right arm, Bud pushed at the ground with his left to propel himself up. Another fiery explosion burst in his right thigh. The useless limb crumpled beneath him, throwing him backwards again into the mucky road.

The hatch of the tank burst open. As C.T. sprang down, Bud yelled, "Back in the tank, C.T.!" His voice sounded as if it were miles away. C.T. materialized by his side, "Ah, man! Ah shit, man! You all shot up. Goddamn Krauts! Goddamn bastards! You bettah hang on, Bud. Don't you go die on me. You hear me, man? I sho' wouldn' be here in dis shithole if yo' white ass wadn' runnin' 'roun' here!"

C.T.'s words washed over Bud, bringing a smile to his face. This was vintage C.T. He sounded just like he had a lifetime ago in Birmingham, Alabama, when they had both been just seven years old. The familiar voice from his childhood wrapped around him and soothed Bud's pain.

§ § § § § §

Blood streaked Liselotte's pale hair and stained her gray cotton dress. A mix of blood and tears rimmed her red eyes and crusted her chapped lips. Shocked at her daughter's appearance, Anna reached out to her, but Liselotte rushed mindlessly past her to pick up the telephone.

"Sepp's number–I need it now, Mama," she commanded coldly. Her stony voice added to Anna's distress as a quick sting of familiar resentment flared in her. Just like her father, Anna thought sadly–unfeeling and imperious, no matter what the circumstances. Anna had little time to nurse her hurt before her daughter's sharp words pierced her pain.

"Hurry, Mama. Papa's life depends on it," Liselotte croaked tersely.

Anna silently surrendered the number. "I've already talked with Sepp. He –"

"You've talked with him?" Liselotte's head whipped around toward her mother and then back to the phone. "Onkel Sepp? It's Lilo. They've taken Papa to the *Türkenkaserne*!"

The Türkenkaserne! Anna knew, as everyone in Munich did, that the dungeon-like cells of the prison were a torture stop on the way to Dachau. Her heart leapt into her instantly dry throat as she leaned in to hear her daughter talking softly with her godfather, General Sepp Dietrich. "Thank you, Onkel Sepp. I will leave in a few minutes."

As Liselotte hung up the phone, Anna launched herself toward her daughter. "Liselotte, you can't go anywhere! Look at you," she cried. "What happened? I am so afraid," her panicked voice weakly fluttered out the words. "I will go to the *Kaserne*– not you. I can–"

Her daughter's disdainful laugh cut off her words. "You?" Anna shivered at the bold disrespect in her daughter's tone. Tears of worry she'd held back ran down her cheeks as her trembling hands smoothed the clean lines of her lavender silk sheath.

Rolling her eyes impatiently, Liselotte declared, "Mama, we have no time for your dramatics. I'm going to get cleaned up. Then I am going to the Türkenkaserne–alone. You would be worse than useless there," she sighed as she turned away from Anna and trudged across the enormous black-and-white-checkered foyer toward the circular marble staircase.

A searing flash of temper burned away Anna's pain. "How dare you!" she screamed at her daughter's retreating back. Her rage powered her tiny purple pumps across the floor. She grabbed her daughter's elbow and spun her to a stop. Her hands

19

shook as she clenched Liselotte's upper arms in her dainty white-knuckled hands. She looked up to face her child's hard stare.

"You are my daughter and you will not talk to me that way. Do you understand?" Her voice trembled with emotion as she shook her daughter forcefully. "You have no right to tell me what to do. I don't know what your father has dragged you into, but he's responsible for being there and he has no right to jeopardize us by asking for your help."

"He didn't drag me into anything." Liselotte jerked her arms away from her mother's grasp, scathingly reproving her, "Your concern right now should be for him–not for us."

Anna shot back, "And I should think that you would realize by now that his involvement with these Jewish actresses–"

The force of her daughter's slap across her face sounded like a gunshot in the cavernous foyer. Its echo chased Liselotte as she sped up the stairs.

1918 - 1938

1918-1938

DATELINE: EUROPE

1918   **Armistice Day – "The Eleventh Hour of the Eleventh Day of the Eleventh Month"**

The signing of the armistice ends the fighting in World War I between the Allies and the Germans on the Western Front. It would take another year to hammer out an official peace agreement.

1919   **Treaty of Versailles Formally Ends World War I**

Nearly 20 million dead. The Entente military (including Great Britain, France and the United States) lose six million, and the Central military (Germany and its allies) lose four million. An estimated 7–10 million civilians die.

1919   **Treaty of Versailles Forces Germany to Pay for Its Aggression**

Germany must agree to the "War Guilt Clause," accepting all responsibility for World War I. That includes the loss of a million square miles of land, payment of billions in reparations to other nations, and limits on its military. Some world leaders fear these harsh terms may cause the German people to rebel in the future.

1919   **France Bestows Its Highest Medal, "The Legion of Honor," on African American Soldiers**

171 members of the 369th Infantry Regiment, known as the "Harlem Hellfighters," receive "The Legion of Honor" for their performance in fighting with the French.

1918-1938

DATELINE: EUROPE

1923   **Failed Austrian Painter Attempts Takeover of German Government**

Adolf Hitler is arrested for treason and begins to write *Mein Kampf* while in prison.

1929   **French Begin Plans for Maginot Line**

Despite limitations on the German military, French government designs defensive network to protect France from German aggression.

1929   **Publication of Classic Novel, *All Quiet on the Western Front***

German author Erich Maria Remarque, a WWI veteran, publishes the book for those who escaped death in WWI, but whose lives were forever "destroyed by the war."

1933   **Adolf Hitler Elected Chancellor of Germany**

Hitler abolishes the German War Ministry and gives himself control of the military.

1936   **African American Athlete Jesse Owens Wins Four Olympic Gold Medals in Munich**

While Hitler looks on, African American Olympic runner Jesse Owens beats German athletes.

1938   **Evian Conference on Refugees Convenes in France**

The United States will accept only 27,370 Jewish refugees. European Jews are in trouble.

1918-1938

DATELINE: THE UNITED STATES

1920s   **Newly Reformed Ku Klux Klan
                  Emerges in American South**

The second KKK preaches "100% Americanism."
Membership swells to 6 million by 1925.
Scandals plummet membership to 30,000 by
1929.

1929   **American Wall Street Crash**

The New York stock market crash ushers in
the decade-long Great Depression in October,
affecting every industrialized country in the
world.

1938   ***Time* Selects Hitler as "Man of the Year"**

The cover of the magazine shows the German
Chancellor playing an organ with the description,
"From an unholy organist, a hymn of hate."

1938   **United States' First Lady Eleanor
                  Roosevelt Challenges Segregation**

Mrs. Roosevelt, already a member of the NAACP,
attends the founding meeting of the Southern
Conference on Human Welfare in Birmingham,
Alabama and refuses to be seated in the
segregated section of the auditorium.

1938   **African American Boxer Joe Louis
                  Defeats German Max Schmeling**

Asked about his strategy against the German
boxer who had defeated him once, Joe Louis
responds, "I plan to come out fighting." Louis
is declared the winner and World Heavyweight
champion by a technical knockout only two
minutes and four seconds into the first round.

CHAPTER ONE

Birmingham, Alabama: 1929

Bud couldn't believe he'd been sentenced to the woodpile again. Why did Ol' Squiggs have to come around the corner just as he'd rolled the first smoke to share with Pee Wee? The teacher's thinning eyebrows shot upwards, wrinkling his bald, pointed scalp as he swooped down and simultaneously nabbed Bud's smoke and Pee Wee's ear. He sent Pee Wee off with a smack on his head and Bud out to the woodpile behind the school. Ol' Squiggs had made it clear that Bud had better chop wood until he returned to deliver Bud to his father.

For what seemed like a solid hour, Bud chopped, distressed about what his father would say about this latest escapade. Pee Wee didn't have to chop wood–Ol' Squiggs probably wouldn't even tell Pee Wee's parents what had happened. They all knew that Bud was the ringleader.

Maybe Dad would be at the church when Ol' Squiggs took him home. Bud's mom would just whip Bud real fast with a hickory switch–but that was wishful thinking. Bud's dad would be at home working on some sermon for the church he pastored. When Dad was around, Mom had him take care of the discipline.

A big drop of sweat rolled off Bud's forehead. He licked the wet smear as it trickled past the corner of his lips, momentarily enjoying the tart, salty sting on his tongue.

Bud didn't mind his mother's whippings–they happened just about every time he turned around anyway. But when Bud's dad heard about his son's latest "sin," he was gonna hurt. Bud could stand a lot, but he always had a hard time when his father's light blue eyes, so like Bud's own, gazed down at him. Then, still staring, his father would let out a sigh signaling that Bud had just done the biggest, damnedest, most disappointing thing in the God Almighty. You'd think that with all those sinners to save at his church, Dad could save the hurt looks for them. No, he knew how to get to Bud. Afterwards, Bud would try real hard for a long time to be good. It was just so hard. The sun was always shinin' just right for swimmin' when it was time for English class. The fish were always bitin' best when it was time for arithmetic.

This time he'd stolen—really only borrowed—the tobacco that old man Benson had brought his dad. Bud didn't intend on usin' all of it. He just wanted to try one little smoke with Pee Wee, but Ol' Squiggs had ended that adventure real quick.

Wait! No, he hadn't.

Bud let the heavy ax slip from his sweaty blistered palms and took a quick look around. The woodpile squatted at the edge of a green thicket, just barely out of sight of the schoolhouse. Squinting, he focused on the squat white wooden building—no sign of Ol' Squiggs. Even if the teacher was peering out of his window, there wasn't a chance in hell that Squiggs could see him—even with those bottle-thick glasses of his. Besides, Bud was an experienced sneak.

Just for safety Bud slowly eased down on the side of the woodpile facing the scrubby stand of pines with his back toward the schoolhouse. He picked his pockets, drawing out a wad of crumpled cigarette papers along with a mixture of dried tobacco and pocket lint. Just like he'd watched old man Benson do, Bud meticulously patted the filthy concoction onto the paper with his stubby, nail-bitten, seven-year-old fingers. Most of the tobacco slid from the thin paper to the ground before Bud managed to lick the misshapen tube. Before sliding the smoke into his mouth, he patted the seam gently. "Not bad, if I do say so myself," he declared proudly.

Bud dug into another pocket to retrieve a pilfered box of matches. Leaning back against the woodpile, he kicked his grimy bare feet out in front of him and struck a match to light his cigarette. He nearly dropped the precious smoke when the fire touched the paper and torched up the crinkled end of the cigarette like a firecracker.

26

But Bud kept his calm and with an air of satisfaction took a deep, grown-up draw from the cigarette–and immediately fell into a coughing fit. Gasping for air, he felt his face and even his ears heat up with the effort of replacing the toxic smoke in his lungs with fresh air. His eyes bulged and then teared as he struggled to breathe. Man, he was gonna choke to death right there in the woodpile. What a way to go.

Just when Bud thought it was all over for him, a heavy thump on his back forced a wrenching cough, a hard swallow, and gratefully–a deep gulp of fresh air into his tortured lungs. He turned to thank his savior, only to see ugly Ol' Squiggs rearing up above him. Jeepers creepers! As Ol' Squiggs reached down and grabbed him by the ear to take him to his father, Bud knew this was it. He'd never live to see his eighth birthday now.

§ § § § § § §

"Son, I'm afraid you've really done it this time. You are expelled from school–expelled, Bud, expelled!" Bud's father couldn't let go of his litany.

Bud sat stiffly on the hard hickory chair in front of the fireplace, his scarred, bug-bitten legs dangling in the air, dirty toes lightly raking the worn pine floor beneath them. His father paced back and forth in front of him, talking first to Bud, then to himself.

This was worse than Bud had ever dreamed. Dad was so upset he was gonna be late for the church service that night if he didn't stop talkin' and pacin' and git goin'. Bud felt kinda bad about that. His dad was supposed to be the guest preacher tonight over at the New Mission African Methodist Church in Baytown. He'd been real proud and excited to git the invite. New Mission folks had never had a white preacher over. Come to think of it, there'd never been a white preacher to set foot in any Negro church in these parts.

"Bud, are you listening to me?" his dad's unusually angry

tone interrupted Bud's musings.

"Yes, sir," Bud quickly replied. He might be lyin', but he was tryin' to pay attention, and that counted for somethin'. Scarlet streaks burned across his father's normally pale face, highlighting the wide cheekbones. His clear azure eyes burned with a frozen blue flame, a look Bud had witnessed only once before when one of Dad's church folks had called a colored person a "nigger."

An elderly colored man had mistakenly opened the church door in the middle of the service, wandering unawares into his dad's church. The minute the ol' geezer had peered into the tiny sanctuary, his eyes got as big as saucers, and he started shakin'.

Ol' Man Jeffers had whipped his head around and shouted, "Git outta here, Nigger!"

The poor ol' man just froze. Bud's normally unassuming father had slammed his fist down on the pulpit. It sounded like all thunder crackin' down from the heavens. The ol' colored man was still standin' there, his slight body rigid with fear inside his too-large shiny black Sunday suit.

Bud's six-foot-six father stepped out from behind the pulpit and strode down the faded blue carpet up to the ol' man. Towering over the shrunken fellow, Reverend Leverett smiled down at him and offered his black robe-clad arm.

Gratitude leapt from the poor man's bulging eyes as his wrinkled brown hand clasped the Reverend's arm. The whisper of the old man's shuffling feet on the carpet was the only sound in the church as Bud's father led him down the aisle and deposited him next to his wife and Bud.

The clattering of his father's shoes on the uncarpeted steps leading to the altar shattered the thick quiet of the sanctuary. As he turned to face the congregation, every eye was cast down, seemingly mesmerized by the hymnals in their laps—

28

except Bud's.

Bud was the first to see old man Jeffers jump up from his seat. Jeffers' face was red and swollen, and he looked like he was having a hard time swallowing. He reached down, jerked his wife up, and yelled, "We ain't stayin' in this nigger-lovin' church!"

Bud's dad had raised his fist and bellowed, "Jeffers, this is a lovin' church, period. You leave now, and I think there'll be no church for you. You'll likely find a building with a cross where you'll be welcome, and Christ will love you in spite of yourself. But make no mistake—you are risking eternal damnation!"

Bud's dad's voice softened as he gravely intoned, "Anyone here care to follow Mr. and Mrs. Jeffers on their high and mighty road to Hell?"

Boy, this was one excitin' church service! Bud reckoned his mom was gittin' pretty worked up, too. She was squeezin' her hands together so hard that her knuckles had turned white, and her lips were movin' real fast. Bud figured she was prayin' up a storm—prayin' the congregation wouldn't decide to string up Bud's dad right then and there.

No one moved a muscle. Dad gave the high sign to the choir to begin the invitation hymn, "Onward, Christian Soldiers"–Bud's favorite. The soldier part of the song seemed more glorious than ever to Bud as he shouted the words with all his heart, if little tune. Bud wasn't sure if he was singin' louder that mornin', or it just seemed that way since his mom on his left and their uninvited guest to his right were both just mouthin' the words. Bud knew he wasn't much of a singer, but what the heck–his normally borin', quiet dad was some kinda soldier this mornin'. By God, Bud was gonna sing.

After church, everyone hightailed it outta there, includin' the little old colored man who'd started it all. Mama said she didn't know to this day why they ever let daddy stay. Six months later, the Leveretts were still in Birmingham.

"Boyd! Why in the name of heaven are you standing there lecturing that boy? He's just sitting there daydreaming, not paying a bit of attention to you. What you need to do is send him out there to pick out a nice long hickory switch. You swat him with that about a dozen times, and he'll hear you."

Bud's unfocused eyes had missed his mother's march into the kitchen. Although her bright red hair was pulled back into a bun at the nape of her neck, he could have sworn that the loose hairs around her face were cracklin' like live copper wires. Was she ever mad. Whooey! For a second Bud was almost grateful that his dad had been at the house when Ol' Squiggs dragged him home. Mama's whippins always burned the fire out of his behind, but when she quit hittin', he quit hurtin'. His father's sad words and grievin' eyes would sting Bud for weeks.

Boyd Leverett smiled calmly at his firecracker wife, "I know, Sweetheart. But you know how I feel about whipping him. Bud's growing up, and I trust him to do right if I just talk to him about it."

Maureen Leverett fastened her inscrutable, deep brown eyes on her son. "Do you hear that, Boyd Theodore Leverett, Junior?"

Bud winced at the words. His mother knew how much he hated to be called by his full name. When she said it, it always sounded like one long word, but Bud's ears always picked out the hated "Theodore."

"You certainly had better appreciate your father's trust. Lord knows, I can't for the life of me see how you deserve it."

"Ma," Bud jumped up from his chair, "I know I done wrong, but you oughtn' be so mad about it. You didn' want Dad to go to New Mission tonight. Now he cain't go on accounta I made him late," he smiled proudly, figurin' how he might avoid

30

the 'talkin' to' from his dad and a beatin' from his mom to boot.

He knew how worried his mom was about his dad goin' to Baytown. He'd heard her tell him that preachin' at the Negro church was gonna bring trouble down on all of them.

Bud's father slapped his hand to his forehead, "For pity's sake. I nearly forgot all about that." He placed one hand gently on Bud's shoulder and lifted the boy's dirty chin with the other. "Look at me, Son."

Bud solemnly looked up at his father.

"I've got to go now, Bud. While I'm out I want you to think about your punishment. It's going to be a long summer, Son." Bud's father smiled at his wife's exasperated huff and leaned over Bud's head to give her a quick kiss on the cheek. He ruffled Bud's jet-black hair before picking up his worn black-leather Bible from the top of the ancient pine desk in the kitchen.

"Maureen, I shouldn't be out too late. What time do you think you'll be back from your Temperance Society meeting?"

Maureen Leverett whipped off her red-and-white-checkered apron and hung it on the rusting iron hook next to the chipped white enamel kitchen sink. "I'm leaving now. If Sue Ellen Smith doesn't get too riled up, I should be home by nine."

Bud's father paused to hold the door open for his wife. As she stopped to smooth back her hair, he warned Bud: "Remember what I said, Boy. Behave while we're out and think about your punishment."

The door latch clicked quietly in place as Bud's parents left.

Think about his punishment? He'd rather think about what kinda trouble Ma had said they were gonna get into since she couldn' talk his dad outta goin' to New Mission. There must be somethin' mighty interestin' over there for Ma to get so

31

worked up about it. Bud wished he could go, too.

The vacuum of silence in the small parsonage mocked his gloom as a germ of an idea sprouted in his brain. He was already in big trouble. No sense in him spendin' these last free hours like a prisoner awaitin' execution. Nope, Bud had a plan.

§ § § § § §

Bud shoved the can of paint and a brush at Pee Wee. "Just take this black paint and brush it on my face. Ouch! Not in my eyes, Pee Wee. You gonna blind me!"

"I don't know why we gotta paint ourselves black anyway," Pee Wee complained as he daubed the paint onto Bud's cheeks. "Why can't we just sneak in and hide behind the pews or somethin' while we listen to your dad?"

"For cryin' out loud, Pee Wee. Sometimes you act dumber 'an a sacka taters. We're sneakin' in, but we gotta be in disguise. Two white boys cain't jus' sneak into a Negro church. Our skin's gotta be black, so's no one'll notice us."

"Maybe we can just hide in these bushes and listen. There's an open window right above us. I already hear some mumblin', so I bet we could hear your dad. He gets real loud, you know," Pee Wee added earnestly.

Even in the darkness of the dense shrubbery Bud saw the fear gleam in Pee Wee's eyes. He took the brush from his friend and dipped it into the can of black paint as he tried once again to explain his plan.

"Look, Pee Wee, we ain't gonna be able to hear nothin' from out here and we sure cain't see nothin'. Quit bein' such a chicken." In his most convincing tone, Bud added, "See, once we're all painted up, we'll just blend in. We'll walk in real casual like, and no one'll even give us a secon' look."

Finally convinced, but never one to pass up a chance to

32

worry, Pee Wee responded, "Bud, you think we'll really fool 'em?"

"Pee Wee," Bud exclaimed with exasperation, "jus' be still. I gotta put some more paint on your big ears. They're shinin' like two lightnin' bugs flyin' outta both sides a your head."

Within minutes the boys parted the bushes beside the front door of the New Mission Church and stepped out into the warm moonlit night. "How do I look?" whispered Bud.

"Jus' like a real spook," Pee Wee grinned.

"Don't say that, Pee Wee. Dad says that's a real big sin. 'Sides, it'll git us caught. Real Negroes don't say words like 'spook.' Let me see the backa your head." Bud examined his friend's closely cropped blonde curls, now glued to his head with a thick, sticky layer of black paint. The boys decided that Bud's jet-black hair could pass without paint, although it was straight as a stick. "All right, Pee Wee, we look great. We'll jus' open the door, stick our hands in our pockets, and sit down in the first pew that's open."

"You hear that? That's your Dad," exclaimed Pee Wee.

"Whoa, sure is. Let's listen to him out here. He might recognize us if we interrupt him while he's preachin'." Bud pulled Pee Wee back into the protective bushes. "I mean I don't really think he would, but why take the chance? We'll go in when the singin' starts. Dad tol' me they sing a lot."

Bud could hear his father's deep bass voice booming from the open window above them. Man, oh man. He sure was goin' to town tonight, and the Negroes sure seemed to like him. Every now and then Bud would hear some folks shoutin' "Amen, brother!" They'd jus' yell it out. Sure wasn't anything like the services Dad preached in the white church.

As they sat in the dirt beneath the enormous bright green

gardenia bushes blooming on either side of the unstained wood doors of the church, the warm, humid, late spring air brought out the heady smell of the flowers, reminding Bud that summer was only a few weeks away. He hoped his dad wouldn't try to get Ol' Squiggs to let him back in school. Seems like gittin' expelled from school would give him an early jump on summertime fun— if his punishment didn't ruin it all for him.

Pee Wee interrupted his dark ruminations. "Hey, Bud. They startin' to sing. Man, they sure is loud," whispered an excited Pee Wee.

"Yeah, and they clappin', too. This ain't no church service. This here's a party!" exclaimed Bud.

"No wonder your dad wouldn't miss it," agreed Pee Wee.

"Well, we gonna miss it, if we don't git in there. C'mon." Bud pushed his friend out from under the bushes and up the warped wooden steps of the church. He pulled on one of the rusted doorknobs and shoved Pee Wee in first.

The handclapping and hallelujahs were deafening inside the old building. No wonder—on both sides of the single center aisle covered in a long threadbare red carpet runner, every pew was packed. It sure wasn't as fancy as their church, Bud observed, taking in the worn wooden pews and the splintered rafters above the enormous white cross that loomed behind a choir of rocking, red satin-robed singers.

Bud spotted his dad sitting in one of the simple, unadorned straight-backed wooden chairs placed to the left and right of the pulpit. His dad's eyes were closed, and he was smiling. Bud was glad his father could enjoy himself. He was gladder still that his eyes were closed—just on the off chance his dad might recognize him. Naw, Bud dismissed the thought. He and Pee Wee had worked way too hard on their paint jobs for anyone to be able to tell they weren't real live Negroes.

Pee Wee poked Bud between his skinny ribs and pointed

to a pew about a third of the way down on the right side of the church. There were only a few people in it, including a large woman in a brilliant flowered dress sitting closest to the aisle.

Good God, thought Bud. She must weigh as much as an elephant. The woman's huge arms jiggled when she clapped her hands, even though they were wrapped in what looked like bright orange, red, and hot pink floral sausage casings. Her large frame took up three spaces on the pew as she rocked from side to side with the music. Bud marveled at how her concoction of a hat stayed perched on her head. Despite her vigorous rocking, only the two long orange and crimson feathers moved–dipping and swaying with the beat.

Bud nodded to Pee Wee to go on, but his friend didn't move. Bud was going to have to go first. He took a tentative first step, and once committed to action, picked up his pace. Before Bud made it past the three pews at the back of the church, the noise quieted a little. As he moved forward, more of the clapping and singing stopped. With about four more rows to go, Bud thought he was home free–until he heard a loud piercing shriek: "Oh, Lawd, what kinda blasphemin' is these chil'ren up to?"

The shrill cry stilled the final note and the final clap as every head in the front row turned toward the voice. Large brown eyes circled in white froze Bud where he stood, stock-still, feeling every eye on him. His dad sat there watching, looking surprised, and then confused. Bud knew the very moment his dad recognized him. It was obvious in the way he shot up from his chair, his face going dead white with the telltale patches of red slashing across his cheeks. Bud searched for a way to duck out, but a swell of people blocked the doors.

Two towering colored men grabbed Pee Wee and held him up by his elbows. His friend looked ridiculous with his bony pseudo-black legs pumping in mid-air. Wheeling around to face the front of the church, Bud saw his father storming his way.

35

There was no exit to the left–hands were already reaching out to grab him. Only the enormous, frightfully frocked woman sat impassively to his right, her huge bulk blocking his only exit. Bud thought fast. He could scramble over her, scurry under the pews, and duck out the front door of the church–not a livin' soul was guardin' that door. Everyone had pressed forward to catch him and Pee Wee.

The pews were too close to the floor for grown-ups to crawl under the pews after him. By the time they figured out what he was doin', they'd never be able to git at him. Bud launched himself into the air at the same time the large woman with the hat leaned forward to see what was going on. He tried to dive past her, but their heads collided. The fine-feathered hat sailed into the air and, to Bud's horror, a mass of lacquered curls along with it. Bud landed face first in the woman's lap. She commenced to shriek and leaned over in an effort to cover her bald head. Her enormous bosom trapped Bud, nearly smothering him. He was dead. He knew it.

His father rushed toward the tightly knit group gathered around the hysterical woman. Bud's black-streaked legs kicked madly as he tried to escape her suffocating hold, damp black paint streaking her flowered dress. Reverend Leverett reached out, grabbed Bud's right leg, and pulled. Surprised by the movement in her lap, the woman jerked upright–just long enough for Bud's father to free him. Bud hit the floor hard, knocking the breath out of him. Dazed, he rolled over on his back and came face to face with his father.

"Oh, God, don't fail me now," Bud prayed fervently and silently. The cold blue flame of his father's normally placid eyes seared him with fear, pinning him to the ground.

CHAPTER TWO

Munich, Germany: 1938

"Papa! Papa!" Liselotte shrieked as she raced down the marble steps, the heels of her red leather shoes echoing in the cathedral-ceilinged foyer.

"Liselotte!" commanded her mother sharply.

Not breaking her stride, thirteen-year-old Liselotte couldn't resist sliding halfway across the shiny floor before coming to an abrupt stop. She loved the way the slick unscarred soles of the new shoes sent her flying across the black and white tiles. If Papa had seen her do this with her flat chest thrust forward and her arms stretched out like wings, he would have applauded her, declaring fervently that she looked exactly like the champion ice skater she momentarily imagined herself to be. Her mother's reaction would be vastly different. Thankfully, her mother had charged into the foyer a split second after Liselotte had come to a full stop, her winged arms now thin flesh and bone, pressed meekly to her sides. She smiled up into her mother's coldly beautiful face, "Yes, Mama?"

Anna Burkhardt stood ramrod straight in front of her daughter. The light blonde hair braided across the crown of her head accented the perfect balance of each of her flawless features. Her clenched jaw and narrowed eyes froze the smile on Liselotte's face until she felt her cheeks would go numb.

Liselotte knew the look in those chilling eyes. She squeezed her own shut, wishing she could stop the involuntary stiffening of her face. She deliberately allowed her tense smile to thaw. If she could keep her face relaxed now, the stinging slap wouldn't hurt as much. Even though her neck was braced for the blow, the force of her mother's hand against her cheek snapped her head backwards so hard that her jaw flew open and slammed shut on her tongue. The slight metallic taste of the blood in her mouth almost soothed the painful gash. She rapidly blinked away the tears rising unbidden by the hot burning of her cheek.

"Look at what you've done to my freshly waxed floor," Anna spat icily, pointing to two long black marks on the gleaming marble. Despite the stinging pain, Liselotte almost laughed aloud. What wonderful skid marks! She had probably set a record today. Too bad her mother would have the floor spotless within the hour. She would like to have used the marks as a measure to see if she could improve her record.

The next time her mother left the house, she *would* skate across the floor again. The thought burst defiantly into Liselotte's head. She immediately tried to quell the quick fire that ignited inside her before her mother's sharp eyes detected the "Burkhardt wrinkle"–the furrow between Liselotte's thick pale eyebrows that deepened and cut toward her right eye whenever she was angry. It was a sign she could only hide by bowing her head. Thankfully her mother considered that a gesture of humility. Liselotte swallowed hard and lifted her brows, trying to smooth out the telltale crease and compose her face into a mask of shame. With her head down and her betraying eyes on her magical new red shoes, she whispered humbly, "I'm sorry, Mama."

"Stop staring at the floor like an imbecile! Look at me."

Liselotte resisted the temptation to jerk her head away as her mother clasped her jaw roughly and twisted her chin upward, probing her daughter's face for the rogue furrow and studying her eyes for the slightest hint of defiance. Liselotte stared back at her mother, looking into her eyes for what she had not seen in so long, hoping irrationally that maybe today it would be there– some sign, some flicker or trace of tenderness to tell her that her mother didn't hate her. She breathed deeply, attempting to keep the sharp hurt from sticking her in the stomach at what she again failed to find in her mother's reflectionless violet-blue eyes.

"Liselotte, are my shoes shined yet?"

Liselotte's mother quickly dropped her hand from her daughter's face at the sound of the deep voice resonating through the cavernous halls of the Burkhardt mansion. Anna bent toward her daughter and whispered harshly, "Now you'll have to explain to your Papa how your wicked behavior caused you to hurt yourself. That will teach you to behave in such an unladylike fashion," she hissed.

"What has happened to you, my Lilo? Are you all right?"

Liselotte nodded and offered him a quick smile.

The worried furrow between his brow, exactly like his daughter's, and his deep voice, so full of concern for her, made Liselotte long to tell him the truth, but Mama would really hate her if she did. And it really wasn't Mama's fault she got so angry. If Liselotte could just behave, her mother wouldn't be forced to strike her.

"I was pretending to be a famous ice skater," she explained, pointing the toe of her right shoe toward the black streaks marring the foyer floor, "and my new shoes made me slide too fast." She couldn't lie to her father, so she just told part of the story–the true parts–and omitted the details, leaving him to fill in the blanks. It was what she always did when she was hurt. She often wondered why her Papa didn't ask more questions.

"An ice skater, eh? Oh, I'll bet you were a lovely one, too," he chuckled as he kneeled down to offer her a hug. Liselotte wanted to laugh with him, but she couldn't. She didn't trust herself to make a sound for fear she would cry.

Sensing Liselotte's vulnerability, Anna broke the troubled silence. "Go get your father's shoes," she ordered before turning to her husband. "Look what a mess she has made of the floor, Georg. At least she did a proper job on your shoes, although why you insist that the child shine your shoes like a servant is beyond me," she added contentiously.

With a weary sigh, Georg Burkhardt faced his diminutive wife. At nearly six feet three, he stood head and shoulders above her. But what Anna Burkhardt lacked in height, she made up for in presence. She squared her shoulders, tilted her head back, and returned his gaze as levelly as she could. Before he could speak, she placed both hands on her hips in attack mode: "Don't give me your lecture about pride in a job well done or learning a sense of responsibility. Our daughter should not have to shine your shoes. The only thing she'll learn is how to be more unladylike." Anna tossed her head disdainfully at the child who stood somberly watching the volatile scene between her parents.

As Liselotte listened to her mother's tirade, she wondered for the thousandth time why her father stayed with her mother. Her mother was mean, and her father was wonderful. Mama was so beautiful–that was probably the reason. Even though she hated her mother at times, she did wish that she was as pretty. She slipped behind her father as her mother continued her harangue. From behind him, she could see her plain reflection in the foyer mirror. The ornate gold-trimmed oval surrounded her washed-out face with as much incongruity as a child's finger painting displayed in a costly frame.

The sounds of the argument faded as she stared at her parchment-white skin, brightened only by the swollen red bulb on the end of her nose. Liselotte did not like her eyes even though they were exactly like her mother's. They were the same unusual violet blue, but her eyes were too big for her face. She looked like the animals her father showed her at the Munich zoo, the ones that lived in the jungle and only came out at night. Her oversized eyes were coupled with her broad forehead and high, too-wide cheekbones. It made the upper part of her face look too big for the rest of it. In her mother's oval face, everything looked perfectly proportioned, unlike her own oddly heart-shaped face with its big, strangely shaped features. As she stared at her own reflection, her too-broad forehead wrinkled as she widened her already overlarge eyes. She grimaced at the protruding cheekbones that narrowed to a pointed chin. Only the fullness of her mouth kept the bottom of her face from disappearing into her neck. But even that was all wrong. Mama had thin elegant lips, while Liselotte's lips looked fat and rubbery–and were as red as her nose. An unfamiliarly sharp tone in her father's voice pulled Liselotte's attention away from further inspection of her face.

"I am tired of you badgering our child," his voice quieted as quickly as it had risen. But now the calm voice held a note of warning, "Anna, I tolerate how you treat her because I know that there are things, women's things, which she can only learn from her mother. But one more time–and I mean this," Liselotte had to strain to hear his voice, but the ominous tone was unmistakable, "another bruise, another drop of blood and–"

The incomplete sentence hung between Liselotte's parents as they glared at one another, oblivious of their daughter.

He knew. He knew! Now he would stop her. Liselotte stared at her parents, forgotten by them both.

Anna's shrill cry broke the silence as tears flowed down her face. She grasped Georg's arm. "What are you saying? Do you think I would intentionally hurt her? She's my daughter." Anna's eyes beseeched her husband's for understanding.

Liselotte saw the moment her father began to melt. Oh, it must feel wonderfully powerful to be so beautiful. A single moment ago, Liselotte had believed that her father was going to stop her mother from hurting her, but now it seemed as if Anna would once again convince Georg that Liselotte needed and deserved her punishment.

"Georg," she pleaded as she clung to her husband's arm, "we live in dangerous times. Liselotte is too bold–too incautious. She will cause trouble for herself and the rest of us if she doesn't learn to control her mouth and her actions. She is too willful–too spoiled, and you know it, Georg." Anna sounded like she was begging her husband for understanding, but Liselotte did not miss the harsh critical undertone in her mother's voice. She looked at her father. The expression on his face told her that he had heard none of it. All he could see were his wife's wet eyes imploring him for pity.

Georg gently loosened his arm from Anna's desperate grip and hugged her close to him. He stroked her cheek softly as she rested her head on his chest and wept quietly. "Anna, don't be so afraid. I will allow no harm to come to her–or to you. She's just a child. You must be gentler with her. You are a good woman, but you have such a temper."

Anna pulled away from his embrace. "I know," she acknowledged, "but look how much trouble some people are in because of their children. One wrong word, Georg, to the wrong person, and–" she broke off with a loud sniffle.

Georg looked down at his tearful wife and shook his head. He could understand her fear. Everyone in Germany was nervous these days with all the political changes and rumors of more changes to come. Since the recent *Kristallnacht*, Anna seemed to live in a near-constant state of agitation.

They had been awakened during the night by the sounds of breaking glass while on a visit to her parents in Nuremberg. On that November 9th many of the synagogues in Germany had been vandalized or destroyed during the night, the window fronts of shops owned by Jews smashed, and some Jews had even been beaten to death in the streets. It had been a night of horror that sickened Georg, and he knew it signaled more difficult times ahead. He was concerned, but it had so unnerved Anna that he hardly recognized as his wife the shrill-speaking harridan who had replaced her since that night.

Before then, Georg had thought Anna was adapting quite well to the changes in the country since the strange little Austrian had risen to power. Georg recalled the note of pride in her voice when she explained to their daughter how Hitler had denounced the hated Treaty of Versailles that had starved and humiliated the Germans for the past twenty years. What Anna failed to explain and what Georg couldn't get her to understand was that the Treaty was not the problem. Anna, like so many other Germans, found it easier to blame the Treaty than to look at the government. Before Hitler ever came to power, the former Weimar government had essentially mortgaged the country's financial future paying for the Great War. The hyperinflation that resulted had allowed businesses to wipe out huge debts with money that was worth far less. Even the average worker thought he was getting along better as wages skyrocketed.

By 1923, even the workers realized that their wages couldn't keep up with the higher prices. By 1924, although the economy had somewhat stabilized, the German people had already been convinced that it was the Treaty that was destroying them. The Treaty had forced the Germans to pay millions of dollars in reparations to other countries following Germany's defeat in the Great War. The proud German people had even been forbidden to form a sizeable army again. The reduction of their army had broken their pride, they were convinced that the reparations had broken their banks, and the post-war partitioning of their land had depleted much of their natural resources.

Georg had to admit the little Austrian was cunning. He pounded the message of the harm of the treaty into the minds of the German people so strongly that the masses cheered any action he took. Shortly after repudiating the terms of the treaty, the Führer had begun rebuilding the economy and the army.

As much as Georg despised Hitler, it was hard to fight Anna when she claimed that times had been better since the Führer had taken over the reins of the government. Before the Kristallnacht riots, Anna had often told Georg how good life had become again, despite some of the stricter laws Hitler had enacted. Germany's economic outlook was the brightest it had been since "Black Friday" so many years ago. That day in 1927 had nearly spelled the end of Georg's trucking company. There had been no work for anyone. Inflation had been so rampant that his wife and their housekeeper Frau Stimmel had had to load a wheelbarrow full of German marks just to buy a loaf of bread.

Sensing that her husband's thoughts had drifted, Anna wept a little harder to regain his full attention. Pulling her close to him, he chastised her once more, "Anna, it seems to me that your thoughtless outbursts of temper could bring us more trouble than any youthful indiscretion by our daughter." Although Anna scowled angrily at him, he continued, "Everything is all right," Georg had assured her. "Nothing bad is going to happen to you."

Releasing his wife and wrapping his arm around her tiny waist, he guided her to one of the two small burgundy brocaded settees lining the cream-colored foyer wall. "Sit down and calm yourself," Georg crooned, as he smoothed Anna's slim gray tweed skirt, sympathetically patting her knee. Next to her, his large frame looked as if it might snap the delicate sofa at any moment. "You must relax a bit, Anna, and you must be kinder to your daughter. She is spoiled," he admitted with a smile, "and, yes, I know that it is my fault. But things are not so bad for us."

Even as he spoke, he shuddered mentally, hoping that his body did not betray his thoughts. Before Hitler had taken power, Germany had been ripe for communism. Members of the *Freikorps*, the young men who had fought in the Great War, had been left without jobs. They had been roaming the country, frequenting the beer halls, jeering the Communist leaders, and terrorizing the German people with their armed support of the new Nationalist Socialist German Workers Party, the Nazis. Germans feared communism as much as they feared the hunger and humiliation they had known since the end of the war.

Georg knew that although Hitler was nothing more than a brutish, little peasant, he had succeeded in quelling the fears of communism. Soon after he had come to power, German men were back at work building the *Autobahn*, developing the Volkswagen, and joining the newly formed army. When Hitler had stopped the payment of reparations to other countries, he had dared any nation to raise a hand against Germany. More important than overcoming some of the shame of their defeat in the Great War, the Germans had begun to hope again.

Burkhardt Trucking was flourishing once again, but Georg detested Hitler nevertheless. He realized that he had unwittingly contributed to his wife's fears when he had told her that Hitler was building the Autobahn so sturdily because he wanted it to be able to support tanks. Hitler was planning war, and Georg instinctively knew it. Despite the improvement in the economic outlook of the country and in his own finances, Georg, who had nearly lost his life in the first Great War, had no stomach for a second one.

Already in October, Hitler had made his first move into the *Sudetenland*, a region of Germany that had been annexed to Czechoslovakia after the war. Several of Anna's friends had showed them photographs of the people rejoicing and throwing flowers at the tanks thundering through their towns, ostensibly thrilled to be a part of Germany once again. Great Britain sent its Prime Minister Lord Neville Chamberlain to sound a warning against Germany's bold step, but no action followed. Hitler was right, the people of Germany proclaimed. Germany could raise an army, stop the payment of reparations, and take back their lands–and no one dared to do anything.

Despite the photographs, Georg was secretly terrified by Hitler's actions. He had begun hoarding his money, meeting with bankers, and insisting that his contracts be paid up front in gold. And, he had started going out at night again–to what he called his "political meetings."

"Georg?" Anna asked timidly, "Do you have a political meeting again tonight?"

It was uncanny, he thought, how she sometimes seemed to read his mind. "No, Schatzie, I do not." Calling her his sweetheart made his wife flash him a brief smile, but he could see that his answer didn't satisfy her.

"You may not go out tonight, but I know you'll go out again," she whined, taking a deep breath.

He stiffened in anticipation of her next attack.

"It's foolish of me to worry that Liselotte will get us into trouble," she noted petulantly. "You will do that instead."

All signs of the delicately weeping woman had disappeared. Georg would have marveled more at the transformation, had he not grown so accustomed to her intuitive chameleon-like ability to sense her surroundings and instantly adapt to them. For all her demonstrative tenderness, Georg recognized that his wife possessed a toughness that he did not. It would have repelled him except for the realization that it was driven by sheer panic and desperate fear. Instead of rebuking his wife, Georg smiled ingratiatingly at her. "I'll be careful, my dear," he said, turning away from her with finality.

"Lilo, you are standing there so quietly. Come and sit on Papa's lap." Lilo rushed to her father and plopped onto his lap. She wrapped her thin arms around his neck, rubbing her soft cheek against the dark shadow that always appeared on his face long before five.

"How's your mouth, Schatzie? Better?"

Lilo nodded, leaning against her father for comfort. It didn't matter that he wasn't going to make Mama stop hitting her. He loved her and as long as he was near, Lilo knew her mother would be careful—or at least try. She felt her mother's stare and looked up at her over her father's shoulder. Mama looked sad—so sad that even though Liselotte was still mad at her, she felt sorry for her, too. Maybe that's how Papa felt when he was mad at her. There was something indefinable in the eyes of her mother that almost made Liselotte want to go and comfort her.

"Mama, are you all right?" she whispered haltingly. The haunted look in her mother's eyes disappeared instantly. Liselotte watched the soft violet gaze turn brittle as her mother turned her face away from them and stood up.

"I'm fine. Don't think you will get away without

cleaning that floor. I will not have Frau Stimmel break her back because your father coddles you when you misbehave," Anna decreed as she turned and walked away.

Liselotte did not see the anxiety that veiled her mother's face. Had she not buried her face into her father's neck, she would have seen Anna turn toward the pair, an ineffably sad expression marring her beautiful features as she stood alone, watching her husband and daughter. The tender way her child embraced her father tugged at her heart and made her eyes sting.

Lost in the image, Anna wondered why her daughter had such power to enrage her. They were so close, the father and daughter. When Liselotte was born, Anna had been thrilled at the thought of having a lifetime companion—a little girl who would mimic her every action. Instead, the child was as close in spirit to her father as she was in appearance to her mother—even though the girl couldn't see the similarities yet. Anna's lifetime companion had instead become her father's shadow.

Anna had thought that nothing but a son would do for Georg, but he had surprised her. Georg Burkhardt doted on his daughter. He had even become a model husband. He had thanked Anna profusely for the treasure of the child she had given him. There were still too many nights out—ostensibly at his "political meetings"—and a few women had even had the audacity to come to her home during these past few months looking for her husband. "Business," they had whispered. "Business" indeed, thought Anna contemptuously. A flash of anger unnoticed by Georg and Liselotte darted in their direction before she left the foyer to be alone with her thoughts.

Beautiful, dark-haired, and dark-eyed women with lavishly full bodies paraded through Anna's mind. She reminded herself that at least one of them could have been a grandmother. Another she recognized as a star of the Yiddish Theatre. What attraction did these women hold for her Georg? Every time they appeared, she railed against him. He would look at her with a faint air of amusement and say nothing. She claimed that she

47

simply didn't want him to soil his "Lilo" with his wanderings.

Soon she needed to convince Georg to stop referring to their child as "Lilo." It sounded so common. She would also put a stop to his teaching her about the business world. The child was already learning mathematics by helping her father with the trucking company's books. Georg claimed he was preparing their daughter to run the business when he could no longer manage it. Ridiculous. How did he think a woman was going to navigate in the business of men?

As soon as the young men discovered their daughter, and she discovered them, he would have to come to his senses. Then, Anna thought triumphantly, she would take over Liselotte's real training in the duties of wife, hostess, and mother. Although, Anna had to admit, with the direction the country was going, who knew what the future held for their daughter, or for her?

She thought back to that night in Nuremberg. Hans, a driver for Georg, had nearly lost a truck in the riot there. Luckily, Hans was unhurt with only a flat tire from driving through miles of broken glass. Anna found it hard to believe that rioters had broken out the windows of every store owned by Jews in the entire business district. Why was there such open violence against Jews? She knew that Jews were quietly leaving Germany. Many of their good friends had left on extended visits to family in America and other countries. Anna knew there were some people who despised Jews, but really, they were just the lower classes. They had no real power, so Anna couldn't understand why her friends felt so threatened—until the riots.

She now recognized that same fear inside herself and she knew it was up to her to protect her family. She had told Georg that it would be best for them to drop their associations with their Jewish friends, at least for a little while. She was confident their friends would understand. No one would blame her. After all, everyone had a responsibility to look after family. But Georg wouldn't listen to her. No one ever did—not even her own child.

1941-1945

1941-1945

DATELINE: EUROPE

1941

Most of Europe and Scandinavia Embroiled in World War II

Only Great Britain remains unoccupied by the Germans. Italy and Japan sign alliances with Germany.

1941

Germany Launches "Operation Barbarossa"

Nearly four million German troops are sent to take over the Soviet Union in the largest military campaign in human history in terms of both manpower and casualties.

1942

Hitler Initiates the Final Solution to the Jewish Question

Mass extermination of the Jews begins. Six million Jews ultimately perish along with five million gypsies, homosexuals, and various other "enemies of the state."

1943

Warsaw Ghetto Uprising

Jews in the Warsaw Ghetto fight to prevent the Germans from sending them to extermination camps. The Germans brutally crush the poorly armed resistance. An estimated 13,000 Jews are killed and another 50,000 are deported to camps.

1941-1945

DATELINE: EUROPE

1944   **Operation Overlord and D-Day**

Operation Overlord is the code name for the
Battle of Normandy. The operation launches
the Allied invasion of Western Europe
occupied by the Germans. The invasion
starts on June 6, 1944, commonly known as
D-Day, when nearly 160,000 troops cross the
English Channel.

1944-1945   **The Battle of the Bulge**

This is the Germans' final offensive, a bloody
but ultimately failed attempt to stop the
Allies. The "Battle of the Bulge" is America's
bloodiest campaign of the war with an
estimated 19,000 Americans dead.

1944   **Massacre at Malmedy**

The 1st SS Panzer Division of Germany
murders 84 American prisoners of war in
the Belgian town of Malmedy. General Sepp
Dietrich is among the soldiers eventually
convicted of the massacre. Although General
Dietrich is not in Malmedy at the time of the
crime, the 1st SS Panzer Division is a part of
Dietrich's 6th Panzer Army.

1945   **Holocaust Uncovered**

Allied soldiers uncover locations used by the
Nazis to exterminate six million Jews, and
five million Romanis, Slavs, homosexuals,
and other minorities.

1941-1945

DATELINE: THE UNITED STATES

1941   **U.S. Congress Passes Lend-Lease Law**

The law results in shipment of $50 billion in supplies and weapons to Great Britain and other Allied nations fighting the Axis powers: Germany, Italy, and Japan.

1941   **America Declares War**

On December 8, one day after Japan's surprise attack on the U.S. naval base at Pearl Harbor, the United States declares war on Japan. On December 11, the U.S. declares war on Germany and Italy.

1942   **Formation of the 761st "Black Panther" Tank Battalion**

The all Negro battalion adopts its motto, *"Come Out Fighting,"* from Joe Louis' response when asked how he planned to beat German Boxer Max Schmeling in their 1938 bout.

1942   **First American Troops Leave for Europe**

Through March 1942, the number of U.S. troops shipped overseas averages about 50,000 per month. That number soars to nearly 250,000 per month by 1944.

1941-1945

DATELINE: THE UNITED STATES

1942　　　　**The Double V Campaign**

At James Thompson's suggestion, the *Pittsburgh Courier* adds another "V" to the Allies' "V for Victory" slogan to stand for victory over racism in America.

1943　　　　**American Jewish Protests**

American Jews hold a mass rally in New York to pressure the U.S. to help European Jews.

1944　　　　**The 761st "Black Panther" Tank Battalion Deploys to Europe**

In October the Black Panthers land on Omaha Beach, France, arriving with six white officers, thirty Negro officers, and 676 enlisted Negroes. General Patton requests assignment of the battalion to his Third Army. The battalion endures 183 days of continuous operational employment.

1945　　　　**Americans Kill 60 German Troops**

Less than one month after the Massacre at Malmedy, U.S. soldiers kill 60 German POWs. The act is thought to be a reprisal.

1945　　　　**Victory in Europe Day**

V.E. Day, May 8, marks the formal acceptance by the Allies of the unconditional surrender of the armed forces of Nazi Germany, thus ending the war in Europe.

CHAPTER THREE

MUNICH, GERMANY: 1941

"Well, Papa, are you going to take the job?" inquired sixteen-year-old Liselotte as she impatiently tapped her foot on the marble fireplace hearth and nervously wound and unwound a thick strand of hair around her finger.

"Stop fidgeting!" Anna commanded from her seat on the overstuffed rose brocade sofa. Liselotte shot an angry look at her mother. Ignoring the impertinence, Anna pressed her husband, "You know that taking this position is Liselotte's only chance to find a decent husband with so many of the boys gone."

"Gone"–that single word had become the code Anna had trained her family to use when discussing the thousands of deaths among Germany's young men. The grown men had gone first–to Eastern Europe, to France, to Norway. Later, the boys, too, were scattered throughout Europe, and now, even in Russia, where they were dying by the tens of thousands. Food shortages had become a part of life for most Germans, sparing the Burkhardts only because their last few years had been prosperous and because Georg could usually barter for some of the food and goods he hauled. But Georg's outspoken contempt for Hitler had already caused his trucking business to grind to a near halt.

Anna believed her family was clearly in danger, but maybe now, with the phone call from Berlin, life could return to some semblance of normalcy. Maybe then she could relax somewhat, not fearing that every knock on the door would be the authorities coming to arrest her husband for his careless comments. For Anna, the offer for Georg to work as Hitler's chauffeur and bodyguard represented the family's last hope to salvage their lives and live in safety. Georg's open disapproval of the Führer made the job offer in Berlin nothing short of a miracle–one brought about only by the efforts of Georg's best

friend, General Sepp Dietrich. It would be nothing short of
folly for Georg to turn down such an opportunity. She waited
anxiously for Georg's reply.

Leaning back in his favorite royal blue damask armchair,
one foot resting on the matching ottoman in front of him, Georg
sat quietly across from Anna. His steepled fingers propped up his
chin and, with his eyes closed, he looked like he was sleeping.
Anna knew better. She leaned forward and rested a gentle hand
on his knee.

"Please, answer me, Georg. Are you going to accept the
offer?" Anna tried unsuccessfully to keep the anxiety out of her
voice. "It's such a wonderful opportunity," she added with a false
brightness. "You want Sepp to know how much you appreciate
him recommending you for his old job."

Georg opened his eyes, his soft leaf-green gaze belying
his agreeable nod and the slight smile on his lips. "Ja, poor
Sepp–leaving his job as Hitler's personal bodyguard to lead
a Panzer division on the front lines." He shrugged and added
dismissively, "The little Führer must be smarter than I had
thought to recognize that Sepp is the best man to lead a division
of tanks."

Georg had managed once again to evade the question.
Was he trying to drive her mad? Surely he recognized how his
actions had already placed his family in danger. Three months
earlier, after Georg had publicly ridiculed the Nazis at a party, the
state had cancelled all of its contracts with Burkhardt Trucking.
Anna believed the word was out that doing business with Georg
was frowned upon since even a few of their private contracts
had been inexplicably cancelled. Their drivers were all gone
too–drafted to join the thousands of German men in uniforms
decorated with the feared red and black swastika armband.

Now Georg had one more chance to protect his family.
Accepting the offer would force him into the uniform he so
despised. As a member of Hitler's elite *Leibstandarte*, the

Führer's personal bodyguard unit, he would be required to join the Nazi party. As far as Anna was concerned, that was simply politics–a small price to pay to keep their heads above water and to avoid imprisonment and financial ruin–or worse, if the rumors were true.

It infuriated Anna that Georg afforded himself the luxury of his unrealistic political ideals. Ideals didn't matter if you were dead or starving. Nearly everyone they knew had joined the party. They didn't like the little dictator any more than she did, but they breathed far more easily for it. It was a small compromise. The relentless tap-tap-tap of her daughter's toe on the fireplace hearth would drive her mad before Georg deigned to answer her.

"Liselotte, stop that idiotic twitching," she snapped, "and remove your arm from that filthy mantle."

The dirt–everywhere she looked she saw evidence of the disarray of their lives. No matter how she tried, she couldn't keep even this single room clean. The room was her pride and joy with its twin Carrera marble fireplaces, muted Aubusson carpets, and two-story palladium windows framed with yards of delicate rose silk. If she squinted her eyes, she was certain she could see a thin veneer of dust resting between the folds of the fabric, dulling its lustrous sheen. How she missed Frau Stimmel.

Even their simple maid had had the good judgment to compromise for her family's well-being. It had been a sad day for Anna when Frau Stimmel had announced that her unemployed musician husband had finally found work. He had been recruited to play in an orchestra touring the various work camps Hitler had opened throughout Europe.

The day had been made sadder when Georg had verbally attacked the poor woman, demanding that she force her husband to forfeit the position. Anna was mortified when he had openly cursed the woman's stupidity because she had dared to express pride in her husband's involvement in the Führer's plan to use

57

music to lighten the souls of the weary workers in the camps–
even though everyone knew that the camps were filled with the
hated Communists and political prisoners. Georg had informed
her that the camps were not work camps but death camps and
that her husband's work was just one more evil duty designed to
make a mockery of the murders of thousands of innocent people.
What might have been a meaningful good-bye turned into a
frenzied shouting match that ended with Frau Stimmel's sobbing
escape from the mansion that had been her home for so many
years.

Anna had been horrified at Georg's insane ranting about
"death camps." Certainly one heard rumors, but since no one
who had been arrested ever returned from the camps, there
were no hard facts. Besides, Anna had thought, most people
should know that in wartime you kept your head down and your
mouth shut until the danger passed. It wasn't easy, but if you
really loved your family, you had no choice. You watched your
mouth. For some reason though, she could never make Georg
or Liselotte understand that. Instead, Georg would make light
of her fears, and Liselotte, always willing to emulate her father,
followed suit.

Then there was the niggling thought that Georg was
seeing other women again. Ach! He was still such a fine looking
man–so tall and handsome with his jet-black hair and dancing
green eyes that sparkled when he laughed. But surely not,
though at times he left the house late at night and didn't come
home until the next afternoon. These days Liselotte kept the
same odd hours. When Anna questioned them, Georg would
wrap his arms around her, drop kisses on her face, and tell her
not to worry.

But she did worry–more than ever since her husband
had put them in such a precarious position. The real trouble had
begun on New Year's Eve. Despite Anna's insistence that their
Jewish friends would understand why Anna couldn't invite them
to her annual party, Georg was equally insistent on inviting their
old friend, Abraham Goldbaum. Anna knew Goldbaum had had

the decency to decline, realizing that his presence at the party with the gold Star of David emblazoned on his jacket would mean trouble for the Burkhardts. But Georg wouldn't give up. Goldbaum was a bachelor who, for years, had joined them for their Sunday evening meal. When he began wearing the star, he had politely declined the standing invitation, but Georg told him to come anyway. Anna knew there was no fighting Georg on this. His friends were his friends–no matter what the danger might be to his family. Even though Anna had thought it was cruel to force Abraham to come to their New Year's Eve party, she knew Georg would never see it that way.

Anna shivered at the memory of the elegant Jewish banker walking through the main salon that night. All conversation had ceased. Georg had broken away from the group of toadying lower-level politicians he'd been entertaining and had marched toward his friend. Lightly draping an arm around the shorter man's shoulders, he had eased him into the group. Each man had looked at Georg, then at Abraham. And as though one thought had been immediately transmitted among them, each one had politely said good night and left. It had taken only until noon the next day for a messenger to bring the news that the state had cancelled all of its contracts with Georg's company.

The next Sunday, Abraham's place at the dinner table was vacant. Despite Anna's pleas, Georg had gone after him. Georg had found the door to Abraham's apartment open, the rooms stripped, and no one at home. Finally, an old woman, furtively looking in the hallway before she spoke, had told Georg that the soldiers had come for his friend on New Year's Day. Seven of them had carried out Abraham's collection of paintings while two others had beaten him. One of them had spotted her watching and had threatened to do the same to her. Still, when she had heard the roar of an engine outside, she'd peeked through her lace curtains and had seen them throw the bloodied man into the back of a truck and speed away.

Liselotte's question interrupted Anna's memories. Still defiantly resting her arm on the fireplace mantle, she asked, "So,

Papa? Do we move to Berlin?"

Anna broke in quickly, "Not do we move, Schatzie.
When we move is the question, right Georg?"

Georg leaned forward and with his face only a few inches
away from hers, he asked, "So you think we must go, Anna?"

Anna leaned away from his unblinking stare. "Think?
What's to think about, Georg? If we don't go, what will happen
to us? This is the perfect chance for you to prove how loyal you
are to Germany–to our Führer."

"Is that what you think I am, Anna–loyal to our Führer?"
His pure green eyes studied her thoughtfully.

"Why of course you are, Georg." Even as she exclaimed
the words, she heard how empty they sounded. Even to her, her
words lacked sincerity. It scared her. Only the ability to lie with
conviction was what saved people during these days. Georg kept
staring at her, and in the deep silence between them, she knew.

Oh, no. He can't do this to us. It was one thing to talk
and lose your business, but it was quite another to turn down a
job with the party. He could lose his life. Surely Georg would
not subject them to such condemnation.

She looked at Liselotte. Strangely enough, her daughter
had a slight smile on her face. Was she laughing at her mother's
obvious discomfort? Surely not, but the child worshiped her
father and always sided with him. Sometimes it was as if some
invisible tether linked their minds. Now, without a word passing
between them, Anna saw Liselotte nod slightly at her father. In
outward appearance, her daughter's face resembled her own.
But instead of Anna's placid features, Liselotte's announced her
fractious temper and her father's iron will. If Georg turned down
the job, Liselotte would happily support him–unless she could
somehow convince her daughter that her father should seize this
chance. Then Georg might consider it.

Anna cleared her throat in an effort to dispel the tension. Liselotte had moved from the fireplace to stand behind her father and rest her hand on his shoulder. Anna ignored her penetrating stare and looked fully into her husband's eyes. "Of course, you are loyal to the Führer." Anna moved her gaze past Georg to her daughter's face. "We can rest well knowing that your Papa will be safe since he will have to join the party to take the position."

"My father is no filthy Nazi!" Liselotte's words exploded at Anna. Her stomach lurched at the attack. But as her husband shook his head, she felt no surprise—only the dull familiar ache reminding her that once again she had said the wrong thing at the wrong time. Once again, she had missed the opportunity to reach her child and to convince Georg to think of the family first. But why should today be any different from any other day—Georg and Liselotte on the inside and Anna on the outside? Only this time, the consequences of Georg's actions would mean far more than just fear and loneliness for Anna. This time, Georg was risking what he loved best—their only child.

CHAPTER FOUR

MUNICH, GERMANY–1941

"She's loaded and ready to go, Papa. Shall I back her out?" Lilo called to her father as she stood on the running board of the truck hanging onto the open door.

"No, Lilo. Leo and Isolde are waiting for you. Go play your tennis game. The load isn't due until tomorrow. We'll take her out tonight. Oh, and did I mention that Leo brought Peter with him?" he smiled lightly.

"Peter's here? Why didn't Mama bring them out here?" cried Lilo as she jumped down from the truck. Georg smiled at his daughter's instant anxiety. Despite the dangers they would face when they went out tonight, her thoughts were consumed by the mention of one name.

"You know your Mama. She probably didn't want that fine Leo to see her little girl behind the wheel of a truck. And wearing pants–filthy ones at that," he teased, raising one eyebrow as he chuckled. "It might spoil your chances with the dentist's son," he winked as he wrapped his arm protectively around her shoulders and guided her down the gravel lane toward the house.

"Chances of what?" she queried. "I'm only seventeen."

Georg laughed inwardly at his daughter's protest. He wasn't blind to how much young Leo felt for his child or how little she felt for him in return. He did notice, however, how Leo's friend Peter's visits affected his Lilo.

"As your Mama says, you can't start husband hunting too soon!" Georg laughed aloud this time as Lilo rolled her eyes and swept a stray lock of hair from her face. The sudden rush of blood to her cheeks belied the disdainful expression on her face.

"Just remember, it's Leo, not Peter, your Mama has in mind for you, even if you think otherwise."

Her blush deepened at her father's teasing. Since Peter Mueller had begun visiting their home so often, Lilo had found herself more drawn to him each time she saw him. She wasn't vain enough to believe that the handsome twenty-year old man could find anything interesting in a seventeen-year old girl, but secretly, she had hoped.

"Mama just likes Leo because his mother is her best friend. She doesn't like Peter because she thinks his mother is common and his father is supposed to be such a big Nazi."

Georg smiled. "You need to walk a little faster, my Lilo, or they'll be gone before we make it to the house. You'll have to change quickly."

She giggled nervously, and Georg could feel her uncertainty beneath her usually confident demeanor. Since she and Georg had begun their "work," his daughter had become a masterful dissembler. It was not a trait that he would ordinarily have admired and certainly would not have encouraged, but when it came to their work, it could mean the difference between life and death.

Georg had resisted his daughter's demands to assist him when she had discovered what he was doing. But there was simply no one he trusted as much as his Lilo. Although she had always helped him with the business, now her assistance went far beyond balancing the books and hauling shipments of boots from the Mueller factory to the warehouses outside the city where they would eventually make it to the soldiers on the various fronts. As they walked, Georg wondered idly if Lilo's feelings for Peter were motivated at all by gratitude toward the Muellers. After all, she knew as well as he did that without the Mueller contract, Burkhardt Trucking would shut down.

He glanced toward his child as they approached the rear

of the house. She was so lovely–so strong and yet so vulnerable. Peter Mueller was in his second year of university, but despite his wealthy father's contacts, Peter would likely have to go to war any day. Leo, a year younger than Peter, had already been called up and was to begin pilot training in two weeks. Georg was concerned about Leo. But because of his daughter's feelings for Peter, he was more concerned about how she would handle the pain if Peter went to war and, like so many other young German boys, failed to come home. They already knew too many heartbroken families who would never see their men and boys again. His daughter was still quite young, although he recalled that he had been barely seventeen when he had first seen Anna and fallen irrevocably in love with her. So long ago, he mused.

"Papa, how do I look?"

His daughter's whispered question broke his reverie. Georg rubbed his chin thoughtfully as he took in the mussed blonde hair, the dirty smudge across one cheek, and the gray wool work pants she wore.

"Beautiful to me, but you'd better go in through the kitchen. Take the back stairs and get your tennis whites on. And make certain you wash your face and comb your hair or your Mama will make me pay. I'm sure she has poor Leo, Peter, and Isolde trapped in the front room. As lovely as you are to your poor old Papa, your mother will be upset if your guests see you even for a moment looking like that."

"You're not old, Papa. You're just perfect," she avowed with an emphatic nod of her head before she turned and raced though the kitchen door.

Georg walked toward the front door so that he might speak with Peter a moment while they waited for Lilo. The young man always asked about Georg's business–as if that would convince everyone that his visits were of a professional nature and not due to the lovely young woman in the household.

Georg walked into the drawing room and saw Anna sitting in the blue silk-covered armchair near the fireplace at one end of the long room, talking with Leo and Isolde—and ignoring Peter, who sat alone across the room on one of the long rose-colored brocade sofas. He wasn't surprised.

Anna was becoming exasperated by Peter's attentions to Liselotte. Unlike Lilo, she did not know that it was Peter's father who had almost singlehandedly saved the business after Georg had turned down his old friend Sepp Dietrich's offer to work for Hitler in Berlin. Georg had secretly feared that Anna's prediction of ruin for the family would come to pass, but as he struggled to decide whether to take the position, the nightmares had become more frequent.

For nearly two weeks while Georg had considered Sepp's offer, he'd been plagued with vivid recollections of the battlefield. The dreams brought back the horrors he'd tried to bury for more than twenty years. There had been several nights when Anna had shaken him awake, her face pale with anxiety because he'd been screaming in his sleep. He knew that she was frightened, but he couldn't tell her about the nightmares. He didn't want her to know about the huge rats in the trenches, floating in rivers of blood as they chewed on the dead, sometimes not even waiting for death before they began ripping apart a screaming man's flesh.

He could never tell her how he had sneaked up the hill to the cook's tent on a rare peaceful Sunday morning to steal food while all the other men in the pasture below him knelt to receive communion from the priests. He was ashamed to tell her that the only reason he was alive today was because he was a sacrilegious thief. While he had stuffed his mouth with molded bread, the enemy had launched a surprise attack on his brothers-in-arms. He didn't even have to close his eyes to see the priests running, their long robes flapping around their legs, as the shelling mercilessly continued. He saw himself race down the hill to take his place with his fellow soldiers.

But it was over as quickly as it had begun, and he was alone, walking among the dead and dying. A strange keening sound, different from the moans of the wounded, had caught his ear. He walked toward the odd, high-pitched whine and found the captain of his regiment lying still in the meadow, his fair hair crowned by the brilliant red poppies whose stems lay crushed beneath his head. Leaning over the captain was the black horse that had been with him since Georg had joined the unit. The horse bent his head gently to his master's face, nuzzling his cheek, and–Georg could hardly believe it–crying. Tears ran from the animal's luminous brown eyes as it alternately whimpered and whinnied, nudging his master with his soft muzzle. Georg pulled on his bridle to lead the poor beast away from his dead rider, but the horse refused to leave the captain's side.

No, these were memories he had no right to inflict on Anna, or anyone else. He had accepted that his decision could ruin him financially and even bring down the wrath of the Nazi regime on his wife and child, but he had decided he could not play a part in the mindless tide that would sweep out as quickly and powerfully as it had swept in, leaving only the dead and those who would live out their lives fighting the same horrific memories that relentlessly tortured him. Up to this moment, Anna's predictions had not come true, but Georg wondered if she would treat Peter more kindly if she knew that it was his family who was preventing them from doing so.

Because the Muellers moved in many of the same social circles as the Burkhardts, they were aware that Georg had not beome a member of the party. When Peter Mueller had approached Georg to propose the business venture with his father's company, Georg was stunned. Hans Mueller was known as one of Hitler's closest confidants. Georg also realized that the few trucks he had left hardly made a dent in the huge numbers of boots that had to be shipped. The only idea that had made any sense to him at the time was that perhaps the Nazis had found a way to keep a closer eye on him–or that Peter was so smitten with Lilo that he had persuaded his father to help the Burkhardts over their objections.

A round of greetings interrupted Georg's musings. He turned and saw his daughter strolling toward her friends, wearing her white pleated tennis skirt and nervously bouncing the face of her racquet against the palm of her hand. Good. Her hair was neatly tied back and she'd succeeded in removing all the dirt from her face.

A quick grin and nod to Leo and Isolde were supplanted spontaneously by a brilliant smile for the young man who had jumped to his feet when she entered the room. Georg almost laughed aloud as Peter rushed to Lilo's side and offered to carry her racquet for her. The tall, lean blonde boy with his light hazel eyes and long thin nose appeared dazzled by his daughter's smile.

As the two looked at one another, Georg was fairly certain his daughter never even noticed poor Leo as the shorter boy brushed his hand impatiently through his dark wavy hair and blew out a light snort of exasperation. Georg smiled to himself as he listened idly to the four young people crowded together talking about their plans for the afternoon. As they hurried from the room, Georg thought how good it was that they could enjoy themselves for the moment.

CHAPTER FIVE

Camp Hood, Texas: 1942

"Hey, hey, lookin' good, man!"

Bud grinned as his friend C.T. made his pronouncement on the fit of Bud's new uniform. He laughed out loud when C.T. began singing the raucous cadence he and Bud now knew by heart:

You in de Ahmy now,

You ain't behin' no plow!

You'll nevah git rich,

You summava bitch.

You in de Ahmy now!

"I look like one tough soldier, don't I," boasted Bud as he saluted himself proudly in the tiny chipped mirror hanging beside his iron cot.

"You do, Bud–you do indeed," nodded his buddy.

"Damn, this uniform's hot, C.T., way too damn hot for Texas." As Bud adjusted the peaked cap he could feel the beads of sweat gathering at his hairline and dampening the fabric. "Yeah, heat feels just as bad here as it does back home."

C.T. pulled up one of the uncomfortable Army-issue iron chairs squeezed between the endless rows of double-decker cots that lined the barrack and blew out an exhausted breath as he fell into it.

Back home–Birmingham, Alabama. Mother, still stern and unyielding, fierce in her protection of the godly man she had married, even more so the last time Bud had seen his parents. But that was because of the halo of impending death shadowing his father's face. His father was so weakened by the pernicious anemia that was stealing his life and yet he remained steadfast in his faith and ministry. Bud didn't get it. God had apparently decided to take one of the finest men on earth before his time. It wasn't fair. His father wasn't even fifty years old. Bud alternately marveled and raged at his father's devotion to such an arbitrary God. Mostly though, he despaired over it, finding not a shred of that same faith in his own soul.

Bud banished his dark thoughts as he checked out the fit of his new uniform one last time. The short tan jacket molded itself across his shoulders, and the pleat down the front of the matching slacks was razor sharp. How proud his parents would be to see him in it. They were jubilant when he had joined the Army the moment he'd graduated from Jacksonville State. He thought they were probably just relieved that he had made it through college. He had wanted to join the Army when all of his friends started turning up in their spiffy new uniforms ready to go overseas and kick the tar outta those Krauts. But when his dad fell ill, Bud had promised him he would finish college first. Bud remembered the sadness in his father's sea-blue eyes when he had told Bud that he believed this war would wait for him.

So here he was now. But God Almighty, he was ready to battle something other than rattlesnakes, tarantulas, and insects. Instead of fighting on a military battleground, Bud had spent six months fresh out of college fighting heat stroke in the hottest and dustiest place he had ever been. Others in his unit had informed him that it could be worse. They allowed as how Camp Hood was a damn sight better than Camp Claiborne in Louisiana. The 761st Tank Battalion had already trained for months in the Louisiana swamps as part of another unit. By the time Bud had joined them, the 761st had become a separate battalion and had moved to Camp Hood for more tanker training.

As if reading his mind, C.T. asked, "Bud, when you think they gonna send us out of this hell pit and let us go fight?"

70

"Don't know. Hope it's soon. I can't stand roasting like a turkey inside these tanks much longer. Of course, we might be bigger turkeys for wanting to go over there at the rate the Krauts are killing Patton's tankers. I prob'ly shoulda just become a preacher like my dad wanted me to."

C.T. leaned back in his chair, roaring with laughter. "You? A preacher? Whatcha gonna preach? Yo two commandments? Booze and broads?"

"Yeah, yeah. You're so funny–wonder how you landed here instead of Vaudeville? You sound like my dad, except he thinks that God could use my–, uh–, my experiences."

"Yeah, dat soun' jus' like yo dad all right. The good Reverend nevah sees no bad in nobody. But jus' how he think yo–, uh–'experiences' gonna work in the ministry?" C.T. could hardly choke the words out through his laughter.

Bud leaned against his top bunk, "Well, Dad said the best preachers were those who knew what they were talking about when they preached against sin." One of his guileless blue eyes dropped a wink at C.T.

"Yeah, and my dad always talked about how *love* was the greatest of the commandments, and you sure do *love* the ladies, Bud."

Even Bud's stern mother had smiled when she overhead his father telling Bud how he figured that Bud's college experiences would make him one heck of a good minister– considering his vast, first-hand experience with sin. Bud never told his father that he would never–could never–consider the life of a minister. He didn't have the courage or the heartlessness to tell his father that–war or no war–he wanted no part of the God he'd met over the years.

Bud knew if he told his father that much, he'd have to tell him the whole truth, and he didn't think his father could bear to hear that. Bud wasn't too sure if there even was a God. Even

71

if God did exist, judging by what he had seen in his twenty-two years, Bud didn't want anything to do with the kind of God that had caused his father the pain he'd had to bear. And he damn sure couldn't stand behind a pulpit and tell others to follow Him.

At least God, or fate, had seen fit to bring C.T. Deeks back into his life. In 1943, the odds of Bud landing anywhere near his childhood friend had been slim to none. The U.S. military made sure colored and white soldiers were segregated, and Uncle Sam certainly wouldn't allow Negroes to do work specializing in the use of complicated machinery or weapons. But times must be changing, because here was C.T. in tanker school. Of course, it was an all-Negro unit, and Bud was only one of a handful of white officers. Even if the Army had decided that Negroes could operate tanks, it sure wasn't about to let them lead themselves into battle.

Bud had heard about something called the "Tuskegee Experiment," where some Negro West Point colonel got a group of Negro pilots together. Eleanor Roosevelt had actually flown with one of them, and after that the program was in high gear. Bud still thought it was a set-up, though. It was just like the Army to try a project like Tuskegee and then stack all the odds against the poor suckers trying to become pilots. Colored guys learning to fly airplanes–in Alabama? Hell, why didn't they bring in a few polar bears and give them marksmen training there, too. Bud figured the odds of success would be about the same for the bears as for the Negroes. He tried not to think much about it, but he knew firsthand how deep the roots of racial hatred ran in his home state.

He remembered the force of that evil all too well. It was especially vivid the moment he saw C.T.'s face upon his arrival at Camp Hood. What a hell of a surprise. Bud couldn't figure out how it had happened until C.T. explained it to him. He confided that while everybody was keeping their eyes on the Tuskegee boys, the Army had long ago integrated their Officer Candidate Schools–all twenty-four of them, including the one at Camp Hood. C.T. told Bud that everybody ignored the Army anyway until they needed a few thousand guys to hit the dirt and take the bombs and bullets. The Army had always suffered so many deaths that it just had no time for all the foolishness of segregation. Anyway, C.T. had shrugged fatalistically, everybody knew no one gave a damn if a bunch of Negroes died.

Bud didn't agree with C.T. on every point. He figured one of the real reasons the Army had integrated its Officer Candidate Schools was because the Army was the largest arm of the service and was considered the "less technically-oriented" branch. It made sense to go ahead and mix the Negroes in there since no one thought they could handle advanced military technology anyway. After just a few weeks at Hood, Bud had figured out that C.T. was much closer to the truth than he'd ever imagined. The number of young dead Army officers was growing, and the Army predicted many more would die as the war in Europe ground on. Bud heard some of his fellow white soldiers say it was about time some coloreds took their place as guests of honor in the funeral parlors, too.

The army didn't mind quietly training its young Negro and white officers together, but they certainly weren't ready for them to fight together. So Bud and C.T. figured that C.T. would go to an all-Negro unit and Bud would be sent to an all-white fighting force. They almost got it right. When all the trainees finished OCS, most of the whites were sent to other units, but not Bud or C.T. Bud wound up staying at Hood as one of seven white officers in charge of C.T.'s unit–another Army snafu: take a southern boy and put him in charge of a Negro unit. What kind of thinking was that? He asked his commanding officer if the Army had realized he was from Alabama.

The boss told Bud they had known what they were doing. They'd tried using officers from the northern states to head up the Negro regiments, but that hadn't worked. Mac said the Yankees could talk a good game, but most of them had never even spoken to a colored person. He explained to Bud that many of the soldiers who came from big northern cities were hard-pressed just to get along with other whites from different ethnic backgrounds. The Poles didn't talk to the Italians, who didn't like the Irish, who despised the Protestants, and on and on.

Bud couldn't quite figure that out, but he knew he was stuck. At least C.T. was there with him, and he knew C.T. would look out for him just as he had since the day they'd met when they were both only seven years old.

It had been the night C.T.'s father had stood arm in arm with Bud's dad and watched the First Methodist Church parsonage burn down. Both men knew it was the price Reverend Leverett's own congregation had exacted from him because he had dared to preach a sermon at Reverend Deeks' African Methodist Episcopal Church. Bud would never forget the tears in Reverend Deeks' eyes as dozens of parishioners from his own church worked in futility to keep the raging inferno from destroying the Leverett home.

But nothing could stop it. All that was left standing was the giant makeshift cross in the front yard. The small cross on the parsonage roof was in cinders, but this one stood solid, like some grotesquely charred sentinel, blessing the evil of that night. Even as the embers hissed and steamed, Bud's father told him the cross the arsonists had planted and set ablaze in the parsonage yard should remind them of God's blessings. Bending down to look earnestly into his son's eyes, Reverend Leverett explained to Bud that God had made sure the Leveretts were not at home that night or the whole family could have died in the fire. Bud tried in vain to understand, but it didn't make sense to him to thank God for his father's pain.

Bud remembered how the vicious act had stunned his father and so many others. Not his mother, though. She had stood next to Bud's father, arms folded across her chest, the light from the leaping flames reflecting off of her shining copper hair. She had repeatedly warned Bud's father about what could happen if he preached at the Negro church, but Bud had wondered if even she had guessed to what extent the gentle Methodist preacher's own flock would punish him. That night, Bud's father

74

asked everyone to join hands and pray for the forgiveness of the people who'd set the fire.

And that's when Bud first met C. T. Deeks. The little boy tentatively reached out his hand to Bud, and as everyone in the circle bowed their heads and listened to Bud's father extol God's infinite mercy, C. T. whispered to Bud under his breath: "We gon git 'em–dat's what I'm a-prayin'! I heah yo daddy askin' dat we fohgive 'em. Not meanin' no disrespec' to him, but I ain't fittin' to fohgive 'em. You watch. I'm gon make 'em pay."

Startled, and seeing every head bowed, Bud looked at the boy. Deep dimples indented his full chocolate cheeks. His enormous brown eyes stared knowingly into Bud's own.

"An' I hear tell 'bout you, Bud Leverett. Uh-huh," he said confidently, "I knowed you wadn' no chicken," and bowing his head once again he finished, "and I'm gon hep you git 'em. We gonna git 'em back together!"

The boy's head popped up as the prayer ended. "AMEN!" C. T.'s rasping whisper rose into a shout as a chorus of resounding amens, hallelujahs, and "praise Gods" broke the night silence.

When C. T.'s grin split his face to show the huge gap where two front teeth should have been and then stuck his tongue out through the gap at Pee Wee, Bud knew instantly he liked this loud-mouthed kid. Bud figured he'd made a new friend, one who apparently had a lot more guts than Pee Wee. Pee Wee had stood back that night holding his mother's hand and watching the fire rage, and, like the dozens of other witnesses, they had done nothing to help.

C. T. and Bud spent that night together plotting revenge. None of the members of the white Methodist church had opened their homes to their preacher. More than the fire, it was that single, collective, gutless lack of decency that had burned its imprint on Bud's mind and heart, never allowing him to forget that night or the "Christians" who'd perpetrated it.

It had been Reverend Deeks who had opened his own home to the Leverett family. The Ku Klux Klan desecration had been a tough lesson for Bud. The bitter smile on old man Jeffers' face that night and the shame on Pee Wee's as he refused to make eye contact with Bud had taught him the harsh reality of Christianity–southern style.

"Hey, Bud! How long you gonna stare at yo'sef in dat mirror? Come on! You ain't dat damn purty." C. T.'s wisecrack jerked Bud back to the moment.

"Better lookin' than you," Bud countered with a laugh. "Alright, C. T. I'm all dressed up with no place to go. Let's practice a little Kraut, what d'ya say?" Bud tilted his cap at a rakish angle, lifted one thick black brow up over his piercing blue eyes, and with a huge grin and a wink tried out his latest German phrase: "*Bitte, komm heah, Schatzie.* Please come here, Darling. Think that'll drive them German broads nuts, C. T.?"

C.T. leaned back in the chair and massaged his chin thoughtfully. "Well, to tell ya de truth, it don' do a whole lot fo me, but dey'll git the message loud and cleah. 'Course what dey do to you, when dey do git yo meanin'–dat's yo' problem." Both men guffawed loudly, even as each man, separately and silently, contemplated the wonders of the war they hoped to see soon.

CHAPTER SIX

MUNICH, GERMANY: 1942

"Get out of here! GET OUT! This is my apartment and everything in it. Any questions, you go call *Obergruppenführer* Sepp Dietrich. Now, move!"

Lilo heard her father's raging all the way down in the street where she stood keeping watch. Within moments, she heard the thumping of boots on the wooden stairs as the SS soldiers raced down from the third floor apartment out into the street. She thought there were at least a dozen of them, but she couldn't be sure since she had to avert her eyes quickly and pretend to look for something she'd dropped on the street. If even one of the soldiers became suspicious, she could jeopardize her father's life. Only when she heard the roar of the truck as it pulled away from the curb and lurched down the street, did she dare to lift her face and resume her watch.

Her father needed to hurry. His impulsive directive for Lilo to stop the truck when he saw soldiers going into the building was dangerous. It was past time for them to be gone. Those soldiers would likely make the call to Dietrich. Even though he would cover for them as best he could, they couldn't necessarily count on his protection. He had no way of knowing about her father's spontaneous action.

When her father emerged from the ornate, granite-faced apartment building, she hugged him with relief. "Papa, are you all right?"

"Certainly," he scoffed as he pulled off the Nazi party pin Sepp had given him and stuffed it into the pocket of his green loden jacket. "Those SS aren't real soldiers. They're just thugs in well-cut black uniforms with silver trappings. Like all bullies, it just takes one little show of authority and they scatter like the rats they are." He laughed and added, "Good thing I had this pin with me today when we spotted those rats going into the building, eh, my Lilo?"

Out of relief Liselotte laughed with her father. He could always make her laugh, no matter how dire the circumstances.

He sobered quickly, "Now go around the corner and get the truck. We have to get the family out of here immediately." Lilo nodded, ran down the block, and around the corner. If anyone thought it odd to see a young woman in a neat white blouse and brown tweed skirt climb into the driver's seat of a large gray truck, no one said a word. These days, few people dared to appear to notice much of anything. Look up at the wrong time or stare a little too long–and trouble with the authorities could follow.

Lilo shifted the gears with ease as she brought the truck to a stop in front of the richly carved double mahogany doors of the building. Even in this neighborhood, the structure's smooth creamy granite façade with veined marble steps leading to the eight-foot tall double doors was an elegant departure from the other substantial stone and half-timbered two-story buildings along the broad tree-lined avenue.

Who would have thought that in one of the wealthiest neighborhoods in Munich people would be forced to flee, leaving all of their belongings behind? This building, along with many of the ones on the block, was nearly empty now. The only families left were those who didn't wear the Star of David.

As Lilo climbed down from the driver's seat, a tiny woman with thick curling black hair walked down the three steps onto the pavement. Two small children, holding tightly to their mother's full black wool skirt, peered around her at Lilo and her father. They were both silent, their brown eyes staring out of fearful faces. The woman was clutching her white sweater closed at her breasts. The gold star hung lopsided down the front of the delicate cashmere. Liselotte saw that the soft fabric was ripped and one long sleeve had nearly been torn away from her arm. The woman stood straight with her shoulders held back as she thanked Georg for removing the soldiers from her home.

But what else was she saying? Surely Lilo had not heard correctly. She was saying good-bye? She wasn't coming with them? Lilo heard her father insist, "You must come with us, Frau Cohen. They will be back. This is nothing but a momentary reprieve."

Lilo jumped into the conversation. "Yes, you must. Papa can get you and your children to safety," she implored. She immediately recognized the look of anger her father flashed at her. In her anxiety to get the family away from their home, she'd broken her father's rule. Never mention their work to anyone–ever–not to her mother, her friends–no one. She looked up apologetically as the woman continued shaking her head sadly. Her fearful resistance was beginning to anger Lilo. "My father risked his life, and you won't come with us?" Lilo blurted, "Why?"

"I'm sorry. I cannot leave. My husband–the lady across the street said she saw them take him yesterday while I was out with the children. He didn't come home last night. She says he told her I should wait for him–that he would be back." The woman's wet brown eyes seemed too large for her lovely heart-shaped face. Lilo could easily read the terror in them.

Georg bent over the woman and draped his arm protectively around her. He spoke gently–solemnly: "Frau Cohen, your husband is not coming back. Have any of your neighbors come back? Some of them have been gone . . . for how long? Months? Years? Frau Cohen, the lady across the street is your block warden. You know that. She is no friend to you. Of course, she tells you to wait. Who knows what luxuries of yours she's been promised once you are arrested. Please, Frau Cohen," Georg entreated quietly. "Bring your children and come with us. But we must go now."

The rich dark curls covering the woman's head bounced emphatically as she shook her head forlornly, tears threatening to overwhelm her. "No, I cannot. I thank you so very much, but I cannot leave. He will be back. We must wait."

Lilo looked away to avoid staring at the woman's sorrowful face and saw three SS soldiers running toward them. The canopy of trees shading the sidewalk obscured their faces but she could see they were waving and shouting. From two short blocks away she couldn't hear them, but she knew they had to go–now!

"Papa," she cried, "Look!"

Her father responded urgently, "We must go. Frau Cohen, I promise you that your husband would want you to leave," George grasped the woman's arm just above her elbow. The threads on the tattered sleeve of her sweater gave way as she wrenched her arm from Lilo's father's grasp.

"No!" she screamed. "I cannot go. I will not go!" Hysterical, she collapsed on the sidewalk, sobbing, her frightened children huddling close as she pulled them into her embrace.

There was nothing more to do. Lilo ducked her head so the soldiers couldn't see her face as she raced in front of the truck, leaping into the driver's seat as her father jerked open the passenger door and bounded into his.

"Let's go, Lilo! Mach Schnell! Quickly!" The words were not quite out of his mouth before Lilo gunned the motor and sped down the street in the opposite direction of the soldiers. She hoped they wouldn't recognize the nondescript truck–or them. Lieber Gott–dear God, they were going to be caught. Then they, too, would be on their way to a work camp. And once there, no one could help–not even Sepp Dietrich.

§ § § § § § §

"Where have you two been?" Anna's strident demand caught both Liselotte and Georg off guard. Anna Burkhardt never visited the large truck garages located nearly a quarter mile down a gravel lane behind their home. Now, she stood inside the double-arched doorway of one of the garage bays sniffing unpleasantly at the stale odor of gasoline and charred wood that permeated the timbered walls of the structure.

She surprised them further as she began firing questions. "Tell me! Where have you been, Liselotte? What have you and your father been doing this afternoon?" At Liselotte's blank stare, Anna turned her full five-foot fury on her husband, "Georg, I have a right to know." Her voice rose with every word. "Sepp has called here three times in the past hour. He says he must speak with you." Looking around distastefully, she smoothed the severe straight lines of her black and white herringbone tweed skirt before delicately picking her way across the oil stained concrete. Her tiny black leather high heels clicked purposefully on the cement. When she reached Georg, she stopped and asked anxiously, "Are you in trouble?"

Georg reached down and drew his wife into an embrace. "No, Anna. No trouble." He said the words gently as stroked his wife's fair hair and looked over the top of her head at his daughter. The expression in his eyes gave lie to his soothing words.

"Lilo, you stay here and take care of the petrol records. I'll go with Mama and see what Sepp wants. He's probably coming to Munich and looking for a dinner invitation from my lovely wife," Georg chuckled at Anna as he put his arm around her to guide her toward the house as she cast a last disdainful look around the dim garage. A quick glance over his shoulder as he walked outside with Anna told Lilo what to do next.

Lilo and her father had planned for this moment. If the authorities discovered the purpose for their evening runs, Dietrich would sound a warning if possible. They would then activate their plan to flee. The only difficult part of the strategy would be to get Anna to stop screaming long enough to leave. If they were caught, there would be no time to explain why they deemed it necessary for her to remain ignorant of their activities. They couldn't simply admit that they didn't trust her. Anna was not stupid–and she loved her family. But her fear for them was all consuming and that made it impossible for them to bring her into their confidence. Already on two occasions when suspicions had been raised and questions asked, it had likely been Anna's ignorance that had saved them. Her righteous indignation at the accusations had been so sincere that without solid proof no charges could be leveled at Georg.

"What nasty rumors!" Anna had raged after both sessions. "How dare anyone accuse us of using our trucks to help traitors escape?" When did they think her husband was doing this, she had screamed at her interrogators. His only contract was with Mueller Leather Footwear, and everyone knew the Muellers were important Nazi supporters. Had Georg and Lilo not been so nervous at the inquiries, they might have burst out laughing at the sight of the tiny woman attacking the two armed Gestapo officers who had responded to her like elephants to mice.

Lilo hoped that today would not be the day they had to relieve Anna of her innocence. As she began preparing for their escape, Georg picked up the phone in the foyer to place his call.

"Sepp, you've been trying to reach me? Are you all right?" Georg could picture his old friend on the other end of the line.

Sepp had not aged well in his position. His five-foot-six frame carried a few extra unhealthy pounds and, knowing him, Georg believed his frustration with the Führer was taking its toll. Dietrich was a career soldier. His men came first, and Georg had heard that it was only his abilities in the field that had prevented Hitler from punishing Dietrich for daring to question him at times. Only Georg and a few others knew that Dietrich had personally approached Hitler about the law that did not allow anyone with Jewish blood dating back to 1750 to serve in the

German military. Dietrich believed the military and the country were hurt by denying these fine soldiers the opportunity to serve. Today, his voice sounded especially weary.

"Georg, I am glad to hear from you. There is no problem. I merely have an interesting story to pass along to you."

Georg knew his friend well enough to know that Sepp did not telephone to relay stories to him, interesting or otherwise. "What is it, Sepp?"

"Earlier today a man called me about another man who had intruded upon the arrest of a woman in Munich. I was in a hurry and did not have time to listen to his folderol and I told him as much, even though he claimed the man had told him to call me. I thought you would find it amusing that the man he described looked a lot like you."

"Me?" Georg laughed incredulously.

Sepp joined him in laughter. "Yes, his story was too ridiculous to even dignify with a response. I certainly couldn't imagine a scenario where anyone would so take leave of their senses as to involve themselves in an SS matter in broad daylight in the middle of the city."

The chastisement in his friend's voice was not lost on Georg as Dietrich continued. "At any rate, I told him I didn't have time to answer his questions but he was quite persistent. When he called again, he was most abject in his apologies–as he should have been. He said they were able to go back to the woman's home and finalize the arrest, but first they had questioned her and asked whether the man who had interfered was named Georg Burkhardt."

Sepp stopped speaking, and Georg let the silence fill while he swallowed hard and forced a chuckle. "I certainly hope you demanded an apology for such an insult to me and to you."

"I didn't have to. He had already apologized and said the

woman had no idea of the man's name. I am curious as to why they would have even brought your name up in the matter. I'll look into that later," he added dismissively.

"Thank you, Sepp. I, too, am curious how or why they would know my name–much less bring it up in association with something as serious as this?"

"I'm sure it's nothing, Georg. In fact, he told me they didn't spend much time belaboring that point. He said they had actually spent more time questioning the woman about the identity of a tall blonde girl who was with this idiot at the time."

Georg thought he would vomit. It was one thing to suspect him, but they also knew of Lilo's involvement. He could not speak.

Sepp continued, "The woman insisted that the man was alone. She was adamant that she did not know the man's name and equally certain that there was no tall, blonde young woman with him."

Georg was weak with relief and gratitude at Frau Cohen's bravery. Sepp's next sentence shattered his relief.

"She denied and denied up to the moment they threatened to shoot her children." Dietrich paused, and Georg's breath caught in his throat.

"But, she was apparently telling the truth. She attacked the officers, and they were forced to shoot her, instead." Dietrich paused to allow Georg to absorb the implication of his words.

Georg considered his response carefully, realizing from his friend's studiously nonchalant tone that other ears might be listening to their conversation. He struggled to keep an even tone as his stomach churned at the news of the merciless execution of a mother in front of her children. "What a tragic end to this very odd tale, Sepp. They say everyone has a *Doppelgänger*–a twin. It's rather frightening to think that I have a double out there somewhere. I just wish mine wouldn't get in so much trouble," he added with an uncomfortable chuckle.

"Don't worry too much, Georg. The authorities promised me that capturing this man is a top priority. You can rest easy knowing they will have him soon."

"I certainly hope so," Georg affirmed with what he hoped sounded like righteous indignation. It took all of his nerve to add, "And let's hope they catch this mysterious blonde, too, if she even exists."

"The good news, Georg, is that if she does exist, I am confident they will find her."

Georg nodded his head in agreement as his shaking knees finally buckled beneath him. He sank down in the seat beside the telephone bench in the foyer. "Yes, thankfully, our Gestapo are very good at their work."

"Yes, indeed, they are, Georg. They are fanatically good at it. It's a pity that these foolish traitors forget that and risk their lives and loved ones for nothing."

Despite Dietrich's casual tone, Georg heard the warning in it as clearly as if Dietrich had shouted an alarm. "Yes, it is," Georg responded woodenly.

"Good-bye for now, Georg, and please give Anna my best. Oh, and a big kiss for my lovely goddaughter. She must be growing up so fast," he added wistfully.

"She is indeed, Sepp. And she would love to see you again. Will you be in Munich sometime soon?" Georg took a deep breath to steady himself and lend to his voice the appropriate note of dismissal of an unpleasant topic.

"I hope so, Georg," Sepp responded warmly. "Of course, they need to catch this double of yours. If this man keeps using my name so freely, despite my obvious loyalty to our Führer, I won't be able to go anywhere." He chuckled lightly, but Georg had known his friend too long to be deceived by the lightness in his voice. "You can imagine how painful that would be for me."

"I certainly can, Sepp." Georg struggled to keep his voice equally sunny as his moist palms gripped the telephone receiver. "Do visit soon, Sepp. We don't see you often enough."

His friend laughed loudly at the other end of the telephone. "That's your fault for turning down that job I offered you a few years ago. Good-bye for now, Georg. Heil Hitler."

"Heil Hitler," Georg responded weakly as his shaking hand replaced the phone to its cradle. He was leaning forward with his face in his hands when he felt Anna grab his elbow. "What's wrong, Georg?"

He winced as her shrill voice stabbed at the headache building in his temples. Georg shook off his lethargy, slapped his hands on his knees, and stood up. "Calm down, Anna. It was nothing urgent, my angel–just business. Sepp said to give you his best and hopes he can visit soon. I'm going back to the garages now to help Lilo a bit." In an instant, he saw his words drive the fear from her eyes. Her voice relaxed into its usual pitch, and his Anna was back again.

"Good, I've already changed for dinner. Perhaps you should do the same," she stated flatly, the telltale smoothing of her hands over the delicate white lace apron that covered her pale green silk dress the only sign of her earlier dismay.

Even though Anna had cared for the house and cooked their meals since the servants had all gone, it amused Georg to see that she continued to dress as though nothing had changed. Every morning she went through her ritual toilette as though she expected her friends might drop in for coffee and a bit of cake. Perhaps in her fantasy, he thought aimlessly, she expected to go walking arm-in-arm with her friends through the shopping districts of Munich, trying to decide whether she needed a new beaver coat or a mink.

As Anna headed back to the kitchen, the sharp click-click-click of her matching green watered-silk high heels on the marble floor mimicked the rhythmic pounding in Georg's chest.

He was still having trouble catching his breath when he walked into the garages. Lilo gasped when she saw the normally bronzed tones of his skin washed out so that his face resembled a drying clay mask.

"Papa," she asked anxiously, "do we need to leave?"

"No, Lilo, not this time. But we must be more careful. I do not want you coming with me anymore on my trips."

The crack of Lilo slamming closed the leather-bound book echoed in the enormous garage. The stained concrete floor and the trucks parked inside the huge structure did little to absorb the sound. The legs of her iron chair screeched against the cement floor as she roughly pushed away from the scarred wooden desk and stood up to face her father.

"Papa, you need me. You can't do it alone. It's too dangerous."

He heard the finality in her voice. He sighed inwardly. She was going to make this difficult.

"I agree," he said soothingly. "It will be a little harder, but Sepp had a warning for us." Georg wasn't certain how much he should tell her about Sepp's call, but it would have to be enough so that she would see reason. He would not tell her about Frau Cohen and the children, but she needed to know the rest. As he told her of his conversation with her godfather, it was Lilo's turn to blanch.

"Papa, you must stop."

Her stoic appraisal of the situation did not surprise

him. "You're right, my Lilo," he lied smoothly. He looked into his daughter's face and felt a powerful wave of helplessness. He understood the risks, but now he chastised himself for endangering her. What had he been thinking? The memories of his harrowing years as a soldier in the first Great War had fueled his commitment to do what little he could to fight the miseries of this war. But Lilo had no such memories to drive her. She risked her life for him alone. He placed his hands on her cheeks and kissed her lightly on the forehead. She smiled so innocently at him, unaware of the turmoil in his heart.

He had wanted his child to have only wonderful memories. A quick spark of anger burned away his melancholy. Thanks to that madman, Lilo and her entire generation would carry their own scars into the future, but at least he could do his best to see that she had one. He would give his life to make certain hers was a future unlike his own–haunted with nightmares of cold and hunger, and the blood of his dead friends running in the muddy trenches. Georg knew he had to keep on. But his beloved daughter's work was finished.

"Enough worry, Papa. Let's go to the house. We have nothing to concern ourselves about."

Georg pushed the painful memories aside as Lilo wrapped her arm around his waist and guided him out into the sunshine. Georg's relief was almost palpable–until she stopped and, arching a single blonde eyebrow, locked her violet blue eyes to his pale green ones.

"You will do what you must do." Then she added with intractable emphasis, "and we will be careful."

It wasn't the first time his daughter had instinctively known his thoughts without his saying a single word. But it always took him by surprise. He should have known it would not be so easy to force her away from his side.

Finally, she broke eye contact with him and shook his

arm lightly, "Come. Let's eat."

Georg took his cue from his daughter's bravado. "Eat?
That's all you think about. You're going to be six feet tall and
as fat as a cow," he declared as he rested his arm across her
shoulders, "but that's fine with your old Papa. No man will want
you, and you can be an old maid who cooks and cleans and reads
to her father. But your Mama will be very unhappy," he warned
her with a smile.

"She's already unhappy since you forced her to accept
Peter. It's a good thing she invited him to eat with us this
evening, isn't it? Now he can see me at least once more before I
grow so fat and ugly."

With the dread cloud of danger temporarily pushed away,
she winked at her father, slipped her arm in his, and they walked
toward the house, each feigning a cheerfulness neither felt.
Each had determined to exert even more caution to guarantee
the other's safety, praying silently that their discretion would be
enough.

CHAPTER SEVEN

Munich, Germany: 1942

"Oh, Peter, no!" Liselotte whispered, her voice nearly soundless from shock.

"Lilo, what did you think–that I would be the only German man not to fight in this wretched war?" Peter's words held a hint of laughter aimed at lifting her out of her despondency.

"Peter, don't go, please! Papa says it's ridiculous. Hitler is murdering you all. Go to England. Just leave." As Lilo saw the stubbornness in his eyes, she felt the air in Peter's tiny apartment close in on her. The room suddenly felt too warm. The stiff gray horsehair sofa scratched at the backs of her legs.

Peter sensed her rising anxiety. "Lilo, please," he spoke in a calm reassuring voice. "I can't do that. You know I hate as much as you do what Hitler has done to us. But I can't just run away and leave my countrymen to fight. And I can't leave you."

She stood up abruptly and paced across the dark pine floor to the fireplace at the end of the small room. She was only standing twelve feet away from him as he remained seated on the sofa, but it might as well have been twelve kilometers. "You will leave me in any case, Peter, and if you go and fight, you may leave me forever. We've lost so many," she whispered brokenly. "Hansi, Albert, Dieter, and now that Leo's flying with the Luftwaffe . . . ," her voice trailed off.

Peter sat dejectedly on the sofa with his shoulders slumped and his hands hanging between his knees. "And if I do as you ask," he spoke as he stared at the floor, "if it were even possible," he stood up and faced her, "what kind of life would I have, knowing that all my friends–every man I know–had gone to war and I was the coward?"

In four steps he was standing beside her. He took her hands in his, "Lilo, that's not something I can live with. Besides, I can do more good within the army than I can running away from it. There have been plots in the military, Lilo. You know what I am talking about. There are rumors that even some generals have been involved–perhaps your own godfather, Sepp Dietrich. You know how close my father is to some of them. He tells me the Führer is losing his hold on them."

She jerked her hands petulantly from his. "No one has the courage, Peter. My Papa and the priest have talked about it. They talk about how sick they are of the war–about the terrible things the Gestapo is doing to people. But no one does anything!"

"Lilo, someone will do something. I promise you." He took her face gently between his hands and looked solemnly into her eyes, "And I will come home to you. I promise you that, too. Do you believe me?" he asked tenderly.

She thought a moment, willing her eyes to remain dry. "I believe that *you* believe you will come home."

Peter leaned down and fervently kissed her lips, stroking her hair with one hand and her cheek with the other. At his touch, she could hardly hold back the tears stinging her eyes. Her heart pounded and she felt the familiar rush of heat to her face–the same heat she felt every time Peter touched her. Peter broke off the kiss.

"Lilo, I must ask you to do something for me while I'm gone."

"Anything."

"Your father told me about Sepp Dietrich's call."

Startled she leaned away from him. She had never talked

to Peter about her work and she was stunned that her father would do so. "What call was that?"

"Lilo, your father must do what he must do, but he worries about you working with him."

Obviously her father had had good reason for taking Peter into his confidence. She felt relieved that this was one important part of her life that she no longer had to keep secret from Peter. Why wasn't he asking her more questions? He didn't seem at all upset that she had kept this important information from him. "I'm sorry I didn't tell you about this, but–"

"Shhh. Did you really think I didn't know?"

She started to speak but he waved her to silence. "Please, let me finish."

She nodded for him to continue.

"Your father has tried to stop you from making these trips with him, but he says you insist. I know how difficult you can be to resist when you insist," he smiled and grazed her lips again with his.

This time she broke away from him, "And I am right to insist. My father needs help. I'm certain you understand that."

"I do," he nodded to her, "but I must tell you that while my father is deeply grateful for your father's work, he knows nothing of your involvement. If he were to find out, he might be forced to cancel your father's contract. He would think it far too risky to have a young woman involved."

Lilo jerked away from him and marched to the small glazed window facing the snowy street. Dark heavy clouds that matched her mood weakened the mid-afternoon sunlight that had streamed through the white airy lace curtains just moments earlier. With her back to Peter, she asked coldly, "Are you threatening us, Peter?"

She paused a moment. Hearing no response, she turned to face him. The small fire didn't provide enough light for her to make out the expression on his face. She shivered as she realized it was also losing its battle against the chill that had crept into the room. She walked to the sofa and turned on the white alabaster lamp. Even that didn't put off enough light for her to read his eyes.

She walked back to Peter and stopped only a few inches away from him. Looking into his face, she made her accusation, "Peter, there is only one way your father would ever know of my involvement–and that is if you were to tell him. Will you? Is that what this is all about? You threaten to tell him, and then I will stop so that our family doesn't lose the precious contract?" The heat of her anger drove away the chill as she decreed, "You will not control me, Peter!"

Reaching out to take her arms, he finally spoke. "Calm yourself, Lilo. Of course, I won't say anything. I'm merely telling you what could happen. I won't tell him, but your determination to continue risks your father's life, your family's livelihood, and the good work you are doing." His voice took on a harsher quality as he finished. "Make certain you understand that your father's worry over your involvement could mean that he can't keep all of his wits about him when he's on a job–and that could be very dangerous for him."

Lilo nodded slowly as the heat of her indignation leached from her heart. He could be right. She settled herself back on the sofa, no longer feeling its coarse fabric scratching against the back of knees. Her father had begged her to stop going with him, but there had been only one dangerous trip since Uncle Sepp's call anyway. When Peter's father had found out about the call, he had insisted that the Burkhardts make certain that leather boots–and only boots–filled the trucks for the next few months.

She would have to reconsider her father's request in light of what Peter had said. But how could she tell him that the only way she knew to keep her fear at bay when her father was on a run was to be at his side? If she were not with him, she didn't know how she would survive those nights, waiting, worrying, frantic with fear until he came home. Besides, she had noticed that a young woman with her father made the authorities much less suspicious. Who would think that a helpless woman would be involved in such things? She had to acknowledge, though, that Sepp's call had been a warning that the authorities suspected both her and her father.

Lilo had accompanied her father on every one of his delivery jobs since the call. They had even scheduled some of them at night to the western border with France so they could establish a pattern familiar to the authorities. Soldiers had even stopped and searched them several times. Each time, the soldiers had appeared surprised and frustrated to find the trucks loaded only with crate after crate of leather military boots. She knew her father felt it was safe now to try another run. She had planned to be at his side again, but maybe it was time to listen to her father and to Peter.

Peter saw the conflict on her face. He sat down beside her, took her hands in his, and pulled her toward him. "I know how difficult this is for you and I know you will make the best decision. Now, I have something else difficult to discuss with you. In fact, if I had not been given my orders to report for duty next week, I would never ask you this, certainly not before talking with your father–and I certainly wouldn't have asked you to my apartment," he laughed gently.

Sensing that something important was about to happen, Lilo typically tried to lighten the moment, "I wondered why you asked me to come here. I thought you were going to try and have your way with me," she laughed.

"Oh, so that's why you ran over here so quickly that I could hardly keep up with you, eh?" He grinned back at her before he became serious once again.

"What is it, Peter? Are you afraid to go to war?"

"Yes, I am, Lilo. I'm no fool, no hero. But it isn't that. It's something far more frightening."

Lilo's breath caught in her throat, "What is it?" she asked gravely.

"Can't you guess?" he asked equally seriously.

Her hands flew to her mouth. She could guess. The hint was when he had said he should ask her father. Even so, Lilo didn't dare voice her hopes for fear of looking foolish if she were wrong.

Lilo knew that Peter loved her, but there were still times when her insecurities made her question it. He was so polished, so mature and handsome. By comparison, she felt ungainly and unfeminine. Her mother constantly reminded her of that fact. Even when Peter's feelings for Lilo had become obvious to Anna, she had constantly reminded Liselotte that no man wanted a woman who was either barreling down the road driving an enormous truck or buried beneath books and ledgers sorting through columns of numbers.

As much as her mother still disapproved of Peter, she took a perverse pleasure in the young man's affection for her daughter. Lilo was convinced that it was because her mother still hoped Leo would be ready to propose marriage to Lilo if and when he returned–but if he had a rival for her affections, he would not delay. Anna seemed to have accepted Peter's relationship with her daughter, but Lilo knew her mother still secretly hoped that Leo would one day become her son-in-law.

Even Peter realized that Anna likely wouldn't have allowed him through the front door, had the Burkhardts not had dealings with the Muellers. He shrugged it off and even found it amusing that Anna forced Lilo to sit down and write Leo a letter every week. But Leo was his good friend, too, and Peter made certain he wrote him often as well.

"Come on, Lilo, guess," urged Peter.

"No. I don't want to. You have to tell me," she replied stubbornly.

"You won't make this easy for me will you, Lilo?"

A wave of shyness swept over her. She could feel her cheeks flush red. She lowered her eyes as he tightened his grip on her hands and moved smoothly from the sofa to position himself on one knee in front of her.

"My dearest Lilo, I have no right to ask this of you right now, but I made a promise to you. Now I want a promise from you. I promise I will come home to you, if you promise you will marry me when I do." Peter, reached into his pocket, took out a simple silver band, and continued, "It is not a diamond. It is not even gold, but it is a symbol of the love I have for you and the promise I make to you today in exchange for the promise from you that you will be my wife when I return. Will you?" His eyes stared anxiously into hers, waiting.

"Peter," she exclaimed as she held out her trembling hand so he could slip the ring on her finger. "Yes, Peter, yes! I will marry you, but," and she reached her hands out to bring his face up to hers as she lowered hers toward him, "Peter, you had better come home. That is my first order to you as your bride. I'll work on more orders so that you have a nice long list waiting for you when you return, but make sure you carry this one out first."

Peter leaned back, rocked on his heels, and stroked his chin, pretending to consider her request. "Hmm, I already promised to obey that first one, but you'd best not make that list too long. I'm not going to allow you to twist me around your little finger the way you do your father," he laughed.

"I don't twist him around my finger. He's just smart enough to listen to me. That's all," she retorted.

"And I thought the army generals were going to be demanding. Ha! They'll be nothing compared to you!" He stood and pulled Lilo up from the sofa. "Come on, Little General. Let's go talk to your Papa. I hope he isn't too angry with me. You are still so young," he added as he held out her dark-green loden coat for her.

"He won't be angry, Peter," she said as she wrapped a warm green woolen scarf over her hair and around her neck. "He cares about you very much. The one you need to worry about is Mama." Lilo grimaced at Peter as he shrugged into his brown, double-breasted leather coat. "Oh well," she added as he tied the belt loosely around his waist and she pulled on her leather gloves, "What can she do? I don't see how she can make our lives any more miserable."

Holding the door open for her, Peter said, "Lilo, I admit that your mother may sometimes be a bit–" He fumbled for a polite way to share his thoughts.

Lilo allowed him to stutter for a moment before she impishly suggested, "Difficult?" They both laughed at the understatement as they stepped out into the bitterly cold weather.

"It doesn't matter, Peter." Lilo reached up to pat his freezing cheek with her gloved hand, "Papa will handle Mama when he sees how happy I am."

They smiled at one another and, holding hands, they ducked their heads and walked purposefully into the howling north wind. Winter-denuded tree branches scraped at the steel-gray skies, their stark brown fingers blurred by the billions of snowflakes the constant gusts whipped up from the streets. Peter leaned toward Lilo and, looking around and seeing no one, put his arm around her shoulder and held her close as they made their way to her home.

For the moment, the war and its horrors–imagined, but still unknown to the hopeful young couple–fell away from them. It was a moment like no other in their young lives, a moment both would relive, over and over, alone, and far away from one another–he in the numbing cold of a Russian winter, and she in a dank prison cell fighting for the life of the only other person on earth whom she loved with all her being. Mercifully, neither of them knew what the future held. All they knew was this moment–and for now, it was enough.

CHAPTER EIGHT

MUNICH, GERMANY: 1943

Lilo squeezed her eyes to slow the tears that wet her cheeks as she began to read the letter. It didn't matter that it had taken more than a year to reach her through the German Feldpost. She would savor every word, every comma, and every period. She half imagined that she could even catch Peter's scent from the wrinkled pages.

January 8, 1942

My Dearest Lilo,

Today I have a little bit of time and I am using the daylight to write you a few lines. We just came across the enemy and the quiet serene life is over. We will lie low in this area for a while. When my mail leaves, I don't know, but somehow it will go out.

If you live like this in danger for so long a time, it is really horrible. If we could just get mail once in a while, then it wouldn't be so bad. Can you imagine a life like this? In half dusk we will arrive in some small Russian village and we will look for a place to sleep. We are waiting until it gets warm again and when it does, we have to get moving again.

How nice it is in our homeland. I think you have to experience this first to really value your homeland. I hope our homeland is drafting more soldiers to come here to Russia very soon so that I can come home, and we can see each other soon. But there is not much hope in thinking that, since there is nothing I can do about it.

I love you so much.

Heartfelt greetings and kisses,

Peter

The thin Feldpost paper felt rough against the tip of her damp index finger as she carefully refolded the letter. She opened her eyes in alarm, afraid the wayward tear that had wet her finger might smear the already fading words on the old letter. She sat up and threw her legs over the side of the bed and picked up Peter's photograph from the ornately carved night table. His solemn light eyes seemed to look through her. She traced his features in the photograph, hating the uniform he was wearing, but lovingly stroking every feature from his long, thin nose to the ever so slightly smiling lips.

Why did she do this to herself? Gazing at his photo and reading and rereading his letters would not bring him home any sooner. While her mind chastised her, her fingers unfolded the next letter.

January 18, 1942

My dearest Lilo!

Thank you very much for your dear letter. Dearest Lilo, if you just knew how much I would rather be with you than to be here. Can you understand that I had to go to the front? If someone says, "Where were you during the war?" I could not say I was at home. I don't want anybody to think that I was not doing my duty. I am not crazy for medals. I will be happy only when I can come home to you..

Oh, Peter! What duty? He'd been gone for so long now. The last time she'd seen him, they had kissed good-bye at the train station—only two days after he had told her he was leaving. Hitler's invasions in Scandinavia to the north, France to the west, Greece to the south, and Russia to the east meant that the huge hungry maw of the military demanded every German son.

She put the letter back in the packet and began her assignment. Her mother insisted that she write a letter to Leo today. She'd already posted three letters to Peter in as many days and she had to agree when her mother told her that writing a friend was the only decent thing to do when those friends were in danger of losing their lives at war.

Not wanting her childhood friend to mistake her feelings, she was hesitant to write Leo. He knew about her engagement to Peter, of course, but she thought that she had detected a hint of romance in his last letter. Her mother had scoffed when Liselotte shared her concerns, claiming that Leo was just another lonely soldier. With the dangers the soldiers faced, it was natural for them to romanticize everything that had to do with home. Besides, there would be time enough to disabuse Leo of any mistaken romantic notions when he was safely home, not when he was God knows where, flying against the English and Americans.

Lilo had to admit it was sometimes a relief to read Leo's letters. He was a typical pilot–invincible. His letters bragged about the exploits and adventures of the mighty *Luftwaffe* rather than detailing the harsh miseries Peter endured in Russia. She unfolded Leo's latest letter so she could read it again and begin a proper response:

> In the next few weeks I think you will see me in the weekly newsreel. A reporter recorded two news strips. The first one is called "Building a New Italian Air Force under German Leadership." I'm flying the "Lilo." We will be taking a few aerial pictures...

Liselotte smiled as she read the last few sentences. She had been surprised when Leo sent her a picture of himself beside his airplane. There, on the body of the plane, was her name– "Lilo." It touched her that he'd named his plane for her, but she felt it was a clear sign that he felt far more for her than she would ever feel for him. Still, she owed him a letter.

Dear Leo, she began . . .

103

CHAPTER NINE

THE FRENCH COUNTRYSIDE: OCTOBER 1944

"Front and center, men, front and center. Here he comes!" The men of the 761st snapped to attention fearfully, yet eagerly. They were finally about to meet "Old Blood and Guts." Bud and C. T. stood side by side, anxious to see the man they'd heard so much about–3rd Army Commanding General George S. Patton. The sea of Negro soldiers stood at attention, the low murmur of their voices buzzing across the cratered landscape.

Bud squinted his eyes against the warmthless October sunshine and spotted the line of jeeps heading toward them. A fifty-caliber machine gun was mounted on each jeep along with a couple of military policemen. As the jeeps bounced towards them, Bud saw one pull ahead of the others and jerk to a stop in front of Colonel Bates. Bud was too far away to see the man's facial features, but he, and every soldier there, recognized the ivory-handled pistols tucked in the man's belt.

"I hear he ain't too thrilled to have us here, Bud," C.T. whispered nervously, blowing on his fingers as a chill wind whipped across the denuded valley stinging the exposed skin on their hands and faces.

"We're all he's got, so he'd better get thrilled," Bud answered. "We'll show him we know what we're doing."

C. T. nodded. "We better be after all that trainin'–in between pickin' up cigarette butts and cleanin' bathrooms," he added with a trace of anger. Bud heard the tamped-down cynicism in C. T.'s voice. He couldn't blame him. They'd had tough duty at Camp Hood, Texas. It was hot as hell, and whether you were colored or white, you were in for a bad time of it. But he couldn't deny that C. T. and the other colored troops had had to carry a heavier burden. Bud was disgusted that the colored men of the 761st could learn to fight in tanks, but they couldn't shop at the Post Exchange. What made it even worse were the smirks on the white faces of the German POWs as they strode into the PX, stepping in front of the colored American soldiers who for a time were barred from entry.

Bud had mixed feelings when he was told that he would remain attached to the 761st when they went to Europe. It was the first all-Negro tank battalion, and everyone was watching the "Black Panthers," as they were called, waiting for the colored men to fall flat on their faces. According to most Army officers, the colored boys were fine for cooking, driving trucks, and the inevitable cigarette-butt patrol and latrine cleanup. But just as she'd convinced many that colored men could fly airplanes, Eleanor Roosevelt believed Negro men could fight in tanks, too.

Bud wasn't sure how the experiment would work until he heard about Lieutenant General Lesley James McNair, the commanding General of Army Ground Forces, who had openly praised the 761st. When the men heard what McNair had said about them, they were ready to fight and prove him right. Bud, along with hundreds of other 761st soldiers, was saddened when he heard McNair had been killed by friendly fire a few months before the Black Panthers landed at Omaha Beach. At least the Training Center Commander had believed in them. When the unit was considered ready to ship out to France, General Dawley had said, "When you get there, put in an extra round of ammunition, and fire it for General Dawley." His vote of confidence had made a difference to the men.

That hadn't been the case with all of the Negro units. Bud had heard from C. T. that the colored soldiers in the 92nd were on the verge of rebellion. Their commanding officer openly hated Negroes. But, as Bud had explained to C.T., being one of only a handful of white officers wasn't exactly a picnic either. Bud was pretty tired of being ridiculed as the "Coon Commander." That was just one of the nicer names some white soldiers had for the few white officers assigned to the 761st. Captain David Williams had told him that would change. He even predicted that before it was all over, Bud would be proud to be a Black Panther. Bud wasn't sure he believed that, but he was proud of his friend C.T.

Something had happened to C.T. during their months in training. The rebellious, quick-witted boy had turned into a serious soldier. Bud didn't know if it was due to the constant abuse by other white soldiers–probably not, since C. T. had been colored all of his life in Birmingham, Alabama. How much worse could it have been in Camp Hood? He knew that C. T. was an expert marksman and a hell of a tank operator, who was ready to fight for his country. With the way his country treated the coloreds, though, Bud couldn't really understand why.

Bud looked out over the field of more than 600 Negro enlisted men, thirty Negro officers, and the six white officers assigned to the battalion. They all stood at attention as the famous general climbed onto the hood of the armored car that had accompanied his jeep. The troops looked pretty good. Of course, they'd only been in France a few weeks. Judging from the nerve-shattering echoes of the heavy artillery firing at the not-so-distant front lines, they wouldn't look this good for long.

"He's about to speak, Bud," whispered C. T. urgently as he poked him in the ribs. "You better get up dere wit de other white boys now, or he's gonna be askin' you a whole lotta questions dat are gonna make the rest of us look bad." C.T. smiled as he poked fun at Bud. "You know questions like, 'Hey, Negro, you already so scared, you done turned white?'"

"Yeah, I do stand out back here, don't I?" Bud made his way to join the other white officers. His friend, Captain David Williams, moved aside to make room for him as the crowd silenced and the General began to speak. Patton's voice rang out over the blackened French countryside.

"Men, you are the first Negro tankers to ever fight in the American Army." A silence followed. "Okay," thought Bud, "tell us something we don't know." If the first words out of

107

the General's mouth were about race, Bud figured the next few words would echo the ones he'd heard from other whites–words like, "Everyone knows you men can't do this," or worse.

"I would never have asked for you if you weren't good." Bud's head snapped up and turned back to where C. T. stood motionless, a huge smile lighting his face. Bud mouthed the words, "Asked for us?" His eyes met C.T.'s, and C.T. shrugged his shoulders in acknowledgement of Bud's surprise.

Patton continued: "I have nothing but the best in my Army. I don't care what color you are as long as you go up there and kill those Kraut sons of bitches! The whole world is looking at you. Everyone has their eyes on you. Most of all, your people are looking at you and I'm looking at you. So goddamn it, don't let them down, and damn you–don't let me down!"

It only took a fraction of a second for those last words to register with the troops before a huge roar of approval rang out. Patton smiled at their excitement, threw up one gloved hand to wave good-bye, and within moments was back on the road, leaving the men of the 761st with a renewed sense of purpose.

Bud prayed the feeling would remain strong enough to get them through the bloody days and nights ahead as he headed back toward C.T. "So, what'd you think of that, C.T.?"

His eyes gleaming, C. T. answered the question wistfully, "I jus' wish Jackie coulda been with us to see dis." Then his usual dimpled smile lit his face as he added, "Course, Jackie would prob'ly have yelled out 'Double V!' or somethin' like dat and dey'd be haulin' him back for another court-martial. Cain't ya jus' see Jackie doin' dat?"

Bud laughed aloud at the picture C.T. had painted. He had to agree it wasn't hard to envision Lieutenant Robinson taking the opportunity to lobby for the Double V Campaign that was all the rage of the Negro newspapers back home.

The articles featured a Double V sign that among the

Negroes represented victory over the Germans in Europe and victory over racism at home. C.T. had shown Bud the letter from 26-year-old Negro cafeteria worker James Thompson that had inspired the newspaper to launch the campaign. Bud could see the questions in his mind's eye almost exactly as they had appeared in *The Pittsburgh Courier*. He remembered them because Thompson's letter had asked all the questions he had always wanted to ask C.T., but just didn't have the guts to.

> Being an American of dark complexion and some 26 years, these questions flash through my mind: "Should I sacrifice my life to live half American?" "Will things be better for the next generation in the peace to follow?" "Would it be demanding too much to demand full citizenship rights in exchange for the sacrificing of my life?" "Is the kind of America I know worth defending?" "Will America be a true and pure democracy after this war?" "Will colored Americans suffer still the indignities that have been heaped upon them in the past?"

"Yep, that would be Jackie's style," Bud laughed. "He's beat one court-martial. I don't think he could stand another."

"Yeah," C.T. said grimly, "still hard to believe dat dey found him 'not guilty' with eight or nine white guys on a nine-judge panel." C.T. snorted, "I wouldn' a made odds on dat bet."

Bud nodded his agreement. "Yeah, but according to the colonel, it was pretty obvious that those guys who claimed Jackie was insubordinate had it in for him."

Bud thought back to those last few tense weeks before they had shipped out from Hood. The only athlete at UCLA ever to letter in four sports, Lieutenant Jackie Robinson was already a celebrity when he joined the 761st. When he clashed with the military police on the post, it had made national headlines. It had all started when Robinson sat down beside a fellow Negro officer's wife on a bus headed off post. The woman's pale skin made it difficult to tell she was colored.

As some white soldiers boarded, they started complaining about the Negro officer sitting next to a white woman. The bus driver ordered Robinson to move to the back of the bus. When he refused, the bus driver called the military police. From that point the situation had heated up. When the word "nigger" was sneered out, Robinson threatened to "break in two" anyone who called him with that word again.

Although Colonel Bates had refused the order to have Robinson court-martialed for failure to obey a direct command and showing disrespect to another officer, Robinson's transfer to another unit had put him under a commander who did sign the order.

By the time Jackie Robinson was court-martialed in August, the 761st had pulled out of Camp Hood on its way to France. Bud remembered how stunned–and how jubilant–he and the rest of the troops had been when they heard that Jackie was found not guilty of all the charges. Having Jackie with them in France would have been a great morale booster, but the "not guilty" verdict was surely the next best thing for the men.

C.T. sounded as mournful as the wind whistling across the barren countryside, "You reckon Jackie wishes he was wit' us? Bet he kinda misses us."

Bud thought about it a moment before he slapped C.T. on the shoulder, "Not if he's got any sense. 'Sides, who'd miss you?" he laughed as he dodged a knuckle sandwich from C.T.

Within a week, the 761st engaged the Germans in battle. It was only the first of what would turn out to be more than six months of brutal combat in an advance that would take the battalion on a trail of agony and death through six European countries. Bud would learn that Captain Williams' promise would come true. He would also learn that in battle that "blood-red" was the only color that counted.

§ § § § § §

"Company, halt!" The order came from the captain of Company A. Lieutenant Bud Leverett's tank ground to a stop. The inside of the monstrous metal machine was freezing. The men shivered in the cold as frozen rain and snow pelted the tank turrets. Bud opened the hatch to see what was holding up the troops. Dozens of colored soldiers marching beside his Sherman trembled in the cold, wet mud, waiting for their next orders.

"C.T.," called Bud, "climb up here and handle her while I find out what's holding up the advance."

Bud jumped down from the tank and landed in an oily puddle of slush that took only seconds to seep into his cracked boots. His toes, already numb and half frozen, stung painfully as he hit the ground. Wet, half frozen, miserable, and stinking, Bud set off to the front of the line. Despite the radios and the communications gear that supposedly made this war so much easier to fight than the Great War, these technological wonders weren't always wonderful. Sometimes, they just didn't work.

Bud had heard the captain's voice crackling through his radio, but he couldn't make out the words that might have told him what lay ahead. He would just have to slog through the mud to get the information.

The 761st was here to support the 104th Infantry in an attack to wrest the French town of Vic-Sur-Seille from the Germans. The dark clouds pressing down on the desolate landscape and the swirls of snow made it tough for Bud to see the thousands of soldiers readying for the battle, but he knew they were there. And he knew they were depending on the Black Panthers. Bud half walked, half ran with his mouth open, trying not to inhale the stench of the bombed and broken sewer mains. The vile smell mixed with the semi-sweet odor of putrefaction from the dead cows and horses dotting the land, their bloating bodies reeking of rot.

As Bud plodded up the mud-rutted road, he saw that despite their wretched state, his men stood still, looking and listening intently for the enemy. Bud hurried on, the newspapers he had stuffed in his shirt for warmth rustling as he walked to where Captain Williams stood beside a tank checking his maps.

"What's the hold up, Cap'n?"

Williams pointed to a ridge of thick brown tree branches beyond the low muddy fields the unit was trying to cross. The wintering branches clawed their way up to touch the low hanging gray clouds that promised more freezing rain and snow. Denying the freezing winter, thick brilliant-green fir trees huddled in clumps, providing the enemy with dense cover from which to attack Bud's unit with impunity.

"The road ahead is loaded with Teller mines, and if our intelligence is right, those woods on the ridge are loaded with Krauts. They've got anti-tank guns up there, too. It may cost us a couple of Shermans and God knows how many men before we can rout them and take the town. Your men ready, Lieutenant?"

"Yes, sir."

"Then head on back and prepare for the worst," the captain said soberly, "and may God be with you."

When Bud returned to his tank, he told C.T. to stay put. He would march in front of his ground troops. Within moments Bud heard the thundering engines of the lead tanks throttle to life. C.T. fired up his tank, and men and machine pushed forward through the muddied, soon to be bloodied, wasteland. Bud explained to his unit that the Germans had likely spotted them and could initiate an attack at any time. The cold forgotten as adrenalin pumped through their bodies, the soldiers kept marching.

The first hail of machine-gun fire erupted so quickly that Bud barely had time to flag his men down and dive into a ditch beside the road. The freezing mud splashed onto his face and hands and plastered the front of his long coat and fatigues like a freezing poultice pack. C.T. loosed his first strike against the machine-gun nest that had assaulted them before another barrage of fire blew a hole in the road less than twenty feet from Bud.

Bud climbed out of the ditch and made his way back toward his men even though he could barely see through the thick smoke-filled air. With the heavy pelting of artillery it was obvious that a sizeable troop of Germans was on the ridge. He could hear the tanks firing, but the howitzer in his unit was silent. "Blake, fire the howitzer! Fire the howitzer!" Bud screamed the order into his useless radio, his voice lost in the furious repetitive thrum of battle.

C.T. blasted another round from the Sherman into the hillside. Flames erupted from the shot, and dozens of German soldiers raced away from the blazing trees in search of cover.

In the momentary lull, Bud turned, and with his shoulders and head bent, raced along the ditch heading toward the howitzer. It took too long to load the tank and, without the corresponding support of the big gun, Bud knew his men were at risk. It took him only a minute to reach Blake's position and throw himself down beside the soldier.

"Blake! What the hell—aw, shit."

Eighteen-year-old Vernon Blake was on his back, his sightless eyes staring at the burning tree tops above them. The other two boys who were part of Blake's team lay to his right. Bright red blood soaked the front of Blake's uniform. Bud couldn't tell the extent of the wounds on the other two soldiers, but both were morbidly still. Bud whispered a quick prayer, passed his hand to close Blake's still warm, staring eyes, and gently removed one of the dog tags from the dead soldier's neck. He checked the other two boys, took their tags, and stuffed them into his jacket pocket. He would never get used to this, but it was time to move.

The huge gun was nearly impossible for one person to manage, but it was already loaded and ready to go. Bud brought it to life. In seconds the pounding of the heavy artillery thumped into the hillside. Bud was gratified when he saw more Germans crawling away from the place where he'd aimed his round.

The firing of the howitzer had bought C.T. the time he needed to load and fire the tank again. He released another thundering salvo, shaking the ground under Bud's feet.

Bud spotted two of his men lying in a mud-filled ditch, their rifles aimed at the unseen enemy. For a split second, Bud savored the pride he felt as he noted the calm deliberate way both soldiers aimed at the hill. The pair and Blake were the three youngest men in Bud's unit. Men? They were boys. In fact, even though Willie Jefferson and Jedediah Leonard claimed they were eighteen, Bud had his doubts. He never doubted their devotion to him or to their country, though.

"Leonard! Jefferson! Get over here and take over the big gun. I'll send some help back to you!" The boys stood, shouldered their weapons, and after glancing up the road, bent low and ran, splashing through the ditch to obey Bud's command. A hail of bullets, so close they ricocheted splinters of icy mud into the soldiers' faces, raced ahead of the pair. They climbed out of the ditch to cover the last few feet when Bud saw Jefferson's frightened but determined face transform into a grotesque blossom of crimson gore. The boy's knees buckled as he threw up his hands to where his face had been just seconds before. In one motion, his body pitched forward into his shallow grave of muddy tank tracks.

Leonard threw his body behind the cover of the big gun, but when he saw Jefferson lying in the road, he sprang forward. Bud grabbed his arm to stop him.

"You can't help him, man. We'll get his tag later, but right now you gotta help me with this gun. We gotta load and shoot and load and shoot. I'm going back up front to get you some help. You hear me, Leonard?"

The frightened soldier nodded.

Bud put his hand on the youth's arm. "You did good, Leonard. You did good, man. We're gonna kick their asses for Jefferson–we're gonna kick their asses all the way back to Krautland for Jefferson. You hear me?"

Leonard swiped at his eyes and nodded grimly at Bud. He took over the weapon and, as he fired off the first booming round, Bud dove forward and raced toward the tank.

First Bud had to get to Jefferson, get the dog tag, and make sure one stayed with the body. Who would recognize the boy with no face if Bud didn't do this? He turned and dove toward where Jefferson lay face down in the mud. The ceaseless barrage of gunfire reverberating in Bud's ears seemed to fade as he lifted the faceless boy into his lap. His hands, slick with Jefferson's blood, fumbled around his neck for both tags. The tag jingled as it landed with the others in Bud's jacket pocket as he raced away from the body toward his tank. C.T. had just fired off another round and the glow of white phosphorus sparkled in the air as the blistering powder ignited the bushes on the hilltop.

As the smoke cleared, Bud shouted to his men, "Keep pushing! We got 'em on the run. Keep firing!"

And with that last admonition, everything slowed to a crawl before Bud's eyes as a torch of heat seared his shoulder and drove him into the mud. Bud lay on his back, stunned by the red-hot embers of pain radiating down his right arm. He took a deep shaking breath as he steadied himself with his left arm and tried to push himself up to his feet again. As soon as he stood up, another fiery explosion burst in his right thigh and the now useless limb crumpled beneath him, throwing him backwards again into the cloying, freezing bed of mud.

Bud saw the top hatch of the tank burst open. "Back in the tank, C.T.," he shouted, his voice sounding hollow as if someone else miles away was trying to get his attention. He tried again, louder, "I said, back in the tank, C.T.! Fire!"

By then C.T. was at Bud's side. "Ah, man. Ah, shit, man! You all shot up. I gotta get the doc here."

"No, C.T., you gotta keep that tank firing or neither one of us is gonna make it. You got that?" Bud grimaced as his lifelong friend ignored his order.

"Butch has the tank. It's firing, Bud, so just shut up, man. Just shut up!" C.T.'s voice was shaking with fear and frustration as he screamed, "Medic! Need some help here!" His voice dropped to its familiar mumble when he spotted one of the medics running toward him.

"Goddamn it! Goddamn Krauts! Goddamn bastards! I'm gonna kill me some fuckin' Krauts. You better hang on, Bud. Don't you die on me. You heah me, man? I wouldn't be in this shithole if yo' white ass wadn' runnin' around out heah'. This is yo' fault, Bud, you heah'? So you better hang in dere. You got dat?"

C.T.'s words washed over Bud, cutting through the pain, cutting through the stink of rot and fire. Damn, he was hurting–and C.T was cussing. He closed his eyes and the pain receded along with C.T.'s voice. He wanted to laugh. The last words he heard from his friend were so typical. He sounded just like he had a lifetime ago in Birmingham, Alabama, when they were both seven years old. C.T. was mad as hell.

CHAPTER TEN

MUNICH, GERMANY: 1944

The skies threatened snow. It was a wonderful night for a trip. "Papa," she whispered, "I can't see you." Lilo walked toward the truck garage, her hands held out in front of her with the groping hesitancy of the newly blind.

A crunch of gravel, a light touch on her arm–"I'm right here, Schatzie. Remember, I will drive the yellow-band. You take the lead in the other truck."

Lilo nodded her assent even though she knew her gesture of agreement was lost in the darkness. "Is it just us tonight, or is Florian driving the third truck?"

"Just us, Lilo."

Georg hesitated, wondering if he should tell her that their third driver had been arrested several days ago, and that making this trip tonight might be an even greater risk than usual. But his contact had told him there were eight people waiting for him and three of them were children. If Florian had talked, then the authorities would come after him anyway, whether or not he made the trip. At least this way, these three children and their parents had a chance. Georg decided his daughter had a right to know the truth.

"Florian was arrested day before yesterday."

He heard her sharp intake of breath. "So we're safe for now, Papa. If Florian had said anything, we would already be under arrest. Don't you agree?" she asked in a matter-of-fact tone that held only a trace of fear.

She was so brave, and though Georg had sworn she would make no more of these trips with him, with Florian's arrest, he had to have her help. They'd finally reached the garage. Georg entered first and held the door open for Lilo.

"Yes, I do. Perhaps the fact that Herr Mueller couldn't get any boots ready for shipping on such short notice may be a blessing. The authorities are used to us having at least three truckloads, but since we're going to pick up wines this time, two are sufficient for a buying trip of such an expensive nature."

"Let's hope they have a change in the guards before we get back to the check point. We don't want them asking to sample our shipment on the way back, do we?" she laughed.

"I've already prepared for just such a moment," Georg assured her as he closed the garage door.

The blackout curtains over the few windows plunged them into an even deeper blackness until Georg turned on the small lamp sitting on a counter just inside the door. The trucks inside the garage appeared out of the darkness, bathed in the light golden glow. Georg opened the door, hopped onto the running board, and reached into one of the trucks. When he climbed down, he held two bottles of wine.

"Here are samples from the vintner. I just have to make sure the guards don't find them on our way to the winery."

That moment a shuffling sound and a short admonition of silence echoed softly in the large garage. Lilo's eyes widened. It was always especially dangerous when they carried children, even though their contact always gave the "travelers" specific instructions. He told them how to get to the Burkhardts, when to go, which truck they were supposed to get into, and what evidence they needed to leave so that Georg would know that his "cargo" was not a trap and was loaded and ready to go. Although they were instructed to maintain complete silence, it was a challenge for the children even though most had long ago been terrorized to the point that they'd learned to obey instantly their parents' orders for silence. Still, by the time they met the guards near the French border, the children would have been cramped in the tall wine casks alone for six or seven hours.

"Lilo, help me load the rest of the barrels," Georg gestured to two large wooden barrels standing near the garage doors. Each of the wooden barrels was roughly three feet wide and five feet high. Even empty, the casks were very heavy.

It took Georg and Lilo twenty minutes to load the two empty barrels onto the truck she would be driving. Georg walked behind the yellow-banded truck and ran his hand under the back fender and across the top of the large right rear tire. When his hand made contact with what he was searching for, he said, "The matches, Lilo."

Lilo struck a match and watched the flame begin to lick the gold-threaded point of the first Star of David badge. Soon the small fire had consumed the eight badges that told them all of the people traveling with them tonight were safely aboard, each one ensconced within one of the eight barrels in the back of the yellow-banded truck.

While the patches were burning, Lilo and Georg reviewed the details of the journey. Usually their trips west consisted of delivering boots to the German soldiers who occupied neighboring France. The Burkhardt trucks never crossed the original border into France, but at least one of the trucks was usually thoroughly checked at one of the guard stations that dotted the new German territory that had been ceded back to France after the Great War. Because so many people in the region were of German descent but spoke French as well, it was easier for them to rendezvous with the Free French Underground between one of the guard outposts and their final normal delivery destination for the boots.

Georg had often tried to convince Jacques Jutard to retrieve his "cargo" at some point before they reached the last guard outpost, but while Jutard was adept at blending with the people in the Alsace-Lorraine region, he would not risk his underground forces by taking one step into Germany. Georg couldn't blame Jutard for his caution. After all, the French were taking great risks in getting the refugees over the border and then to the safe houses in the town of Philippsbourg.

This time, even the trip home would be dangerous because the barrels would be empty on the way back to Munich. Georg had neither a contract, nor any money to purchase wine to make the trip legitimate. Without any official paperwork, the guards would likely search more thoroughly. Every detail of the trip was carefully calculated to use any advantage. They were leaving at nine o'clock at night–dangerously early, but it would be between three and four in the morning when they met the border guards. Tired guards increased the odds of a less thorough search.

The two bottles of Rhine wine that he'd found in their wine cellar would have to serve as a bribe of sorts if the German guards insisted on checking the trucks again on the way back. If they asked to sample the wine, which even Georg had to admit was unlikely, he would simply offer them the bottles, explaining that the bomb-rutted road back to Munich required them to nail the lids securely to the barrels to prevent accidental spillage, making the lids difficult to remove.

Since the lids obviously had to be nailed down when the casks were full of wine, it was not unreasonable that they were loosely nailed down now to insure they didn't find themselves short a lid when the barrels were full. The guards would certainly pry open a few barrels, but the casks that held the stowaways were lodged at the back of the yellow-banded truck. The guards would have to make a special effort, climbing over other empty barrels in the tightly packed truck to examine the ones in the rear. To thwart them further, Georg hammered those lids down more tightly so that they would be too troublesome to open without a special crowbar. If the guards should ask for one, Georg had regrettably lost his.

Georg finished hammering as Lilo ground out the last

plumes of smoke escaping from the small pile of ashes on the garage floor. She swept them away with her booted foot until they mixed with the rest of the oil and grime on the concrete.

"Are we ready?" Georg asked, jumping down from the back of the truck.

Lilo nodded as she wrapped her arms around her father's neck, kissed his weathered cheek, and whispered her traditional blessing, "Safe travels, Papa."

§ § § § § §

The rain had long turned to sleet when Lilo saw the dim lights of the sentry post break through the darkness ahead. So far their luck had held. The snow that had threatened in Munich had only fallen for a few kilometers outside of the city so that despite the rain that had accompanied them for most of the trip, they had arrived at the guard station according to schedule. The loud roar of the engine faded as she shifted into low gear to roll to a stop where her truck would be easily positioned for the search. As planned, Georg would stay several yards behind in the hope that the guards would be satisfied searching the truck nearest them.

Lilo pasted on her most brilliant smile as two young, solemn soldiers walked wearily toward her. Their wrinkled uniforms and sleep-encrusted eyes bolstered her hope that their plan would work. Their uniform insignia told her the short, light-haired youth with the petulant expression was a corporal. The sergeant was a taller blonde man, probably in his late twenties. Lilo took a deep breath to revive herself, then bit her lips, and pinched her cheeks to bring some color to her pale face.

She'd already rolled down her window to greet them when they reached the truck. Two pairs of bloodshot eyes met her own as she spoke, "Heil Hitler! A long night isn't it, gentlemen," she smiled in commiseration. Both men were instantly and self-consciously alert at the sight of the lovely blonde woman poised behind the wheel of the large truck. Lilo

121

pointed behind her where her father's truck was idling. "My father and I are visiting several vineyards around Hornbach today. We are buying wine to take back to Munich."

"So your trucks are empty?" asked the sergeant, stifling a yawn.

"No, we carry our own wine barrels that are filled at the vineyards. Regrettably," she added with a small laugh, "we don't have enough money or trucks large enough to carry even one of the huge wine vats from the vineyards." Her cheeks dimpled coquettishly as she smiled at the sleepy soldiers.

The young corporal puffed up with juvenile self-importance: "We shall have to search your trucks, of course."

"Of course," Lilo replied cheerfully. The sergeant grunted his half-hearted agreement as the corporal strutted toward the back of her truck. Lilo's mind raced, trying to think up some conversation to keep the sergeant with her. If the corporal handled the inspection alone, then perhaps he would only look through Lilo's truck. He would be bored soon enough and wave them through.

"Has it rained here all night?"

The sergeant replied, "Most of it, yes. You'll have to drive carefully along the road into Hornbach. How many vineyards will you visit?"

Lilo's mind faltered a moment as she thought back to their previous trips. "Oh, as many as it takes to bring back a variety of some dry and some sweet wines. If we're fortunate, perhaps the first one will have enough to sell so we don't spend our day and our petrol driving around the countryside," she said with mock exasperation.

"Are you going to help me here?" the young corporal shouted.

The sergeant scowled his response to the young man.

Lilo looked over her shoulder at the corporal. Lieber Gott, oh dear God! He was heading toward her father's truck! In an instant Lilo hurled open the truck door. Its weight slammed into the sergeant. His pained yelp of surprise broke the early morning silence.

Lilo tumbled out of the truck, apologies falling from her lips as she threw herself into his arms pretending to help him catch his balance.

She shouted over her shoulder, "Corporal, please help me a moment. I'm afraid I have accidentally hurt your sergeant. Oh, I am so sorry," she wailed grievously as she leaned heavily against the tall man.

The corporal ran toward them.

"What's happened here, Klaus?" The annoyance in his voice forced the question to end in a nasal whine.

Embarrassed, the sergeant growled, "I'm fine. I'm fine," but he did nothing to stop Lilo's hands from fluttering up and down his arms soothingly.

"Klaus? Your name is Klaus? My favorite cousin's name is Klaus," she gushed effusively while her heart pounded in her ears. "Why, you even look like him. I've always said how I hated that he was my cousin. It's embarrassing to go places and have all your girlfriends ignore you while they bat their eyelashes at the handsomest man in the room," she said coyly. "You are truly all right, aren't you?" she asked, her eyes melting into his with grave concern.

Lilo was grateful her father was too far away to witness the humiliating spectacle she was making of herself.

Before the sergeant could answer, she turned with annoyance to the corporal, "Do you have no respect for your superior? Either help him back to your station where he can rest a moment or hurry and finish your search," she ordered peremptorily, hoping the corporal was just young enough to be awed by the authority in the voice of an "older" woman.

He was. The words stuttered out of his mouth: "I-I must search, Fräulein."

"Of course, you must," Lilo responded, and with a last glance at the sergeant who was tentatively rubbing his abdomen, she turned the full force of her charm on the underfed boy. "Come." She took his elbow and guided him to the back of her truck. "Shall I help you? You may have a bit of trouble removing all of the lids from the barrels. We have to nail them down or they'll rattle constantly on these rutted roads and drive me to distraction," she added with a sweet smile.

The youngster was no more immune to Lilo than his sergeant. She glanced around the corner of the truck to make sure Klaus didn't try to redeem his manhood by deciding to engage himself in a search of her father's truck. No, he was still standing where they had left him. She turned to face the corporal who was slapping his hand against the side of the barrels. This one was not stupid. With each slap of his hand the barrels echoed hollowly.

"Oohh," she sucked in her breath piteously. "Poor Klaus. He certainly looks as though he needs some help. Tell me," she brought her voice down to a pseudo whisper, "I know he is the sergeant, but do you always have to do all the work for both of you?"

The corporal looked at her admiring smile and grinned back arrogantly as he jumped down from the back of the truck and swaggered close to her. His thin, drawn cheeks pinked with pride as he answered her, "It does seem that way," he sniffed.

"It certainly does," she exclaimed, hoping the concern in her voice didn't sound too false. She looped her arm through his and rested her hand on his forearm. "Would you be so kind as to help me back into my truck? It's still so dark, and I twisted my leg yesterday stumbling around these horrible roads. I'm afraid if we don't get to the vineyards soon, we'll never get our wine loaded and back to Munich before tomorrow." She glanced out of the corner of her eye to make sure the corporal was appropriately moved by the worry in her fawning voice.

The corporal glanced hesitantly at her father's truck. She jerked her arm from his. "Of course, you don't have to help me since you're still too busy. I'm sure Klaus has recovered enough to assist me," she sniffed haughtily as she opened her mouth to call to the sergeant.

"No, no," he said reaching for her hand and tucking it into the crook of his arm again. He called to his sergeant instead, his voice matching the swagger in his step, "Klaus, please open the door so I may help our Fräulein back to her truck."

"Certainly," Klaus responded so unctuously that Lilo had a difficult time holding back her laughter as his smiling eyes met hers. He rolled his in ridicule at the pompous corporal's affected manner.

"Thank you so much. Klaus, I am so sorry about our accident. You are all right now, aren't you?"

"I assure you I am fine, Fräulein."

Lilo turned her attention to the corporal who was standing impatiently waiting for his accolades. "And thank you, too, Corporal. I hope I shall see you later this afternoon. Perhaps I can convince my father to purchase a bottle of wine for two such fine young soldiers," she said as the two assisted her into her truck.

As she pulled away from the checkpoint, she gave them a final wave before speeding out of sight.

Lilo had driven several miles before the shaking in her

125

arms and legs fully subsided. "Danke, lieber Gott, danke." Thank you, dear God, thank you, she repeated over and over. Despite the frigid early morning chill in the air, her brow still shone with the sickly nervous sheen of sweat that had begun pouring from her the moment she was safely out of the guards' sight.

Within fifteen minutes they would meet Jacques at the rendezvous point. Only then, when the children and their parents were safe with him, would she dare to release the hysterical laughter threatening to overwhelm her. It was a habit she'd never outgrown. In pain, under stress, Lilo had always laughed. It was the only way to keep from crying.

§ § § § § §

Lilo cut off the engine and rolled the truck silently into the dense forest. She moved far enough into the cover of the sheltering trees so her father could pull his truck behind hers and shield it from the view of any passers-by. The rising sun streaked the sky, lighting the tops of the green firs with brilliant golden crowns, though thankfully it had yet to penetrate to the dark forest floor beneath them. Lilo hopped from her seat and ran toward her father's truck. He was already heading to the back.

There was no sign of Jacques, but Lilo knew that once he arrived he would wield his crowbar with speed, open the barrels, and transport their cargo out of sight within minutes. Georg and Lilo would then have to find a place to wash away the human waste they would find in the barrels before heading back home. Father and daughter were hoisting an empty barrel from the truck when Jacques and one other man materialized from the forest. Armed with crowbars, they crawled into Georg's truck and made short work of moving the empty barrels out of the way and prying open the others.

Georg remained on the ground and kept watch as they worked while Lilo climbed into the back of the truck to help their passengers. Her eyes widened with stunned disbelief as a tiny, filthy hand reached over to grasp the rim of one barrel. She

126

instinctively clasped the thin, dirt-encrusted fingers and peered down into the darkness. The acidic smell of urine pierced her nostrils and the long-lashed brown eyes of a little girl blinked back at her as she raised her other thin arm imploringly toward Lilo. As Lilo lifted the child out of the barrel, the toddler's arms wrapped tightly around her neck and she sighed deeply as she tucked her head under Lilo's chin. Wordlessly, Lilo stroked the child's fine dark hair for a moment and then gently unwound the child's arms.

"I'm going to put you down now. I have to help the others. Ja? Yes?" Lilo lowered the child to the floor of the truck where she wobbled for a moment before her thin white legs crumpled beneath her. Instead of the howl of pain Lilo had expected, the child scowled, made an impatient motion with her hands, and fastidiously brushed the dirt off of her hands before purposefully struggling to her feet. Lilo picked the child up once again as she walked to the front of the truck bed. She buried her face in the little girl's hair to wipe away the hot scald of tears that burned her eyes. Sensing Lilo's distress, the child used one still grubby hand to brush at the moisture on Lilo's face.

"Esther!" A woman's cry broke the communion between Lilo and the child as a disheveled young woman reached into the truck, snatched the youngster from Lilo, and began cooing to her, "Esther, *mein Kind,* my child."

Lilo looked again toward the back of the truck where two women and two children–perhaps a few years older than Esther– quietly tested their cramped legs and stretched their aching arms. The smell escaping from the barrels fouled the air. Lilo felt sorry for them, especially the women whose cheeks flushed with embarrassment at the waste that soiled their skirts. A tall, emaciated man unfolded himself from the last barrel and smiled graciously as Lilo offered her arm to help him.

A long, low whistle from outside the truck immediately froze the travelers inside with silent terror. "It's all right," Georg whispered into the back of the truck. "That is the signal. Jump

down, speak quietly, and follow your guides. You must hurry.
Can everyone walk?"

At the universal nods, Lilo and the two French men
jumped down from the rear of the truck and began lifting the rest
of the women and children onto the ground. Within seconds,
hands were coming from every direction, touching and patting
Georg and Lilo as the voices, in the hoarse whispers of those
who have been silenced for too long, all offered prayers of
thanksgiving. The thin dignified man who'd emerged last from
the barrels grasped Lilo's hand and bent low to kiss it gently. He
lifted his deeply shadowed slate grey eyes to meet hers.

"Thank you, Fräulein. I will remember your face always
and I will always thank you for the life of my wife," his arm
reached over to encircle the shoulder of the woman who carried
the smiling baby Esther, "and for the life of our child." He then
turned to Georg, "Thank you, sir, for the chance you've given us
this day." He nodded toward Lilo, "Your daughter?" At Georg's
affirming nod, the man added, "May we raise our daughter to be
as fine and brave as yours. Shalom." Her father's eyes looked
suspiciously bright as he thanked the man for his kind words.

A short, heavily muscled man dressed completely in
black and carrying a rifle emerged from a thicket, waved his free
hand urgently and called in a loud whisper, "Nous allons! Nous
allons! Ici! Ici! Let's move, let's move. Here, here!" The
bedraggled group melted into the thick forest.

CHAPTER ELEVEN

U.S. ARMY FIELD HOSPITAL NEAR CHERBOURG, FRANCE:

CHRISTMAS 1944

Mail! Thank God. Bud was getting tired of talking to wounded soldiers and visiting brass. He did like the string of pretty nurses, though. Must be the Army's idea of a Christmas present. Not that he had anything against the nuns, but Bud felt a little funny when a pretty sister took care of him. He couldn't talk to her the way he could to some of the bright-eyed Army nurses. Those nurses had a way of making you feel that even if you were down now, they knew you were man enough to make a comeback.

Bud glanced at the pathetic little tree tucked in the corner of the sterile hospital ward. It looked as wounded as the soldiers in the unit, but the tiny cherry-cheeked French girl who'd dragged it in yesterday had been thrilled at her gift to the Americans. Bud couldn't understand what she said, but one of the guys who spoke a little French said the people in the town had cut down the tree and donated the ornaments so the American soldiers could enjoy some Christmas cheer. Pretty decent of them, Bud thought, considering that a few houses and this church-turned-hospital were the only buildings left standing by the time they drove the Germans from the village. Now finally, he had a real Christmas present–a letter from someone who was out there, someone who might tell him what was really going on. Bud ripped open the letter from C.T. Deeks.

Bud, you lazy grunt–Sir.

Bud laughed out loud at the appellation. C.T. had no respect for a superior officer.

I don't know if you'll get this in one piece. I gave it to Captain Williams

because I figured they'd probably censor it
to bits if I didn't. I hope you're on the
mend. You gave me a real scare when you
got hit but that's what you get for being
such a sucker.

Bud laughed again. He did feel like a sucker. One
month in battle and he was down for the count. But the Army
docs were right when they had promised him he'd be as good as
new and ready to slug it out against the Germans again. Now
he was all healed and just waiting to leave. He probably didn't
have a chance of rejoining the 761st–God only knows where they
were. Uncle Sam had told him he'd join the next group of grunts
marching through the area on the way to Germany.

It's been tough, Bud. We're doing all
right, but you'd be one lonely white boy
if you were with us now. Only one left is
Captain Williams. Guess he's enough. When
I'm not mad at every cracker in the world–
except you and you don't count, I can see
the Captain is a pretty good egg. There
don't seem to be too many like him.

I did hear that some general at Hood
said that we Negroes stood pretty high in
the Tank Destroyer classes at OCS. Of
course, this guy was surprised about it,
but at least he bothered to tell somebody
we could do the job and do it pretty damn
well, too. Not good enough for the Army,
though. I thought Birmingham was bad. My
four years at Wilberforce University were
like a breath of fresh air–my own people,
my own place. Even OCS wasn't too bad.
Now, even getting killed isn't enough to
satisfy the white man.

The day you got knocked out of action,
we took Vic-Sur-Seilles. I don't know how
these Frenchies spell their names–so just
ignore the spelling. Anyway, the next day
we took some castle town called Chateau-
Salins. It took us four hours of straight
fighting in a monster of a snowstorm, but
we did it. Then we moved on to some place
called Morville-les-Vic. I told you to
ignore the spelling!

130

> Those first two days from November 7th–9th,
> we lost you and every other white officer
> except Williams. Even the battalion
> commander got hit. We lost nine Black
> Panthers, too—not saying the white officers
> weren't Black Panthers, but you know what I
> mean. I mean Negro Panthers.

Bud read the names of the dead and saw each face. Sometimes he lay awake in the hospital bed at night, not daring to fall asleep because his nightmares would wrench him from sleep so hard that his screams would awaken everyone else in the ward. In those sweaty nightmares, he saw Blake lying there shot to hell and saw Jefferson get his face blown off again. In those brilliantly colored recalls, Bud always ran to save Jefferson, but he never made it. Over and over again, the boy's face exploded, saturating Bud's own uniform with blood and gore.

> Captain Williams says I shouldn't even
> write you this stuff, but I figure by now
> you're getting pretty sick of all the fine
> food and bullshit they're feeding you at
> the hotel-hospital.

> Back to the story: By November 16, we
> were headed to someplace called Guebling.
> That's when the shit really got to me.
> Remember Ruben Rivers? Light-skinned Okie?
> Remember that time early on when we heard
> all those mines blowing up, and it turned
> out some crazy guy had hooked a cable from
> his tank to a tree and then pulled the
> tree out of the road with mines going off
> like popcorn? Well, that was Rivers. The
> brother got a Silver Star for that—won't do
> him no good now.

> Anyway, we were headed to another French
> town when the Krauts started kicking the
> crap out of us. We were getting mortared
> and shot up like you wouldn't believe.
> Rivers' tank hit a mine that blew out half
> the bottom of the tank and about half the
> meat off Rivers' leg, too.

> Captain Williams told me the medic had
> bandaged Rivers up and got ready to give

131

him his morphine and take him out of there, but Rivers told the Doc he wasn't leaving the fight. He told the Captain that he was going to need him. Williams told me he begged Rivers to leave, but he wouldn't.

By that time, the snow and sleet was falling hard and we hit a nest of Krauts that wouldn't turn us loose. We got pinned down and were fighting like hell. It got so bad Williams ordered us to get out of there and take cover.

Then Rivers radios in and says he sees where this anti-tank shit's coming from. He tells Williams he seen them so he was going to fight them. Long story short—Rivers got those Krauts, but he died doing it. If it hadn't been for him, you wouldn't be reading this letter.

A couple of days later Williams tells me he took a recommendation to the brass to get Rivers the Medal of Honor for saving the unit. I don't know for sure what happened next. Williams won't say too much about it, but you can tell he's angry if anybody brings it up. Word is that when he brought the recommendation, the senior officers just laughed at him and threw it in the trash.

So you tell me, why should a colored man take another step in your white man's Army? If you come up with an answer while you're vacationing there, you let me know. I'll tell you right now, if it wasn't for the guys we lost and Captain Williams, this Negro would be anywhere but here. I'm thinking something like what you got right now—pretty women bathing you, breakfast in bed—that kind of thing. And if anyone called me "Nigger," I would kick some ass! Guess that means I better not go home to Birmingham when we're done here.

So long now. I know this letter cheered you up. Don't know when we'll see each other again, but don't forget our promise. I get it—you know what to do. Of course,

if you don't get your lazy ass out of that
soft bed, the only thing you'll be fit for
is driving a desk.

So long, and pray for the Panthers. God
knows we need it. V V

Pray for the Panthers. If his words had not made it
clear, the hastily scrawled double-V symbol evidenced C.T.'s
frustrations. How could C.T. still pray with what he was going
through? Since he'd seen Jefferson's face blown off, Bud wasn't
doing much praying. He didn't understand why God let this shit
happen. But he'd been questioning God for so long, it was just
second nature. It really didn't surprise him, or even hurt as much
any more when God let him down.

Sometimes, for brief moments, his father's letters helped
him understand, but Bud's dad had never seen this kind of soul-
searing devastation. He wondered idly if even his saintly father
would hold so tightly to God if he knew what God was up to
here. Even as he posed the question, Bud knew the answer.

Time to pull out one of his father's letters, he thought
with a sigh, or C.T.'s letter was going to have him wallowing in
the depths of gloom for days. He didn't want to be there today.
It was hard enough to fight off the clinging miasma of misery
surrounding the fact that it was Christmas, and he was in a ward
with twenty men, some of whom he might have called friend.
When he first got here, he'd dared to make friends. They had
died.

Why, Dad? Give me an answer, Bud demanded silently
as he sat up in bed and reached for the packet of letters he kept
in his knapsack on the metal nightstand. He untied the graying,
once-white string that bound the slim packet of papers together.
Hmm—he hadn't even been here long enough to amass a decent
cache of letters to look through when he needed respite from his
own dark daydreams. Where was the letter he was looking for?

Sometimes Bud tired of his dad's constant preaching, but

133

he had to admit that his father didn't just speak the word. He lived it, as Bud had never seen another human being live it. Bud figured his dad was trying to be good enough for both of them. He thought guiltily about how his dad had probably had to work doubly hard to try and ensure Bud's salvation, considering all the trouble Bud had gotten into during his years at home and in college.

He had caused his father no end of embarrassment. One particular night he'd stumbled home drunk as a skunk. God, he was so sick he'd just fallen onto the front porch swing and vomited between his knees. He might have gotten away with it if a member of his mother's Women's Temperance Society hadn't seen fit to make an early call on the Reverend and his wife.

Bud laughed out loud. Not so funny then, but it sure was funny here. Just another example of God's twisted sense of humor because his father had never done anything Bud could see to deserve a son like him. But Reverend Leverett always told Bud he loved him and was proud of him, saying he figured God was saving Bud for something so big that He had to teach him some lessons early.

There it was. He unfolded the already yellowing sheets of paper and scanned his father's words until he found the verse he was looking for.

> . . . who comforted us in all our tribulation, that we may be able to comfort them which are in any trouble. Whether we be afflicted, it is for your consolation and salvation, or whether we be comforted it is for your consolation and salvation.

Bud often disdained his father's lengthy Bible quotations, but this one made some sense.

> We are troubled on every side, yet not distressed, we are perplexed but not in despair—

Bullshit! Bud threw the letter down. He was not just perplexed. He *was* in despair. And Goddamn it, he *was* distressed! Why? Why? WHY? Bud's fist hit the pillow beside him with a soft whump. The move was enough to catch the attention of one of his fellow patients.

"Hey, Merry Christmas to you, too, Leverett. What happened, man? Santa not gonna bring you what you want? Hey, me neither, unless that red-headed nurse gives me a back rub or–" The man's words stopped abruptly, bitten back by the look of rage Bud leveled at him. The unexpected jocularity of the man's comments hit Bud right between the eyes.

"Hey, sorry, man. I just–" His words stuttered away as he looked at Bud.

"S'okay, Crenshaw. No big deal," Bud lied smoothly trying to tamp down the anger that threatened the hard shell of equanimity he'd worked so hard to construct. "Just gets to me every now and then. Know what I mean, Buddy?" Bud's smooth white smile slid into place, one thick black brow arching up as the other eyelid closed over a crystal clear blue eye in his trademark wink.

Bud knew that even though his lips felt stretched to the point of cracking over his dry white teeth the face he presented to Crenshaw and to the rest of the world offered no hint of his inner anguish. As he leaned back against his battered pillow, the thin strains of a heavily French-accented rendition of Silent Night mocked his emotions, but still managed to send him into an uneasy slumber.

CHAPTER TWELVE

MUNICH, GERMANY: 1944

The air raid siren shrieked its series of deafening blasts across the city. It was not an unusual occurrence anymore. Lilo and her father joked about her own personal early warning system. Whenever American or English bombs dropped nearby, Lilo's hair filled with static electricity and lifted like a gauzy halo off her shoulders. It was such an accurate sign that now whenever her scalp started its familiar tingling, she would alert her family and they would move to the nearest bomb shelter. It was one of those inane jokes that people who find themselves in unthinkable circumstances learn to make in order to bear the unbearable.

Lilo deftly steered the truck to the curb and had hardly shut down the engine when she and her father jumped out and raced into a basement-level restaurant. The streets, already filled with people going about their daily duties, instantly transformed into congested avenues as the throngs rushed to shelter.

The raid was a short one. A mere ten minutes later as Lilo and her father walked back to the truck, Georg joked, "Your system failed us this time, Lilo."

"Of course, it did, Papa. The bombs fell too far away. You don't see fires here, do you?" She hopped into the driver's seat and waited for her father to join her. They'd driven only a few miles before they saw the damage the bombs had wrought. Thick, oily plumes of black smoke billowed into the sky, high above the multi-story apartment buildings. Months of such bombings had left most Germans inured to the sight of blackened rubble. Lilo and her father looked at one another with relief. While the devastation was terrible, it was miles from their home. The familiar mixture of sadness, mingled with guilt at the relief she felt, tightened her throat as they drew close to the first of a

137

block of flaming buildings.

Lilo was amazed at how quickly the fire and medical personnel rallied to the scene. Moments from the time the bombs had burst, the wailing ambulances careened around corners and skidded to stops. Doctors and nurses, the coats of their already soot-soiled uniforms flapping behind them, ran from group to wounded group, trying to identify those who needed them most urgently.

Just one year ago, there had been no bombs in Munich. But 1944 Munich and other southern German cities now suffered the same barrage of Allied bombing that the cities in the north had endured for several years. A burning beam clattered onto the road showering sparks onto the hood of the truck. She slammed on the brakes and shut down the engine. They would move no further for a while.

She heard her father sigh and turned to him as he leaned back into the seat, closed his eyes, and massaged his forehead. Her eyes widened as she looked past him to see a harried young man drop to his knees beside the immobile form of a small tow-headed boy. The man, a medic or doctor, judging by the nearly shredded Red Cross pinned to his sleeve, grabbed the child's wrist, bent low, and put his ear to the boy's mouth. Seconds later his shoulders slumped as he gently placed the tiny hand over the child's chest. He looked around, his eyes scanning the crowds, perhaps for the child's parents. As he rose heavily to his feet, he seemed loathe to leave the toddler who was obviously beyond medical help. Muffled sounds of keening and crying leached in through the closed windows of the truck.

Lilo saw the doctor look down once more at the unmoving child before he ran toward the next group of men, women, and children who lay bleeding in the streets, while dozens more raced frantically from one burning building to another calling out for loved ones. Firefighters sprayed sparkling plumes of water into the cool, smoky air trying to douse the leaping flames. The brilliant orange tongues of fire crackled and hissed noisily, heaving puffs of thick, black acrid smoke into the silent breezes that lifted and spread the noxious fumes through the streets. Civilians worked to help the firefighters unravel lengths of massive hose, hoping for enough water to drown the raging infernos. A few others, bravely or foolishly, raced in and out of the burning buildings trying to salvage what they could before the flames finished the job that the bombs had begun.

Amidst the frenzy, Lilo's eyes rested on one of the few still images in the chaotic scene. An old man sat on a sidewalk curb, his bumpy spine lumping the thin fabric of his brown coat as he bent forward, hands cradling a woman's head in his lap. She appeared to be sleeping in his arms, but the blood seeping from her mouth and ears, staining the frayed collar of her white blouse and coloring the silvered wisps of hair near her ears, made it clear that she would not awaken from this sleep. The old man seemed oblivious to that fact as he gently rocked her back and forth, stroking her forehead lovingly, blood streaking her face with every tender touch.

Stopping had been a mistake. Theirs was the only truck or car that was not a military or hospital vehicle. Lilo saw people push toward them. Their backs bent with the weight of chairs, pictures, even pots and pans as they frantically tried to save what they could from the all-consuming infernos. Within minutes they surrounded the truck pounding on the doors, their frightened faces pressed against the windows.

"Please, please, take this on your truck."

"Please," cried another, "a ride to Erding–to my brother's." Lilo opened the door slowly and stepped down from the truck to push the crowd back. Within seconds, wet, entreating, blood-smudged hands pulled on her dress and raked her long hair as the growing cluster of people jockeyed for attention. Her eyes teared as the choking smoke roiling from the blazing buildings stung her eyes and nose. Lilo knew it was impossible to accept and deliver the stacks of household goods that the desperate people were loading on the truck. She and her father tried to stop the frantic crowd, but their voices were lost in the din. Finally, her father moved his enormous frame to block off the back of the truck.

"No more," he yelled as he waved his arms in the air. "We can carry no more! Those of you who have belongings in the truck may climb in. No more than six people. The rest of you must go." His voice sounded uncharacteristically ugly and harsh, but Lilo knew her father. He never cried, never wrung his hands, and never let anyone except her know the depth of his rage and frustration over the war. The crowd kept pressing toward him, pushing him, trying to climb around and over him to get into the truck. A burly middle-aged man grabbed Georg by the lapels of his brown wool jacket and pulled him forcefully out of his way so he could climb into the truck.

"Goddamn that stupid devil, Hitler!" Georg hurled the words into the crowd as he snatched the interloper's pants leg and pulled him from the truck. The silence was nearly instantaneous. Those who couldn't be forced away before drew back as though burned. Her father had just committed the unspeakable. Lilo thanked God that the noise and furor of the tragic scene had likely drowned out her father's momentary lapse of his senses. Nevertheless, the crowd had heard, and the knot of desperate people melted away as quickly as it had converged. As they drew back, their nervous eyes darted back and forth, scouring the crowds for the uniforms of the Gestapo, those spies who moved among the people, always ready to arrest any traitor who showed the slightest hint of disloyalty to Hitler.

Lilo climbed uneasily behind the wheel, while her father listened to directions from the few people who had already climbed into the truck and decided that a way out of the blazing neighborhood was worth the risk of riding with a traitor. Georg was walking toward the front of the truck with Lilo watching in the driver's side rearview mirror when it happened. Two Gestapo officers came out of nowhere, grabbed Georg's arms, one on each side, and lifted him off the sidewalk. Georg had not seen the pair and, surprised and at the end of his patience, he wrested his arms away from them, turned, and landed a fist on the chin of the shorter of the two men. The man absorbed the blow, but before he could strike back a third Gestapo officer materialized behind Georg and brought a heavy truncheon down across his back.

"You will come with us, Herr," thundered the tallest of the trio. Lilo jumped out of the truck as her father fell to the ground. The men and women in the back of the truck did the same, running from the scene leaving Georg and Lilo, and their belongings behind.

"What are you doing?" She screamed as she fell down beside her father and tried to help him to his feet. Her father leaned heavily on her as he got to his knees.

"Out of the way, Fräulein."

Lilo barely heard the snarling command before an enormous black boot kicked her in the face, causing her to fall backwards and strike her head on the pavement. Only the blood streaming from her mouth and nose kept her conscious long enough to hear her father yell, "Leave her alone! I'll come with you," and to see his face before hers as he whispered forcefully, "Stay down!"

Rolling onto her stomach on the sidewalk, Lilo yelled as loudly as she was able, "Where are you taking him?" Her voice sounded tinny and shrieky to her, as though some child was screaming at her. The blood rushed to her head, and she could hear it pounding in her ears as it renewed its flow from her nose and mouth and mingled with the tears streaming from her rapidly swelling eyes.

The same pock-marked Neanderthal who had driven her father to the ground fixed her with a baleful glare and spat menacingly, "To the same place you'll be going if you don't be quiet–the Türkenkaserne!"

"Call Dietrich," was all her father had the chance to say

141

before the man with the club brought the weapon down heavily on Georg's skull. Catching him in his arms, he dragged her now unconscious father to a black car and unceremoniously dumped him into the back seat. He slammed the door and climbed in the front as the driver incautiously pulled away from the curb scattering the crowds. Dimly aware of her knees prickling from the hard gritty pavement, she watched helplessly as the car raced out of sight through the hellish scene of fire and blood. Involuntarily, she leaned forward and vomited into the gutter.

CHAPTER THIRTEEN

MUNICH, GERMANY: 1944

"I don't know where they are, Sepp," Anna cried into the telephone.

"Anna, calm down and think. Think. Anna, let me explain again what I was told. You tell me if you can remember where Georg and Lilo said they were going today." Dietrich quickly reviewed the call he'd received from the young SS lieutenant. The man had asked whether General Dietrich knew a civilian arrested this morning and accused of treason for denouncing the Führer and assisting people to escape the law.

Dietrich had been unnerved by the call. He remembered how he and his boyhood friend had tried to squeeze out a living during those first months after the war ended. Everyone knew that when times were hard, one could count on the farmers to have something. So Sepp and his friend Georg had spent their days traveling to various farms and selling "holy" relics. The devout wives of the Catholic farmers in Bavaria and throughout southern Germany always had enough money for a piece of St. Peter's sail or a shard of wood from the cross of Christ. If there was no money, there was meat or flour–something that could be sold or traded back in the city. Those were hard times, thought Sepp, but infinitely easier than the present.

No time for reverie right now–Anna's hysteria was rising. "I can't remember anything, Sepp. There's nothing to remember. You know how Georg and Liselotte are–they tell me nothing," she wailed bitterly.

"Anna, please. Whatever has happened, you or I will hear from them. If you hear first, you must ask where they are and call me right away. Do you understand?" Anna voiced her assent, and Dietrich quickly hung up. Anna should hear something soon enough, and he would hear from her. He would be ready when the call came.

Anna paced distractedly across the marble foyer trying to fathom what Sepp had told her. Why did he think that it was possible Georg was under arrest? True, the authorities had questioned them several times, but there were no problems. Anna's pacing stopped instantly as the front door swung open and her daughter stood before her.

"Where have you been, Liselotte?" cried Anna, racing toward her daughter. "Oh!" Anna stopped in her tracks as she stared at her child. Blood streaked Liselotte's pale hair. Bright splotches of it stained her gray cotton dress. A dry salty crust of blood and tears rimmed her bloodshot eyes and chapped lips. But it was the expression in those eyes that chilled her. Their empty stare swept past her as Liselotte moved calmly toward her mother, gently pushed her aside with a limp gesture of her left arm, and walked to the telephone table. As she picked up the telephone, she commanded coldly, "Sepp's number–I need it now, Mama."

Her stony voice added to Anna's distress and a quick sting of familiar resentment flared in her. Just like her father, Anna thought sadly—unfeeling and imperious, no matter what the circumstances. Anna had little time to nurse her hurt before her daughter's next sharp words pierced her pain.

"Hurry, Mama. Papa's life depends on it," Liselotte said tersely. Anna gave her the number and added, "I've already talked with Sepp. He –"

"You've talked with him?" Lilo's head whipped around toward her mother and then back to the phone. "Onkel Sepp? It's Lilo. They've taken Papa to the Türkenkaserne!"

The Türkenkaserne! Anna knew, as did everyone in Munich, that the dungeon-like cells of the Kaserne were a torture stop on the way to Dachau. No one knew what happened there or at the other camps rumored to exist. Anna knew of only one person who had ever made it out. The story he told–or more precisely, the one he refused to tell–spoke volumes about the unendurable hell that existed there for Jews or other Germans who simply couldn't keep their mouths shut–like her husband, she thought resentfully.

While Lilo listened to Sepp, Anna thought back to the night she had first learned about Dachau. It had been some years ago. She, Georg, and Liselotte were enjoying a quiet meal at home when someone knocked at the door. Frau Stimmel had still been with them. When she had answered the door, everyone heard her surprised exclamation, "Herr Goldbaum!" Georg had rocketed out of his faded tapestry armchair and sped toward the door.

"Abraham, can it be?" A moment later an emaciated shadow bearing a fleeting resemblance to Georg's old friend walked into the dining room, leaning on Georg's shoulder. It was indeed Abraham Goldbaum. What in God's name had happened to him? Anna couldn't believe the skeletal man with the ravaged face and prematurely white hair was the same man who just some years earlier had been the picture of an affluent Munich banker. The only resemblance she could find was in the eyes of the figure that bowed deeply before her now.

Goldbaum couldn't miss Anna's shocked stare. As he rose, his eyes–those same warm expressive brown eyes–looked into Anna's violet ones as his mouth twisted into a wry smile.

"Ah, Frau Burkhardt, please accept my most profound apologies for disturbing your family at this hour. I know you worry, but I promise I will stay only a moment."

His voice shook slightly, and Anna felt herself blushing at the implication that one of her husband's dearest friends was not welcome in his home. She could feel Georg's censorious eyes on her. She answered in the most welcoming tone she could muster. "Nonsense, Abraham!" She hoped her voice registered a reasonably sincere amount of warmth without the fear Abraham had obviously discerned in her upon his arrival. He was a wonderful man, but times had been so hard on the Burkhardts because of him. That was not fair, she reflected–it was because of Georg's foolish and outspoken devotion to him.

"Sit down, Abraham, sit down." Georg guided his friend toward his own comfortable chair. "Frau Stimmel, a brandy for Herr Goldbaum, please." Anna wondered if she was the only one who had noticed Frau Stimmel's brief hostile glare before she ducked her head and rushed to comply with Georg's request.

"Abraham, where have you been? We have been so afraid for you. I was told you had been arrested." Georg pulled another chair up to the table and sat across from his friend.

"Georg, I can only tell you that I have been in Dachau. I came tonight only because I knew you were likely worried for me and because you have always been the only family I had. Selfishly, I wanted someone to whom I could say farewell. I leave Germany tonight."

"Oh, thank God for that, Abraham. But how did you escape? Or did they release you? What is it like there? We hear very little about the camp–only that it is horrible." Georg leaned in more closely to hear his friend's hoarsely murmured response.

"I did not escape, Georg. I was released and was allowed this visit before I leave, but I can tell you nothing about Dachau. It is not allowed. One word about it, and they will send me back there. Georg, I cannot go back. I will not go back." Abraham's empty eyes pleaded for understanding as he continued, "My leaving Germany is a blessing, Georg, though it breaks my heart to leave the land of my birth. Tomorrow I go to Russia."

"Russia!" Georg exclaimed. "That's insane! We are at war with Russia. The fighting is terrible there. I don't know what news you received at the camp, but thousands of Germans and Russians are dying there every day. Everyone knows the

Führer can't possibly continue fighting on two fronts. We only hope it comes to an end soon, and Lilo's fiancé can come home."

"I know all this, and I, too, hope the fighting ends soon," he smiled gently at Lilo. "Who knows? Maybe I will help keep him safe. I'm going to Russia because the Führer has a special assignment in mind for me. I, along with some others, will be used to find and clear mines."

The Burkhardts sat in silence, stunned with incredulity at what they'd heard. Georg was the first to recover. "That's outrageous! You're no trained soldier, Abraham! Surely they have professionals for such work?"

"I'm certain they do, Georg, but it's dangerous work. Why waste the life of one German soldier if you can use a German Jew as a human mine sweep?" he shrugged fatalistically. We will walk in front of the soldiers and we will find the mines–ja, when we step on them and they explode–which is why it was so important for me to come and say good-bye to you."

Georg recovered his voiced and boomed, "Why you simply can't go, Abraham. It's ridiculous–suicide. You must go back to the camp. They can't force you to go–or better still we will arrange for you to join me on a little trip."

Anna froze in horror. A little trip? With Abraham? What was Georg talking about? She glanced briefly across the room, her eye detecting a flicker of movement. Frau Stimmel again? Listening? Ridiculous. I am losing my mind. Frau Stimmel has been with us for years. Still, Anna's every nerve wanted to shout at the men to be quiet. But be quiet about what? She didn't understand what they were talking about.

"That's the primary reason I had to see you, Georg–your trips." Georg held up a silencing hand to Goldbaum and spoke to Anna.

"Liebchen, Darling, bitte, would you check on Frau Stimmel and the brandy?" Anna nodded and jerked up from her seat, desperate to get away from the disconcerting conversation. She too wondered what was taking Frau Stimmel so long.

Once Anna had left the room, Georg motioned for his friend to continue.

"Georg, I heard of these trips in the camp–heard a few of the prisoners talking about the secret mark on one of your trucks. Georg, I promise you, if the prisoners know, then so do the Nazis. If you are caught, you will join me in the minefields, or worse."

Georg shook his head stubbornly, "There is no worse, my friend. Let me help you."

"No," the emaciated man answered flatly as Anna joined them bearing a silver tray with two snifters of brandy. Abraham stood as she entered the room and took the glass she offered him from the tray. With the beautiful flourish that she remembered so well, he bowed to her once again and lifted his drink.

"To you, Anna," he nodded as he and Georg sat down once again. They nursed their brandies for a few moments in silence. Then, placing his still half full glass on the table, Georg's friend rose painfully from his chair.

"Please do not get up. I will see myself out. They are waiting for me." Georg ignored him and rose immediately saying, "No, Abraham. Listen. We must think. They can't make you go."

What Anna remembered most about that night was how calmly Goldbaum had responded to Georg. He stood at the front door and, with an arm looped around his friend's shoulder, answered without a trace of the earlier tremble in his voice.

"Georg, they are not making me go. I volunteered and was fortunate enough to be chosen. My choice is the minefields over the camp, Georg. And I will not go back to the camp. I cannot! You cannot imagine the horrors there. They defy description," he whispered bleakly, seeming to have exhausted all his energy with his vehement declaration. A brisk blast of cold air chilled them all as he opened the door to leave. With a brief nod he added quickly, "Good-bye, my dear friends. It has been a rare privilege to count you as my family." With that, Abraham Goldbaum accepted Georg's bear hug, broke away to offer one last bow to Anna and Lilo, and walked out into the frozen night.

He had said nothing about the camps that night. But he had made it amply clear that choosing certain death in a frozen minefield thousands of miles from home was a far better fate than Dachau. It was the unbidden memory of that night that terrified Anna as she listened to her daughter speaking frantically to Dietrich. Her husband could well be on his way to that same camp. If that happened, it wouldn't be long before she and Liselotte wound up there as well.

"Thank you, Uncle Sepp. I will leave for the Türkenkaserne in a few minutes." As Lilo hung up the phone, Anna launched herself toward her daughter.

"Liselotte, you can't go alone! Look at you," she cried. "What has happened? I am so afraid," her panicked voice fluttered out the words weakly, "but I will go with you."

"No, Mama. You cannot. Uncle Sepp was very clear about that."

"Liselotte, you must tell me what's happened. I have a right to know. Why has your Papa been taken into protective custody?" Anna fired the question at her daughter's retreating back. Liselotte whirled around to face her mother.

"Protective custody? That stupid statement is exactly why you can't go with me. You won't face the truth. There is no such thing as protective custody. That's the term the Nazi filth uses. It is an arrest–for nothing!"

Anna recoiled at Liselotte's tirade. Her hand flew to her

mouth as tears of worry and now pain at her daughter's treatment of her stung her eyes.

"Forgive me, Mama, but I don't have time to explain. I must get dressed and go now. I am sorry. Honestly."

Sensing an opening in her daughter's armor, Anna blinked her eyes dry and drew herself to her full five feet. "Liselotte, I am sick with worry for your father, yet he runs around all day and night doing God knows what, and you protect him. It's no wonder he was arrested as you insist on calling it. Now what exactly has he done? Tell me."

Liselotte's cuts and bruises were beginning to hurt, and the pain was grating at the edges of her patience. Here she stood listening to her mother's idiocy in the comfort of the marble foyer hung with tasteful gold-framed landscapes while her father languished in the dripping dungeons of the Türkenkaserne. Liselotte took a deep breath, wiped her palms on her torn and blood-spattered gray dress, and tried to respond calmly to her mother's diatribe.

"He has done nothing–nothing." She shook her head forlornly. Seeing her child's obvious anguish brought Anna under control. She reached out her perfectly manicured hand and brushed Liselotte's arm tentatively. "I am his wife, Liselotte– your mother. Tell me, please."

Liselotte looked at her dainty mother. Her hair was perfect, as always. Her perfectly pressed lavender silk day dress with its perfect Belgian lace collar made her blue-violet eyes look almost purple. Liselotte shook her head in amazement. Even in these difficult times, her mother insisted on maintaining appearances.

Standing in the foyer, Liselotte could see four massive pairs of twelve-foot mahogany doors closed tightly. They shone, and no one would guess what lay behind them. Anna had covered all of the antique furniture in them with sheets.

They had no more servants and since it was futile to try to keep up with the household work, Anna had left only two rooms open downstairs–the grand parlor and the library dining room. As she'd often heard her mother say, appearances must be maintained. "One must do what one must do and if we keep our heads down we will emerge with them still on our shoulders when this is over." The temptation to relieve her own burden passed. No, her mother could not be trusted.

"I don't know what happened. There is nothing to tell you, Mama." She turned and wearily put her hand on the ornate black iron balustrade beside the marble steps that would take her to her room. She was so tired, but she had to hurry.

Her daughter's ability to completely shut her out, so like that of her father, enraged Anna. "I will find out for myself what is happening. I will go with you!"

What little patience Liselotte had maintained evaporated at her mother's words. She deliberately took her foot off of the first stair, scowled at her mother and sneered, "You?"

Anna shivered at the bold disrespect in her daughter's tone.

"Liselotte, you will not go to the Türkenkaserne alone. It's simply no place for a young single girl. It's unseemly–with all those SS barracks there," her mother sniffed. Liselotte almost laughed out loud. She so wished and had been so tempted to pour everything out to her mother, but with every word Anna uttered Liselotte knew that she and her father were right to make certain she remained ignorant.

Anna's peremptory demand ended on a sorrowful note, "I need to see him–" The tears of worry she'd held back ran from her eyes as her trembling hands smoothed the clean lines of her lavender silk sheath.

Typical. But Liselotte was not her father, and she needed to hurry. Dietrich was making arrangements, but the timing was critical. She had to do her part–and quickly. Rolling her eyes impatiently Liselotte declared, "Mama, I have no time for your dramatics, to see to *your* needs. I'm going to wash and then I am going to the Türkenkaserne–alone. You would be worse than useless there," she remarked pointedly as she turned away from Anna and began her march back up the circular marble staircase.

A searing flash of temper burned away Anna's pain. "How dare you!" she screamed at her daughter's retreating back. Her rage powered her tiny purple pumps up the steps behind Liselotte. She grabbed her daughter's elbow and spun her to a stop. Her arms trembled slightly as she clenched Liselotte's upper arms in her dainty white-knuckled hands. She looked up to face her child's hard stare.

"You are my daughter and you will not talk to me that way. Do you understand me?" Her voice vibrated with anger as she shook her daughter forcefully. "You have no right to tell me what to do. I don't know what your father's dragged you into, but he's responsible for being there and he has no right to jeopardize us by asking for your help. I want to make sure your father knows the position he's put us in so I will go to the Kaserne, not you."

Jerking her arms from her mother's grip, Liselotte exclaimed, "He didn't drag me into anything," she scathingly reproved her mother, "and I should think your concern should be for him right now, not for us."

Anna shot back, "And I should think that you would realize by now that his involvement with these Jewish actresses and these–"

The force of her daughter's slap across her face sounded like a gunshot in the cavernous foyer. Its echo chased Liselotte guiltily as she sped up the stairs to her room.

CHAPTER FOURTEEN

THE FRENCH COUNTRYSIDE: JANUARY 1944

God, these assholes were pissing him off. And he'd thought it would be better to be around some white southern boys. Damn! Give me the Black Panthers any day, Bud thought sourly as he trudged along the muddy roads through the bomb-blasted French countryside. He recalled how both Colonel Bates and Captain Williams had told him that one day he'd be proud to be part of the 761st. Forget being proud, he was just tired of this bunch of rednecks.

"Hey, grunt. Gotta smoke?" One of the paratroopers jostled Bud with an elbow to his ribs, nearly knocking him off balance.

"Cut it out!" Bud spat out angrily.

The gray sky with its low, moist-looking clouds added to the grayness of Bud's mood. The damp freezing temperatures penetrated Bud's heavy overcoat, but despite the chill, Bud caught the unpleasant aroma of his own sweet and sour sweat. The effort it took to lift each heavy boot out of the sucking mud warmed the soldiers up quickly enough, but each time they stopped marching, their perspiration evaporated, leaving only the pungent smell of their unwashed bodies lingering in the freezing air.

"I told you last time you asked that I don't smoke." Bud decided to let the "grunt" remark pass. These paratroopers thought they were the elite of the Army, but they certainly weren't the only guys who called Army foot soldiers grunts. Sure, Bud could remind them that he was no foot soldier–he was a tanker, Goddamn it, but that would just open up a new round of jeers about the Black Panthers.

The young trooper's smile curled into a mocking grin anyway as he hooted, "Oh, yeah, that's right. Preacher boy don't smoke. Don't drink or fuck either, do you?"

Bud wished for the thousandth time that day that he hadn't given away the cigarettes in his ration packs. If he still had 'em, he'd light 'em up, and shove 'em down this little bastard's throat.

"Don't let him get to you, Leverett," advised the captain, who'd walked the last three miles beside Bud without saying a word. "Dave's always Mr. Cool Cat. I thought he'd drive me crazy in Toccoa. Every word out of his mouth was 'F' this and 'F' that. I thought the boy had no vocabulary whatsoever. But it's not that–he was just brought up so strict in those Georgia backwoods that he didn't know what to do with himself once he got away. The boy just went crazy, smoking, drinking–you name it–every chance he got." The captain smiled slightly at Bud as Dave glared at the two and fell back behind them.

"Is that where you guys trained–Toccoa, Georgia?" Bud was familiar with Toccoa. It was the home of a private Baptist College that he had visited a couple of times with his father when Reverend Leverett traveled to Georgia for Methodist Church conferences.

"Yeah, it was tough, too. If you wanted to be part of the 506th Parachute Infantry Regiment, you had to work like a dog. More than 500 officers volunteered and more than 5300 enlisted guys tried to get in. Out of all of those guys, only about 150 officers made it–and most of the enlisted guys washed out. I think we might have ended up with slightly fewer than 2,000 of those 5,000 guys."

"After awhile it was guys like Dave who kind of kept us laughing through the pain. One guy, some preacher's kid, said he'd rather wind up speaking German than succumb to the outhouse oral offerings that passed for the English language. You know this guy just had to be talking about our buddy

Dave back there." He laughed and pointed his thumb over his shoulder.

"What I can't figure out is why you guys want to jump out of a perfectly good airplane?" Bud grinned, warming up to the low-key captain.

"For me, it was that extra hundred bucks a month. Even the enlisted guys get an extra fifty."

A smattering of distant machine-gun fire stopped the conversation. The men could hear the fire, but they couldn't see anyone. The thick hedgerows on either side of the road turned fighting in this area into a treacherous game of hide and seek. You heard a shot, and if you weren't hit, then you tried to figure out where it came from so you could shoot back. The thick green shrubbery was one of the worst enemies the American GIs found in parts of France.

The hedgerows dated back to Roman times when the now rock-hard mounds of earth, overplanted with shrubbery, had been used to mark property lines. The tall dense bushes were perfect cover for the German defensive forces. Bud was almost grateful he wasn't driving a tank. When a tank tried to go through a hedgerow, the earth that had been packed down for centuries wouldn't give–even under the weight of a tank. Instead, the tank would rise up like some rearing metal monster giving the Krauts a clear shot at its unprotected underbelly. No thanks, thought Bud.

Another burst of machine-gun fire broke the early morning silence. Bud was already on his stomach when the captain yelled, "Hit the dirt, Leverett. That last burst sounded pretty close."

Bud and the captain rolled into a shallow ditch. The rat-a-tat-tat fire continued for several minutes as the dozens of soldiers ahead of Bud and the captain returned fire. Bud squinted his eyes but the enemy remained hidden. Fine wisps of smoke curled and hung in the frigid air ahead of them as the sound of the bullets died away. At least it was only small arms and machine gun fire–no mortars.

The captain was already on his feet and offering a hand up to Bud when an enormous blast blew open a wet crater in the road ten feet in front of Bud. Gritty black mud shot into his eyes as he threw himself blindly back to the ground, face first, nearly suffocating as the wet clods packed his open mouth and nostrils. He turned his face sideways and blew the muck from his mouth. He kept his eyes closed and allowed his ears to scan the sky above him. Bud marveled at the sharp acuity of his senses. He could hear the eerie low-pitched whistle of the north wind and nothing else for a few seconds. The skin on his back registered the caress of his shirt and coat as the wind whipped them up and down on his prone body. There were no more mortar blasts, but the rifle and machine-gun fire started up again.

Slowly Bud opened his eyes–to find himself staring into a pair of wide lifeless ones just six inches away from his own. The lusterless gaze of the captain's eyes didn't fully register with Bud until he saw the thin trickle of blood oozing from his newfound friend's mouth and nose. A biting blast of the wind made his eyes water and sting. Bud kneeled beside the captain and released the metal chain with its identifying dog tags from the body before passing his hands over his new friend's eyes to close them. Distant shouts from American voices told him medics were on the way.

Bud stood up and saw the men with the red crosses on their sleeves already kneeling among the dead and the dying, trying to get the wounded out of the open roadway and under the hedgerows, where they could treat them without attracting any more bullets. In addition to the captain, three other soldiers lay still in the reddening mud, and about fifteen yards ahead, Bud could see dozens more on the ground.

Bud watched as one young medic flew to the side of a soldier close by and began working on him. Apparently the guy had been hit badly because from Bud's vantage point, it looked as if the medic wasn't getting any help from his patient in trying to get him to the side of the road. When the medic was finally able to drag the soldier to safety, Bud saw him dash back to the road to pick up several objects lying in the dirt, his head bent low to avoid attracting any gunfire. In a momentary lull, Bud made a quick run ahead, firing his machine gun in quick spurts and sprays to try and give the medic a clear path back to the wounded man. Another burst of machine-gun fire answered Bud's volley, but the medic made it safely back to his patient.

Bud admired the Army medics. In the training camps everybody made fun of them. That changed when the troops entered the fighting. Many of the medics performed so heroically in the field that contempt had long ago changed to respect. Bud understood why as he raced toward the medic and the wounded man he was tending. The medic's own bag was apparently empty, but he found one of the Syrettes that the wounded soldier carried in his musette bag. The Syrettes contained doses of morphine. The medic plunged the Syrette into the soldier's chest and then attached the empty tube to his collar. Whoever treated the soldier down the line would know to avoid giving a second– and potentially lethal–dose of morphine.

Another round of fire drove Bud into a ditch before he could reach the medic, but he was close enough to see a sight that nearly made him puke. The medic was kneeling beside the soldier and trying to reattach one of the soldier's arms to his mutilated torso. The soldier's left leg lay useless in the dirt beside his still body. As Bud's head cleared and his stomach stopped gurgling, he crawled the remaining few feet to the medic's side. Good God. This boy wasn't even twenty years old, yet the effort he was making to save the hopelessly ruined soldier aged his hairless face with every frustrated crease of his pimpled brow. It was obvious that the medic's efforts couldn't help.

"Hey, Doc," Bud said, paying the young teen the respect he so obviously deserved while resisting the impulse to say,

"Hey, kid." Bud placed his hand on the boy's shoulder. "Doc, he's gone." The blood that had been pumping out of the stump of the man's severed right arm and leg had stopped. The medic just shrugged off Bud's arm and his words, still engrossed in his work. Bud tried again. The medic's dog tags had fallen out of his shirt and were swinging in front of him as he bent over his dead patient. Bud lifted the tags, read the man's name and called to him, "James, Michael James."

The boy medic looked up, "Mikey–everyone calls me Mikey." His vacant shell-shocked eyes stared vapidly at Bud.

"Yeah, Mikey. Look, let's give this guy a rest, okay? Come with me. It's pretty quiet now. I think some of the boys up front are gonna need you. This guy's gonna be okay now." As he talked, Bud took the teen's elbow and helped him to his feet. The stinging smell of white phosphorus still hung over their heads, but the air was mercifully quiet. Bud saw a knot of soldiers heading towards them.

"All clear," one of them shouted.

"You got a medic up there?" replied Bud.

"On our way. How many you got down?" Bud glanced at the youth who had melted away from his side and was crouching down again beside his "patient." "Just one, guys–just one," Bud said sadly, wondering how many more men would make it home with their bodies intact, but their minds forever crippled. Before the pain could dig too deep, Bud heard a call.

"Hey Panther! You goin' on a little ride with me." It was Bud's nemesis, the frog-belly pale, red-headed, trash-mouthed Dave.

"I'm not going anywhere with you, jerk."

"You are if you want to meet up with your Nigger buddies again," laughed Dave.

Bud's astonishment defused the quick spark of rage ignited by the man's slur against his fellow tankers. "What are you talking about?"

"Some of us are gittin' sent up to Belgium. The Krauts are all lined up there, and we're gonna go meet the 17th Airborne. Your guys are spearheadin' for 'em. God help us," he added derisively, "but orders is orders. At least we got some Airborne guys there. Anyway, the major says you need to go. They's in a bad way and needin' some experienced tankers. You any good?" he asked.

"Not bad. When do we leave?"

At that moment a canvas-covered transport truck lurched up to a stop in front of them. A filthy-faced sergeant leaned out of the passenger side, a cloud of cigarette smoke wisping to his nostrils and hiding his eyes. With the cigarette dangling and waving from one corner of his mouth, he yelled at the pair, "All aboard to no-man's land!"

CHAPTER FIFTEEN

MUNICH, GERMANY: 1944

Eyes cast down, Lilo made her way through the shattered streets of Munich. She huddled into her thin cloth coat, not so much seeking warmth from the worn brown wool but to blend in with the other colorless defeated masses who wound along the buckled walkways running beside the potholed streets. The Germans' usual penchant for orderly progress was ruined. The crowds lurched crazily with people bumping into one another, sometimes murmuring *Entschuldigung*–excuse me, but more often just shuffling past aloofly as they tried to pick their way through the stones and broken bricks littering the landscape.

The buildings on both sides looked like open mouths with black, rotted, decaying or even missing teeth. Stone buildings squatted by the road, their second and third levels blown off. Tall buildings lurched ominously, barely holding their own with great chunks of brick and mortar gouged from their sides.

The painful throbbing in the right side of her face kept pace with the rapid nervous beating of her heart. Lilo knew she probably presented a gruesome figure to the people who stood in the long queues waiting for food. If they noticed her swollen and blackened right eye and raw oozing cuts on her right cheekbone and upper lip, they did not register it. She scanned the crowd, knowing that if she caught anyone's eye, they would look down, look away, and pretend not to see. It was their way–Anna's way, the only way, of staying safe: see nothing, remark on nothing, know nothing.

The hundreds of people forced to stand for hours waiting for rations kept their discontented mutterings to a minimum. Everyone knew that the Gestapo mingled with the populace, ready to arrest or even shoot on sight anyone whose grumbling included disparaging remarks about the Führer. Grateful that her father had not met that fate, Lilo hoped that the bribe Sepp Dietrich had advised her to take to the Kaserne would allow her to bring her father home.

The Türkenkaserne was in the heart of downtown Munich. Afraid to drive one of the trucks left in her father's once large fleet, Lilo opted to walk. Dietrich had warned her that the Gestapo might have enough of a description of the trucks to use against her and hold her if she drove one. She had told Dietrich she certainly would not take the yellow-banded truck they parked at the garage behind the house, but he had advised her it was still best to go on foot. There was hope that her father's arrest had come about solely because of his rash and contemptuous remarks against Hitler in a public place.

Sepp had warned her that thousands of people were picked up without a shred of evidence, but often broke down in fear and confessed to things that the authorities knew nothing about–that was how the Gestapo worked. Silence, he cautioned. He counseled her that if she were questioned about any of her father's activities to admit nothing–no matter what they promised, and no matter what she might see them do to her father. Lilo's heart had frozen at that, and Dietrich had refused to say more.

Arriving at the Kaserne, an imposing three-story building with a network of cells and tunnels rumored to run below the building, Lilo took a deep breath and repeated Sepp Dietrich's warning in her head–admit nothing. She stepped out of the weak sunlight of the gray day into a dark and cavernous hallway. It was freezing. The heavy smell of ammonia failed to mask the cloying, musty scent of damp decay that permeated the stone walls and floors of the building. She showed her papers to the armed sentry, who scanned them and wordlessly pointed to the stone steps descending into the earth.

Before the daylight completely receded, she saw a light flicker ahead of her, illuminating the pale patches of moist moss clinging like a second skin to the stone walls. As she reached the final step, she felt before she saw the huge presence that materialized beside her. The dim bulb glowing from the wall in front of her and the dusty moats of intermittent light shining from the grates of the street above the subterranean cavern helped her eyes adjust quickly.

"Your papers," demanded the guard, his expressionless pale, gray eyes boring into hers. She handed him her identification papers and said in a voice that startled her with its strength, "I'm here to visit my father." Dietrich had warned her not to cower before the guards. He said that despite the ghoulish skeletal death head the SS guards wore on their uniforms, they were lowly idiot-beasts. Like animals, the scent of fear could drive them to attack, while a show of strength gave her the best chance of success in her mission. A wayward shaft of lemony light haloed the lower third of the guard's face. Lilo was surprised to see the sheen of pale blonde fuzz on a boy's chin.

"His name?" the teen tried to bark gruffly.

"Herr Georg Burkhardt," she replied calmly.

"You cannot see him now," the guard said abruptly as he wheeled on one shiny boot heel and stalked away.

"Wait a moment. I was promised." Lilo stated flatly.

The guard spun around to face her. "Promised? By whom?"

Lilo realized that in her desperation she had spoken too soon. Uncle Sepp had told her this would happen. The guards would forbid her entry, waiting for the accustomed bribe, but she was to keep calm and keep them guessing about whether she truly had connections that could wield power over them, should they prove too harsh. It was a fine line. He had specifically explained to her that using his name at this point could jeopardize her chance of getting her father out of prison.

Lilo drew another deep breath and smiled as best she

could, feeling the raw skin on her upper lip split wide with the effort. She brought her hand up to stanch the threatened flow of blood and said, "No one really. I only hoped that perhaps you and I could negotiate so that I might just see my father for one moment." Lilo saw the spark of interest in the guard's eyes.

"What did you have in mind, Fräulein?"

Lilo reached deep into her overcoat pocket. Sepp had told her that the guards were easy to bribe, but that the bribe must be of value, easy to hide, and untraceable. The guards were always searched at the end of their shifts, and if they were found carrying large sums of money or a valuable object that could be traced to an individual, they would be shot.

Lilo and Dietrich had agreed she would pry a diamond and two pigeon-blood rubies from a ring her father had given to her mother. Lilo pulled a handkerchief from her pocket and unfolded it, carefully revealing its contents in the flat of her palm. The matching one-carat rubies and the single two-carat diamond glowed in her palm. She heard his quick intake of breath before she saw him look cautiously from side to side. He pulled her roughly by her elbow into a dark corner. A wave of panic washed over her—he was going to overpower her, steal the stones, and throw her out. She tried to calm herself again. Dietrich told her that the penalties for anyone threatening a German woman were so stiff that she would be safe. She needed to stay calm.

"I see my father first. Then you get the stones."

"Be silent. Or find yourself arrested, Fräulein. Give the stones to me if you want to see him."

Lilo shook her head, "Understand, please. I must see my father. You will have the stones." She tried to smile engagingly as she flattered him. "We both know that if you were not such an honorable soldier, you could take them from me anyway," she added.

The striped half-light from the street burrowed into a dark corner of the room as the sun shifted in the sky. In the shredded light Lilo thought she saw a glimpse of sympathy in the young man's eyes.

"Fräulein, you must give them to me." The sibilance in his whisper hissed menacingly in the gloom. "They will search you, and if they find them," he nodded towards a dim stone passageway, "they will keep your stones and then arrest you for trying to offer a bribe. Do you understand?"

Lilo used the shifting half-light in the room to look into the young man's face and made her decision. Despite his harsh words and tone, he had kind eyes. She almost laughed at how quickly and decisively she had determined that. The past few years of war had taught Lilo and many others to trust their instincts over words. She handed him the handkerchief with the jewels wrapped in them. He snatched it from her, quickly shook the stones from the fabric, handed her back the linen square, and then drew his gun from his holster.

"Oh, please, no!" Lilo cried out, her voice echoing in the darkness.

"*Sei ruhig*! Be quiet!" he snapped at her as he quickly released the magazine from the Walther PPK, put the gems inside, and slid it back into the gun.

Once he had holstered the weapon, he motioned for her to follow him down the narrow cobbled passageway. Flickering electric lights placed every few feet overhead kept enough of the darkness at bay so that Lilo could avoid tripping over the uneven stones on the floor. The passage finally opened into a small anteroom. As her eyes adjusted to the onslaught of bright light, Lilo saw a slovenly guard sitting at a scarred wooden desk, his feet propped up, head thrown back and eyes closed. The young teen with Lilo slapped the soles of the man's boots with the leather baton he pulled from his belt.

"Heinrich, the keys. The old traitor has a visitor." The unkempt guard snorted awake. Seeing a visitor, he licked his thin lips and ran his freckled hand across his thinning gray hair to smooth the long strands across his scalp. His leering smile revealed a row of perfectly even, long, yellow tobacco-stained teeth. Lilo was unable to still the shudder of repulsion that ran through her.

"Here you go," the guard said curtly as he tossed a ring of keys to Lilo's escort. "He has some visitors with him now, but I don't think they'll mind one more. By the time they're finished with him, he may not feel like having any more guests. She had best see him right now," he chuckled unpleasantly.

His words intensified Lilo's fears for her father and, as the young soldier unlocked the gray metal door leading down another dim hallway, her hands itched to shove him aside and run down the tunnel screaming for her father. Within moments, the soldier stopped abruptly at a blackened iron door. The heavy metal muffled the sound of raised voices.

He turned to her and ordered, "Stand back and wait until I call you."

"No, please. You promised." Again, Lilo thought she saw the guard's pale eyes soften as he reached out his large mitt of a hand, looked furtively around again, and then patted her clumsily on one shoulder. "Bitte, Fräulein, you will wait out here. It will only be a moment."

She nodded in mute agreement, and the guard pounded on the iron door demanding entry. Lilo heard the gruff response, "Come in."

The guard unlocked the door with the ring the older guard had thrown him. He offered Lilo a slight encouraging smile as he pulled open the creaking door and stepped inside. As the door slammed shut, she could hear short staccato murmurs of conversation but couldn't make out the words.

166

After a few moments, the door swung open wide, and the guard stood before her. Over his shoulder she could see a single electric bulb throwing harsh light on the damp, moss-slicked walls of a small stone cell. The young guard stepped aside as Lilo walked as calmly as she could into the tiny dank cell. Pale, cleansing sunlight shone through a tiny barred window set at least eight feet high in the thick stone walls. The natural light comingled with the harsh aura of the bulb dangling at the end of a thin black wire, and in its brilliant aura she could see her father trying valiantly to smile at her.

Something wasn't quite right though, and before she could even register his welcome, she gasped in horror. The left side of her father's face was drawn down in a dreadful rictus. His left eye was open and staring, while his right eye was swollen nearly shut, the flesh ringed with black and purple bruises. Dried blood caked his right eyebrow and ear.

"Oh, Babbi!" She cried, the name she hadn't used for her father since she was a child. "What have you done to him," she shrieked accusingly as she rushed toward her father. A hand reached out from behind her and wrenched her arm so painfully that she nearly fell to her knees on the filthy stone floor.

"Be quiet," commanded a strange voice. "You will not approach the prisoner unless we allow it."

Lilo's father waved his right hand for her to obey the guard. She could see now that his left hand lay useless and claw-like in his lap. Her heart stabbed in her chest when she saw the shackles around her father's ankles. It was obvious they were not necessary since the entire left side of his body seemed shrunken into itself. All of the strength that had fortified her for her mission seemed to run from her body and puddle around her feet. She wanted to do nothing more than to put her head in her father's lap and sob.

He felt it. Although his words were slurred, she clearly heard her father say, "No more tears, Lilo. We will be home soon." The guards heard him, too, and raucous laughter burst out in the room. Lilo realized that there were two more guards in the cell other than the young soldier who had brought her to her father. The laughter stopped abruptly when one of the guards spoke.

"Not likely." A short, round man, his belly hanging grotesquely over his tailored black slacks, stepped between Lilo and her father to address her. His bald scalp shone in the light, as did the greasy brown fringe above his ears. Fat pig. These SS—they were all young hoodlums or rejects of society.

"Of course," the pig squealed again, "we can arrange for him to go home with you," he added slyly. Rubbing her injured arm, Lilo took a step toward him. "How?" she asked more timorously than she had intended.

"Simply. All you have to do is verify a few facts for us." His small washed-out blue eyes glowed from within their bed of thick, pock-marked flesh.

This was the moment Dietrich had warned her about. In a voice that sounded much more relaxed than what she felt, Lilo responded, "Of course."

Her father's right-eye opened wide as he slurred, "No, Lilo."

At that, the pig in uniform took his ham-sized fist and brought it down on Lilo's father's head like a sledgehammer.

"Stop!" Lilo screamed. "You've hurt him enough, already. I will tell you anything you want to know, although I can't imagine what that might be," she pleaded.

"He's used to it by now, Fräulein. Unfortunately, your father is quite stubborn," smiled the fat guard, shaking his head in mock mournfulness as he continued. "It is such a shame that he went into that little fit after we had our first chat with him. We've not had any fruitful conversations with him since."

He turned back to Lilo's father, "You will not speak again, or we will have to talk to your daughter and perhaps a bit more harshly than a father might like. Do you understand?"

Georg's half-ruined face suffused with blood as he attempted to stand up.

The guard brought his fist down again, this time across Georg's shoulders slamming him off the chair onto the hard cell floor. He rested one dull black boot in the small of Georg's back, pinning him on his stomach to the ground. The man threw out his hand to halt her approach, threatening to grind his foot further into her father's back.

"You see how stubborn and clumsy he is, Fräulein? What's a poor soldier to do with such a charge?" He posed the question with a light shrug of his shoulders as he removed his foot and gestured toward an empty rickety wood chair. "Perhaps you'd best sit down. You look quite unwell," he added unctuously.

"Not until you let me see to my father," she declared.

"Very well," the pig smirked. "Run to Papa."

Lilo fell on her knees before her father. As she placed both hands under his arms, Georg looked directly into her eyes. She understood. The bond that united them made words unnecessary. She was reminded that no matter what happened, she could say nothing. No matter what they did to him, they would get nothing from her. From the moment she'd seen her father, she had wondered whether she had the strength to heed Dietrich's advice. In her father's beseeching eyes, she found it.

"Help me with him, please. I will tell you anything you want to know," she lied dully.

"Of course, Fräulein," the guard said magnanimously. With a nod of his head he motioned to the young guard. He helped Lilo pull her father up and get him back into his chair.

169

Lilo could tell from the disapproving frown on the fat guard's face that the youngster's treatment of her father was far gentler than he would have administered. "Please sit down and let us visit, shall we?" His smile creased the oily pitted skin of his cheeks.

With a tight smile in return that belied none of the boiling rage and hatred she felt for him, Lilo held his gaze and sat down in the hard wooden chair.

"Fräulein Burkhardt," he drew a similar chair across from hers and sat down to face her, "allow me to introduce myself. I am *Oberführer* Otto Schmidt. Please, call me Otto." He reached over and started to give her a pat on her knee, but something in her eyes stopped him and he pulled back his paw.

"I hear you and your father have been busy now for quite a number of years, haven't you?"

"We are fortunate. Yes, business isn't what it used to be, but we manage."

"Oh, come now, Schatzie," he leered the German endearment, turning it into a vile utterance. "Why don't you tell me about your father's visits with some of his 'friends'?"

"What visits? What friends?" Lilo sounded innocently confused.

"Come, come now. I am not a patient man. We know all about your father's unhealthy predilection for Jewish women. I heard that once your father threw a rage when some of our soldiers paid a visit to one who needed to move out of her house. Surely you remember. You were there with him."

The incident with Frau Cohen. That was so long ago. So, they knew—or suspected. A spark of hope tingled in her heart. If they had nothing more recent than that . . . Lilo took a deep breath and lied. "I don't know what you are talking about. All I know is we helped some people in a bombing raid yesterday, and some of your soldiers attacked me and my father and brought him here."

"Fine, perhaps there has been a mistake. We are obviously wrong about you." He grunted to a standing position. "Erik and Sebastian, take the shackles off the old man. We've made a dreadful mistake," he tisked annoyingly. The two surprised guards hesitated but a moment before Lilo's former escort did as he was told.

"As you can see Fräulein, your father probably cannot walk very well since he had his unfortunate episode. Quite a sight. Really, it's just too sad you weren't here to minister to him while he was seizing on the floor and foaming at the mouth," he smiled icily.

Lilo forced herself to sit stone still in her chair and let the words wash over her. Get Papa out. That's what mattered. Stay calm. Seeing no reaction from her, he continued, "So you'll need to bring your truck around to the rear exit of the Kaserne. It's much closer, and there are no stairs."

"I didn't come by truck. I walked."

"Well, that's quite impossible for your father to manage." He paused to rub his chin theatrically. Within seconds, his eyes sparkled gleefully as he snapped his fingers. Lilo almost laughed at his transparency. The only detail he had missed was to yell "Eureka!" as though he were some mad scientist.

"I tell you what we will do, Schatzie. Since we've made such an awful mistake and we really do feel quite ashamed of ourselves, I will send Erik around to get your truck." Lilo was stunned. Perhaps she had misjudged him. The Oberführer's voice had even lost its sarcastic tone.

"That's very generous of you. Thank you," she stuttered in confusion. She managed a courteous nod toward him and glanced at her father. His eyes screamed an alarm at her. What was he trying to say? Careful, careful, she repeated to herself.

171

"Which truck shall we bring Fräulein, the one with the yellow bands on the side?"

"No, the–" and it hit her.

They knew. But how could they? No one knew except Lilo, her father, and the handful of people fortunate enough to be told about the network and live to use it. Even Lilo's mother had never noticed that intermittently one of the trucks sometimes parked in the garage had a pair of thin pale yellow bands painted from the front to the rear of the truck. The truck was not used often, but when it was, the nearly invisible yellow bands were the sign of hope to the hunted.

The two other gray trucks that were part of their normal runs were filled with Herr Mueller's leather boots so that a cursory search at any roadblock would reveal nothing. On the rare occasions it was used, the yellow-banded truck was always placed in the center of the convoy because Lilo and Georg had discovered that the roadblocks were thinly manned these days. With the constant discordant flow of traffic over the bomb-ruined roads, the guards did not often have the luxury of time to check every truck. The first in the convoy or the last were usually inspected, so it was critical that the stowaways board the truck with the light yellow bands.

Lilo smoothed the expression on her face and tried to add an innocent note of puzzlement to a voice she hoped would not betray her fright. "Yellow bands? Our trucks are all gray, sir."

"All gray, you say?"

Lilo steadied her voice further. "That's correct, but we only have a few left. As I said, my father's business is hardly what it once was, but we are proud to be able to help our soldiers. Most of our business is shipping boots from the Mueller factory to the lines." It was an honest response. Never mind that Herr Mueller had made it clear that if several hundred pairs of boots were accidentally left behind to make room for other cargo now and then, it was fine for the boots to go with the next shipment. Yet, even with Mueller's tacit complicity, Lilo's relationship with his son, and his important connections with the Party, she wondered now if they were more vulnerable than she'd realized.

There was silence in the room. The guard nodded and smiled at her. He looked from father to daughter and back again.

"Erik, you have the Burkhardt address?"

"In his papers," responded the youth.

"Fräulein, the keys?" He held out his hand.

"They are in the trucks."

"Very well. Erik, on your way."

The teen guard clicked his heels together and bowed–an awkward little jerk at the waist as though someone had pulled a string attached to the base of his skull and snapped him back to attention.

"And Erik, be careful. We know you children like to run those engines, don't we?" The boy's ears reddened at their tips, and Lilo could see by the set of his jaw that he was embarrassed at the reference to his youth. She caught his eye as he turned and flashed him a commiserative smile to let him know that she thought far more of him than his superiors. His quick, shy answering smile warmed her for a moment. He had taken her stones, but she found herself feeling sorry for this boy who seemed to lack the utter brutality needed for such a position.

"Now, while Erik is away, why don't we continue our conversation? We'll talk of pleasant things, shall we? You seem to be a nice girl. You're certainly a pretty one, aren't you?" The SS guard smiled as his fat beringed hand reached out to smooth her cheek. "And look at all that fine blonde hair." Lilo stilled the impulse to jerk her face away from his repugnant touch as his stubby fingers slid down the length of hair. His hand paused

173

where her hair ended, just at the top of her right breast. Lilo heard a choking sound as her father tried to stand.

"Papa, no. I'm all right," she smiled tightly. Her outburst stopped the guard. He leaned back in his chair. "So, Fräulein, I understand you have a fiancé–a fine soldier who is doing his duty to his country."

Was there anything they didn't know? She thought longingly of Peter and smiled tremulously. The stinging in her eyes caught her unaware, and she gulped down a breath of fetid air to hold back the threatening tears. "Yes," she swallowed, "his name is Peter Mueller. He was sent to Russia. He is somewhere on the *Ostfront*." The Eastern Front.

"Ah, Russia's proved difficult. Do you hear good news of him?" Lilo was again surprised at the kindly air the guard assumed in asking the question. "I hear no news of him, so I hope that is good news."

Her nemesis nodded his agreement. "It is hard to get news from the front, unless it is bad news. You know, he could be a prisoner. The Russians have taken many of our soldiers as prisoners." The guard's obscenely fat red lips twisted sullenly as he added, "Our Führer does not send our good soldiers the fuel, food, and weapons they need to achieve victory. And the Russians are pushing us back."

She was stunned at this outburst against the Führer. Hitler's Death Head SS guards were slavishly loyal to him.

He continued, "You could find out if he was a prisoner, you know." He gazed guilelessly at Lilo.

She rubbed Peter's silver ring with her thumb. "How would I do that?"

She asked the question innocently, but she knew. It was plain on all the posters plastered throughout the city. They depicted a man, bent over in the covering darkness, ear furtively pressed close to a radio. The title on the posters shrieked *Verräter!* Traitor! The posters were meant to stop the growing number of people who violated the law by listening to Russian radio broadcasts. The Russians would tell listeners how many German troops they'd killed or imprisoned. The Nazis discouraged people, on pain of death, from listening to the Russian radiocasts, claiming the messages were false and were an attempt to lower the morale of the German people.

Lilo listened anyway as did so many others. At times, the Russians would put a German soldier on the microphone and let him speak. When Lilo stopped getting letters from Peter, she began to listen, too.

The *Oberführer* answered her question sharply. "You know how, Fräulein," he snapped as he stood up and kicked the chair toward the wall. "You and all the other traitors in our midst," he exclaimed angrily.

Lilo stared at him calmly until he turned and stormed away from her. She stood up silently and moved her chair next to her father's. Otto the pig was sulking in a dim corner of the cell whispering with a guard whom she'd forgotten was with them. He scowled at her but made no move to stop her. She tried to talk with her father, but he used his right hand to wave her silent. The guards left the room. Lilo heard a key grating in the rusty lock. Would they come back?

An hour later the iron door banged open and Erik marched in behind the fat guard. With a sharp salute and a "Heil, Hitler," he handed Otto the truck key.

"Did you bring the truck with the yellow bands," commanded the Oberführer.

"There was no truck with yellow bands—only two gray trucks that looked almost exactly alike," the boy responded.

The fat soldier spun on his dull black boots and whirled to face Lilo and her father. "Get out of here!"

175

She sprang from the chair at the command. Erik stepped toward her and proceeded to lift her father from his chair.

"Leave him alone," barked the commander. "She'll handle him alone or leave the old traitor here."

Lilo leaned forward, stooped, and wrapping both arms around her father with more strength than she had imagined she had, lifted her father to his feet. Georg could barely stand, but he found his balance by leaning his weight on his strong right leg.

"Come, Papa" she beamed in his face. "It's time to go home." Once again she read the message in her father's eyes: "I am proud of you, my Lilo. I love you, my brave child." Had anyone asked her at that moment, she would have sworn he'd spoken the words aloud. She heard them so clearly that they lightened a heart that was cracking in pain–a heart that would break apart in the days to come.

CHAPTER SIXTEEN

THE FRENCH COUNTRYSIDE: JANUARY 1945

Bud trotted along the tank lines greeting old friends, seeing so many strange new ones and missing so many more. An edge of anxiety was gnawing at his nerves. He still hadn't found C.T. Before his apprehension grew more intense, Bud decided he would muster up the courage to ask someone. He spied Otis Johnson. The soldier chortled his response to Bud's query.

"C.T.? Shit, you know where C.T.'s at, Lieutenant. Wait 'til you see him. The rest of us got uniforms hangin' like croaker sacks off our skinny asses, and C.T. look like de damn fat man in de circus." The tall, ebony-black soldier laughed at his own joke. "You gonna find him at the head of de chow line, man. Where else?" He pointed to the front of the tank column where Bud could see a camp of sorts taking shape for the night.

"Chow line? Oh yeah, you think I'm gonna believe that you got a mess tent set up ahead? Shee-ut." Bud laughed a little too hard at Otis' description of C.T., relieved now that he was assured he would find C.T. in one piece. He had to admit his old friends in the 761st looked like they had been ridden hard and put up wet. He had been looking forward to hearing all the news of what he'd missed while he was in the hospital. Now he wasn't so sure. Bud threw up a hand to wave good-bye as he walked on searching for C.T. He spotted him sitting on a camp chair practically buried in a shroud of frozen snow and hugging a box of C-Rations to his chest. Bud waved his arms and yelled at the top of his lungs, "C.T., it's me!"

C.T. looked up to see who was causing the commotion. He shaded his eyes from the blinding sun reflecting off the surrounding four-foot drifts of oil-stained snow. Bud hollered, "What the hell's wrong with your eyes, C.T.? You got battle blindness or somethin'? He saw the moment a grin of recognition split C.T.'s face. The rations tumbled to the ground as C.T. lumbered forward to greet him–arms thrown wide threatening a bear hug that Bud knew was probably going to squeeze the breath out of him. God, it felt good when it came– Bud and C.T. pounded one another's backs, then stepped back from one another, and traded mindless male, knuckle bustin' shoulder thumps.

"Look at you, Bud. You so well fed and purty. I don't think we should put you out in the battlefield. You might get dirty," C.T. hooted good-naturedly.

"You're one to talk, C.T. You're so fat they must have to squeeze you into a tank, and then there's probably no room for anyone else in there. I believe you're stealin' C-rations." Both men laughed uproariously as C.T. gave Bud a final payback thump on his shoulder.

"How the hell did ya git back to us? Last we heard you was stuck with a bunch of cracker paratroopers outta 'Jaw-juh.'"

"Yep, I was turned loose with the 501st Parachute Infantry Regiment. When some of 'em had to meet the 17th, they sent me along so I could get back into one of them tanks."

C.T.'s face sobered, "Man, we sure are glad to have you back." He shook his head back and forth. "It's been tough, Bud. We don't have enough tankers, we don't have enough riflemen, and Jerry's been givin' us hell."

Bud knew the story. The Germans had been putting up a brutal defensive in the Ardennes–what would one day be called The Battle of the Bulge, one of the bloodiest fights and the final decisive Allied victory of the war. It would eventually cost tens of thousands of lives on both sides. The German U-boats were so successful in keeping fresh American troops from getting to the battlefields that in Bud's own 761st, young tankers were learning in days what the original group had learned and practiced for more than a year before seeing any action.

"I heard, C.T. Didn't make for much of a Christmas, huh? But I bet you guys have been kickin' ass."

"We ain't been doin' too bad," admitted C.T. "We got some big advantages. Jerry's tanks got those big 88-millimeter guns. Those mothas hit you, and you be singin' with the angels. But dey so goddamn big dat de Krauts gotta turn 'em by hand. Wid de turret guns, we just hit the switch–and boom! Our guns move 360° in two seconds flat. By the time the Krauts take aim, we done blown 'em right back home to hell. But damn, Bud. We got so many greenhorns. We still need pros at the wheel. Jerry ain't stupid."

Since C.T. had taken the conversation into a more serious vein, Bud decided to go ahead and broach what he knew was a pretty chancy topic.

"I 'preciated the letter you sent me, C.T. Really hit home while I was with those Georgia rednecks. Things goin' any better now for the Panthers?"

"Ha!" C.T. snorted as he snapped to attention, placed his hand over his heart, and began singing in a deep reverential voice.

"*My country, 'tis of thee, sweet land of bigotry,*" he shook his head as he stopped the mournful refrain. "Nothing's changed. Swear to God, the only reason I'm still here givin' it my all is 'cause of the 'Great White Father' and Captain Williams–and 'cause I be damned if I'm a gonna live down to the bad shit people say about us."

Bud smiled at the nickname the guys used to refer to the commander of the 761st, Lieutenant Colonel Paul Bates.

"I'm glad Bates is back with us, but I thought the captain had gotten hit?"

"He did, but he come right back to us soon as he got outta de hospital. He sho' gonna be glad to see you, Bud. It'll take some of the strain off 'im. We ain't got much respect for some of dese other white officers. Williams need another decent white guy to hep him out–even if it someone as goofy as you."

He and Bud both laughed as C.T. leaned back, and Bud's knuckle sandwich flew lightly through the cold air.

"You ain't gonna believe some a de crap we still have to take," he resumed. "Make ya tired. 'Specially out here."

Bud saw the weariness behind C.T.'s smiling façade. The fading afternoon sun highlighted the deep perma-set wrinkles beside C.T.'s dark eyes. Bud knew what the Panthers had had to put up with. Before he was taken out of action, he had thought the unit had resolved most of the problems with the white officers who were determined to treat Negroes like third-class citizens.

"Same shit as Hood?"

"Same shit. But it feel like a helluva lot worse when ya here gittin' yo ass shot off. You wanna stick me in a uniform and make me pick up yo garbage," he shrugged. "I'm a gonna survive dat. But don't make me take a Kraut bullet and den tell me I got to cook and clean foh 'em."

C.T. read Bud's quizzical look.

"Oh, yeah. I didn't tell ya 'bout dat. Couple a weeks ago, we took some Jerry prisoners. Dey wadn't givin' us no trouble. Hell, I think dey was relieved–no mo' war for dem. Anyway, we got a few days off to settle 'em in–and it's a damn good thing it wadn't any longer or Uncle Sam woulda had a mutiny on his hands."

Bud looked around. "This sounds like a good, long story, and I need to sit down. I'm tired of freezin' my ass off in this snow bank. Got another chair?"

C.T. laughed uproariously. "You was in dat hospital way too long, Bud. Got kinda' soft dere." He poked his forefinger at Bud's stomach. "C'mon. Let's go sit in one of dem tanks. Looks

180

like it's about to snow again. You eat yet?"

Bud shook his head.

"I got some extra C-rations in dere. Let's go."

"You got extra C-rats? You sure you ain't just tryin' to slip me a dog turd?"

Bud referred to the D-bar, an oblong chocolate survival bar that could be eaten on the run when nothing else was available. Problem was the chocolate was hard as a brick, tasted bitter, and so hard to digest it was sometimes called "Hitler's Secret Weapon."

"Naw, man. Can't you see I'm eatin' good?" C.T. patted his flat stomach and the two laughed while they picked up their pace to avoid the light drizzle of freezing rain as it began to fall.

"So finish telling me what happened, C.T."

C.T. nodded as they plodded through the dirty slush. "Remember when dey brought dem German POWs to Hood and dey could do whatever dey wanted?"

Bud nodded. The memory still stung him with shame.

C.T. continued, "I figured dat shit was ovah since we saved a lotta white asses ovah heah. But I be damned, Bud. Dese Krauts shot at us–and dey did the same shit. Dey's eatin' in de mess tent, while our Negro asses be stuck outside. When we pulled out, I heard some of de guys complainin' that dey was gonna use us to pick up trash in de Krauts' prison area. Dat wudda sent us ovah de edge, I'm tellin' ya."

"Good thing you got away from 'em," Bud responded shaking his head in disbelief at C.T.'s story. "Say, did Williams ever have any luck gettin' Rivers the Medal of Honor?"

"Shee-utt!" C.T. declared. "You know when dey'll give Rivers that medal? When hell freezes over."

181

Bud held out his arm, gesturing toward the sweeping vista marred with charred stumps of what were once lush stands of trees, pools of filthy frozen slush, and the ice encrusted fissures left in the muddy road by the tanks. He grinned at C.T as he surveyed it all.

"Well," Bud said drily, "Seein' this, looks like Rivers ought to get that medal real soon. Thanks for the welcome to Hell, buddy. Frozen stiff," he proclaimed flamboyantly.

CHAPTER SEVENTEEN

MUNICH, GERMANY: JANUARY 1945

The shriek of the air raid sirens awakened Lilo from a deep sleep. She was so exhausted and numb that for a moment she thought about simply not getting out of bed. It just wasn't worth it anymore. Since she had brought her father home from the Kaserne, their already difficult lives had become nearly intolerable. Although her father had fully regained his speech, it was slow and slurred at times. He could walk, though with a pronounced limp, but his left hand and arm were still lifeless. The doctors didn't give Lilo and her mother any hope that would change. Dr. Braun reminded them how fortunate they were that Georg had not suffered irreversible brain damage from the cruel treatment he had received at the hands of the SS.

It fell to Lilo to keep alive what little they had left of the business. She carried out the odd contract that came their way, and there were days when she was forced to stay awake behind the wheel for a tortured twenty-four hours to haul a load of boots for their primary customer. She found herself grateful for the bomb-blasted roads whose craters often lurched her awake just in time to avoid an accident. If only Papa could drive again.

In an effort to banish the sleep from her eyes, she walked to the porcelain basin in her room and splashed herself awake. Not vain by nature, even Lilo had to admit that the scarecrow countenance peering back at her in the mirror was frightening. A frame of deep purple and black smudges overshadowed her violet-blue eyes. The normally pale-rose flush in her cheeks had drained away leaving her skin an unhealthy shade of aging parchment. Even though her mother berated her daily for her appearance, Anna took pride that her daughter's shoulder-length blonde hair, though darkening, was still thick and shiny. The hair was a nuisance, but she didn't have the strength to listen to her mother's harangue if she cut it off.

Peter wouldn't care. He loved stroking the thick mass, but he would never say a word. *He* would understand–her perfect partner. The tears that sprang to her eyes surprised her. She must be tired if thoughts of Peter could bring her to tears–a luxury she rarely allowed herself. It interfered with her daydreams of him coming safely home to her.

Thank God, the war would be over soon. Since the Russians had retaken the city of Stalingrad and the Ukraine, the Germans were in full retreat. Peter could possibly be in Warsaw even now–on his way home to her. Even though she'd had no word from Peter in slightly more than a year, she refused to worry. The last letter he had written her around Christmas of 1942 had not reached her until the day after the new year in 1944. It had only been a year, she rationalized, as she tied her hair back with a faded black cotton ribbon and finished dressing. The house was still quiet so she knew she had a few minutes before she had to leave.

She pulled open the top drawer of the antique Biedermeyer dresser where the stack of Peter's letters lay invitingly. She untied the purple satin ribbon that held the soiled papers. God knows how these missives ever reached her from so far away. The last one had dried coppery stains on it. Mud? Blood? She didn't want to think about it right now. She repeated her morning mantra: perhaps this is the day a new letter will arrive.

She pulled his last letter from its stained envelope. He'd written it after she had met him in East Prussia two years ago when he'd earned a short leave. Her face burned with shame as she thought back to how she had almost not recognized him–until the shrunken soldier standing in front of her at the train station had croaked out her name.

Peter's once brilliant pale gray eyes were so deeply sunken that no light shone from them. When he gave her a pained lopsided grin, she gasped and almost cried aloud. His once beautiful smile now consisted of his upper teeth bordered on the right side by a large gap where two or three of them were missing. And he'd seemed so sad at first, but by the time she took him to the room where they spent his three-day leave together, he was her Peter again.

As she reread his last letter, it seemed that he was unable to hold on to the beautiful moments they'd shared together in that room. Her cheeks warmed, this time remembering how she'd avoided the landlady's eyes when she brought Peter to the room she had secured at a boarding house near the train station. The woman had asked no questions, but Lilo wasn't sure whether the silver band she wore had convinced the woman that she was indeed "Frau Peter Mueller."

December 22, 1942

Dearest Lilo,

Now a few hours have passed since your departure, and I am so terribly unhappy. I feel that this is the last time that we will see each other. I don't want these unhappy thoughts, but these really sad thoughts keep coming back.

I hope the fight with your parents will not be so bad, and you will have a happy Christmas. I think if you explain it to your mother very clearly, it won't be so bad because your parents were once young.

Lilo couldn't help but smile. The fight with her parents had been very bad. Anna had refused to allow Liselotte to go and meet Peter, claiming it was unseemly–and for the first time, her father had agreed with her mother. He tried to tell Lilo that the trip east was too dangerous. She ignored them both and told them she could either go with their permission or without it. In the end, they capitulated and Peter was proven right. She heard a door slam downstairs and quickly scanned to the end of the letter.

Live well, and think always of me and don't ever
forget me. Will you promise me that?

She planted a kiss on the paper before putting the letter
away and whispering a quick prayer for Peter. He would be
home soon–she knew it. Lilo's father had told her the war was
over the day that Hitler had decided to fight in Russia and that
Germany's defeat was inevitable once the Americans decided
to fight on European soil once more. Her father had battled
them during the Great War, and he said they were worthy and
admirable soldiers with more money, manpower, and machinery
than any other country on earth.

Lilo had once met an American. Before the war, her
father had an American friend who had visited a few times. Lilo
remembered him because he was her father's only business
associate who had ever paid any attention to her. If he was any
example, these Americans loved children. This man had even
seemed like a bit of a child himself. He had always brought her
funny little American toys–and he could even make Mama laugh.

A knock on the door interrupted her thoughts.

"Papa, is that you? I'm coming."

"Liselotte, it's Mama. I'm coming in."

Her mother's face was ashen as she walked into the
room. Liselotte noted how thin her mother had become and
that the thinning braids crowning her head were now woven
with thick bands of gray. She felt the trembling in her mother's
hands as she wrapped her fingers around Liselotte's and guided
her daughter toward the bed. Liselotte sank into the thick white
down comforter. Her mother, still clasping her hands, sat down
beside her. Only then did she release them.

"We have some news, Lilo," she said gravely.

Lilo's hands flew to her mouth, "Oh no, Mama, not
Peter!" With unexpected tenderness, Anna reached out and

stroked her daughter's cheek.

"Nein, Liselotte–no word about Peter," she said as she reached into the pocket of her starched white cotton morning apron. "And right now, that is good news." She opened the letter she had pulled out, "This came today." Anna handed Liselotte the single sheet of paper.

ACHTUNG!

The single line in bold script jumped out at her as she read the note aloud.

LISELOTTE KRISTINA BURKHARDT, YOU ARE TO REPORT . . .

The paper fluttered and landed silently on the dusty surface of the dark wooden floor. "Mama, I have to go to Austria," she said anxiously allowing her mother to wrap her arms around her. There had been an unspoken truce between Liselotte and her mother since her crippled father had come home from the Kaserne. At first it was an uneasy peace, but Anna had gained Liselotte's respect with the fastidious way she now cared for her dependent husband. "Mama, how will you care for Papa? Who will drive the truck? Earn money?"

"Shh, *Mädchen*. Young girl. Your Papa felt this was coming. He has done everything possible to stop it. You realize you are not the first girl from the *Bund Deutscher Mädel* to be asked to serve away from home. It was only a matter of time." She patted Liselotte's hand comfortingly.

"Asked? You know this is not asking. This is an order. I am the sole support of our family. I thought that meant they wouldn't do this. I have not caused any problems in the Bund Deutscher Mädel. I knitted socks for soldiers until my fingers fell off," she said furiously. Lilo's contempt for Hitler's *Das BDM–Werk, Glaube, und Schoenheit* was evident in her voice. She had been forced to be a member of female branch of the

Hitler Youth until she was eighteen, but when her entire group decided to join the all-volunteer Work, Belief, and Beauty Society for girls up to twenty-one and even older for some, her father told her she would be looked on with suspicion if she was the only one in the club who failed to continue.

"What good will I do in Austria?" The warmth of her anger felt good as she stood and reached to help her mother up from the bed. "Let's go talk to Papa. Surely Uncle Sepp can help," she added confidently.

Anna seemed to have used all of her strength in delivering the news to her daughter. Weakly, she pulled her daughter back down to sit next to her. "*Liebchen*, Papa has done all that he feels he can. Your Uncle Sepp is too far away–in France or Belgium. We don't know." Her mother buried her face in her hands and moaned, "So many boys dead now–all gone. Ach, mein Gott." She began to cry thinly, "And now my daughter–my only child." Rather than her usual impatience or disdain for her mother's tears, Liselotte felt an odd tug of empathy. She wasn't afraid to go to Austria, but the government that was sending her certainly wouldn't feed her family.

"Come, Mama. Don't cry. I will be fine." Liselotte felt the landscape slide back to its familiar orbit. She pulled her mother up from the bed, wrapped her arms around her, and comforted her–and that comforted Liselotte.

"It's terrible for your Papa, Liselotte. He feels so helpless, but for some reason he is afraid that if we fight this "request," it might go badly for you. I don't know why. He did ask the messenger to wait so he could write an appeal and send it with her, but then he decided against it."

Anna allowed Liselotte to herd her through the door and down the hall toward the long, curved marble staircase. Walking slowly toward the stairs with her hand on her mother's elbow, Liselotte couldn't miss seeing the thin veneer of dust cloaking the tables and lamps that lined the wide upstairs hallway. Her mother tried to keep up with the housework, but it was a losing battle without the help she had once commanded to keep every corner of the three-story mansion shining.

"Your Papa will find a way for you to come home again quickly, Liselotte. But it will be weeks before we know. The letter is clear. You must be on your way to Austria within twenty-four hours."

"That's simply not possible, Mama. I have a delivery today that will take at least twelve hours to get there and back again.

"Lilo."

The name took her off guard–her mother never called her that.

Noting her daughter's surprise, Anna stopped on the top stair and smiled sadly at her daughter's willful scowl. "Papa says you must go–or there will be trouble for you. He says he will find someone else to drive today's shipment, and then we will work to get you home again."

Once more Lilo was struck by her mother's newfound strength. It was almost as if now that she felt truly needed, she could rise to the challenge.

"Well, thank God that at forty-six, you are one year too old, Mama." Liselotte tried to laugh a little, "Or we would be going together."

Without a trace of answering laughter her mother responded, "If I could go with you–if I could go for you, I would."

Liselotte caught the shine of tears in Anna's eyes as she wearily started down the stairs.

CHAPTER EIGHTEEN

NEAR VIENNA, AUSTRIA: JANUARY 1945

Out of the iron bed, into the drab uniform, drink the watery chicken broth. March through the radio room, climb up the tower, plug in the headset. The strict regimen had Lilo's days and nights running together in a mindless haze of habit in the two weeks since she had left home. She still could not believe what they expected of her and the other girls. If her father knew, he would find a way to bring her home immediately. Because most of the parents would have reacted the same way, the girls were not permitted to write home a single word about their duties. Their parents all thought their daughters were working as telephone operators to help with communications. According to the Führer's public stance, the only activities the women of the Bund Deutscher Mädel engaged in that paralleled the male arm of the Hitler Youth were regular athletic events. Their reality was quite different.

On their second day at the camp, the commander ordered the girls into a long barracks filled with radio and telephone equipment. Lilo had never seen anything like it. Huge aerial maps hung on walls painted the color of dirty, wet sand. The walls devoid of maps held giant boards full of small evenly-spaced holes set above rows of scarred wooden desks.

The activities of the women seated at each desk fascinated Lilo. Never acknowledging the presence of visitors, they yanked black cords of from one hole in the boards and plugged them into another, working at astonishing speeds. The women spoke in quick, hushed tones into headsets that curled around their chins and flattened their hair. It was impossible to hear any conversation because of the dull roar of their incessant low-pitched chatter. It looked confusing, but she would learn.

Each new recruit stood beside an operator to observe.

Lilo marveled as she watched the operators repeatedly issue unintelligible commands. She sometimes caught a few phrases: "All clear," "watching at forty-five degrees," or "find cover." Judging from the bland looks and unchanging expressions on the faces of the busy operators, she doubted the conversations were any more interesting at the other end of the line.

The next morning the group commander came into their barracks at 5:00, ordered the women out of bed, and divided them into two groups. They had five minutes to dress in their uniforms and the heavy greatcoats they wore to protect themselves from the wintry weather. One group waited, while the other followed her to the communications barracks.

Lilo turned to Annette, one of the girls she'd met the first day. Although both had celebrated their nineteenth birthdays, Lilo thought Annette was much younger. She looked more terrified than Lilo felt when they had first arrived at the camp. Lilo felt instantly protective of the plain, dark-haired girl who'd been raised on a farm in the Bavarian countryside. Lilo had first noticed her when she'd boarded the train in Munich. She was waving to an elderly couple at the station, and the old man and woman were both crying so loudly that the people around them had stared distastefully at them.

When Lilo recognized Annette at the camp, she told her how sorry she had felt for the two old people who had seen her off at the station. Annette shyly confided to Lilo that she was the youngest of five children and that all four of her brothers had been killed: one in France, two in Russia, and her youngest brother had died after he was arrested as a dissident and sent to Dachau for crimes against the state.

Annette described to Lilo how her brother had been caught distributing leaflets denouncing the Führer. "My Mama and Papa are almost dead from grief. When my oldest brother was first called up to join the Army, my father was proud. Even when we were told Wilhelm had been killed, my parents managed. Then Joseph and Hans had to go–both to Russia."

"My fiancé, Peter, was in Russia, but he is on his way home now." As soon as the words were out of her mouth, she regretted them. Lilo nervously rubbed Peter's ring with her thumb, embarrassed by her thoughtlessness. Annette immediately sensed her discomfort.

"Please," she patted Lilo's arm, "don't feel bad. I am happy if your fiancé is alive. I wish my brothers were, too. You should know, though, that the notice telling us of Hans' death took more than a year to get to us." She saw Lilo's immediate concern and added, "but now with our soldiers pushed back to Poland, I am sure the fighting is not nearly so harsh, and your Peter is fine." She patted Lilo's hand comfortingly.

"Thank you, Annette. I wish Peter had done what your youngest brother did. He was at the University and didn't want to fight." She glanced around the barracks to make certain there were no listening ears, "He never thought we should be at war."

"I don't know, Lilo. Even though three of my brothers died, I am afraid Wolfgang may have suffered most. They told us he was sick with a cold that turned into pneumonia and he died at Dachau. But they wouldn't send us his body for a proper burial. They said they had cremated him. Why would they do that? They knew he was Catholic. It has destroyed my poor parents."

Lilo saw the suspicious shine in her new friend's large, dark eyes.

The girl took a deep breath and continued, "He was my twin brother, and they wouldn't let me bury him. Mama and Papa think I was sent here because they kept going to the authorities to find out why Wolfgang's body wasn't sent to us."

At that moment the commander marched into the barracks: "All of you, follow me!"

Lilo and Annette fell in at the end of the hastily formed line. As they walked across the slick mud and wet patches of frozen grass, she saw several thin men in chains hammering at a pile of timber. As she glanced at one of the men, he smiled and waved at her. She lifted her hand in response.

"Eyes straight ahead," the rough command came from the dumpy woman leading the girls. "We do not speak or acknowledge the Russian prisoners."

Russian prisoners? What were they doing here? Lilo resisted the urge to glance toward the men again. She'd have to ask her questions later.

Lilo was so absorbed in her thoughts that she almost ran into the girl in front of her. The contingent had stopped beside one of the tall wooden towers that dotted the perimeter of the camp. Lilo was surprised at how sturdy it looked up close. From the barracks, the tower looked like a six-sided disk with a small peaked room perched on four wooden toothpicks. Standing beside it, she saw the legs supporting the platform were as thick as tree trunks.

"We will climb the towers in groups of six—one girl at a time," shouted the commander. "You! Amanda Eisele, you will go first." The commander nodded tersely toward the girl at the front of the double line. "Maria Schaeffer, Anna Buchen, Rita Rentz, Annette Toller, and Liselotte Burkhardt, you will follow— in that order. When you reach the top, you will find six pairs of field glasses and headsets. The tower has six sides. You will station yourselves one on each side. Look for the place to plug in your headset and make sure you can hear voices coming from them. Make certain you can understand what you hear. Next, check your field glasses. If everything works, leave it all in place and climb back down. If not, bring the malfunctioning piece of equipment with you. You have ten minutes to climb up, check your gear, and climb down. Now hurry. *Macht schnell,*" the commander trumpeted.

The first girl climbed nimbly up the wooden-laddered steps to the top of the platform. Lilo shaded her eyes against a rare ray of morning sun as Amanda neared the top of the platform. Gott, she looked so tiny up there. The other girls quickly followed until Annette and Lilo were the only ones left on the ground.

"After you, Annette," smiled Lilo.

Annette turned to her, "God, I am so frightened of heights," she whispered as she placed her foot tentatively on the first step.

"Toller! *Mach schnell*," the stocky commander snapped at Annette. She was a woman of indeterminate age, somewhere between thirty-five and fifty. Her body was thick and looked as straight and strong as an oak tree. The short gray-streaked mud-blonde hair that peeked out from beneath her brown cap looked as though it had been hacked to its uniform three-inch length by some untutored butcher.

"Go on, Annette. If you fall, you'll just land on my head."

Both girls laughed as Annette took her second tentative step. As soon as she was on the fourth one, Lilo followed. Their progress was slow because Annette tested each stair on the ladder before placing her full weight on it. Lilo resisted the temptation to look down, keeping her eyes instead on the retreating figure in front of her.

Within moments she was on the last step and peering through the rail at the tower platform. It was much larger than it had looked from the ground. She pulled herself onto the deck. The open-air platform was built with solid but oddly gouged and splintered wood. At its center was a small open shelter with a wood and tin roof. At least it would offer some cover against the inevitable snow and rain that had pelted them almost constantly since they had arrived.

Lilo walked to the vacant section of the tower, picked up the headset, and plugged it into the metal box bolted to the waist-high double wooden railing. Even before she had placed the set firmly over her ears, she gritted her teeth at the high-pitched squeal issuing from it. Almost instantly, the squeal was replaced by the voice of a woman uttering unfamiliar commands.

Lilo returned the headset to its place and picked up the heavy military issue binoculars. As she held them up to her eyes and twisted the focus ring at the bridge of the glasses, the desolate monotone landscape came to life. Brilliant green fir trees dotted the dirty white, brown, and gray landscape, the only spot of color within miles. Holding the glasses firmly to her face, she bent her head down over the railing. The ground looked so close she felt she could take only one step over the rail to reach it.

Returning the glasses to their place, Lilo stretched her arms wide, taking deep cleansing breaths of the crisp air. It was colder up on the platform than on the ground, but thankfully her heavy gray coat kept the whistling wind from biting through her. The view was stupendous and even better–if they only sent six girls up here with no supervisor–this job, whatever it was, might not be too bad.

Lilo held the glasses up to her eyes again. This time, she spied a few tiny houses in the distance. "Annette! Come and look at these cottages. I wonder how far away they really are?"

Annette joined her, and looking through her own glasses replied, "They look like Hansel and Gretel houses, don't they?" she laughed.

"They do. And look," Lilo responded pointing down at the ground below the tower, "there's the evil witch!" The commander's sour face loomed in the glasses as she gestured furiously for the girls to climb down. Annette's laughter brought out the deep dimples in her round face, making her appear even younger.

"You'd better not let anyone hear you say that, Lilo, or

she'll put you in the oven and cook you for dinner. Look how fat she is. I wonder how many children she's already eaten?"

"Many, I'm sure," answered Lilo as she wrapped the strap of her field glasses around the headset and put them back onto the small shelf built under the first railing.

Amanda Eisele was already beginning her trek down the ladder and the other girls lined up to follow. When everyone was on the ground, the *Kommandantin* had the next assignment ready.

"Now you will learn how to follow the instructions you will hear in your headphones and how to issue them as well. We go to the classroom. Follow me." She turned on one thick-soled black shoe and walked purposefully along the muddy path that had been cleared between two banks of dirty snow.

Annette whispered to Lilo, "What kind of instructions are we supposed to give?"

"I have no idea, but I will ask." She was just as curious about their duties as Annette. It was obvious they would not be working as operators. She made her way to the front of the single-file until she caught up with the Kommandantin. "*Entschuldigen Sie*, Frau Kommandantin. Excuse me."

The woman looked up at Lilo. Her thick brown-gray brows furred together above her nose, making her scowl look especially menacing.

Lilo ignored the look and pressed on, "What exactly is it we are to do? We thought we were to operate telephones or–"

The woman interrupted her rudely. "You girls are not here to talk on telephones," she responded curtly. "Our Führer needs every able body to work–to do the meaningful tasks since the men are away fighting to keep our homeland together. You will learn how to spot the English and American airplanes that are attacking us and how to direct fire so that they cannot murder our people."

At Lilo's shocked stare, she continued, "You should be very proud. Very few women have this honor." She ran her eyes up and down Lilo's thin frame and added scathingly, "especially for girls like you, focused only on *Kinder, Kirche, und Küche*– children, church, and kitchen."

Lilo finally found her voice. "We can't do that. We don't know how. We are not soldiers," she added sullenly. "We were told we would operate telephones or cook for the soldiers here."

"Fräulein Burkhardt," smirked the commander, "Do you see any soldiers here?" She gestured around the camp with a shrug of her shoulders.

Lilo saw only the lines of low-roofed barracks where she knew only women slept. Toward the front of the camp was a stone and timber building that housed the officers of the camp. The commander was right. The only men she had seen were a few SS officers in their telltale black uniforms and the prisoners who she knew cooked the meals.

"Your job," the commander continued, "is to honor the Führer and keep as many airplanes as possible from killing our German citizens. Do you understand?" she asked harshly.

The woman's attitude and her apparent blind devotion to Hitler angered Lilo. She tried to keep her rage and disgust from her voice as she responded, "This is still work for trained soldiers, and the Führer says he does not want German women fighting."

"And you are not fighting," the Kommandantin snapped back, "but you will do more than merely knit socks and gloves. You were assigned here for a reason–one I do not know, but I would suggest that you do not want to be insubordinate. I don't believe there would be much patience for that, and it would not go well for you or your family."

Lilo gasped at the threat. The beetle-browed woman ignored her and continued sarcastically, "Fräulein Burkhardt, apparently it has somehow escaped your notice that we are at war."

Before she could turn away, freckle-faced Amanda Eisele slid silently beside Lilo. "Burkhardt is right," she stubbornly reiterated, "we are not trained."

The Kommandantin turned her marble-brown gaze to her. "Fräulein Eisele, there are women operating searchlights and serving as flak helpers–and we may even have to carry arms if the Russians, British, and Americans are not stopped. Be grateful to be of service to your country. *Schweigen Sie sich*! Be quiet." She addressed the entire group that had now closed in to hear what was being said.

"All of you, listen well. You will protect your homeland. You will do as you are told. I will hear no more complaints. You will find that I will treat you as you treat me. Disobey, and you will be punished. Obey, and you will find me an amiable leader. It is your choice."

With a cursory wave of her leather-gloved hand, she moved toward one of the low-slung barracks. "No more chatter– we never know when the bombers will strike. You must learn quickly."

As Lilo and the rest followed the squat woman, she thought how naïve she had been to think that perhaps somewhere during this war she might find carve out a few minutes where fear and worry weren't her constant companions–a few moments of laughter with a new friend. She had yet to learn that her naiveté lay in the notion that one could make–and keep–friends.

CHAPTER NINETEEN

West of Klingenmünster, Germany:

March 23-24, 1945

"Mornin', Bud. D'ya git any sleep las' night?" queried C.T. as he settled down beside Bud, sipping hot coffee from the tin mess cup clutched between his hands.

"Oh, yeah. Like a baby. Man, it didn't take me long to get used to how cozy the inside of a tank can be with a group of guys fighting for the covers."

"Yeah, but I promise ya–it's a damn sight better in March than it is in January. Did I tell you what Redd started doing last January?"

"Nope. What?"

"Dat's a crazy bastard. Say he rather be shot dead by de Krauts dan freeze to def wid a bunch a guys in de belly of a tank. Every night Redd crawl outta de tank an' sleep on de motor. He got me out dere one night fo 'bout five minutes, and I tell you what–after dat engine been runnin' all day, it be warm as toast out dere–not warm enough fo me to chance gittin' picked off by Jerry. But I tell you de truf, dat damn Redd was Mr. Sunshine every mornin' while de res' of us was drag-assin' aroun' fightin' for some coffee."

"He's lucky one of you ill-tempered Panthers didn't just knock those smiling pearly whites down his throat," Bud chuckled.

C.T.'s rumbling laugh joined Bud's causing the other sleepy men who'd gathered around the mess tent to look over and see what could be so amusing on a sunlit March morning

201

with the sound of gunfire already rolling down the still icy slopes in the distance. C.T. was the first to acknowledge the distant roar.

"God almighty, Bud. I jus' don't see how dese Krauts can keep fightin'. To heah de brass tell it, we cleaned house in de Ardennes. God knows, dey took enough of our guys out."

Both men stared into their coffee, watching small puffs of steam rise from the battered tin cups, only to settle again, frosting the dented containers. Bud was first to break the contemplative silence.

"Well, we better hope everybody got a good night's rest, C.T. Jerry's not gonna give up the last of the Siegfried Line without another hell of a fight."

"Yeah, but we'll take 'em. Those paratroopers from the 17th are good. They've figured out exactly how to travel with us. We lost some of the greenhorns a couple of days ago because they didn't have the sense to follow in our tank tracks."

The tankers usually led the charge against the German troops, but because the Germans had had plenty of time to fortify their positions, there were usually hundreds of mines surrounding the position of the enemy. Seasoned soldiers knew to follow in the tank tracks, but some of the young ones, tired of slopping through the mire in the wake of the tanks, struck out onto the solid frozen ground and often onto a deadly mine.

Bud thought about what lay ahead of them. Who would live? Who would die?

C.T.'s thoughts obviously echoed Bud's. He scanned the sky with a worried expression on his face, "Hope de weather holds out through de night. We don' need our tanks slidin' all ovah de place on ice."

"Looks like we'll be okay, C.T., but we'd better get busy," Bud motioned toward the mess tent where a group was packing the ration kits. A few yards beyond, several of the Shermans roared to life.

C.T. nodded toward the tanks, "Uh-oh, Bud, what if they leave us?"

"Fat chance, Buddy. Me—they probably wouldn't miss, but you turned into a real heavy hitter while I was 'vacationing' in France."

Both men got a good laugh from the joke—glad that Bud's hospital stay had healed him, and gladder still that they were together again. If the laughter was tinged with a hint of uneasiness, no one else was listening anyway.

§ § § § § §

"Keep it up! Keep it up, men!" Bud could barely hear the crackling transmission in the thundering storm of the battle.

It had to be after midnight, and still the fighting was going strong. The tank driver revved up the motor until the Sherman was running at a steady thirty miles an hour. Bud almost smiled as the gargantuan machine sprinted nimbly across the snowy field. When it came to facing the Germans' Mark IVs or their Tiger Royals, the Shermans could easily outrun them. Because they were much lighter, the Shermans could weave and dodge far better than the formidable enemy tanks.

From Bud's vantage point in the commander's turret, he could barely make out the vast forces of the 761st, the 17th Paratroopers, and the dozens of other units that had come together to form part of Task Force Rhine, the massive sweep into Germany by the Allies. A flash of fire illuminated the scene for a moment. It was long enough for Bud to take aim and fire on another anti-tank position. These nighttime battles were the worst. In the darkness Bud lived in fear of shelling one of his own men or falling victim to friendly fire himself.

"We got a hit, men!" Bud exclaimed as the volley from

the 75-millimeter gun flashed in the night air. The brilliant yellow-orange luminance of the blast lasted long enough for Bud to see a shower of stone and steel catapult into the star-strewn blackness. Another transmission, clearer this time, broke through the din. "They're on the run, boys. Full speed ahead and keep the guns goin'! Keep the guns goin'!"

Bud saw a dark hulking shadow veer toward him in the night. Shit! What the hell were the German Panzers doing this close? The Colonel had said they were retreating. Before he could give the order to fire, the shadow materialized into a tank with the single white American star on its side. Bud nearly passed out in relief. When the words "Hot Stuff" emblazoned on the side of the tank rolled by, he nearly wept with gratitude. If Bud hadn't seen the star, C.T.'s tank would surely have been hot stuff. It woulda been a Goddamn Ronson.

The tankers sometimes morbidly referred to their tanks as Ronsons or Zippos because while the Sherman was fast and nimble, when hit, it torched up like a cigarette lighter. As soon as the wave of relief swept through Bud, a wave of anger followed.

"Goddamn it, C.T., I coulda wiped you out," he mumbled.

"You say somethin', Lieutenant?"

Bud realized the other guys in the tank could hear him because an eerie silence, almost as deafening as the previous tank blasts and machine-gun fire, now pervaded the valley.

The radio crackled to life again. Its message split the heavy smoke-filled night air: "Roll on in, men. It's our town."

§ § § § § § §

Bud crawled out of the tank, climbed to the ground, and strode purposefully to C.T.'s tank. His fists echoed hollowly as he pounded on the steel body, "Get out here, C.T!"

C.T.'s smiling face looked down on him from the high

turret. "We got 'em runnin', don't we Bud?"

Bud ignored C.T.'s greeting and yelled his response. "C.T., I almost blew you to your maker. Didn't you see that you cut right in front of me? For a minute I couldn't make you out."

Responding to Bud's harsh tone, C.T. climbed down from Hot Stuff. "I saw ya, Bud," he answered quietly. "What you didn't–"

Bud's temper blew as he cut C.T. off in mid-sentence, "Then why in the hell did you cut in front of me that way? Goddamn it–that was stupid," he yelled.

In the weak moonlight Bud could see C.T.'s mahogany skin flush a shade darker but instead of raising his voice, C.T.'s words fell an octave lower.

"Because, Sir, what you didn't see was a heap of scrap metal loaded with Teller mines in front of you. I had just enough maneuverin' room to keep you from gittin' blown to smithereens without hittin' 'em myself–Sir," he added sarcastically before turning on his heel to begin his climb back into his tank.

Bud absorbed the information. Son of a bitch!

C.T.," Bud called to his friend's retreating back, "I'm sorry. You did it again, Buddy. I've just been outta this too long." He shook his head with embarrassment as C.T. stared impassively down at him. "Must be losin' my nerve. Thank you, C.T."

After what seemed an interminable length of time, C.T.'s natural good humor restored itself. "It's fine, Bud, but you betta watch ya mouth or nex' time I'll jus' letcha blow. You got dat?"

Still stung by his attack on C.T., Bud answered with relief, "Got it. Now let's get some shut-eye. I have a feelin' those Krauts will be givin' us hell again tomorrow. But I promise ya, C.T., if anyone's givin' ya hell, it won't be me."

§ § § § § §

"Rise an' shine, Ladies. Rise an' shine! Colonel says we movin' out!" shouted the First Sergeant as he rousted a group of sleeping tankers.

Bud moved in the opposite direction to wake the others. The Colonel had allowed a few of the men to get some much needed rest, but he said it was critical that they move ahead to Klingenmünster. Once they took the town, the infamous Siegfried line would be history. Defeating the Germans' famous western border defense would allow the men of Task Force Rhine to sweep into the Rhine River plains. Then nothing could stop them from marching into Germany's southern heartland and the Bavarian capital city of Munich.

"Rise and shine! Rise and shine!" The call multiplied as the sleeping soldiers awoke and repeated the greeting to one another, fully knowing the harmless words carried with them the unspoken dark weight of the fearful battles that lay ahead.

CHAPTER TWENTY

Near Vienna, Austria: March 1945

Lilo and Annette marched to the tower in the pitch-black night with the sure-footed steps of those who trod the same path day after day. For the past two months nothing had interrupted the monotonous routine. Up at four and up in the tower before sunrise. Lilo hoped something would eventually happen to break up the dull days, but she wondered idly if either one of them would remember what to do if anything were to happen.

"Annette, would you know what to do if we saw a plane?" Lilo could almost see her words form in the frosty air. She rubbed her leather-gloved hands together and huddled into her greatcoat against the freezing early morning temperatures.

"I don't know. I guess so," Annette answered tentatively. "Why? Do you think something's going to happen?" She scanned the dark skies above them nervously.

"No, no, Annette. They were just trying to scare us. The only harm that will come to us is that we'll be dead of boredom before the war is finally over."

"Do you think we will have to stay here until then, Lilo?"

"I don't know," she shrugged. "I just worry about my family. The work here is a lot easier than driving a truck. I certainly wouldn't mind a change in the food, though," she quipped as she reached into her pocket to pull out a bundle wrapped in plain brown paper. The bag contained two slices of bread, each with a pat of usually rancid butter on it, and, if they were fortunate, an apple or a boiled potato. Today's bag held the weekly ration of a pack of nine cigarettes and a box of matches.

"I don't know why they give us cigarettes. It would be great if we could get to a village or farm and trade them for something delicious."

"Amanda and Rita smoke and they don't cough so they must be used to it. I always give them my cigarettes," Annette shrugged. "I can't bear to have cigarettes near me ever since my brother Wolfgang and I once sneaked one from Papa. I did all the smoking, but when Papa caught us, Wolfgang told him that he had smoked them and that I had not. Papa put his arm around him and told him if he liked to smoke so much, he had a real treat for him. He put a big cigar in Wolfgang's mouth and made my brother puff on it until he turned green. Poor Wolfgang was vomiting on the ground before Papa allowed him to stop. I felt so guilty that I promised never to smoke another one."

Lilo laughed with Annette, happy that her friend could talk about some of her warm memories of her twin, but she hurt for her, too, just imagining how heart-broken she would be if she lost Peter or her father.

Annette broke the silence with a plaintive wish, "I want to go home."

"I know, Annette. I miss my parents, too." Lilo tried to think of a way to break the melancholy. "Don't worry, Annette," she patted her friend's shoulder, "we'll get you home. Of course, you'll be an ugly old toothless woman by then," she ran ahead laughing over her shoulder, "but you could never be as ugly as the Kommandantin!"

"That is wicked," Annette laughed back at her as she began chasing her friend and calling, "Just for that—take this!" Annette pulled the mushy, nearly rotten apple out of her lunch sack, hurled it at Lilo, and then sped past her running toward the tower.

"Ha! You missed me, you shameful food waster! You'd better run faster. When I catch you, I'm going to rub your face in the dirt," yelled Lilo as she gave chase.

The laughter of the two girls echoed in the pre-dawn

208

silence. Although the others in the camp were up and on their way to their duties, the morning was usually a quiet time with so many sleep-deprived girls still shaking off the dust of their dreams.

Much smaller and faster than Lilo, and now used to climbing the tower, Annette was already settled at her station by the time Lilo breathlessly climbed the last few steps. "What took you so long?" Annette chirped, "I thought you took your lazy self back to bed."

"You just wait. I'm going to–"

"Shh!" Annette snapped sharply, put one hand to her lips and cupped the other around her ear, while she tilted her head slightly.

"I don't hear anything," Lilo whispered.

Annette wrinkled her forehead and motioned for Lilo to be quiet. Then she heard it–a dull, droning sound, not high or low-pitched–just a steady monotonous drone. She'd heard that sound before–in the city, right before the bombs fell.

"Quick, Annette, our headphones, and get your binoculars!" Lilo rushed to carry out the orders she'd barked at Annette, but her hands were trembling so much she could hardly get her headset plugged in. Finally, with the set askew on her head, she shouted into the microphone.

"We think we hear an airplane–no eye contact, no coordinates yet. Stand by."

Her headset sputtered and crackled before a sharp voice responded calmly, "Please do not shout. It distorts your words. Repeat message."

Lilo repeated her words as she scanned the treetops nervously with her binoculars. The glare of the rising sun made it difficult to see to the east as its rays reflected harshly on the glass. She turned west, and the dull vibrating noise seemed imperceptibly louder. Lilo understood now why the tower had a six-sided platform. She had to constantly turn around to check east, west, north and south. She wished she and Annette had waited for the others this morning. She glanced at her watch. They were not due for another fifteen minutes.

Seeing nothing, she took the glasses away from her eyes to check where Annette was posted. Her friend stood only a few feet away scanning the skies with her binoculars making quarter turns every few seconds. As Annette made a final turn toward Lilo, she let loose a shrill scream and dropped her glasses. The lanyard looped around her neck was all that kept the binoculars from crashing to the platform.

"Lieber Gott! I thought you were some sort of monster! All I could see were two enormous eyes." Both girls burst into a brief near hysterical spate of giggles betraying their anxiety.

"Annette, it's getting louder. I think it may be more than one airplane and they're coming from the northwest. I'll look north, northwest and northeast. You do the same for the south. We have to manage all sides until the others arrive."

Annette nodded and quickly moved to the opposite side of the platform. Halfway there, she stopped and looked alarmingly at Lilo as the dull roar of engines throttled up.

Lilo brought her glasses up to her eyes and turned west. She spied two airplanes shooting up over the dense forest surrounding the camp. Through her glasses they looked close enough to touch.

"Mustangs," Lilo tried not to shout the information into her headset. "I believe I have two American P-51s–they have red tails."

Lilo prayed that the information was accurate. If P-51's were in sight, the big American bombers would be here, too. The instructors had been thorough in teaching Lilo's class the difference between the English Spitfires, the American Mustangs, and the planes in the German's own Luftwaffe. Lilo hoped she'd learned her lessons well. The lives of the people in the local villages and in the camp depended on it. Now she had to tell them how high above ground and how far away. God, they seemed so close! Even without her field glasses she could see the planes would be on them in a minute or less.

"Tower to base: Mustangs at about 300 meters above ground level. Repeat: three-hundred meters A-G-L." A crackling sound accompanied the clipped voice in Lilo's headset. "300 meters A-G-L? Confirm."

"Confirm," Lilo answered.

The voice crackled again in her headset. "300 meters A-G-L. Take cover immediately! Repeat! Take cover immediately!"

For the first time since Lilo had arrived, the normally cool voice on the other end held a hint of alarm. Cover? What? The little cabin on the platform? Lilo's thoughts were interrupted when the incessant ear-numbing roar of the planes suddenly turned into a screaming whine as both planes plunged in unison toward the platform.

"Annette," Lilo screamed. "Into the cabin, now!"

Lilo jerked off the headset tethering her to the rail just as the first staccato sound of fire broke from the planes. She threw herself onto the floor of the tiny sheltering cabin. Rolling on her back, she saw Annette only seconds behind her. Her soft brown eyes were dark with fear in a face pulled taught in a grimace of exertion as she raced for the shelter.

The rat-a-tat-tat of machine-gun fire punctuated Lilo's scream to her friend, "Hurry, Annette!"

Oh, God. She could see the planes looming behind Annette as her friend covered the last few feet, her eyes wide with terror.   Lilo threw herself forward, almost out of the protective shelter and reached out to pull Annette inside.

Relief flooded her as she locked her hand around Annette's wrist and pulled.   In that instant she felt a weight trying to pull Annette's hand from her.   Her friend's grateful smile slid out of place as her slight body began jerking spasmodically.   Her knees locked instinctively, bracing her tiny frame against the onslaught of fiery lead.   Her hand slid wetly from Lilo's palm, the soaking river of blood making it impossible for Lilo to hold onto her.

Annette took another step toward Lilo, her eyes wide with surprise, bloody palms up, a supplicant begging for release from agony, before the sparkling light in her pain-blackened pupils flickered and died.   Her knees gave way, and she pitched forward into Lilo's arms.

Lilo leaned back and eased Annette gently onto her lap. "It's all right, Annette," she whispered as she pressed her hands against her ears and screamed to drown out the incessant piercing sounds of the shells hammering the tower.   They rained down, splitting the platform, gouging huge bites of wood from it, and spitting them at her in splinters sharp as razor blades.

The shelling stopped as suddenly as it had started.   Lilo sat, rocking back and forth, holding Annette's motionless body in her arms.   She squeezed her eyes shut tightly and whispered her friend's name over and over.   The ceaseless roar of the airplanes faded away.   Complete silence followed their departures as though in leaving they took with them every vestige of the sounds of life from the air around her.

Lilo sat in the red-glowed darkness behind her tightly closed eyes and waited.   Someone would come soon.   She would open her eyes then.   They would know that she and Annette might be hurt and they would come.   She would just sit here, unmoving, until they came.   She would not open her eyes until they came.   But even with her eyes closed, Annette's blood-splattered face floated in front of her. She squeezed her eyes shut even more tightly, trying to expel the specter of her friend's hurt-filled face.

When would they come? A magpie's high shrill whistle penetrated her brain. A light breeze blew a strand of her hair under her nose, where it clung wetly to the mixture of mucus and tears that filmed her upper lip. She licked at it, but the annoying strand of hair wouldn't move. Every ounce of her consciousness focused on that strand of hair. All she had to do was slide her hand from beneath Annette's head and move it. She couldn't. She was afraid if she moved her hand, Annette's head might slip from her lap to the dirty wood floor beneath them. She would have to open her eyes and look to make sure that didn't happen. And she couldn't open her eyes. She would wait until they came. Perhaps if she called them–she opened her mouth and felt her lips crack dryly.

"Help us," she screamed shrilly, the force of the effort causing tears to flow from her eyes again. Once she'd uttered the words, she couldn't stop. "Help us! Help us! Oh, dear God, help us," she cried inconsolably.

"Burkhardt, is that you?" The disembodied question floated through her weakening screams.

"Yes, thank God, you're here. We need help," Lilo responded gratefully.

"Come out of the shelter, Burkhardt," the voice ordered. It was too faint for her to recognize but the note of authority in it was unmistakable.

"No! I can't. Please hurry! We need help," she begged.

"Burkhardt, we can't come up. The planes may be on their way back. If you can walk, you must come to the platform. Can you walk?"

"Yes, but I can't leave Annette."

"Burkhardt, get out on the platform now. That is an order. You have to watch for the planes. You know those red tails protect bombers. They could be here any moment. You must watch."

Were they mad? How could she possibly watch for planes? Annette was dead. But they didn't know, of course. She had to tell them. She had to move so she could tell them, and they would know the horrible thing that had happened here today and they would come and they would get Annette, and she could leave and go home. She wanted to go home. She had to go home.

Lilo flung her head forward, opened her eyes, and stared into her friend's own dull lifeless ones. A small cry escaped her as she stroked the blood away from Annette's paper white cheeks. Gently, she moved Annette's head and slid out from under the weight of the body. She stood on her numbed and trembling legs and walked stiffly out of the shelter to the edge of the platform. She looked down and saw the Kommandantin standing alone at the base of the tower.

"Help me! Annette is dead. Do you hear me?" she raged hysterically. "Annette is dead!" She saw the Kommandantin move closer to the tower base and wave to her. Lilo turned around and began making her way down the tower ladder.

"No, Burkhardt! Go back." Lilo ignored the order and continued down the steps, willing her shaking hands to hold on to the railing.

"Get back up there," the commander snarled. "Do you hear me, Fräulein Burkhardt? Not one more step." Lilo ignored the rising fury in the Kommandantin's voice and kept moving toward the ground. She felt a slight pinching in her right leg. It hurt, her mind registered dully. Never mind–she would tend to it once she was back in the barracks.

She finally reached the ground only to have the

Kommandantin grab her by her shoulders and with a hard shake snap, "I told you to get back up there. We have no time for your nonsense. You are endangering everyone with your dereliction to duty." She shook Lilo again cruelly to emphasize her words. Lilo slapped wildly at the restraining hands.

"Don't touch me," she screamed, "get away from me. I will not go back up there. Where are the other girls? Annette is dead, do you hear me?"

The Kommandantin's small brown eyes bored into Lilo's own. Lilo stared into them and was stunned to see them soften. The woman released her iron grip from Lilo's shoulders and instead put her arm around them, pulling her close. She looked up and scanned the now empty skies before she spoke.

The unexpected tenderness started Lilo's tears flowing again, "She is dead," Lilo intoned softly.

"Shh, Liselotte." It was the first time Lilo had ever heard the Kommandantin use anyone's first name. "We can do nothing for her now. This is the time when you must be strong. The planes may be back. You must help direct the fire. Do that–for Annette," she implored.

A deadly calm male voice interrupted them. Lilo wheeled around to the SS officer she had seen at times strolling through the camp. The silver buttons on his black uniform glinted in the early morning sunlight as the rays reflected coldly against the muzzle of the Walther PPK he pointed casually at her forehead.

"You will go back up into that tower immediately or you will be shot–here, now. It's your choice," he added coldly.

"But–"

"You choose the bullet?" He arched his thick blonde eyebrows up questioningly as the Kommandantin interrupted him.

"*Herr Gruppenführer,* bitte. The child–"

Keeping his gun leveled at Lilo's temple, he turned easily toward the Kommandantin. "Frau Kommandantin, I am beginning to question your ability to train these girls. Where are the others? Why aren't they up there?"

Lilo heard the chill in his voice and for the first time felt sorry for the stout homely woman who'd made their lives so difficult. "They are on their way–"

"You need say nothing more, Frau Kommandantin. You and I will have this conversation later, once you have the other girls at their posts and this Fräulein is back where she belongs."

He pressed the gun more firmly against Lilo's forehead, nudging her back toward the tower. With a stretching of his thin lips emulating a smile, he spoke reasonably to Lilo: "Fräulein, it is up to you."

He used the gun to gesture toward the tower. "You may go back up into the tower and do your duty, and yes, you may die. That is true," he said matter of factly.

In a measured pace to match his words, he moved the gun back to her temple adding, "Or you may remain here," he pushed the gun painfully into the soft temple area next to her right eye, "and you will most assuredly die."

The finality in his voice was unmistakable. "You choose. But I think you are a smart one, Fräulein," he smirked as he holstered his gun.

Lilo looked briefly into his hooded reptilian eyes and, seeing nothing human there, began walking toward the tower as he strode toward the communications barrack.

"Liselotte?" The whisper was accompanied by a light touch on the small of her back as she placed her foot on the first rung of the ladder. She turned toward the voice.

The Kommandantin told her, "At the end of the day, we will bring Annette down together. I am sorry, Burkhardt. War is difficult. But you will survive–because you must survive."

She gave Lilo a light ineffectual pat on her forearm and hiked away, her clumsy thick-soled black shoes making light squishing sounds in the snow-melt muck.

As Lilo climbed the ladder, her right leg throbbed each time she placed her weight on it. When she reached the platform, she saw a wide drying streak of blood leading into the shelter. She'd forgotten to ask if the other girls would join her or if she would be left alone with Annette all day. It didn't matter, she thought dully as she wearily checked her headset. If the planes returned, she would die anyway. She would not follow the blood trail and seek shelter in the cabin. Annette was there, and she could not bear to see her friend lying alone on the rough wooden planks, so still. She would rather die.

The next few hours were quiet. Lilo huddled alone on the shredded wooden platform, ignoring the other girls, who'd arrived with awkward pats on her shoulder and their hushed whispers of horror. She had removed her headset. The only sound was the intermittent shrill whistling of the bitterly cold north wind. A rare sunshine poured over her shoulders as the day aged, failing to bring an ounce of warmth to her body.

She stood up to stretch her cramped leg muscles and was surprised to feel her stomach growl. It was well past lunchtime, and she was ravenous. How could she think of eating without becoming violently ill at the thought of what had happened here today? But she was hungry. Leaning against the railing of the platform, she reached into her coat pocket for her sandwich. Instead of the rough brown lunch bag, her fingers closed around a sodden lump as a sharp pain arced in her upper leg. She opened her coat to inspect her leg and saw a gush of bright red blood form a large reddish-brown stain on her gray uniform slacks. She trembled as she realized she was wounded.

She pulled the wet bag from her pocket. The paper had disintegrated into a bloody mush, but the folded buttered bread slice was whole. Her stomach growled again more forcefully. She glanced toward the shelter and saw her friend lying here. Her shame staggered her. How could she possibly eat? Her friend was dead, her pale face and limbs lying in the now congealed pool of blood. But dear God, forgive her. She was hungry.

CHAPTER TWENTY-ONE

MUNICH, GERMAN: LATE MARCH-EARLY APRIL 1945

"Liselotte, how's your leg?" Anna Burkhardt swept into the living room and yanked back the rose damask drapes.

Liselotte grimaced as the bright sunlight poured into the room stabbing her eyes. She moaned slightly as she sat up on the sofa, "I'm fine, Mama. Stop worrying so much. I just wish I didn't have to go back."

"You are not going back, Liselotte. Your Papa will not allow it," Anna said firmly as she reached down and awkwardly patted her daughter's arm. "But you cannot be so careless," she added quietly.

Liselotte resisted rolling her eyes at her mother. Instead, she lay back on the worn rose brocade sofa and asked evenly, "What do you mean, 'so careless,' Mama?"

Anna looked furtively around the cavernous room before answering.

Her behavior annoyed Liselotte, but instead of commenting, she focused on the diaphanous motes of dust floating like an ephemeral halo around her mother's head. Since she had come home injured, Anna had removed the dust covers and opened up the formal drawing room so Liselotte wouldn't have to mount the dozens of steps up to her room each day. She tried to help her mother keep the room clean but the three ornate seating areas flanked by huge twin marble fireplaces at each end of the room created more work than the two could manage.

"You know what I mean, Liselotte," Anna snapped impatiently as she thumped the pillow behind Liselotte's head.

"Stop it, Mama," she waved her mother away with both

hands. "I have no idea what you mean. Just tell me. No one is going to hear you. What would they hear, anyway?"

Anna pulled a small royal-blue silk side chair close to Liselotte's head and leaned down to make sure her daughter could hear her hushed voice. "You never know, Liselotte. They didn't arrest your Papa for nothing, you know." She eased more closely, "and I'm certain that's why you were sent away." Her voice dropped another octave as she continued, "I think they are watching him and he still–even while you have been gone–he still goes out, not as often, but he still goes out sometimes in the night." She arched one pale-blonde brow. "You believe what you want, but remember, your Papa is no saint–and no model husband, either," she added firmly.

Liselotte sat up angrily, "Enough, Mama," she said roughly. "I won't hear anymore. You don't know what you're talking about. I am sorry for you that you have no more faith in Papa than that."

It was such an old and tired argument now. Liselotte remembered with longing that when her father had been so utterly dependent on Anna after he'd had his stroke, all of her tortured accusations and fears had ceased. With every gain he made in strength and independence, there was a commensurate loss in Anna's newly found aura of equanimity. Rather than argue with her mother until the words degenerated into a battle of acrimonious barbs, she drained the passion from her next words.

"Please leave me alone for now, Mama. I'm tired," she said listlessly. Anna nodded and hastily left the room. Liselotte stared at her mother's retreating back and sighed. She had looked forward to returning to the woman she thought her mother had become after Georg was injured, but instead Anna's paranoia seemed to have grown. She would be glad when she was no longer a near-invalid trapped in the house with her mother.

The familiar slam of the front door cheered her. Seconds later, her father strode into the room throwing off his heavy winter coat onto the matching rose sofa across from Lilo–missing it entirely. She laughed as he picked the coat up off the floor with his withered left arm and held it proudly in front of her.

"Getting stronger every day," he pronounced.

Lilo agreed, noting that even his limp was not as noticeable as long as he walked slowly. The problem was, he didn't. He never had. These days his haste was a particular source of dismay to Anna since it made him clumsy. He was already responsible for a fairly regular pattern of broken crystal and pottery.

Her father dropped into the dainty blue silk chair positioned next to her. His leaf-green eyes sparkled, and his cheeks had a rare healthy color in them. The warmer spring weather allowed him to spend more time outside despite the occasional frigid early spring windblasts that assaulted the city. So many buildings had been bombed to ruins that Munich seemed colder, even in spring, as the leveling of dozens of tall structures created vast shattered concrete plains across which the howling winds whipped furiously.

"My Lilo, I have good news today," her father announced ceremoniously as he dexterously pulled the leather glove from his bad hand. She was amazed at how he so readily accepted his new handicaps, as if they had always been a part of him. Seeing her pensive expression, he slapped her soundly on the shoulder with the glove.

"Thinking, thinking, thinking–come now. Your leg is almost healed. Let's go for a walk around 'The Garden.' The exercise will be good for you," he exclaimed merrily.

She laughed as she rose from the sofa. "The Garden" was their private code for going outside to discuss delicate matters. Georg and Lilo never spoke of important issues when Anna might accidentally overhear them. Lilo thought back to those years when she and her father had begun their late night "work." The early plans were hatched in "The Garden" when it still bloomed with towering lilacs and bushy dahlias, delighting the senses and overcoming the noxious fumes of the betrayingly beautiful foot-high blood-red geraniums. Desperate food shortages meant that now turnips grew where tulips had once flourished, and bouquets of bright green dill stood two feet shorter than the once hot pink and brilliant yellow dahlias. The lilacs were still there, though—faithful old sentinels patiently pushing on, despite neglect, their sweet scent reminiscent of happier days long past.

Lilo linked her arm through her father's strong one as they strolled between the lilacs. "So, what is this good news you have, Papa?"

"You are not going back to the camp, Lilo. Your Uncle Helmut will be here in an hour with the lawyer. You remember Hans Weiss—a good man, a quiet man." This last was drawn out— and the implication was not lost on her. Weiss could be trusted. The authorities would learn nothing from him if there were anything to learn. She nodded, not quite understanding what her father had in mind, but curious to know how he could prevent her from going back to face the horrors she had left behind in Austria. She shivered at the memories.

The day after Annette died, Lilo had been shaken out of her bunk. All of the other girls were getting up as well. Her drug-induced sleep from the morphine the doctor had finally given her after the ordeal the day before had caused her to forget where she was for a moment until the pain burned through her thigh.

"Up, Burkhardt!" the commander had ordered.

Lilo had tried to sit up, but had fallen back heavily in her bunk. "I cannot. My leg is hurt."

"The doctor is here to bandage it and give you another morphine shot. You will be fine. You have work to do."

222

In the pre-dawn darkness, Lilo saw an elderly man bearing a black medical bag approach her. His arthritic knees creaked as he kneeled beside her cot and pulled back the blanket to expose her bare leg. The bandage was soaked in blood.

"Frau Kommandantin," he stood and turned toward the shorter woman. "She cannot make it up the tower today. She is still losing blood and is likely in great pain."

The Kommandantin frowned at the news. Any trace of sympathy Lilo had seen in the frowzy woman had evaporated during the night.

"We have no choice. Yesterday's events require that we have every person on duty. Give her a shot, make sure she's bandaged appropriately, and we will allow her to see you at lunch, should she require more care."

The doctor shook his head, and leaning forward, rolled up the long sleeve of Lilo's coarse bleached woolen nightshirt, and plunged a syringe into her arm. Within a moment her pain had receded to a dull throbbing, and she felt an overwhelming sense of peace. She lay back dreamily and closed her eyes.

"Get her up and bandaged, Herr Doctor." The woman's voice grated on Lilo's ears as she turned to the others and asked querulously, "Why aren't you girls dressed?" She barked at the girls clustered around the cot.

Amanda had been the first to speak, "I'm not going," she stated flatly. "I'm not going to die like Annette."

Lilo wanted to warn them. She wanted to tell them about the SS officer with the death's head cap, and the death's head smile. But talking seemed too great an effort. The doctor finished bandaging her leg and pulled her up, settling her bare feet on the hard wooden floor. The other girls huddled around Amanda, nodding and murmuring their assent.

The commander sneered at the girls, turned, and walked

out of the barracks.

"Where do you think she's going?" asked Rita.

"I don't know and I don't care," replied Amanda. "Annette is dead less than one day, and I'm not going up there to get killed, too. They can go up there themselves," she added vehemently.

Lilo tried to speak again. She knew where the Kommandantin was going. She would bring back the SS officer with the gun. She tried to stand, but her leg gave way and she fell back heavily onto her cot.

"What are you doing, Lilo?" scolded Amanda, "You're going to hurt yourself. Be still."

Lilo shook her head. Her tongue felt thick and dry in her mouth as she spoke to Amanda, "We must go. They will kill us all if we do not."

Amanda looked at her in astonishment as the heavy door to the barracks slammed open and banged loudly against the wall.

"Alle Fräulein! Line up." He was dressed in the same unrelieved black from the top of his black and silver cap to the tips of his highly polished knee-high boots. He marched into the barracks, unholstered his large Walther pistol and used it to gesture toward Amanda. "You!" With his left hand he grabbed Amanda's forearm and jerked her roughly to the front of the line. "So, you are the first person to volunteer to die today, eh?" He tapped the muzzle of his gun against his muscled thigh.

Lilo knew what was next. The adrenalin coursed through her body and steadied her as she stood.

"No, she is not," Lilo said hoarsely.

She cleared her throat and took a step toward the SS

officer. "Amanda was concerned about me, but I am fine, and we are all going." She limped to the front of the line and saw another SS soldier in the doorway gesture with his rifle for them to follow him.

"That is good news. Friedrich will wait outside while you dress, and he will accompany you," he added magnanimously as he holstered the gun.

Lilo now recalled those agonizing steps to the tower that morning as her first steps back home. As she had walked with the others, her wound had begun bleeding heavily and she had fainted. The doctor had insisted that she required hospitalization, and within two days she was home in Munich recovering with her family.

"Lilo, you are not listening to me," her father reproached her gently.

His insistent tone dragged her back from the painful memory.

"You are not going back. I swear to you. Never."

She gave him a tremulous smile. If he said it, it was so. "Tell me your plan."

Quickly Georg explained that bombers had destroyed an apartment building that her Uncle Helmut owned in the city. Helmut was Lilo's favorite relative. He had never married, so she was the benefactor of the exotic gifts he collected in his worldwide travels. Although he had invested his considerable income into apartment buildings throughout Munich, he chose instead to live in a quaint medieval hamlet northwest of the city. During the summers when she wasn't visiting her grandparents, Lilo had spent many days at Uncle Helmut's. She remembered the bicycle rides they would take together through the old trails and logging roads that wove through the forests surrounding his cottage.

"Tonight, Lilo, you become the proud owner of a bombed-out pile of rubble," Georg pronounced heartily.

"Wonderful, Papa! Now please explain to me why I would want such a thing," she responded as she steered him toward a rusted iron bench beside the gravel garden path.

She saw that despite his cheerfulness, his limp was becoming more pronounced. The tight whitened lines around his mouth betrayed the effort it took for him to drag the withered limb. He sat down gratefully and patted the seat beside him as he explained to her the new law allowing property owners to take leave from their duties to handle issues dealing with their damaged properties.

"Tonight Helmut will deed you this bomb-ruined building, and you, as the owner will be allowed by law to stay home and handle all the problems that come when your property is lost. The plan will only buy a little time, but with the Russians and the Americans on their way, it may be enough. If not, we will find a doctor who understands that it is not acceptable for a young girl to help shoot down the men who will hopefully"–at this last, in deference to years of habitual caution, Georg's voice dropped a bit–"liberate us." He added with quiet joy, "Lilo, the Americans are coming. They have the men and the machines. Remember I told you that after the Great War, it was the American president who tried to show us some compassion."

Lilo had heard all about the dreadful Treaty of Versailles, the post-World War I document that everyone claimed had pushed the Germans so far down that many had initially welcomed Hitler's leadership. Anna had once described how she had witnessed her own mother using wads of worthless paper currency to light her breakfast fire in the kitchen. In her history classes Lilo had learned that a few years before she was born the value of a *Deutsch-Mark* was four billion to one U.S. dollar–an incomprehensible figure.

France and England had been adamant that the treaty

assured that the Germans would never again be in a position
to wage war. Only the American president, Woodrow Wilson,
seemed to understand that the armistice terms to end the war and
bring Germany to its knees could backfire. But it was doubtful
if even he could have imagined how craftily someone like Hitler
would use it. In January of 1917, before the Great War ended,
Wilson uttered a shrewd prophecy. A punitive peace, he warned,
would "leave a sting, resentment, a bitter memory upon which
the terms of peace would not rest, not permanently, but only as
upon quicksand."

"Child," Lilo's father whispered joyfully, "we are so close
to the end–to the destruction of that monster." He smiled, closed
his eyes, and took a deep breath of the lilac-perfumed air.

"You say this plan is only for a short period of time.
What are you thinking of, Papa, in case we need another plan?"

"I'm certain there is a doctor who will see that you cannot
go back because of your injuries–or some disease," he said
matter of factly. "If you are not healed, you cannot go back."

"What?" She understood her father's words, but she
knew that it was a certain death sentence for a doctor to swear
to a false statement. When it was time for her to return to the
camp, the SS would be there to take her. They had already been
around to check on her progress three times in just the few weeks
she'd been at home. Transferring the ownership of the apartment
building carried its own risks, but Helmut was family. Lilo
questioned whether her father truly knew a doctor willing to use
his own life as a stake in such a deadly gamble.

§ § § § § § §

"Liselotte, Herr Doctor Braun is here to examine you,"
Anna announced.

"Here I am, Mama."

Liselotte extended her hand to the small rotund graying

man carrying a large, worn black leather satchel.

"Go get your Papa while I see to the doctor," Anna ordered as she took the doctor's gray felt bowler and worn gray overcoat and ushered him into the grand parlor. She invited him to sit on a small forest-green velvet settee directly in front of one of the marble fireplaces. He stood and warmed his hands briefly at the small fire before taking his seat.

Georg limped into the room and extended his hand to the doctor. "Please don't get up, Herr Doctor. My friends tell me you are very busy. Please relax while I tell you of my daughter's unfortunate accident." He smiled back at Lilo who had followed him into the room.

"No need, Herr Burkhardt. I am fully acquainted with the details of your poor child's misfortune." The doctor lifted his heavy satchel and began removing some of its contents. He looked around the enormous salon until his eyes paused on a long mahogany sideboard. Gesturing toward it, he asked, "May I use one of the larger tables if this room is going to serve as our clinic?"

"Clinic?" asked Anna, "Why would you need a clinic here?" The doctor shot a warning glance at Georg, who smiled down at his wife, took her gently by the elbow, and steered her toward the double mahogany doors leading into the foyer.

"Anna, the doctor is just giving Lilo her final examination to clear her for work. We can take care of his needs here. Why don't you take care of our meal?"

Georg turned back toward the doctor, "You don't want to miss my Anna's cooking, so you will stay for our evening meal?"

The doctor nodded, and Anna blushed with pleasure at her husband's unsolicited praise. She knew it had been months since they had eaten anything close to what they would once have considered a fine meal but even she had to admit that with leeks, a few potatoes, and some stringy chicken, she could make a fair goulash.

"Certainly, Georg," she nodded as she smoothed the light-blue linen skirt of her dress and left the room. When Anna was safely out of earshot, the doctor asked, "She does not know?"

"She cannot know," Georg replied.

"I was assured that in no way would anyone discover what we are doing." A network of deep wrinkles sprouted across the doctor's high forehead.

"And no one shall," Georg stated calmly as he gestured for the doctor to make himself comfortable once again. "Now may we serve you a brandy?"

Sinking into the soft velvet cushion, the doctor nodded. "A brandy would be delightful, Herr Burkhardt," he smiled conspiratorially as their plan unfolded.

"Lilo, would you please go to the dining room and bring the good doctor a nice brandy."

"Of course, Papa."

Within minutes, the crash of breaking glass on marble, accompanied by a shrill scream of pain brought Georg, Doctor Braun, and Anna running into the foyer. By the time Anna arrived, Georg and the doctor were already on their knees beside her daughter, who lay writhing in pain.

"My leg, Mama," she wailed, "my leg!"

Anna circled the three anxiously, running her hands down the front of her white apron. "Is it your wound, Liselotte?"

Liselotte grimaced and nodded, "Yes, it's my wounded leg, Mama, but the pain is inside."

She let out a yelp as the doctor pressed tentatively on her thigh. He splayed his fingers down the length of her leg. He

229

stopped again halfway between her knee and her ankle and shook his head as she tried to pull the limb from his hands. "Be still," he warned, "you have a serious break, perhaps more than one."

Lilo lay still while Anna disappeared into the kitchen returning with a mop and broom. She swept nervously at the crystal shards glittering on the checkered marble floor as she kept an eye on the doctor while he completed his examination.

"I'm afraid her leg is broken. The upper femur appears to have snapped and the tibia also, here," he stood and pointed at her calf. "I can set it here, but we need to bring her into your drawing room. She will be fine. I believe the breaks are clean. No need for any x-rays. It's too difficult to find a machine these days, and she is so thin it is easy for me to tell."

Anna stopped mopping up the brown liquid on the foyer floor, and asked suspiciously, "Herr Doctor, how could such a healthy young girl snap her leg this way?"

"Likely, it is because she was immobile for an extended period of time, and if she was rushing through this foyer,–"

Anna interrupted the doctor to scowl at her daughter. "She is always rushing!"

The doctor nodded sagely, "So the force of a clumsy fall on this very hard floor coupled with weakness in the limb," he shrugged fatalistically and nodded for Georg to help him carry Lilo into the other room.

Georg knelt down beside her, "Hold tight to my neck. The doctor and I will lift you."

Lilo let out such a shriek of pain as they lifted her that Georg had to hide his face in his shoulder so that Anna would not hear the quick bubble of laughter that escaped from his lips. Lilo moaned as they lay her back onto the couch that had been her home for so many weeks. The doctor took a long syringe from his bag. Lilo's eyes widened.

"Anna," Georg addressed his wife who was fluttering around them unable to assist and unable to leave for fear her daughter would need her. "Why don't you go prepare Lilo a bit of soup? The doctor and I will manage."

Anna's relief at being assigned a task was almost palpable. "Yes," she nodded firmly. "First I will finish clearing the glass and the spill in the foyer before someone else is hurt."

As soon as Anna left the room, Lilo exclaimed, "Get that needle away from me, please, Herr Doctor. It looks vicious," she laughed. The doctor put the needle away.

After Georg brought him some water, Dr. Braun began mixing up a plaster cast for her leg. When he finished, the cast wrapped around her leg from the ankle to the top of her thigh, and she was once again immobilized on the brocade sofa.

"Papa, please plump the pillows behind my head," she whined as the doctor began packing his satchel. "Then I will need soup and perhaps a book read to me," she sighed. "I am in such pain," she added with a grin.

"I'll make you more comfortable," Georg said as he pulled a pillow roughly from behind her head and began pummeling her with it. "How's that little sick one?" Even the earnest doctor broke out laughing as Lilo tried to ward off her father's gentle blows.

"What's going on here?" the shrill question echoed in the room.

The doctor recovered first. "Why, nothing at all, Frau Burkhardt. It is the morphine. Some patients go to sleep immediately and others laugh uncontrollably. At least we know your daughter is in no pain."

"None whatsoever," added Lilo impudently.

Anna eyed the three suspiciously before she turned away.

"I will finish our meal preparations then."

Once she had gone, Georg turned to the doctor. "My apologies to you, Herr Doctor. We will have to remain very circumspect in consideration of my daughter's latest injury."

The doctor nodded seriously. "So you shall, Herr Burkhardt." With that final utterance the three were bound together in a deadly pact that, if but one of them broke, would condemn them all.

§ § § § § § §

This time the knock came long after nightfall. As Liselotte, her mother, and father sat in the drawing room, each looked anxiously to the other as Georg stood to go answer the door.

"Heil Hitler," declared one of the two raven-dressed SS soldiers. "Where is your daughter?"

"Come in if you wish to see her. She cannot walk well yet." Georg motioned the pair inside.

"Still in a cast?" one of the eagle-eyed officers demanded contentiously.

As the officer stooped his lanky frame to step through the door, Georg caught his first look at him under the bright light of one of the two large crystal chandeliers in the foyer. A child, he thought, just a boy. As if reading Georg's thoughts, the teen stood tall again.

"I am Lieutenant Hans Studt," he stated with more force than necessary, as though his stern tone would negate the youthful impression of his pink-cheeked hairless face.

The hardened expression in his light eyes, the black uniform with the double silver lightning bolts on the collar, the black jackboots and gloves, and the pistol in his belt left no doubt that this boy was to be taken seriously. It was not Georg's first encounter with boys whose minds had been forever twisted with the message of the Hitler Youth. Sadly, however, they were all Germany had left to take care of military duties at home.

"Follow me, Lieutenant." Georg walked into the drawing room with both SS soldiers on his heels. "This is my daughter, Liselotte." Georg gestured to the sofa where Lilo sat, her leg with the confining ankle-to-thigh cast propped on an enormous rose damask ottoman.

"Heil Hitler," snapped the lieutenant.

Lilo and Anna each made the obligatory straight-armed salute–disheartened gestures fearfully put forth as a semblance of what they hoped were appropriate responses to the soldier's fanatical greeting.

The youth pulled a packet of papers from the breast pocket of his uniform. Reading from them, he listed her most recent injury.

When he finished, Lilo nodded wearily. The SS visits had become more frequent these last two weeks. Each time the visiting soldier would read a statement of her injuries, then read a statement from Dr. Braun. Lilo knew the youth's next visit would be to Braun to make certain the doctor was telling the truth about her injuries. She was alternately amazed at his bravery and fearful for his life each time the doctor swore that her injuries were in fact so serious that she could not return to the camp in Austria. Her father had told her that there were more and more people who, like Braun, were willing to take risks since life had become so difficult and brutal under the Nazis and since it was apparent that the war would end soon.

"You are needed back at your camp, Fräulein Burkhardt. When will you be well?" He poised a pen over a small notebook ready to record her response.

"Dr. Braun says I am no worse but no better since your

comrade asked me the same question day before yesterday. I have not seen my doctor in one week. He comes tomorrow, and I shall know more then, but–" she couldn't resist adding sarcastically, "I'm certain you will have that information before his visit is even complete, won't you?" Lilo added a charming smile to soften the impact of her words. She felt her mother's unease and added, "It is a difficult job you have, Lieutenant. I see you do it thoroughly." Another smile accompanied the ingratiating words.

The teenager's already pink cheeks reddened as he fought to keep his demeanor as dark as his uniform. With a brisk nod of his head, he barked his farewell, threw up the Nazi salute, and with his footfalls echoing on the polished foyer floor, he and his silent partner dissolved back into the darkness outside.

§ § § § § § §

It had been a wonderful day. For the first time in months, Lilo had enjoyed an afternoon with her friends Gudrund and Anne. She was so overjoyed at an afternoon of friendship and gossip that she had stayed too long. The last bus that would have taken her close to home had already left. The people of Munich were enduring such horrific bombings that even though it was only six o'clock at night, the streets were already deserted. The blackout curtains in each apartment were so effective that not a single ray of light shone to help her navigate her way in the encroaching darkness.

She picked her way carefully through the rubble that littered the streets and sidewalks, careful not to trip over the stones, bricks, and boards scattered before her. A rare spring snowfall was already melting away, leaving her struggling through the dirty piles of slush.

She had begun the two-mile walk with enough energy. Now into the second mile, the wet snow had soaked her cast and doubled its already irritating weight. She lumbered along as quickly as she could. Her parents were probably already very worried. With her next step, her knee broke through the soaked plaster. Now, she could actually bend her leg and walk much more quickly and less clumsily. It was fully dark when she took her final steps toward the lamp-lit front porch. Before she could get there, the door opened. Her father peered inquisitively into the dark beyond the pale halo of light.

"Papa," she exclaimed with a beckoning wave as she sped toward the light, "I'm here!"

As his eyes adjusted to the gloom, Georg saw his daughter nimbly stepping toward him. Unseen by her, his face registered dismay as he watched her walk in unfettered haste toward him.

As she took her final step onto the porch, he grabbed her upper arm with such force that she cried out in pain: "Papa?"

He pulled her into the house and slammed the door. "You foolish girl!" he berated her in a tone she had never heard him use with her before. "How could you jeopardize all those who have helped you?" He looked down at the sopping wet cast, now shredding soggily above and below her knee. "Are you trying to get all of us, including the poor doctor, shot for treason? Do you realize you look about as crippled as a gazelle?" His green eyes glittered with anger and fear.

Lilo shrank back from his onslaught.

"Papa," she stammered, "I'm sorry. I didn't think—"

"No, you didn't think," he leaned forward and stabbed her temple with his forefinger, "you behaved foolishly."

Lilo hung her head, watching the water shedding itself from her cast and pooling onto the polished black and white checkered marble floor. "I am so sorry," she mumbled. "I was having such a good time with Gudrund and Anne." Her dismay was evident as she reached for her father, her aggrieved apologies still rushing from her lips.

235

Georg sighed, pulled his daughter toward him and stroked her damp hair. He had made an adult of her far too soon, he thought guiltily. A crushing red wave of anger forced the blood to his face. This was the first time he could ever recall her behaving with the least bit of childish abandonment. He was so proud of her. By the time she was thirteen years old, the Third Reich had stolen her childhood as she became his partner in deeds that many grown men would never have dared.

He sighed again, his eyes misting as he held her. Her life was so far from what he'd dreamed for her when he'd first held her in his arms. God knows, she deserved at least one day of joy, but he knew first-hand the harsh consequences of a single unguarded moment.

He cleared his throat and pulled away from her and looked down into his daughter's remorseful face. "I am sorry for being so harsh with you, Lilo. But you know the SS have not been here for several days. They could have seen you," he warned. "Ah, well, they didn't." He smiled and wrapped his arm around her shoulder and escorted her to her permanent place on the rose sofa. "Sit now, while I go find your Mama and have her mix some plaster. I think we can patch this without troubling Doctor Braun."

§ § § § § § §

The knock came later than usual that night. Liselotte's cast was already roughly patched when the sharp knocks reverberated through the ground floor of the house. Georg winced slightly as he pushed himself up from the deep-green velvet settee by the fireplace. The knock sounded again, frantic and somehow softer than it had been the moment before. Georg heard a low moaning as he approached the door. He hurried his step and swung the door open. Two thin women stood huddled against the cold. Their faces were pale even in the warmth of the golden porch light. Their red-rimmed eyes squinted at him as he stood there. He knew them both, but the older woman, whom he had seen only last week, had moved from middle to old age in that brief period. The younger woman looked lost as her dark blonde hair swirled in the brief blast of wind speckling it with melting snow as it whipped stingingly across her pale cheeks.

Georg stepped out onto the porch and reached his strong right arm out to encircle them both. "Herta? Katherina?"

The women, whose tears had evaporated in the cold air, began softly weeping again. The older woman buried her face against the soft dark-green loden fabric of his jacket. "He is gone—my son, my son"—her last words a mournful whisper ripped from her lips and tossed away as the howling wind replaced them with its own eerie wail.

Georg gently pulled both women inside and ushered them into the foyer, guiding them to a small wine damask upholstered bench against the wall. "Sit down a moment. I will have Anna bring you something to warm you."

Georg took his time walking to the kitchen to find his wife, wishing desperately that the two women would disappear. A portion of the sorrowful burden they brought to his home that night would not leave with them.

"Anna, two glasses of brandy, quickly," he called as he approached the kitchen on heavy legs, "in the front hall." Anna joined him within a moment carrying a small tray with a decanter of brandy and two glasses. Georg steadied the tray when she stopped abruptly as she recognized the two women huddled together on the settee. He took the tray from her and set it on the round mahogany table under one of the chandeliers as Anna flew forward toward the pair.

"Herta, oh no! Mein Gott. Please, you do not come to tell us–?" The cadence of her words lilted up anxiously. Both women nodded in unison as she bent to embrace them. Georg placed his hand on the small of his wife's back and whispered that he would carry the brandy in the drawing room while she ushered their guests in.

Lilo smiled at him as he walked into the room and placed the tray on the sideboard next to one of the marble fireplaces. "Oh, so now you serve the SS brandy?" She laughed as she tried to peer around him for their visitors. He moved her legs gently from the sofa to the large ottoman and sat down beside her.

"Lilo," he began haltingly as he placed the palm of his hand on his daughter's cheek. His back faced the doors to the foyer, but the expression on his child's face told him the moment Peter's mother and sister entered the room.

"No!" Her heart-rending scream echoed in the large space as she launched herself from the sofa. She looked about wildly as though searching for some escape from the room as the three tearful women rushed toward her in their shared grief.

She turned away from them to her father and wrapped her arms around him sobbing, "Papa! Oh, Papa! He's not coming home, is he? He is never coming back to me, is he?" she cried out as Georg pushed her back down to the sofa and held her.

Anna guided the two other women to the sofa across from them. Desolate, they wept–one, a mother who'd lost her only son, another who'd lost her only brother–both crying as they buried the memories of yesterday. And the third, sobbing for the memories she would never make tomorrow.

CHAPTER TWENTY-TWO

Near Munich, Germany: April 29, 1945

C.T. opened the tank turret and breathed in the rare clear air as he surveyed the bomb-blasted countryside. Despite the metal wreckage and the fallen, charred, and still smoldering trees at the edge of the vast plain, the last few weeks of spring sunshine had teased the field into sprouting a bold green carpet through the ashes of the burned landscape. Even with the American observation plane droning above him, the German countryside presented a hushed serenity that C. T. marveled at this morning.

The 761ˢᵗ had broken up into several "bastard" outfits since they had smashed through the last German stronghold, the Siegfried Line. Now, he and Bud and a couple of other tankers were leading a company of riflemen and grounded paratroopers toward their next objective, the city of Munich, capital of Bavaria. It was ironic that what was likely the end of their bloody trek would take them to the place that marked the beginning of Hitler's bloody Third Reich.

C.T. heard a move below him as his other tank mates slowly awakened, no doubt brought to life by the bright beam of sunlight he'd loosed into the belly of the stinking tank when he'd opened the turret. He had always been an early riser, but thankfully the company cook was always up first. Since C.T. didn't like to eat alone, he figured it was time to give his fellow soldiers a little push out of dreamland.

"I'm gonna lay down my burden, down by the riverside, down by the riverside, down by the riverside." C.T. bellowed the old Negro spiritual joyfully into the quiet morning, his warm rich bass voice stroking each note.

"I'm gonna lay down my burden, down by the riverside.

Down by the ri-ver-side." He paused to get his fellow tankers ready to deliver the rousing chorus with him. Leaning into the tank he blustered, "Come on, guys, it's Sunday morning! Clap yo hands wid me!"

He laughed at the chorus of "Shut the hell ups" that echoed up to him from the belly of the tank. He was not deterred. Instead he slapped his palms together and sang out.

"*Ain't gonna study war no more, ain't gonna study war no more–Ouch!*" C.T.'s cry interrupted his jubilant chorus. "Whicha you heathens is hittin' my leg down there? That you Cap'n?"

"Naw, C.T., not me," came the reply. "But since you got all of us awake down here, how 'bout movin' your ass so we can git out and git some breakfast? And cut out the singing, if that's what you call it."

"No way, Bud. It's just too damn pretty a day out here," he responded as he climbed out of the turret onto the side of his heavily armored home and dropped to the ground.

He pounded his meaty fist on the side of the tank and laughed as he heard the responding groans and grumbles. If anyone was still asleep in there, the reverberating thumps had surely wakened the last of the somnolent soldiers.

"Well, good mornin', Captain," C.T. welcomed Bud with a smart salute as Bud crawled from the tank and joined him on the ground. "Welcome to my beautiful day, sir."

Bud answered with a nod as "Tree" Tyson popped his head out of the turret and yelled, "It a been a damn sight mo' beautiful if we hadn't had to hear you crankin' up the church choir fuhst thing this mawnin'!"

"Aw, come on, Tree. You know you thought you 'as back home in Mississippi when you heard my fine voice," C.T. yelled back as the lanky soldier unfolded his limber frame and climbed down to join them.

"You think that even with all the bullets and bombs we've had flyin' past us these last few months that that hell-hole of a state is any place I'd even think 'bout goin' back to? Hell naw, uh-uh." The lean young man shook his head vigorously back and forth to make sure the meaning of his message was clear. "But you is right 'bout one thing. Let us gib thanks fo' this day what the Lord has done made!" Tree Tyson's brilliant white teeth shone in the daylight, resembling perfectly gleaming piano keys as he turned his ebony face up to the sun.

"Amen, brother," answered one of the last two soldiers exiting the tank.

"I'll say "amen" after I've had me some breakfast," added Humphrey. "Jaybo got it ready yet?"

The men of the 761st were dearly enjoying the luxury of a few regular hot cooked meals. It had been a different story on the battlefields, but for the last few days the tankers had had some relief. They had met with some resistance as they rolled through the southern German countryside but most of it had been limited to some small arms fire by rabid SS soldiers caught far away from their units. In fact, Bud and C.T. had hardly fired the 75-millimeter or even the .50 and the two .30 cal guns since their last firefight nearly a month ago when they'd smashed the Siegfried Line at Klingenmünster.

Bud pulled out his map to figure out about how long it would take them to get to the city of Munich. C.T. leaned over as Bud perused it. "Wacha' think, Cap'n? How long?"

Bud rolled up the map and swatted C.T. in the head.

"Knock it off, C.T. Quit callin' me "Captain" every time you open your mouth," he growled good-naturedly.

Since the commander had pinned on Bud's captain bars, C.T. had made it a point of using his new rank instead of his name. C.T. also thought it was great fun to snap to attention and salute Bud every single time he was within earshot–or armshot.

Bud pointed to a small mark on the map. We're about seventy miles away from some place called Dock-ow. It's a little Kraut town with some kind of labor camp there. Colonel told me last night he has something he needs me to get to a colonel with the 20th Armored. They're somewhere around there so I'm gonna head out and meet up with you guys in Munich."

"Hot dog, Cap'n, we sleepin' in feather beds pretty soon!" Tree whooped it up, excited at the possibility of having a little space to stretch out and sleep. They'd been forced to sleep inside the tanks so much instead of outside on the ground. Tree's height assured he got the worst of it.

"Maybe so, Tyson," nodded Bud, "but remember we've bombed the livin' daylights out of Munich for weeks. Findin' that feather bed may take a little time," he added with a smile.

"And findin' one long enough for you is gonna be impossible," interjected C.T. as he reached into Tree's overflowing mess kit dish. "You prob'ly oughta gib me dat biscuit just so you'll slow your growth some, ya know?"

C.T. snatched the biscuit, and Tree dropped his mess kit to chase him down. C.T. raced away from Bud, then looped around the tank back toward him, waving the biscuit tantalizingly over his head before stopping and tossing it back to Tree, minus a big bite. Resting his hands on his knees, he leaned forward to catch his breath.

"Say, Bud, you ain't goin' to make that delivery by yourself, are you?"

"Naw, they'll pick some poor sucker to go along."

"That's me, then. 'Sucker C.T.' I'll go along with ya, Cap'n." He added his faithful salute.

"No, hell, you won't if you don't knock it off with the salutes."

"Roger that, Bud. Oww!" The rock-hard half-bitten biscuit hit C.T.'s head with a thunk.

"That'll learn ya, durn ya," yelled Tree as he took off with C.T. not far behind. Bud grinned as the innocent sound of their laughter rang out across the deceptively new green and sweetened meadow. He couldn't know that the sight that would greet him and C.T. that afternoon would render it impossible for them ever again to recapture the last shred of the boyhood that they had so briefly shared at this moment.

§ § § § § §

"Eat up, fellas. You'd better enjoy this last meal together. They're splitting us up again." The Colonel strode in front of his troops relaying this latest round of dispatches.

One of the men asked, "What's goin' on, Colonel? Ain't nothin' left but a few old men, those poor little Hitler Youth boys, and those crazy SS sons a bitches. Geez Colonel, these Krauts been surrenderin' by the thousands like sinners hit by the spirit at a tent revival!"

"They lookin' to be saved!" a loud voice shouted.

"Hallelujah!" laughed another.

"Yeah, Colonel. Who needs Black Panther armor against that?" added another soldier.

"I don't know, fellas, but I've got an armload of dispatches here from everybody and his brother, and every last one of these units is begging for a Black panther." This last he had exclaimed with a proud grin.

A corresponding roar rose from the crowds of men scattered before him "Yeah, they can't lynch us fast enough back home, but now they split us up and beg for us to cover their asses," hooted one soldier.

"You're right," agreed the Colonel, "but we'll meet up again somewhere between Munich and Austria–and we're going to hoist a few beers together when we do. Until then, I've got requests from everybody from your old friends in the 17th Airborne to the 103rd Infantry. Finish up while I hand out your assignments, and we'll get moving again. And men, until we meet again, what do you do?"

From the throats of hundreds of men who'd already lost more than half of their friends on frigid, frozen battlegrounds from France through Belgium and Germany rose the motto of the 761st. The motto had enabled them to brave the worst and come out as one of the best. In one communal voice, the words, *"Come out fighting, Sir!,"* rose to the skies like ground dew evaporating in the early morning daylight.

§ § § § § §

"They'll find that colonel soon, C.T., as soon as we start moving again."

Bud and C.T.'s jeep was at a dead stop wedged between two idling tanks. They had fallen in with the 20th Armored about five kilometers back. Driving through the rutted tracks on the heels of a tank had delivered both bone-jarring bumps and throat-clogging dust, but it beat freezing to death in snow and mud.

They could tell they were close to a town since the distance between the stone and stucco houses was decreasing. In some places the symmetry of the neatly ordered houses standing beside the road was ruined by a heap of stone and charred wood, or the single chimney left standing like a lonely sentry reaching toward the crisp blue sky.

A young G.I. sprinted up to them. "Captain Leverett, sir?"

Bud nodded.

"Captain Blount, I Company. I've got some info you guys need to hear."

Bud jumped down from the jeep. "C.T., if we start moving again, just drive on. I'll walk with the Captain here." Bud reached out to shake Blount's hand and added, "Bud Leverett. We've got a message for Colonel Alford, but no one's located him for us yet."

"Yes, sir, that's why I'm here. He's at the head of the column somewhere, but the message might have to wait a bit. I'll take it up to him for you when I go back up there, but we may have a priority situation here. Let me introduce you to Corporal David Abramowitz, lately from Teaneck, New Jersey, by way of Munich."

Blount gestured to the small corporal who had been standing at an inconspicuous attention beside Blount. The man's sallow skin looked pale, almost to the point of illness. His large dark eyes glowed.

Blount continued. "Abramowitz made it to the U.S.A. when he was a teenager." Bud wondered idly how long ago that could have been since the young corporal still looked like a teenager to him.

"David, Captain Leverett's a tanker with the 761st. If we get into any big trouble, he can help. Right, Captain?"

Bud nodded and gestured toward C.T.

"Let me introduce you to Lieutenant C.T. Deeks. He's a tanker, too. Anything we can do to help, we'll do. But we haven't been running into much trouble for a little while. What's going on here?"

"Not yet sure. But we've got our doubts about whether our intelligence has the dope on Dachau–at least to hear David here tell it." He turned to the diminutive corporal. "Abramowitz, tell him what you heard."

The young corporal's Adam's apple was bobbing soundlessly in his scrawny throat as though he was trying to take

245

in enough air to form the words his Captain had ordered him to speak.

"Well, it's like this, sir. I know we've been told Dachau's a work camp for political prisoners, but my folks had heard some other stories." The youth rushed this last and then abruptly stopped his narrative.

Bud was surprised at how difficult it was to detect a German accent in the boy's speech since he had could not have lived in the United States for too many years.

"Go ahead, David. Tell him the whole thing," Captain Blount prompted gently.

"Even though I was born in Munich, my grandparents were from Krakow, Poland. When we were getting ready to go to the States, my father wired my grandparents some money so they could come with us. We waited a week for them to get there. My father called dozens of relatives there, but couldn't reach a soul. Finally, he contacted the priest at the Catholic Church there. That's how he found out that my grandparents along with everyone else who had lived in the Jewish section of the city had been forced on a train—not a regular train sir, but on cattle cars heading west. He said they had been loaded up after a series of pogroms." The young man explained earnestly, "Those are like riots, sirs. They—"

"I know what pogroms are, David. Keep talking," Bud interrupted.

Bud's father had taught him about how the Jews had been treated throughout history. He knew it all from the story of Moses to the pogroms in Russia during the first Great War.

The roar of a tank starting its throaty engine stilled the conversation. The three men waited for the giant machine's engine to throttle down to a dull idle.

"The priest told my father that he had learned they were

taking the Jews to a work camp called Belzec. He said it was a 'tough camp, like Dachau.' When Father asked what he meant by 'like Dachau,' the priest told him, ' You know, like Dachau–a slave labor camp where you work until you drop dead.

He told my father that he could never repeat what he was telling him but that he had heard from some of the Catholic priests from Germany that Dachau, and some other camps like it, had been deliberately set up to kill Jews. My dad didn't believe it at first, but he said that the priest had been so scared when he told him that it was impossible to ignore it. Although we were not scheduled to leave for another week, that night my father was so upset that he awakened us in the middle of the night and told my mother and me that we had an hour to pack. We were cautioned not to say good-bye to anyone."

The young teen's eyes misted at the memory and he cleared his throat in embarrassment before finishing his story.

"That was in May of 1942. After we arrived in the U.S., we tried to contact friends and neighbors–all Jewish. But we have not been able to contact anyone since August of 1942. For nearly three years we haven't heard a single word from anyone."

While the teen finished his story, the column of tanks, jeeps, and soldiers had started inching forward. The trio walked slowly, keeping pace with C.T. as he drove in the dusty wake of the tank growling forward ahead of him. Bud wasn't certain what to make of Abramowitz' story.

Captain Blount quickly informed him. "Captain Leverett, the bottom line is that we thought this camp would just be guarded by those *Volksturm* folks, but when you put together a few of our intelligence reports with David's story here and a couple of others we've heard, we might be in for a tougher fight than we had thought. Even though we're pretty strong here, the colonel asked if you might just hang around until we find out what's what."

Bud looked at C.T., who shrugged his shoulders noncommittally, before responding. "I don't know, Captain. The 761st is getting busted up right now and they may need us. You look pretty stout here."

Before Blount could answer, Corporal Abramowitz interrupted. "Captain," the young man swallowed again before he rushed his next few words. "Captain, sir, I don't know what's true and what's not, but when I was younger, we used to say a prayer if we were being punished." He cleared his throat uncomfortably before he began reciting a prayer in German.

Bud understood only the final few words, "… dass ich nicht nach Dachau komm'."

The young man quickly translated for them all, sending a brief chill up Bud's spine.

"God, help me be a good boy so I don't have to go to Dachau."

Bud saw that C.T. had been transfixed by the prayer and was slowly nodding his head. Shit! Just invoke the name of God and you could get C.T. to do any damn thing!

§ § § § § §

It took less than an hour to reach the town of Dachau. In the towns they had passed through earlier, some people had hidden in their homes, but others, especially the children, swarmed the streets enthusiastically greeting G.I. Joe. Today, though, most of the people remained inside. Bud thought it was because there were fewer infantry men walking beside the tanks of the 191st Tank Battalion. That meant fewer soldiers handing out candy bars and becoming welcome pied-pipers instead of menacing invaders.

Today the tanks rumbled noisily through the otherwise silent town. Bud and C.T. enjoyed the bracing sunshine now that the column was moving, and they could put some distance between themselves and the tank in front of them. The roads were dry and rutted, but it was better than riding with the nose of the jeep inches away from the rear of the tank and choking on the dust kicked up by the metal beast.

Dachau was a pretty little village with picturesque cottages, most of which sported the obligatory window box filled with scarlet geraniums. Some of the window boxes were hidden by the great white sheets hanging out of the windows of a few houses, giant flags of truce acknowledging, and in many cases welcoming, the arrival of the Americans.

A squad of armed G.I.s waving machine guns materialized from around the corner of a tiny stone church, their animated gestures interrupting Bud's mental meanderings. C.T. slowed the jeep as the tank in front of them shuddered to a clanking stop, and the tank commander opened the top turret.

Bud couldn't see where the head of the column had stopped, but more soldiers were pouring around the tanks. About a dozen riflemen were running toward the tank commander. Bud stepped out of the jeep to walk ahead and find out what the hubbub was all about. As he approached, he saw a butter-bar lieutenant, yelling and gesturing to the tank commander. The young soldier's face was pale and a light sheen of unhealthy sweat glistened at the rim of his helmet.

"Oh, God, sir. It's awful. You, uh, you, uh..."

The soldier grimaced and cleared his throat before starting again. "What I'm trying to say, sir, is that, well, there's nothing up there anyone needs to see," he finished grimly.

The tank commander started to ask the obviously distressed young officer a question when a short, burly major strode up to them.

The lieutenant snapped to attention and saluted the higher ranking officer. Bud's own salute was ignored as the man's bushy dark eyebrows furrowed over his hard brown eyes. He leaned forward, his face only inches from the lieutenant's.

"Smith, get back to that train, now! There's no going backwards. Are you nuts?" The major's exasperation seemed to run out of steam as the young lieutenant drew back from the superior officer's tirade.

"You need to buck up, son–just buck up now," the major added with a light pat to the young man's back. "Now go do your job, Lieutenant." With a parting salute to the major and to Bud, the lieutenant hurried back toward the group of riflemen.

"You!" The major stabbed his finger in the air at the tank commander still leaning out of the turret. "Get that tank moving."

He turned and gave Bud the once-over. His eyes lingered on the Black Panther insignia on Bud's shoulder.

"You 761st? Didn't know you guys were here. How many tanks you got back there?"

"Sir, it's just me and Lieutenant Deeks," Bud gestured to where C.T. sat in the idling jeep, watching the scene. "No tanks. Fact is our unit's miles away. We were sent here early this morning to deliver a message, but we'll do what we can to help if you'll fill me in."

The major nodded curtly. "You'll see for yourself, but you'd better have a strong stomach," he added dourly as he turned his full attention to the group of infantrymen who had materialized around them.

"Okay, men. Let's get through those gates," he ordered as he waved toward an opening in a stone wall further down the road.

Bud signaled C.T. to pull ahead. As he climbed in the jeep, C.T. asked, "What's going on?"

Bud shrugged his answer, "Not sure–just know it's not good. Let's park the jeep by this wall and walk in. We'll just get stalled in the shuffle with all this traffic headed through that gate. I don't think it's more than a half-mile or so ahead."

Within ten minutes Bud and C.T. had reached a group of soldiers knotted around a train stopped on the tracks. The tracks ran under an enormous iron arch featuring an eagle perched on a swastika and into a gated compound. Beside the train lay piles of dirty clothing that smelled to high heaven. Bud saw that each open car in the long train was also filled with more piles of clothing. What a stinking mess. As Bud pushed forward, the cloying, putrid scent hit him in a noxious wave at the same moment his eyes registered to his brain what they were seeing.

Beneath the grayed piles of rags Bud detected a face, a hand, an arm–all motionless. Some were spotted, and some soaked with deep, drying crimson stains. The sight struck him in the chest forcing the air from his lungs and nearly forcing out the contents of his stomach as well. He swallowed.

As Bud struggled to make sense of what he was seeing, he heard C.T. whisper behind him: "Jesus Christ, Captain." Too shocked to move for the moment, they listened as the major shouted orders to his troops, many of them, like Bud and C.T., stunned speechless by the horrific scene. On these battle-hardened faces Bud saw every emotion from confusion to rage at the revolting sight.

"Count them!" The major's words smacked Bud's eardrum, shattering the cacophony of repulsion swimming in his brain.

Left foot, right foot, left, right . . . His mechanical steps marched him from car to car. He studiously stepped around mounds of shredded rags, not daring to look too closely at the final swaddling of a mother, a father, a child, in infinite sleep.

Count them.

251

One, two, three . . .

Huge mountains of rags. Of human beings. Long waves of dark hair shrouded some of the mounds of cloth like some departing gift left on an inhuman altar of wicked sacrifice. He saw faces, too. Wide, heavily lashed staring eyes and thin arms stretched out in petrified beseechment. Grimly, Bud swallowed down the bile that rose and burned the lining of his throat.

"Did you hear me, soldier?" The major stood in front of Bud. "You need to help me keep these grunts moving. No need to stop and stare at all this. Just keep these boys busy counting. They need to keep moving. Understand?"

Bud saluted his agreement and pulled his eyes away from the scene toward a knot of men wandering aimlessly from car to car. He took a deep breath. "Alright, soldiers. You heard the major. Quit amblin' around and get busy. Count 'em all. Every one. That's an order." Bud was gratified to hear the calm steely edge in his own voice.

Four, five, six . . .

Please, dear God. This would take hours. The dancing spring sunshine cast an unholy light on the corpses as Bud and the men moved from car to car counting and cataloguing the mountains of men, women, boys, girls–and the babies. All so still. Their ghostly white cheeks and fuzzy bloodied heads offering no trace of who they might have been.

Good God Almighty, Bud smirked to himself as the habitual words rattled around in his head. Only the men with him, biting their lips and stoically moving from mound to mound, kept him from laughing out loud at the irony of his unbidden prayer. *Good* God?

The brilliant sun moved behind a cloud, graying the day and finally offering some measure of dignity to the desecrated.

Seven, eight, nine . . .

This was the last time. He swore it. "God" would never hear from him again. With a certainty as dark as the day had become, Bud accepted God once and for all–a cold, calculating, vengeful, murderous, almightily cruel-beyond-human-capacity God, a God he would never serve.

The finality of his decision fueled a feeling of relief–an odd peace in him, as the eternal questions in his once hopeful heart drained away.

Ten, eleven, twelve . . .

He would count them–every one.

Thirteen, fourteen, fifteen . . .

And he'd remember every single one in case he was ever tempted to reopen the door he'd slammed shut today–the door to his heart he'd kept cracked open all of his life, wishing for God, waiting for God, wanting God.

Sixteen, seventeen, eighteen . . .

CHAPTER TWENTY-THREE

NEAR MUNICH, GERMANY: APRIL 29, 1945

"Go! Go! Go!" The shouted order hurtled Bud into action a mere second after he heard the first long bursts of machine-gun fire. The flurry of activity snapped him out of the near state of catatonia he'd self-induced by counting the victims of the ghastly massacre.

"C.T.!" Bud yelled, his machine gun spewing fire as he raced in a zigzag pattern toward the guard towers where gunfire was spitting on the American soldiers. Dozens of G.I.s swarmed ahead and behind him. He spotted C.T. in a group of soldiers whose venom-laced visages told the tale of men at war who had finally seen too much and were determined to end it.

The deadly aim of the Americans momentarily stopped the strafing, but when the gunfire stilled, Bud heard a long low wail begin. From a series of broken-down wooden buildings at the edge of the dirt yard ringed by the guard towers, Bud saw an endless throng of emaciated humanity pour toward the electrified fence that encircled the area. Baggy, faded black-and-white-striped pajamas hung from their bodies. Some wore patchy threadbare jackets. Most of them shuffled forward, with not enough strength to pick up their feet–shuffled toward the sounds of battle that had begun again.

Suddenly, there was another brief respite from the barrage of bullets bombarding Bud and the rest of the U.S. troops as the German soldiers turned their machine guns on the starving rabble. The outrage of the scene galvanized the American soldiers and their unified roar soared through the air as they made their final deadly push for control of Dachau.

§ § § § § § §

The bodies of the German guards lay scattered in the dusty yard. Dozens of other German soldiers came forward, hands held high, moving without the slightest resistance as the outraged American soldiers pushed them roughly ahead, the barrels of their weapons stabbing between the ribs of the vanquished men.

The Germans moved quickly, knowing that the sight of the thousands of living skeletons who kept pushing forward had driven the Americans to the point of near insanity. Their barely controlled rage showed in the way their forefingers twitched against the triggers of their guns as if anxious to lay the deadly pressure against the part of their weapons that would release a hail of bullets on these men whom they considered unworthy of life. All they needed was the slightest provocation. Like caged animals, the Germans sensed the blood lust waiting to be unleashed on them.

Bud didn't want any part of it, but he didn't know where to cast his eyes. To the right, the SS–a glance at them forced such a black anger into his brain that he thought he would suffocate from it. To the left, the beaming skeletons–and yes, they were beaming. Unbelievable, thought Bud, unbelievable! One look at them crippled his guts.

"Captain! Bud! Give me your candy bars and cigarettes. Jesus H. Christ, come on! These poor guys are starvin'!"

Bud followed C.T. to the fence and began passing out the candy and cigarettes he'd miraculously kept after they'd been issued when he and C.T. had left for Dachau. Had it only been this morning?

He stretched his arm with his unopened pack of Lucky Strikes toward a bony limb covered with a thin parchment of skin. The filthy frayed sleeve of the black-and-white-striped shirt hung on the arm that reached weakly toward Bud.

Until now, Bud had passed his rations out quickly to each

of the anonymous red-knuckled grasping hands, making certain that he kept his eyes cast down, pretending he needed to search each pocket of his uniform to find the goods. But when he heard the quiet hoarse whisper ask in elegant, slightly accented English, "A light? You have light?" Bud made the mistake of looking up–and into the face of the wraith–the person attached to the arm that reached so hopefully toward him.

Bud saw the slightly shaky voice belonged to an equally slight man, his wasted limbs enveloped in the oversized striped pajamas. His boney wrists and twig-like fingers, each one interrupted at the joints by a huge swollen knot, looked as though they didn't have the strength to hold the cigarette pack Bud had been about to hand him, before the voice had frozen his actions.

"A light?" Bud repeated dully, his mind unable to absorb the connection of a human voice issuing from the pathetic creature standing before him. He saw the deeply shadowed orbs, sunken back into a broad bony skull as he stared into blue eyes so like his own that he almost gasped in amazement. The eyes were young! And full of a joyful fire that Bud's shock-numbed brain recognized as hope. And the light in those crystal blue eyes! It danced, lighting a spark in Bud's soul and awakening him from his fugue.

"Light? You have light? Yes?" The man-creature croaked again.

Bud ripped open the pack of cigarettes, clumsily tapped one into his hand, and then passed the open pack through the fence. The hot current that had electrocuted at least one of the prisoners during their mad dash for freedom had been cut off, enabling the American liberators to pass out every ration, every candy bar, every cigarette they had.

"A light? Sir?" The latent dignity in the man's sparkling eyes demanded the respectful appellation, "Well, I don't smoke, sir." The man released his slight breath in a whispering sigh of disappointment and a fatalistic shrug of his shoulders.

"But, by God, I am gonna start," Bud exclaimed. "Wait just one minute. I am going to find a light, and we are going to smoke one together. Understand?" Bud smiled at the unutterable hope that blazed in the man's eyes. The smiling eyes pierced Bud's own as the large head nodded understanding on its knobby stalk of a neck. Bud turned away, but not before he saw the prisoner's answering grin issued from swollen lips and toothless gums, as the mouth moved in a rusty, obviously rarely used whisper: "Americans are good! God bless America! God bless Americans!"

CHAPTER TWENTY-FOUR

Near Munich: April 30, 1945

"Let's move. Let's move. Let's move! C'mon, soldiers! We're outta here." Bud shouted the orders into the cool sunlit morning air. A fresh spring breeze carried a faint scent of lilacs that almost masked the remnant smells of charred, bombed-out tree stumps and houses.

"C.T., make sure Tree and Davis got the word about their new assignment. Tell Tree we'll save him that feather bed whenever he gets to Munich."

Bud flashed a smile at C.T. but got no response. It looked as though it was going to take a while for C.T. to get over it all–not that the sights at Dachau had been any easier for Bud to handle. Oddly, C.T. was taking the deaths of the German camp guards there a lot harder than Bud had thought he should. Hell, they deserved a lot worse than what they got–considering what they'd witnessed at the camp yesterday.

C.T. needed to shake it off. Bud was counting on his friend to help him forget the horrors they'd seen at the camp. Even if it took C.T. a while to get squared away, Bud was glad the army hadn't separated them. It was a minor miracle since so many units were begging for the support of the 761st. They were already scattered throughout the countryside escorting various troops and now another call for more of them had come during the night.

So far though, Bud, C.T., and a couple of other tankers were still attached to the units heading into Munich today. It would all change once they arrived in Munich. The Colonel had already told Bud that C.T. would keep moving south, while Bud was destined for some desk duty in the city. If C.T. didn't come around soon, he thought sourly, he'd be glad to get rid of him.

Bud kept shouting orders up and down the line to make sure everyone understood the last minute changes. He hoped the boys wouldn't see much firepower. Personally, he didn't want to test his own self-control with a rifle in his hand if he ran into any more of those filthy Krauts. C.T. had handled it all okay until he saw the pile of uniformed soldiers lying at the base of a concrete wall surrounding the camp.

Word had reached them about the murders of the German guards at the hands of the Americans, but Bud and C.T. were so busy handing out food to the prisoners that they hadn't seen what had happened. When their new friend with Company I had told them about it, C.T. had insisted on dragging Bud to the yard on the other side of the concrete watch towers to see the scene for himself.

The story was that the Americans had rounded up a bunch of German camp guards. They were a pretty nervous, dejected-looking bunch except for one guy who was all spruced up in in a spotless, jet-black SS uniform. According to one soldier who had witnessed it all, the entire episode centered around that one Nazi. The Americans brought him in with several other German prisoners dressed in some kind of camouflage.

This guy was different. The more than a hundred other German prisoners milled anxiously around the concrete wall where they'd been ordered to stand while this guy smiled and acted as though he was out for a day in the park. First, he wanted to speak to the commanding officer. When he arrived, the officer told the American C.O. that he was surrendering the camp to the Americans. No kidding!

The soldier who told Bud and C.T what had happened said that when you looked at this fellow, you saw the Goddamn poster boy for the Nazis. He was a tall, blonde man who, despite his status as a member of a vanquished army, still saw himself as a big wheel. Apparently he had been the head honcho there. Certainly the other German soldiers saw him that way because the moment he showed up, the prisoners who had been skulking

260

around nervously now had a little swagger in their step and little smirks on their faces.

The Americans, who had mostly been keeping a somewhat nonchalant eye on the prisoners, noticed the perceptible change in their charges. They had a machine gun mounted on a tripod aimed at them, but most of the American soldiers were still busy searching the camp looking for any more guards or prisoners. Now the atmosphere changed. The increasing self-assurance on the part of the Germans now that their spit-polished leader was part of their pack grated harshly on the already frayed nerves of the American guards. A couple of them began mumbling curses and threats at the prisoners. They responded in turn with sneers of scorn and derision. The scene was intensified by the background noise of the tortured camp inmates who were alternately screaming and crying from pain or relief–sometimes it was difficult to tell which.

It was too much for one soldier. When a couple of the G.I.s started yelling, "Kill 'em, kill 'em!" he loosed the first deadly spray of machine-gun fire. About a dozen of the German soldiers fell to the ground. But instead of stopping the G.I. doing the shooting, the entire squad joined in the melee, screaming for blood.

"More, more! Kill 'em all!" they yelled. It was all the encouragement the enraged G.I. needed to pull the trigger again. Another–this time longer–sweep of the machine gun. Thirty more fell. The smart-aleck SS officer was in this group, but even his death couldn't stop the slaughter. Another spray. Fifty more down.

The mass murder continued until the unit's major raced to the scene. As the machine gun-wielding soldier loosed his final volley, the major hurtled his body the last few feet and kicked the trigger happy soldier to the ground. It was too late. The last three prisoners crumpled and fell beside their fellow soldiers. Even though all 122 Germans lay dead, the G.I. who'd killed them all lay motionless as well, weeping incoherently and still mumbling softly, "Kill 'em. Kill 'em."

Bud shuddered at the remembrance. Still, unlike C.T., when Bud saw the bodies lying there yesterday, a part of him was glad that some measure of vengeance had been taken against the monsters that were responsible for the bodies he'd counted on the train and the living skeletons he'd fed.

C.T. felt differently. He told Bud that he had prayed there would be no more murders, knowing that before the Americans had discovered Dachau, the American soldiers traveling through Germany had dealt humanely with both the civilians and the thousands of German soldiers who had turned themselves over to the American troops. C.T. was afraid that it would be different now, especially for those Germans who wore the black uniform of the SS. Shoot 'em first. Ask questions later.

"You ready, Cap'n?" C.T.'s voice brought him back to the present.

"Yep. You feelin' better? You been kinda lame since yesterday."

C.T. shook his head solemnly. "I don't know what's happenin', Bud. When we start actin' like dem, we got a problem."

Bud stilled his quick flash of impatience. "C.T., it's gonna take me a lifetime to forget those people starving in that camp. But I promise you, I won't waste a minute's sleep on the German guards. They had it comin'. And you heard what another unit did to some of our guys in Belgium–near some place called Malmedy? Massacred an entire unit. This is just payback. War is hell, Buddy."

Bud saw a quick flash of anger in C.T.'s eyes.

"All due respect, Cap'n, but I don't need you to tell me that. They were unarmed, and American soldiers murdered 'em. And as far as whether they had it a comin', that's just not for you

262

to say. 'Judgment is mine sayeth the Lord.'"

Bud's temper flared at C.T.'s pious pronouncement. Cruelly, he mocked his best friend's words. "You seen any sign of the Lord in any of this, C.T.?" he asked sharply, his blue eyes shooting cold sparks of anger at C.T.

His best friend just stood and stared until the flame of Bud's rage died in his eyes. Then, quietly and very unlike the cocky irreverent man that he knew, C.T. answered: "Not this minute and certainly not in you. But He's here. I just pray you figure it out."

"Shee-ut," Bud blurted his disgust and turned to finish getting the troops moved out. It was gonna be a long goddamn time before C.T. was good company again.

CHAPTER TWENTY-FIVE

MUNICH: APRIL 30, 1945

"Are you ready, Papa?"

"One moment, Schatzie," Georg boomed.

Listlessly, Lilo finished packing the food for their trip. Almost one month. It seemed like such a long time ago since she'd learned Peter was never coming home. It didn't matter that she had not seen him in three years. Her certainty in their future had made the days fly by. Now she swam in time, drowned in tears.

She had not wanted to leave the house today, but her father had insisted. She'd hardly moved from her "bed" on the rose brocade sofa since she'd heard the news. With the end of the war so near and the crippling blow of losing his only son, Hans Mueller had abruptly closed his factories. He had barely been able to keep them open because of a shortage of laborers. Because he was unwilling to use the slave labor that the state would provide him, his loyalties had been called into question. Now without the Mueller contract, business for Burkhardt Trucking was almost nonexistent. Lilo was ashamed at how grateful she was for the lack of work. She could hardly push herself to do it–not even for her father.

On those days when she could rouse herself from the sofa, she would trudge up the circular marble staircase to her bedroom. With the blackout shades drawn, the thick film of dust over everything was invisible. She would sit in the darkness, alone, eyes dry and open, imagining what life would have been like had Peter been coming home. Sometimes, she would light a small kerosene lamp and loosen the lavender ribbon from her packet of letters and pretend that all the passion pouring from those pages would be hers again one day.

It was when she tried to envision the long years ahead without Peter that her imagination failed. All she could conjure was darkness–no end to the war, no end to hunger and food lines, and no end to the bombings that had turned the once vibrant Bavarian city into a shattered smoking ruin.

It was only the two visits she had made to Annette's parents that had pulled her even temporarily from her pain. She'd taken her first trip to see the Tollers because she felt her friend's parents deserved to know the truth of how they had lost the last of their five children. She wanted them to know that even in the confines of the camp Annette had known some happy moments and that she and Annette had tried to take care of one another.

Despite their losses, the elderly couple welcomed Lilo and listened raptly and joyfully to stories about their daughter's last months. Talking to them helped Lilo to awaken for brief periods from her lightless daydreamings of Peter. She wished someone would come home and tell her what it been like for Peter before he had died. Had he thought of her? Dreamed of her? Talked of her? Had he died with her name on his lips?

The smooth silver metal rubbing against her thumb brought her back to the present–Peter's ring. Her mother had told her that she should remove it one day. Liselotte's response assured that Anna would never bring the topic up again.

As Liselotte stroked the smooth circle around her ring finger, she wondered idly whether her mother was right. Blinking back tears, she called to her father again. Today he was going with her to visit the Tollers.

Lilo had volunteered her father to contact Sepp Dietrich to see if he could learn anything about the circumstances surrounding the death of their youngest son, Annette's twin brother. Though they could never bring their son home, these days there were so many rumors of torture in the camps that the Tollers believed that perhaps something other than pneumonia had killed their child. If only they could know the truth, they could find peace.

Georg had been unable to contact Dietrich who was rumored to be fighting with his troops in either Berlin or Austria, but when he saw how the search for answers for the Tollers had revived his child, he vowed to help.

§ § § § § § §

Leaving the city was a relief. The further they drove, the smoother the ride. The countryside had not suffered as many of the incessant bombing raids that had cratered the city streets and highways. It was a relief to see another farmhouse standing every few kilometers rather than miles of bombed and blackened shells or the mountainous piles of rubble teeming with rats that festered in the city.

The truck rocked almost smoothly along the roadway. Through the open window, Lilo heard a familiar sound–the high melodious tune of a songbird. It was music she had not heard in years. Her eyes drank in the colorful palette of flowers along the roadside and the fields checkered in shades of bright green and olive, testifying that some food was growing once again.

Lilo and Georg had the road to themselves since the petrol shortage didn't allow most people to use their vehicles. It was only because of Georg's trucking company that the Burkhardts had been able to modify the trucks to convert wood into fuel. Lilo wasn't sure she would ever get used to how the trucks handled with the extra weight of the conversion tank, but the change had kept them in business.

Lilo's eyes wandered beyond the kaleidoscope pattern of plantings to the mountains beyond–majestic mountains, their snowy caps jutting into a sun-baked cerulean sky. She caught an intermittent waft of the fecund richness of the earth, an odor that had become so alien to her that at first she had no idea how to identify the scent.

Lilo glanced over at her sleeping father. The motion of the truck, the bright springtime sunshine, and the beauty of the Bavarian countryside had lulled him to sleep twenty minutes ago. If she concentrated hard, Lilo could pretend they were on a Sunday outing to visit her grandparents. So they were, in a manner of speaking, as she brought the truck to a creaking halt at the Toller's front door. Her father awoke with a start and smiled the lopsided smile he had worn since his imprisonment.

The Tollers immediately came outside to greet them. "Liselotte, come in! Come in. *Willkommen*, welcome, Herr Burkhardt," Frau Toller beamed as she ushered Lilo and her father into their home.

§ § § § § § §

"So, Herr Toller, you will join us in Munich tomorrow?" queried Georg Burkhardt with a hearty slap on the back of the now smiling Victor Toller.

"Yes, we shall. I cannot thank you enough for your invitation. You have convinced me that it will be far worse to meet the Russians who we know rape and murder than the Americans who—"

"Only steal a little," both men shouted in unison, laughing and holding up their beer steins in a mock salute before drinking the last bit of lager from their mugs.

"I just pray they get here soon, and this terrible war can finally end," added Eva Toller meekly. She abruptly stopped speaking and dropped her chin quickly to her chest to hide her emotions. Victor reached for his wife and drew her close, dropping a kiss on the top of her graying head.

"I know, Eva. Too late for our children, but, maybe soon enough to save others," he whispered to his wife, his eyes meeting Lilo's over the top of her head.

The tender moment caught Lilo off guard, misting her

eyes with tears. No, I will not cry. I am so tired of crying–crying for Annette, for her once vital father's infirmities, and for the still searing loss of Peter. No more tears, she swore vehemently as she reached out to hug Eva good-bye.

§ § § § § § §

"Papa, wake up! Wake up! *Soldaten*! Soldiers!" Georg stirred himself to see what Lilo was shouting about. Soldaten? He shielded his eyes against the bright late afternoon sunlight and tried to see what was causing his daughter's outbursts.

Lilo brought the truck to a rolling stop as it crested the top of a small hill. It cast a shadow on the fields at the base of the knoll, but in the sunlit distance along the horizon, Georg could see it–an interminably long phalanx of soldiers clogging the entire width of the road.

As he stared at the approaching column, Georg saw tiny dots of people in the farmhouses closest to the hill come out into their yards. At least one person in each huddle carried what looked like a white bed sheet tied to a stick.

"The flag of truce," he said quietly to Lilo, "they're foreign soldiers."

"But are they American or Russian?" she asked worriedly.

"They must be American, Lilo," he pointed into the distance. "See how the column curves from the right? They come from the west toward Munich. Oh, thanks be to God. Look at them, Lilo, there must be thousands of them!"

At that moment the soldiers at the head of the column disintegrated into a disorganized melee. From their vantage point Lilo and her father watched as the column quickly formed up again minus several small groups.

"Your binoculars, Papa? Do you have them?"

"Under the seat, Lilo."

She reached down and felt for the small leather case. As she held the glasses to her eyes and focused, the ant-like column jumped into plain view. She could see that the groups of soldiers who'd broken rank were rushing in and out of a cluster of cottages that stood near the crossroads. She handed the glasses to her father.

"What are they doing, Papa?"

"I don't know, Lilo–searching the houses I suppose," he responded as he continued to look through the glasses. "Drive down the hill."

She eased the truck in gear and began slowly rolling down the gentle slope.

The villagers below did not notice them. They all stood talking and cheering and waving their makeshift flags excitedly. Even though the soldiers were going into their homes, these people did not seem afraid. City by city and town by town, the Americans marched through Germany. Yet, unlike any other time in history, when foreign soldiers had marched into another country, the people almost universally welcomed the Americans. In the past, foreign soldiers had taken the spoils due the victor. But with the occupation of each German town, the news of the goodwill of the young G.I.s spread ahead of the advancing army, and the stories were enough to give most of the German people a favorable opinion of G.I. Joe.

Lilo drove the truck through a small crowd gathered in the roadway waiting for the troops who were still several miles away. She waved back as the people waved her through. Despite the rumbling of the truck, Lilo's sharp ears picked up the all too familiar rat-a-tat-tat of machine-gun fire in the distance. Quick short bursts. Silence. Another burst. And silence again. Georg heard the final volley as well. He used his strong arm to reach out and give his daughter's shoulder a comforting pat.

"Don't be so nervous, Lilo. These men are honorable soldiers. When I fought against the Americans before you were born, they were good men–decent. " He gave her knee a quick pat and added, "Still, they are soldiers, and I think it is best if we take the small side roads home. We need to get back to Mama before they reach the city."

"Do you want to take the village road to Uncle Helmut's? We can stop and make certain he is all right. Perhaps he should even come with us?"

Georg nodded in agreement.

"Papa, you don't think they can possibly be in Munich by nightfall, do you?"

"Of course not, but when your mama hears they are nearby, well–" he waved his hands in the air and pretended to scream.

Lilo laughed at his comical caricature of her mother. It was accurate, though. In the past weeks as the Americans had advanced from the north and west and the Russians had trooped in from the east and south, Lilo's mother had grown more and more frantic. She swept through the house moving items, hiding her china, wrapping and storing her silver, only to take it out again within days and move it elsewhere. She mumbled incessantly during her frenetic activities, fearful the Americans would steal her prized possessions. While Lilo and her father eagerly welcomed the fall of the Third Reich, Anna Burckhardt greeted this change as she did any other–with fear, trepidation, and her own personal brand of preparation.

Lilo and Georg drove the rest of the way in silence, bumping along the hard-packed dirt road that narrowed as they entered a thick sheltering forest. The tall evergreens dimmed the bright afternoon sun as they arrived at the tiny village. The dwellings here were a bit grander than the far-flung farmhouses. In these small hamlets the tradesmen lived in their two-story homes. The butcher, the baker, the greengrocer—each had his own store below and his home above his business. Although they were townspeople, most were still close enough to their farming origins so that each home had a small barn or outbuilding behind it.

Driving through the center of the nearly deserted village, Lilo noticed a few faces peeping around the corners from the alleys that separated groups of three or four houses from one another. These alleys allowed the trades people to bring trucks and livestock into the barns behind their homes. Torn white bed sheets and even a pair of white bloomers, fluttered outside the windows of almost every home. Word had reached them: "The Americans are coming!"

"Almost there, Papa," Lilo announced as a startling burst of small-arms fire rang through the surrounding forest. The shots were sharp, loud, and obviously close by. The short bursts of gunfire were nearly shrouded by faint shouts. Lilo's father sat up and ordered her to pull the truck into a dirt alley between two houses. She was puzzled as he got out of the truck and walked around to the driver's side.

"Lilo, take the truck and go home, now. The shots are coming from near Helmut's house, and I don't want you anywhere close by. "

"Papa, I–"

"Do as I tell you, Lilo," he interrupted harshly. "There's no time to argue. Get to Mama and let her know where I am and that I will be home soon."

She nodded tersely at her father, "How will you get home, Papa?"

Georg answered his daughter's question with a burst of laughter. Gesturing to his wilted leg, he quipped: "Obviously I won't walk, but Helmut and I will find a way. Now hurry and get out of here."

"Papa, I'm afraid for you."

"Afraid?" He almost roared at her. "My Lilo, afraid?" He guffawed. "You're going to have a reason to be afraid–of me, if you don't get home now." He winked, patted her cheek quickly, and turned to begin his halting trudge toward Helmut's. As always, Lilo marveled at his strength. Despite his withered arm and leg, his other limbs still evidenced his short tenure as a semi-professional boxer, a period in his life he often discussed with open pride while his wife, equally often, looked on in embarrassment.

Another quick burst of encroaching gunfire punctuated his directive, and Lilo pulled further into the alley to turn the truck around behind the house. The area couldn't be seen from the road, but it was still remarkably well kept. The garden between the house and the barn had obviously been planned, planted, and cared for as though it we would be on constant public display. A row of brilliant red poppies nodded under the lengthening shade of an enormous lilac bush. Lilo caught the scent of its strong perfume. If not for the ever-increasing staccato of the small arms fire, the sight and smell of the flowers would have transported her back home–back before the war.

She pulled the truck into the empty roadway and headed toward the city. She hated leaving her father almost as much as she hated the thought of dealing with her mother when she arrived home without him. Anna would be outraged that he'd put himself in harm's way for his brother. It was exactly what he had always done, and Lilo knew she could count on her mother to do what she had always done. It wouldn't be the first time she had had to sit through a tirade as she tried to explain her father's actions to her mother.

Within ten minutes she was bouncing gently along the road leading back to the city. The countryside was eerily quiet, but she couldn't shake her concern for her father. She shouldn't have left him–no matter what he had said. She rotated the thin silver band around her finger and bit at her lower lip. Only the

273

screech of another set of brakes alerted her to the large, black, dust-covered automobile that sped through the crossroads, its horn honking rudely at her. She slammed on her brakes and the transmission thunked in protest as she deftly wrenched it into first gear.

That idiot had almost broadsided her and he had the nerve to lie on his horn as though it were her fault. Shaking at the near miss and fuming at the driver's carelessness, she watched as the car finally screeched to a stop, and then turned around in the middle of the roadway. Obviously he was heading back toward her to apologize, but as he approached, he blasted her with his horn again and whipped the car around her truck heading in the direction from where she'd come–back toward her uncle's village. The car had slowed perceptibly to take the turn, and she saw the lone driver, his distinctive black and silver braided cap pulled low over his eyes. The whining noise of her engine nearly deafened her as she threw the truck into reverse, turned around, pulled forward, and shot back down the road to follow him. Her father's orders be damned–she wasn't leaving. She silently thanked her near-miss with the maniac in the black car for helping her make her decision.

As she drove into the village, she saw the offending automobile pull into the first alley. She slowed as she passed and saw that the driver had parked the car in a barn behind one of the houses. Years of summer visits to her uncle meant that Lilo knew almost everyone in the village. The butcher who owned this barn was married with three young girls. This man did not belong.

She brought the truck to a stop and hoped that he would not notice her sitting in the seat and watching him. He was slamming the trunk of the car closed. Maybe he was a distant relative. She itched to get back to her father and get him and Helmut to the city. She certainly didn't need any trouble with the SS. As she began to move forward again, she heard a sharp command. The soldier was waving for her to approach him. She was hesitant but the expression on his face made her fearful of ignoring him. She kept the engine running as she stepped out of the truck and walked toward him.

As she approached she saw that his black uniform was wrinkled and his knee-high boots were thick with dried mud almost to his ankles. His hand rested easily on the gun in his black leather holster and a network of fine wrinkles around his eyes nearly obscured their cold stare.

"Why did you follow me?" he barked at her.

"I wasn't following you," she stated flatly. "You almost crashed into my truck," she added sharply.

He ignored her accusation and stepped closer, "You were coming from this direction," he answered suspiciously. "If you weren't following me, then why did you come back this way?"

She took a step backwards away from his menacing face.

"My family is here, and I was thinking about turning around anyway. There are American troops in the area. When you nearly hit me, I decided to come back and bring my family members back to Munich with me–for their safety."

He stared into her eyes, assessing her story, then abruptly turned and walked back to the car and opened the rear passenger door. Uncertain whether she was dismissed, Lilo stood motionless as he pulled out a large red metal can. He twisted the cap off and began sprinkling the contents on the hay around the automobile. The acrid smell of gasoline penetrated her senses.

"What are you doing?" she screamed as she ran toward him. "Are you mad?"

He spun around to face her. "How dare you interfere with official state duties," he sneered at her.

"How is it an official state duty to burn down someone's barn," she yelled as she stood facing him eye to eye.

"You idiot," he snarled. "I have no time to deal with you. The Americans are minutes away. The people who own this barn should be proud to help prevent what's in this car from falling into their hands. Now, get out of my way!"

Lilo felt someone watching and glanced toward the house. Her uncle's friend and his wife stood with their children staring at the scene. The woman had one hand pressed to her mouth while the other gripped her smallest child's shoulder. Lilo reached out and touched the officer's elbow as he turned away from her again.

"Please, sir, I don't know what you have in there, but I beg you, please don't burn down this barn," she entreated.

"I should shoot you right here," he spat. As if in response to his statement, both heard the quick volley of gunfire. It sounded much closer than before. The soldier glanced nervously toward the sound.

"All right, Fräulein." He stepped so close to her that she had to stop herself from lurching backwards to escape his tobacco-poisoned breath. "They will keep the barn," he nodded toward the house before taking her by the shoulders. The loose skin around his aging jowls shook slightly as his fingers pressed into her flesh. "But make no mistake, if the papers in this automobile fall into the hands of the Americans, I will be back to make certain you pay for it. Do you understand me, Fräulein?" He slapped his hand against the gun holster, and Lilo nodded her assent to him as he pressed the car key into the palm of her hand. "The trunk is locked," he said before nodding curtly at her. Then he began pulling off the jacket of his uniform.

Lilo was surprised to see that underneath–instead of his military issued black shirt–he wore a plain white cotton farmer's blouse. From the back pocket of his muddied uniform trousers. he pulled out a worn brown woolen cap with a small front brim. Lilo would have been shocked when he released the belt to his trousers, but she had realized by then that he would have the rest of his disguise beneath it. To complete his quick conversion from SS officer to farmer, he untucked the brown woolen pants from his mud-spattered jackboots and smoothed the rough wool over the boots. Finally, he reached into the front seat of the car and pulled out a pipe and a pair of gold spectacles. He seated the thin wire-framed glasses on the bridge of his nose, stuck the carved bone pipe into one corner of his mouth, and tucked his heavy silver pistol into the waistband of his slacks..

The transformation astonished her, and as she turned back toward her truck, she was even more stunned when he offered her a benign smile and a wave that had her nearly questioning her earlier encounter with him. Lilo pulled the truck forward and drove to Uncle Helmut's. As she parked and climbed down from the seat, a middle-aged farmer rode by on a rusting bicycle. He doffed his brown cap, and she thought she saw a slight wink behind his glasses before she reached Helmut's front porch.

Lilo pounded on the heavy oak door of the stucco and timbered two-story cottage. As she waited, she heard the sharp crack of rifle shots. They were close by—in the village. She cocked her head and renewed her assault on the door as she tried to determine exactly where the gunfire was coming from. The door finally opened, and Lilo's Uncle Helmut stood before her.

"Stop that noise and come in," he ordered brusquely. "What are you doing here," he asked as he closed the door behind her. Helmut was several years younger than her father, and like all the Burkhardts, he was blessed with the same smooth tanned skin and bright green eyes so familiar to Lilo. Even in his casual country slacks with the loden jacket, rather than the business suits he favored when he visited them in Munich, he still exuded authority. Despite the peremptory tone in his voice, Lilo knew he wasn't angry with her, and she hugged him quickly before asking about her father.

"Where's Papa?"

"What do you mean? He is not with you?"

"No," her voice rose anxiously. "I let him out about thirty minutes ago in the alley by the butcher's shop. We were on our way home when we heard the gunfire, and he made me let him out to come and check on you while I drove back to Mama."

Helmut shook his head. "Big brother, always checking on little brother. So if you are to be on your way to Munich, why are you here," he asked sternly.

"I couldn't just leave him, Uncle Helmut. We have to go and find him," she pulled at her uncle's sleeve and motioned toward the door.

Helmut shook his head again. "No, Lilo. We stay here. Your father will arrive. The gunfire is too close now. We shouldn't wander about."

"Uncle Helmut, we can't just sit here. He should have been here by now. Something's wrong."

Her uncle sighed heavily. He knew his niece. If he didn't go with her, she would go without him. She was a foolish girl when it came to her father. He nodded at her, and they left through the back door.

Nearby, Georg was equally intent on finding his brother. The main street was empty and oddly silent so he'd decided to pick his way furtively behind the houses, cutting through back yards and gardens across the dirt-packed alleyway toward Helmut's. His leg was hurting so he had to stop and rest it more frequently than he liked. Just a few moments ago the roar of a large truck racing through the town had broken the silence. It had sounded oddly like his truck, but thankfully Lilo was far away from the village by now. The noise motivated him to try and pick up his pace, but his bad leg was weakening painfully beneath him. He heard a few cracks of rifle fire and tried again to hurry, half-hopping and half-dragging his nearly useless limb. "*Verdammt*! Damn!" He hated his weakness.

Another short burst of bullets stopped him again, so close

this time that he could hear voices drifting from the main road. Cautiously, he peered around the corner house and was shocked at the sight that greeted him. Three lifeless bodies lay not more than fifteen yards away from him at the feet of two foreign soldiers. Schwarze! Das waren schwarze Soldaten. Negroes! They were Negro soldiers. They had to be Americans.

Georg could see that two of the bodies wore the familiar black uniforms and highly polished jackboots of the SS. The third wore plain clothing, the back of his white shirt turning a dark red. A pair of gold wire-rimmed glasses and a silver pistol lay in the dirt beside him winking in the late afternoon sunlight. One of the soldiers stooped to pick up the cap of one of the dead men. As he twirled it on his forefinger, Georg could see sparkles of sunshine reflecting from the revolting skeletal death's head insignia above the silver braided band that adorned the cap. It was odd to find SS men in the village, but he'd heard that many German soldiers were deserting as the Americans pushed through the country. Still, the SS were fanatical Hitler loyalists, and Georg couldn't imagine them as deserters.

"SS bastards," one of the American soldiers snarled. "Dese people got 'dem Goddamn white flags flyin' out de windows and dey prob'ly sent dese summava bitches to nail us."

"You can't trust dese damn Krauts," agreed the other soldier.

The American language grated harshly on Georg's ears. His fluency in English had given him the idea that he would have no problem communicating with the occupying forces, but these soldiers spoke in an unfamiliar dialect. Although he had to strain to understand the words, the tone was unmistakable. These Americans were very angry. At the mention of the flags, Georg glanced up to see the white pillowcases and bed linens fluttering in the breeze. The airy bits of cotton were dipping and waving a tentative welcome in the warmth of the late afternoon sunshine.

Another whirring hail of fire exploded from the second-story window of the house that hid Georg. The taller of the two Americans yelped in pain and grabbed his forearm as he ran under the shelter of the recessed doorway of the house. In the same swift movement, the other soldier jerked his machine gun toward the window and answered the volley with a shattering burst of bullets.

In a moment a lone SS officer emerged from the building, arms behind his head. He wasn't a tall man, and his uniform looked disheveled, but he stood straight as he said, "I am–" The sudden spurt of gunfire startled Georg as the soldier with the bleeding arm loosed two quick shots from his rifle.

As the man slammed face first into the black dirt, George had no trouble understanding the soldier's words as he pronounced without emotion, "Dead. That's what you are. You a dead motha fucka."

His companion took a piece of cloth and began wrapping it clumsily around his partner's bloody forearm as they moved back under the sheltering eaves of the house. Georg dared not move.

A deep low rumble sounded in the background–tanks, or at least one. With his stomach churning in fear, Georg turned away from the scene to continue through the alleys to Helmut's. A bit of loose gravel at the base of the house where he'd been hiding shifted. The sharp cry of pain was out of his mouth before he could stop it as his leg crumpled painfully beneath him, and the sharp white gravel lacerated the palms of his hands.

"Did you heah dat?" asked one of the soldiers.

Georg couldn't hear the other man's whispered reply before the first soldier responded angrily, "I'm tellin' ya' I heard somethin' behind that buildin' oba dere. Covah me."

The wounded soldier crept cautiously toward the back of the building where Georg was trying desperately to get to his feet. The tank's engine was so loud now he couldn't make out the soldier's voices anymore but he knew they were heading toward him. Georg hopped away as fast as he was able and was trying to make the turn around the next house when the soldiers rounded the corner and spotted him. As he gratefully turned the corner, he saw a young woman and–it was his brother and Liselotte. What was she–

The crack of the rifle shot had barely receded as an agonizing heat in Georg's leg exploded. The already crippled limb couldn't take this final assault, and Georg pitched forward, his leg on fire. The pain was short lived as another bullet cut through his mid-section driving him to the dirt. His face rested in the dark gritty earth just a few yards away from his brother's house. A warmth enveloped him just as a crushing weight descended on his chest for a single second before it was replaced by an indescribable feeling of euphoria.

Georg smiled and thought with joy of his beautiful wife Anna. He could see her lovely oval face before him. He remembered the first time he had seen that face and how he'd fallen in love with its perfect beauty. Now he saw his lovely Anna cradling a small baby in her arms. Georg saw himself peek down at the tiny sleeping form. Tears gathered in his eyes as Anna's face melted away to become a stronger, yet equally lovely visage–his beloved Liselotte, his Lilo. She stood before him like a Valkyrie warrior, her hair blowing around her flushed cheeks. Her beautiful eyes were nearly squeezed shut as she smiled and waved to him.

Good-bye, Papa. Good-bye, Lilo. She wasn't smiling– she was crying. Her eyes were staring into his, tears falling warmly from them onto his face. "Don't cry," he tried to say. Then the image shattered in a cloud of darkness. Harsh voices slammed him back to near consciousness and into indescribable pain. As Georg felt a thick wet substance spilling from his mouth dampening the ground beneath his cheek, he prayed: *"Lieber Gott, ich danke Dir für deine Güte.* Dear God, I thank you for your goodness. *Und für meine Lilo.* And for my Lilo. *Bitte schütze meine kleine familie.* Please protect my little family."

The taller of the two Americans stared at Helmut who didn't dare move. He watched achingly as his brother lay bleeding in the shelter of his niece's arms, both of them oblivious to the armed soldiers looming above them now and glancing anxiously, nervously at one another. Helmut's eyes locked hatefully into the brown eyes of one of the American soldiers. Murderer! The thought resonated so loudly in his brain that he wouldn't have been surprised if they had heard him. When the soldier with a bloodied rag hanging from his forearm lifted his rifle pointedly at Helmut, he wondered if perhaps in his shock he had spoken aloud.

The other soldier placed his hand on the barrel of the man's rifle and pushed it down forcefully. "Shit, man! What you doin', Bartow? You fuckin' crazy? He's a civilian an' he ain't armed. Git yo goddamn gun offa him." Bartow grudgingly moved his rifle to his side as he looked up for any faces or weapons in the windows of the neighboring houses.

"Yeah, that last fuckin' farmer wadn' s'posed to be armed either," he grunted.

Gazing down at Georg, the younger soldier exclaimed, "Well, he ain't armed. Shit, Bartow," the younger soldier was in a full panic now. "We killed a fuckin' civilian. Goddamn, he's an old man." His voice rose with the pronouncement of each syllable as he dropped to his knees beside Georg and Lilo.

"Miss, please, lemme' check 'im." Lilo merely looked up and stared uncomprehendingly into the soldier's eyes. He tore his gaze from her accusing one and saw a slight flutter of the old man's eyelids. Jumping to his feet, he waved his hands at Helmut. "Hey, mistah, spreken zee de English? Huh? Speaka de English?"

Stunned into stillness, Helmut found it difficult to move his head in response. He croaked, "Yes, I speak English."

"You got a doctor in this place?"

Helmut shook his head sadly.

"Look mistah, man, I mean"–the soldier's eyes were wild with fear.

Helmut saw the black letters stitched on an inch-wide white ribbon above the breast pocket of his drab olive uniform, S-T-E-V-E-N-S.

"We thought, you know,"–he held up his hands as though leveling a makeshift rifle–"SS. We thought he was SS. The SS shot Bartow here." His madly gesticulating hands flapped in the direction of his partner's blood-soaked bandage as he continued his halting diatribe. "You know this man? That girl?"

"My brother, his daughter," Helmut responded tonelessly.

The taller soldier, Bartow, broke the agonizing second of silence.

"Shut up, Stevens," he yelled at his partner with a vengeance. "Just shut the hell up." He turned his frustrated rage toward Helmut.

"We didn't know he was a civilian. He coulda been another one of dem SS bastards."

His voice broke with rage–and fear. His next sentence was laced with a whisper of remorse as he stared in the dirt at the blonde woman sitting at her father's feet pressing the palms of her hands on his stomach wounds trying to stanch the flow of blood soaking her fingers. The background rumble of the tank stopped suddenly with a phlegmy cough and a sputter of the engine.

"The tank's right over dere. Bartow, go git de Cap'n. He'll know what to do."

Eager to be away from the scene, Bartow raced around the building, calling for Captain Leverett.

Bud and C.T. had pulled their jeep up beside the tank and were getting out to inspect the four bodies lying next to the road. "What happened here, Bartow?" Bud asked as his eyes swept over the bodies and landed on Bartow's wounded arm.

"They ambushed us, Cap'n, but I got to tell you 'bout dat later. We need you to come quick. We got a civilian down–an ol' man and dey don't got no doc here. You gotta hurry, Cap'n."

Calling for C.T. to go find the medic, Bud raced after Bartow. It took less than a minute for Bud to reach the gruesome scene. An old man wearing the traditional Bavarian loden-green jacket and derby was standing beside a young woman who had her fingers pushed into the bloody mess of another old man's stomach. The earth around the man was stained darkly with blood. Through a curtain of pale hair, Bud could see the water dripping from the woman's face onto her bloodless knuckles as she pressed into the old man's middle in a desperate effort to slow the bleeding of the wound.

"Shit," C.T.'s expletive gave voice to Bud's unspoken disgust. The medic who had arrived with C.T. knelt down and gently tried to pry the young woman's hands away from his patient. The touch on her hands seemed to startle her. When she looked up to see who was interrupting her deathly vigil, Bud's gaze met a pair of breathtaking violet eyes, eyes that contained such a look of shattered grief that if his own soul could have borne her pain at that moment, he would have done so–for her.

"Ma'am, I need you to move aside, please." The medic pointed to the Red Cross on his helmet. He pressed his fingers into the ragged hole in Georg's gut as Lilo slid hers away. She wiped her bloody hands on the wide skirt of her faded red and green *dirndl*. Her father's eyes squeezed shut and his mouth flinched with pain. She stroked his hair with her still blood-smeared fingertips and cooed soothingly to him as her tears dampened the black earth beneath them.

The tank's engine idled in the background. Its rumble

stilled the songbirds and made the unearthly silence of the village more palpable through its low drone. The shadows from the two houses on either side of the dirt alley where Georg lay were lengthening. Occasionally, the light flutter of a lace curtain in a window betrayed the inquisitive eyes peering onto the scene. No one dared leave their homes though the guns were now silent. Bud, C.T., and the other two American soldiers stood by, watching, not a word from them breaking the heavy stillness.

"Need some help here, Captain," the medic shouted the words over his shoulder pulling Bud from his stupor. Bud squatted beside the medic, his shoulders touching Lilo's. She jerked away from him as if burnt.

"Quick. Open my bag and get me a few packets of sulfanilamide." Bud tossed two packets to the medic. "Need you to open them, Captain, and then get some dressings and that brown canister of adhesive plaster. Next, get the tourniquet out and wind it around his leg, just above the wound, while I finish here."

Bud ripped open both packets, and the medic quickly removed one hand from the wound to sprinkle the crystalline white powder on the injury in Georg's side. He worked with efficiency while Bud wound the tourniquet around Georg's thigh.

The medic called to C.T., "You got two big boxes of Carlisle dressings in my bag. Hand them to me–and then get some of that adhesive plaster off the roll. I'll hold the dressing while you lay the first piece across it." C.T. grimaced at the assignment.

"You can handle it, soldier," the medic asserted. C.T. lightly patted the strip of sticky tape over the gauzy white dressing. The medic finished the job and turned his attention to the wound in Georg's leg. "Nice job on the tourniquet, Captain." The medic went through the same procedure on the leg wound. Georg winced again and began writhing in pain.

"Papa," Lilo cried gently.

"Ma'am, I'm going to give him some morphine now. He'll be much more comfortable in a moment."

"*Onkel Helmut, bitte frage, Papa stirbt ja nicht?*" Uncle Helmut, please ask, "Papa isn't going to die, is he?" In heavily accented English, the tall thin man in the green wool jacket with strange deer antler carvings sewn onto each lapel asked the medic, "She wants to know if her papa, my *Bruder*, is going to die." As the man waited for a response, his hands nervously twisted a dark green felt fedora-type hat decorated with a knot of small feathers and colorful pins on its crown.

"We'll do everything we can to make sure that doesn't happen, but he's lost a lot of blood."

Lilo looked at the medic quizzically.

"Blood–bloot," the medic tried the German pronunciation and gestured at the red pool in the dirt. "He needs bloot."

Lilo nodded her understanding and turned her palms up, the universal gesture for "how."

He had no answer for her.

"*Entschuldigung, Fräulein.* Excuse me, Miss."

He turned to talk with Bud again.

"Captain, I know you've got your orders to move ahead, but if this guy's going to make it, we need to get him back to the clearing station fast and get some blood in him. It's too far back to the rear to get an ambulance up here in time. You've got the rank here. It's your call."

The medic turned back toward Georg and pulled a booklet from his brown canvas pouch. He began filling out one of the Emergency Medical Tags describing Georg's wounds and his treatment of them. Before he attached the tag to Georg's chest, he asked the English-speaking man his brother's name and wrote it on the EMT.

While the medic attached the card, Bud waved at the tank driver to shut down the beast. He and C.T. instructed the tank's riflemen to maintain their positions and remain alert. Bud motioned for a few of the riflemen to follow him and circle him and C.T. while they fashioned a makeshift litter using the medic's litter strap to tie their field jackets to their rifles. Usually there were litter bearers attached to an outfit, but since they were getting so little resistance, the medic had walked ahead with Bud's advance team. The litter bearers were a few miles back with the main force.

"Here's what we're gonna do," Bud raised his voice to make certain everyone could hear him.

"C.T., you go with the medic and get this guy back to the clearing station while I keep moving with the rest of the unit."

The medic shook his head. "Tourniquet's off the leg now, and the dressings are tight, but I can't tell what kind of internal injuries he's got."

He eyed Bud's jeep and then the tank.

"That's not going to work. It's at least three miles back— no way he can stand the ride in that little jeep–and we damn sure can't get him in the tank."

Helmut had kept Lilo away from her father while the soldiers worked on Georg. Now he pulled her close to him and whispered something to her. She nodded, and he called to the medic, "Herr Doctor, we have a solution."

"I'm no doctor, but we're going to try and get him to one."

"I understand you have a transport problem."

The medic had to listen closely to understand the old man as he laid out his plan.

"My niece, Lilo, has a truck. It is parked at my home," he pointed down the street to a whitewashed two-story house, the window boxes on the second story merrily draping red blooms and greenery toward the somber scene below.

"Big truck," Lilo added, nodding vigorously at the medic.

"Captain, she's got a truck here. If you trust them, Lieutenant Deeks and I can ride with the patient in back and one of the riflemen can sit up front to give her directions."

Bud looked at the lovely woman, expecting her to implore him to help her. Instead, she stared at him, daring him to refuse her offer. The look in those violet-blue eyes as she glanced toward Stevens and Bartow reminded Bud with a start that she was German. She might be a civilian, but she was the enemy. She had a damn good reason to be angry at them, but if she was a Nazi, she probably hated their guts anyway. They had to help the old man–he was obviously an unarmed civilian, but Bud wasn't too sure he could trust her with the medic or any of his men.

Turning to the girl's uncle he said, "Tell her to bring the truck around, and we'll get her father to a doctor. But she stays here with you."

She apparently understood enough to say, "*Nein*! No!"

Bud ignored her and directed his words again to her uncle. "Tell her I'll send someone back with the truck and to let her know how the old man's doing," he added impatiently.

She surprised him when she uttered her first full sentence in English. "I don't care for de truck, but you cannot make me leaf my fadder. I bring de truck. I drive," she said with finality.

Bud saw a slight smile on the uncle's face. "She always

like this?"

The elderly gentleman offered Bud a tight smile through the lines of fear that etched his face, "Since she was in braids."

Bud made up his mind in an instant.

"Fine. I'll just go with her myself." Bud knew for certain that she understood every word he had said when she turned her back to them and raced toward her uncle's house. He called a young second lieutenant to his side. "You're the C.O. now. Keep the guys going toward Munich. We'll catch up. C.T., you come with us."

Bud saw an old gray truck lumbering toward them and motioned for two of the riflemen to pick up the makeshift litter and load the patient into the back of the truck when it stopped. When the old man was secure, C.T. climbed in with the medic, while Bud explained to Helmut that he would make certain someone brought him word of his brother's condition.

"Ich spreken nicht goot Deutsch," "I don't speak good German," Bud told Lilo as he climbed into the passenger seat of the truck and motioned for her to turn it around. Bud tried to keep his eyes from lingering on her face, but he couldn't help glancing at her profile as she expertly steered the truck around the few holes and debris in the road.

Her tears had dried, and now her mouth was set in a thin line of fear and determination. She seemed utterly focused on the task at hand. The only sign of her unease was the constant movement of her thumb massaging a worn silver band on her left hand–a wedding band?

Bud made a stab at conversation: "My name's Bud. Your name?"

She glanced at him and repeated, "Butt?"

He guffawed, "Nein, no, not 'Butt'–'Bud.'" He

enunciated the "d" slowly.

A fleeting smile accompanied her response. "Bud," she mimicked. "Mein Name ist Liselotte." "My name is Liselotte."

"You married?" he asked. At her quizzical look, Bud searched for the word in German. It wouldn't come to him, so he pointed to her ring.

Bud's breath caught in his chest at the look of utter grief revealed on her face as she shook her head sadly, "Nein," no, she whispered, her voice catching with anguish. "Gestorben." "Dead."

Dead–not surprising. "Soldier?" he asked.

She nodded sadly.

Bud was satisfied that he'd made the right call going with her. Oh, yeah, Nazi husband, Nazi wife. The sudden high-pitched whine of the truck's engine as it strained up a steep hill interrupted his thoughts. In clumsy half-German, half-English words, he told her to keep her truck in low gear since the clearing station was just on the other side of the rise.

She seemed to understand. As they reached the top of the hill, she gave a small gasp at the site before her. Hundreds of tents dotted the vast field below them. Grouped in a tight circle stood several larger dark green tents, each with an enormous white square emblazoned with a red cross.

She headed toward them as Bud waved at the groups of soldiers eyeing the gray truck suspiciously. As soon as the truck stopped, she cut the engine off, jumped from the driver's seat, and ran to the back to check on her father.

Several soldiers, seeing C.T. and the medic struggle with Georg's litter, were already on hand to help unload him and rush him into one of the tents. Bud could feel the soldiers all gawking at the beautiful and obviously German girl in their midst.

Lilo paid no attention to anyone, instead murmuring to her father as she walked beside the litter holding his hand. They passed through the one rolled-up flap on the tent that provided entry. An armed soldier stepped directly in Lilo's path, forbidding her to go inside. "Sorry, ma'am, only patients and medical personnel in here."

Liselotte slapped ineffectually at the stock of the rifle he had pushed toward her to physically bar her entry. Bud stepped forward ready to calm and comfort her, but he was met with an icy stare. "I vill go in mit meinem Papa," she stated coldly.

Her haughtiness rubbed Bud the wrong way. He chastised himself with the reminder that whatever the circumstances, she was the enemy and beyond getting her father some good medical help she obviously had no use for him.

"You seem to speak pretty fair English, so you need to understand this."

She stared at him as he enunciated the words while shaking his head and finger at her.

"You will not go into the medical tent. If you want your father to live, then you will let the doctors do their work."

It was bad news that they'd shot her father, but he'd seen enough of these goddamn arrogant Nazis and he damn sure wasn't gonna put up with any shit from any of 'em—no matter how pretty they might be.

She wrinkled her brow, and despite her heavy accent, the scorn in her voice was apparent.

"You shot my Papa and you expect me to believe you will help him?"

"What do you think we brought him here for, huh?" he

lashed back at her.

She could speak English well enough to attack him, but not well enough to offer more than a few words of conversation on the drive–not a thank you, not a nothing.

He had orders to move, and instead he had turned the unit over to some wet-behind-the-ears junior lieutenant just to make sure her old man got the care he needed, even if it was a long shot that the guy would make it. His men had fired the shot and he was responsible and he'd be damned if anyone would be able to say that he didn't try to make it right. Her lovely face had nothing to do with it or the depth of pain in those beautiful violet eyes when he had first seen them.

His next words were edged in steel as he tried to contain his rising temper, "Ma'am, that was an accident, and I am sorry for it, but you Nazis have killed plenty of my boys here," he waved toward the sea of tents. "Now your father here–"

"Nazis! How dare you! We are no Nazis." She spat the words at him, her face alive with rage.

He didn't have time for this. "Yeah, yeah," he said dismissively. "To hear you people tell it, there's not a Goddamn Nazi among you." He turned away from her and threw his next words over his shoulder, "Just stay out of the tent." Fuming, he strode away, rubbing his forehead and fighting the conflicting roar of emotions racing through his brain. His heart ached for her pain, but her thanklessness and her superior attitude were more than he was going to stand. He was done here.

§ § § § § § §

Lilo watched the handsome American officer stride away. Her anger fueled her desire to run after him and demand that he retract his words. Bah! *Macht nichts*! It doesn't matter. She had no time to waste explaining herself and she was almost grateful that the heat of her rage had allowed her to put away some of the fear for her father.

She turned and offered a sweet smile to the sentry. She could hear the murmur of excited voices coming from the tent. She tried to peer around him to look inside. His scowl softened, and she thought he deliberately edged slightly to the right to afford her a better view—even as he shook his head when she put one foot forward to try and step through the open tent flap.

She couldn't see much. The inside of the tent was so dim. Suddenly a large, very dark man materialized within the tent heading toward her.

C.T. stepped out in the fading sunlight and stood before her, blocking the small view she had inside. She tried to look around him but he stood still. Removing his helmet and swiping his hand across the top of his cropped head, he looked down at her. Lilo could see the compassion in his velvety brown eyes.

"My Papa?"

"Ma'am, the doctor is working on him. Someone will be out in a minute to tell you more." He replaced his helmet and nodded his good-bye to her as she began to pace back and forth in front of the tent, ignoring the sly glances and sometimes outright glares of the dozens of people rushing back and forth across the camp.

As nightfall approached, the activities of the soldiers became more hurried. She couldn't understand the shouts and yells as they waved and gestured to one another. So many men—and some of them looked so odd to her. In different uniforms she would have mistaken many of them for Germans. She saw hair in shades of blonde, brown, and even the occasional red peeking out from under the caps of those soldiers who weren't wearing helmets.

At the edge of the camp was the strangest sight. Groups of soldiers gathered around a long line of tanks whose idling engines provided a low thrum of noise. There were dozens of men, and each one was some shade of brown. Some had skin the color of old parchment while others were nearly ebony. She caught flashes of brilliant white teeth as the men worked. Some of them were inside the tanks with half their bodies hanging out of the open turrets as they listened to the instructions of the men on the ground. They were apparently moving the tanks into some sort of position. She watched as one by one the tanks rumbled into a formation that looked as though it would eventually encircle the entire area–a solid ring of machines and colored men surrounding the inner circle of olive tents and white soldiers.

The medic who was taking care of her father finally came out of the tent. "Come in," he said gravely. Lilo held her breath as she followed him inside the dim gloom. A bright circle of light illuminated the table where her father's prone body lay motionless. Relief washed over her as she saw the slight rise and fall of his chest. A rail-thin man with beads of sweat dotting his thinning gray hairline stood beside the table. He wiped his gloved hands on the blood-spattered butcher's apron that covered the front of his wrinkled olive drab uniform.

Wearily he spoke, "English?"

She nodded mutely.

"The wounds are closed and he is resting." Over her head he said to the medic standing behind her, "Brown, you did a great job. He shouldn't have made it this far."

His gaze returned to Lilo. "He has to go to a field hospital now. The closest one was set up a few days ago in Ingolstadt about fifty miles away. You know it?"

She nodded again.

He gestured into the darkness. "We have a few more guys who need to go, but we can't travel at night. They'll have to go in the morning–if they all make it through the night," he said matter of factly.

"Danke, Herr Doctor. May I stay with him?"

"No," he said evenly as he removed the bloodied apron and tossed it into the gloom. "He is critical. We've given him all the plasma we have. His situation is touch and go. You can't be in the way."

She nodded, "I will sleep in my truck outside. May I sit with him for awhile?"

"For a moment. Then he and these other men need their rest."

Lilo thought the doctor could use a rest as well. He seemed weary to the bone as he disappeared further back into the dimly lit tent.

§ § § § § § §

Bud nearly ran the doctor down as he turned the corner. He grabbed the man by his thin shoulders. "Whoa, Doc. Sorry about that. I was just coming to see you."

"Uh-huh, what about?"

"That German guy in there–is he gonna make it?"

The doctor looked up at Bud.

"I don't know. He has lost a lot of blood, and I don't have any more plasma. The Second Platoon of the Forty-Second Hospital unit's located about fifty miles back. We'll get him there in the morning. He's got a shot. Seems like a tough old bird, but he's got some stroke damage. We just don't know."

He thrust his thumb over his shoulder, "She's in there with him if you want to check up on him."

"Thanks, Doc. I appreciate it."

"Yeah, I bet you do," the doctor stated sardonically.

Bud's face flushed with heat. "It's not what you think, Doc. One of my guys shot the old man."

The doctor nodded his understanding, "Got it. Sorry 'bout that. Best not to fraternize with the enemy. Not just because it's against the law either. You saw what they did at Dachau, didn't you?"

At Bud's nod he continued, "Yeah, I did too." He balled his fists by his side and looked back toward the tent. "I'm a doctor and I took an oath, but you beware the pretty face, Captain. These people are animals–worse than animals."

"No worries on that score, Major. But like one of my buddies here says, we gotta be careful that we don't behave that way towards them or we're no better."

The doctor grunted his assent as Bud saluted him and turned to enter the hospital tent.

Lilo was leaning toward her father. The tight fist that clenched in Bud's chest prevented him from taking another step forward. She sat so still that under the illumination of the single bulb she shone like a marble statue. The only movement was the silent trail of tears running down her pale cheeks. He tried to steel himself. He didn't need those tears washing away the anger he felt at her lack of gratitude.

He approached her warily.

She must have heard him. The mask of superiority slipped over her features so quickly when she looked at him that Bud thought the naked pain and vulnerability he had just witnessed must have been a mirage of his own making.

He asked brusquely, "How is he?"

Lilo couldn't understand why a hot flare of anger raced through her at his benign question. "He's just an old Nazi. What do you care?" she tossed at him before turning back to her father.

Bud threw his hands up, palms toward her, and backed out of the tent–to hell with her. He stuffed his hands into his pockets and strode angrily away from the tent. A high-pitched scream interrupted his escape.

"Papa! Help me, someone!"

Bud raced back and reached the tent just in time to see a medical technician shove the girl rudely away from her father. Two other med techs leaned over him, their hands flying over the man's inert body. Another one blew past Bud yelling for the doctor.

Bud saw the doctor shed his lassitude like an old coat as he raced to the tent, the tech running beside him, talking animatedly.

"Turn on the operating light–now," the doctor commanded as he tried to catch his breath.

Bud stepped further into the tent and heard a thin mewing cry issuing from the dim interior.

"Liselotte," he whispered softly, sneaking toward her. He saw her huddled in the corner where the tech had pushed her. She held her hands up to her mouth trying to stifle her sobs.

"Don't we have anymore Goddamn plasma anywhere," the doctor yelled to no one in particular. Knowing the answer, the doctor snapped his next question, "What's his blood type?"

"He's O negative, sir," the red-haired med tech snapped back.

"Well, that's just great," the doctor said glumly, "not a donor among us."

Bud broke in. "What do you mean? He's O. I thought just about everybody was O. Hell, I'm O."

The doctor gunned out his reply. "Yeah, so am I, and

297

these two," he pointed at both medical technicians, "but we're O positive. O negative is a different story. We got a seven in a hundred chance of finding someone with that type. And we don't have time to type her," he nodded toward Lilo. "We should have thought to do it earlier, but I figured he'd get through the night," the doctor recriminated himself quietly.

Bud rolled up his sleeve.

"I'm O negative. Go ahead." He thrust his bare arm at one of the nurses.

"Sorry, soldier, no can do. You're in combat, and I can't take blood from you."

"Why the hell not?" Bud yelled angrily.

"Because, soldier, he's a German civilian, and you are U.S. government issue. We are in a war zone and we need all hands on deck. I can't compromise you in any way–not here, not now, and not for him."

The doctor turned to Lilo who was silently witnessing the conversation, "Fräulein, I am sorry, but–"

Bud saw that her tears had dried as she interrupted the doctor.

Coldly and without an ounce of emotion, she attacked.

"You are a doctor. He is dying."

Her glacial voice broke and as she pointed to Bud and then back to the doctor and the medical technicians, "and you are killing him." Her finger pointed back to Bud as she continued berating the doctor, "His men shot my father. He should help, and you won't let him?"

Her English was broken and labored, but they all understood.

Bud reached out to pull her away from the medical team.

"Nein," "no," she shouted as she shook him off, now pointing again at the doctor, "You are killers–all killers!"

Two soldiers heard the commotion and rushed into the tent. They grabbed Lilo's arms and began physically pulling her out of the tent.

"Leave her alone," Bud ordered the two privates.

"Yes, sir," they answered in unison as they dropped their hands from Lilo's arms.

Bud motioned for her to stay silent.

"Doc, I'm going to say this once. You outrank me so I can't order you. But I am begging you. Help me make this right. My guys did this. Please. Don't we all have enough miserable memories that we're gonna have to carry around for the rest of our lives? Please, Doc, don't make me carry this guilt, too."

Imploringly, he held out his arm again.

One of the med techs picked up a large needle and attached an empty vial to it. "I'm ready, Doc."

A deep rattling breath from Georg broke the silence.

The doctor nodded, and the tech pushed Bud down into a chair and tied off his arm. He felt a small soft hand touch his shoulder lightly from behind.

"Get her out of here," roared the doctor to the two privates.

They bolted toward her, but at his command Lilo had already begun walking out of the tent.

§ § § § § § §

The contrasting smells of motor oil and antiseptic

filled Bud's nostrils as he watched the medical team load the ambulances for the trip ahead. There was no sign of Lilo or her father. The miles of tents that covered the dirt and grass plain gave off a rosy glow as the rising sun threw its first rays over the charred and barren landscape. The chow line already looked like it was a mile long, but that's the way it was when the soldiers had a chance to eat a hot breakfast. It might be SOS, but it beat the C-Rats.

A cloud of gaseous fumes added its offending odor to the air as the drivers cranked up their ambulance engines. Bud was glad he'd made it over to check on the old man before they left for the long ride to the field hospital for the 42nd. He hadn't slept well last night. His dreams were filled with images of Lilo. He had awakened out of sorts, both eager and dreading to see her face again.

Lilo emerged from the medical tent. He held his breath as she ran her hands through her sleep-tumbled hair–spotted him, and smiled.

Lilo was shocked by the joy that ran through her when she saw Bud standing by one of the ambulances. She could read no emotion in the pale blue eyes that stared into hers and though she wanted to run to him, to thank him, to–to–yes–to kiss him in gratitude, she wasn't certain she would get the words out without losing her composure.

She had slept only a few hours in the truck before sneaking back into the hospital an hour earlier to check on her father. He was still pale, but the technician watching him said that he had rested well and there were no problems.

Lilo took a deep breath to still the rapid race of heart, wiped her damp palms on her rumpled skirt, and began walking toward Bud. With relief she saw a smile spread across his face as he took a half step toward her. Suddenly, he stopped and threw up his arm in a salute.

Lilo saw the doctor round the corner of the tent.

"Morning, Captain, coming to check on your patient? How about lending us a hand? We're a little short today, and I'd like to get these boys to the 42nd as soon as we can."

Lilo saw Bud nod his assent as she tentatively approached them.

"Bud," she was careful to pronounce his name correctly, "I dit not haff de chance to tank you." Before he could respond, a young G.I. with a headset dangling from his neck and waving a sheet of paper in the air raced toward them screaming, "He's dead! He's dead!"

"Whoa, soldier," the doctor stepped in the man's path, "Who's dead?"

The youngster could hardly contain his joy. "Hitler! He killed himself yesterday! That Kraut coward," he added with disgust.

Both Bud and the doctor heard Lilo as she burst into tears. Repulsed, Bud followed the doctor into the tent. The boy took off again, a modern-day town crier heralding the news.

Lilo heard shouts of joy erupt from various groups of men. Hitler was dead. The war would finally end! She clasped her hands together in a thankful prayer. A ray of sun reflected from Peter's ring, and an overwhelming grief enveloped her. The war was over, but he was never coming home. Lilo felt a dam break inside her as she walked toward her truck, trying to get away from the prying eyes staring at her as she sobbed her pain.

She climbed into the driver's seat and pressed her face to the steering wheel. Finally, a brief search yielded one of the linen squares that her father always left littering the inside of the truck. She wiped her eyes and drew in a deep calming breath. Peter was gone. But that devil Hitler was dead, and her Papa was alive. It was something. A loud metallic knocking on the door of

301

the truck startled her.

Bud's angry face materialized before her eyes. "They're bringing your father out," he said brusquely before he turned to walk back toward the tent.

Lilo scrambled after him, "Wait, is he awake? Does he know?"

Bud turned toward her. "Know what?" The scowl on his face hid the expression in his clear blue eyes under thick black brows.

"About Hitler? Does he know?" she beseeched him.

Bud leveled his stare at her and smirked, "I doubt it." He added in a voice loaded with sarcasm, "I think that bit of bad news might be too much for him to take in his shape. *Auf Wiedersehen*, Fräulein," "Good-bye, Miss." He punctuated his last words with a mock straight-armed salute, "and Heil Hitler."

Lilo felt as if he had struck her. Her face reddened as her fury took control of her. She marched past him into the tent and took a deep breath as she approached her father's cot, leaving Bud to follow as the first litters were taken out to the waiting ambulances.

"Papa," she breathed the word lightly in her father's ear and was rewarded with his eyes opening and a responding whisper, "Lilo."

"Papa, Hitler is dead," she smiled at him.

"No!" Her father croaked in disbelief.

"Yes, that filth killed himself," she said vehemently.

Georg tried to sit up and winced as he fell back on the cot.

Lilo wiped the tears of joy from her father's eyes as they

302

both alternately laughed and cried waiting for the next leg of his journey.

Bud tried to stay within earshot of their discussion, but he couldn't understand a word they were saying. He caught the name Hitler, then the old man started crying, and next they were both laughing. They talked too fast for him to make any sense of it, but he had his suspicions, especially with the smirks she flashed his way during the conversation. He approached one of the med techs to help him load a patient on the ambulance. He needed to stay busy until she got out of there. He had so much he wanted to say to her–so much he could never say.

The doctor stopped by Georg's bedside and remarked to Lilo how much her father had improved. To Georg he added, "Speak English?"

Georg answered hoarsely, "Ja, I do. I studied it after the first war."

The doctor could tell his patient was eager to try his skills. "I hope you can understand this," he said roughly. "You owe your life to that man," he nodded to where Bud was loading another litter onto an ambulance.

Georg looked confused, "I don't understand."

"I thought you said you spoke English," the doctor's annoyance was clear in his tone.

"No, I understand your words. I want to understand why I owe my life to him," he gestured weakly toward Bud.

"He gave you his blood when no one else had your type. Do you understand?"

"Does he have time to speak wit me ein moment," Georg asked hesitantly.

The doctor was back in a moment with Bud in tow.

"Captain Leverett, Herr," he strained to read the hastily written medical I.D. badge on Georg's chest.

Georg filled in, "Burkhardt. I am Georg Burkhardt. My daughter tells me I am going to an American hospital. And that doctor says I have you to thank for my life." His feeble hand reached to clasp Bud's as tears filled his eyes. "I thank you, Captain. This is such a wonderful day."

Uncomfortable with Georg's effusiveness, Bud quipped, "I don't know how you can think it's such a wonderful day– you're lying in a hospital and you nearly died."

Lilo giggled as her father gave Bud a wink and wagged a finger at him. "Ja, but I am in an American hospital rather than a German one with no medicines," he laughed before he added darkly, "and that monster Hitler is dead–and from the shameful death that he deserves. I would have hated for him to die in battle like an honorable soldier."

Bud stared in stunned silence. Either the man was a hell of an actor–or Bud was a damn fool.

§ § § § § § §

When Georg was comfortably settled in the ambulance, Bud turned to Lilo and addressed her stiffly. "You can ride with him to the hospital. I checked with the doctor."

"Thank you," she said equally stiffly, "I don't have enough fuel to follow. What will happen to my truck?" She surveyed the camp where the tents were now almost all dropped to the ground with men folding them away. "You won't be staying here, I see."

"Don't worry about the truck. Someone will get it back to you." He pulled out a small notebook and a pencil from his breast pocket of his field jacket. "Address?" When he finished writing it down, he tentatively offered his hand to help her climb into the passenger seat of the ambulance. He closed the door as

304

the driver revved the engine, impatient to be on the road now that the sun was fully up.

"Auf Wiedersehen, Bud, and thank you," she smiled at him.

Despite the filthy dirndl and the dark blue smudges under her violet eyes, Bud was nearly speechless but he managed to clear his throat and offer a smile of his own. "Goodbye, Liselotte, and don't worry about the truck," he added as he moved his arm from the roof of the ambulance, and the vehicle eased away from him.

§ § § § § § §

"Wait!" Lilo grabbed the wheel from the startled ambulance driver. Before the tires stopped rolling, she was out of the truck and running toward Bud. The driver leaned out the window and yelled, "Mach schnell! Hurry up!" The other drivers slowed down to make certain they remained in a convoy. The jeeps behind them carrying their riflemen escorts idled to an impatient stop.

"Bud," she yelled at his retreating back, waving her hand in the air. He turned around and shaded his eyes against the brilliant morning sunshine. She stopped shyly in front of him, "I didn't thank you properly. I'm so sorry–"

He shrugged as he cut her off. "I didn't let you. Sorry this war–"

"Will soon be over," she declared. "You will be happy to go back home to America, ja?"

He nodded and swallowed hard, wishing–wishing something different than what was.

She nodded back to him, her eyes glistening–wishing too, but for the first time, hopeful, for something.

Impulsively, she wrapped her arms around Bud's neck, kissed him on the cheek, and whispered fervently into his ear, "I wish I had time to know you."

The ambulance horn blared impatiently, but she still heard him as she pulled away to race back to the waiting ambulance. Heard him clearly as he whispered back to her, "But you do know me."

THE END

Sequel to *The Reason of Fools*:

A REASON TO FEAR

COMING SEPTEMBER 2013

"When so many hours have been spent in convincing myself that I am right, is there not some reason to fear I may be wrong?"

Jane Austen

The cavernous waiting room was empty. Three U.S. Army clerks chatted amiably waiting for the throngs of people to arrive as they did every day. Corporal Boyle was the first to look their way. His pocked face scowled his recognition before he opened his mouth.

"You again," he stated flatly. His small, hard eyes brushed over her new escort. He smiled derisively. "Found another G.I. sucker, huh? Hope he's more help to you than the last one," he smirked.

Captain Stanley's placid expression belied the quick spark of anger the man's words incited in him. This girl didn't deserve this kind of treatment. Her concern for her crippled father and her poise under the man's attack were impressive.

"Look, Buddy, let's just get this show on the road," he said evenly. "Miss Burkhardt and her father need to get their denazification papers. Why don't you just pull the file and we'll get this done and get out of your hair."

Boyle nodded tersely. There wasn't really anything he

could do, short of ignoring a direct order from an officer. It killed him how so many of his brothers in arms got tied in with these filthy Krauts. If it were up to Boyle, there wouldn't be a Goddamn denazification program. A leopard doesn't change his spots.

"I have the last set of papers you gave me already filled out for you, Corporal, since the last three sets I've completed seem to have disappeared." Lilo handed the sheaf of papers across the wooden countertop. Boyle refused to take them from her, so she laid them on the scuffed dark wood counter and waited for him to pick them up. Instead he glanced down at the name and walked to an enormous gunmetal-gray file cabinet centered on the back of the clerks' work area. After several long minutes, he pulled out a thick file.

"Burkhardt, Georg. That you?"

"My father, yes," she answered, nodding to the stooped old man who sat impassively on the wooden bench beneath one of the many boarded-up windows in the waiting area.

Boyle picked up the documents she'd placed on the counter and compared them to those in the file. "I guess everything looks okay here," he mumbled grudgingly as he continued his perusal of the papers. "Wait a minute." He looked quizzically at Lilo. "Says here your old man was arrested by the SS." He looked back down at the papers in the file. "Locked up and released in a day. How'd you guys swing that?" This was unusual. Boyle had the good grace to appear a bit embarrassed at his treatment of the family. Obviously if the old guy had been arrested by the SS, he wasn't much of a Nazi. The guy was lucky he'd been released. In the short time the Americans had occupied Germany, Boyle had learned enough to know that once you were in the hands of the SS, the chances of coming away from the encounter in one piece were slim to none.

"A family friend helped us," she responded.

"Hmm." Some "friend." This friend had to have some real juice to effect a person's release from SS custody. Something didn't smell right here. If you were the kind of person who got locked up by the SS, then you sure didn't have any friends with the kind of pull that could get you out.

"So who is this family friend?" Boyle's eyes narrowed again and bored into her own with the familiar expression of disdain he customarily wore when dealing with the Germans.

Lilo thought a moment. Sepp Dietrich was in the custody of the Americans. He had surrendered to the American General George Patton near Krems and was being held at the prison camp for generals at Augsberg until the Americans decided what to do with him.

"His name is Sepp Dietrich."

Captain Stanley who had been leaning quietly against the counter snapped to attention. "General Sepp Dietrich?"

"Yes," she answered calmly.

"You know him. You're friends with him?" His rapid-fire questions stunned Lilo with their ferocity.

"Y-yes." She stuttered uncertainly. "He was an old family friend before the war. He helped keep us out of trouble with the authorities," she finished lamely.

"Well, you can just call on him to help you now," the captain fairly spat the words at her before turning on his heel and stalking out of the office. The slam of the door echoed in the room, a fitting exclamation point to Boyle's mocking laughter.

§ § § § § § §

"You okay, C.T.?" Bud whispered the question as his eyes swept worriedly over C.T.'s disheveled appearance. His friend sat glumly on the edge of the lone piece of furniture in the dingy

309

eight-by-eight foot cell. The small iron cot covered only with an inch-thin blue-and-white-striped mattress looked as though it would buckle any moment under the huge man's weight.

C.T.'s only response to the question was to turn his head slowly in the direction of Bud's voice. The single unshaded light bulb dangling about six inches from the water-stained ceiling threw a harsh glare on the upper half of C.T.'s face. The rest was lost in shadow, but even in the half-lit darkness, Bud could see the spiritless slump to his friend's shoulders.

"I'm gonna get you out of here, C.T. Just hold on, Buddy. They didn't give me any trouble when I said I wanted to see you, so I think I can get you out of her in no time."

C.T. gave Bud a lethargic half nod as he turned his face away to stare again at the concrete floor beneath his once shiny boots.

It worried Bud to see C.T. like this–no fight in him. He wouldn't even get up from the cot to walk the two steps toward the iron bars where he could talk to Bud face to face.

"I'll be right back, C.T." No acknowledgement.

As Bud walked out of the cellblock, an armed soldier fell into step beside him. When they reached the main intake room, the guard returned to the cellblock while Bud addressed the two M.P.s who were slurping noisily on their steaming cups of coffee.

"Hey, First Sergeant, I need your help, please." The older of the two soldiers gestured for Bud to take a seat in front of his desk.

"Sure, Captain. Can I get you a cup of joe?" His arm held the insignia of three chevrons, three rockers, and the hollow diamond-shaped lozenge between them that told Bud this guy had been at soldiering a good while and probably knew his stuff.

Bud waved the offer away and explained that he had

come to pick up C.T. The first sergeant leaned back against the torn padding of his metal armchair. "Sorry, Captain. No can do." His voice told Bud that he likely was sorry. "Your man there attacked another soldier. We can't let him go."

Bud snorted out a quick laugh. "Aw, come on, Sarge. If you locked up and then held every G.I. who got into a tussle, you'd have this place filled up in an hour."

The grizzled sergeant nodded his agreement. "Right you are, Captain, but I think you know this is different. Colored soldier working over a white one—I can't do a thing 'til legal gets here. That's serious stuff."

The iron folding chair clanged to the stained concrete floor as Bud leapt from his seat.

"Sergeant," he snapped, "You weren't there. The white man you're talking about was an enlisted man who disobeyed a direct order from an officer." Bud added sternly, "If anyone should be locked up back there, it's him. I don't think I need to remind you, Sergeant, that the last time I checked corporals are supposed to obey orders from captains."

The sergeant had risen to his feet as soon as Bud had launched himself from the chair.

"Yes, sir, I do know that, sir. I didn't earn these stripes by ignoring orders from officers, sir. This isn't about rank, though. This is a Negro man attacking a white one. Don't mean any disrespect, sir, but even you have to admit that's a little different," he added uncomfortably.

"Is it, Sergeant?" Bud snapped at the poor man. "Please explain it to me, would you?" Even as the words left his mouth, Bud felt sorry for the poor guy standing at attention in front of him, his cup of coffee rapidly cooling in the chilly dank air of the room. Bud knew he was pulling rank on the guy, but he didn't care. Grudgingly, Bud had to admire the guy. No wonder he had made first sergeant. It took some guts to stand up to a captain.

311

Bud could see from the set of the man's mouth and his clear-eyed hazel gaze that he was wasting his breath trying to strong-arm him into releasing C.T.

"Sir, meaning no disrespect, but I don't make the regs–I just follow 'em. You take it to someone up the chain and get the okay, and I'll be glad to turn him loose." He leaned forward companionably, "You have my word, Captain." He looked around to where two other M.P.s were straining to appear as though they weren't listening to every word, "I'll keep him on suicide watch, and I'll make sure no one touches him while he's in here."

"Suicide watch?" The words took Bud by surprise.

"Well, yes, sir. We had to take his belt and boot laces from him earlier."

Bud nodded for him to continue.

"He tried to hang himself, sir," the sergeant finished quietly as he looked down sheepishly at his own glossy boots.

What in God's name had happened to C.T.? Bud knew he'd better get to work.

To be continued . . .

Watch for "A Reason to Fear,"

Coming September 2013.

The Reason of Fools is based on a true story. The battles and heroes of the 761st Tank Battalion as well as the origins of the "Double V" campaign are accurate. On January 24, 1978, nearly 33 years after the war ended, President Jimmy Carter awarded the Presidential Unit Citation for Extraordinary Heroism to the 761st. More than fifty years after David Williams recommended Ruben Rivers for the Medal of Honor, finally on January 13, 1997, President Bill Clinton presented the medal to Rivers' sister.

The impact of the Treaty of Versailles on Germany and the descriptions of *Kristallnacht* are well documented. Much of what you've read here about numerous historical figures is easily verified. One of the most prominent figures in this book is General Sepp Dietrich, about whom much has been written. What has not been written and what I have set forth in these pages is the personal relationship of my mother's family with him. I have no physical or corroborative evidence of this connection, but ultimately, what my mother and my grandmother, independent of one another, told me about him, coupled with my research into his life, convinced me of the authenticity of their stories and that their oral histories are worth memorializing.

It is by no means my intent to paint Sepp Dietrich as someone who actively assisted any Jews in escaping Hitler's "Final Solution." I found no evidence to support that, nor did my mother ever intimate in any way that was the case. Furthermore, in the Nuremberg Trials Dietrich was convicted in connection with the massacre of American soldiers at Malmedy, and the German courts convicted him in association with the murders of German SA soldiers in 1934. However, the information that I gleaned from various sources includes the assertion that Dietrich had voiced his displeasure at the laws that prevented Jews from serving as German military officers unless they could prove they had no Jewish blood dating back to 1750. There is also a notation on the website, www.Jewishvirtuallibrary.org, that claims Dietrich personally protested twice to Hitler about the shooting of Jews. Yet, there is no question that he was a member of Hitler's inner circle.

Nevertheless, my mother was very clear that Dietrich was a good friend of the family who wanted her father to take his former position as Hitler's chauffeur and bodyguard and that she did call on him for help when her father was arrested. She said she did not know what he did, but she told me she had no doubt that without his intervention she would not have been able to take her father home. Her primary theme was that she hoped that my brothers and I would never have to watch someone we loved tortured and not be able to utter a word for fear that a wrong word could result in his death.

My grandmother often joked about the period in her husband's life when he and Sepp Dietrich sold holy relics to Bavarian farmers' wives. While I could find no corroboration of this story in my research on Dietrich's life, in *Hitler's Gladiator: The Life and Wars of Panzer Army Commander Sepp Dietrich*, Charles Messenger writes of a short period after the war where records and Dietrich's own words about his employment at that time are unclear. The conflict lends enough credibility to the stories of my mother and grandmother that I felt they, too, were worth putting to paper.

In regard to the "work" of my mother and grandfather during the war, I have no idea how many "trips" they made. My mother described at least two trips. In one, she told me how her father had built a "false back" in the truck where he could hide a few people. Another time, she told me of the mock wine-buying trip. I would love to state that my mother was some great heroine. The fact is that when I once told her how much I admired what she and her father had done during the war, she laughed and told me that there was nothing to admire. She said that during war you "did what you had to do." She added that she and her father did not "look for trouble," but that when occasions presented themselves, there was no option but to help. She believed many people presented with similar opportunities felt compelled to help, too. Since these acts required the utmost secrecy, there is often little evidence of people behaving the way my mother described. I asked her if she knew the names of any of the people she and her father had helped. She said she never knew any of their names and she was so terrified that she only clearly recalled the one little girl I described in this book. I admit that I do nurture a vague hope that this little girl might recognize herself in this story if she and the others survived. The Mueller Boot Company is a product of my imagination.

My mother and grandmother told me the story of Herrn Goldbaum volunteering to walk in front of the German soldiers as a human mine sweep. As I did with each of their stories, I researched, and while I could not find evidence of this single event, there are accounts of the Germans using Jews for this purpose in Russia during World War II.

There are conflicting accounts of the shooting of the German troops at Dachau. Some reports claim that thirty died, while others insist there were more than 500 killed. Because of the disparity in the numbers, I would urge interested readers to conduct their own research.

The excerpts of letters in this book from Peter and the one from Leo are authentic. I found them hidden in a desk after my mother's death. The pictures on the back cover of this book were both with her letters. It seems reasonable to assume that the man standing beside the plane with "Lilo" painted on it is the "Leo" who writes of this same plane in the letter I found.

The scene with Annette is true. I only learned of it when I accidentally walked in on my mother dressing one day and saw scarring on her leg. When she shared the story with me, what struck me most was my mother's contrition. She was so very ashamed of having eaten the sandwich the day Annette died. At that moment, I hurt for her.

Bud and C.T. are characters I invented, mostly from stories my father told of his childhood, including the time he painted himself black. I modeled Bud after my father because he was the son of a Methodist minister and his knowledge of the Bible and his struggles with his faith were apparent to me. He is also the person closest to me who regularly insisted that we are "our brother's keeper." I have vague memories of my father telling me of the heroics of the 761st Tank Battalion, likely inspired by the fact that my father was stationed at Ft. Hood, Texas, the home of the 761st, when I was born.

The interaction with Bud, C.T., Lilo, and her father stems from my imagination. My mother's father died at age 54. She believed his early death was due to injuries he sustained in World War I and from the beating he received in the Türkenkaserne.

Selected Bibliography

The research on this novel began at least a decade before anyone had ever heard of the Internet. As a result, I had the opportunity to read and study many published works on World War II. Below is a short list of those books that I found particularly valuable to my research.

Ambrose, Steven, A. *The Victors*. New York: Simon & Schuster, 2005.

Crocker, Lawrence P. *Army Officer's Guide*. Harrisburg: Stackpole Books, 1996.

Elting, John R., Dan Cragg, and Ernest Deal. *A Dictionary of Soldier Talk*. New York: Scribner, 1984.

Gilbert, Martin. *The Second World War: A Complete History*. New York: Holt Paperbacks, 1989.

Kurowski, Franz. "Dietrich and Manteuffel." In *Hitler's Generals*, edited by Correlli Barnett. New York: Grove Press, 1985.

Messenger, Charles. *Sepp Dietrich: Hitler's Gladiator*. London & New York: Brasseys Publications, 1988.

Read, Anthony. *The Devil's Disciples: Hitler's Inner Circle*. New York: W. W. Norton, 2005.

Sachar, Abram Leon. *A History of the Jews*. New York: Alfred A. Knopf, 1964.

Sasser, Charles W. *Patton's Panthers: The African-American 761st Tank Battalion In World War II*. New York: Gallery Books, 2005.

Shirer, William L. *The Rise and Fall of the Third Reich*. New York & Toronto: Fawcett, 1950.

Young, Peter. *The World Almanac of World War II: The Complete and Comprehensive Documentary of World War II*. New York: World Almanac Education, 1981.

Weigley, Russell F. *History of the United States Army*. New York: Macmillan, 1967.

DODIE CANTRELL-BICKLEY

Dodie Cantrell-Bickley is a self-proclaimed Army brat. Among the various stops at Army posts throughout her childhood was the transfer of her family to France, where her German mother opted to send Cantrell and her two brothers to the French public school rather than the American school on the Army post. As a result, she is conversant in both German and French.

A more profound result of growing up as the daughter of an American World War II veteran and a mother who had spent her youth under the oppressive rule of the Nazis, Cantrell became a passionate First Amendment advocate. Consequently, she spent more than three decades in broadcasting. During her career, she worked as a reporter, news anchor, news producer, and television station president and general manager, garnering numerous awards for her consumer and investigative reporting. After the fall of communism in the former Soviet Union and Eastern Europe, Cantrell-Bickley volunteered to travel to Bulgaria and Macedonia to work with journalists learning how to function in their new environment. She also sponsored and worked with journalists and media managers from Ethiopia, Ghana, Kenya, Nigeria, Peru, Romania, Serbia, Sri Lanka, Uganda, and Ukraine.

Cantrell-Bickley retired from broadcasting in 2012 to complete a manuscript begun some twenty-five years ago–a developing version of *The Reason and Fools*, her first novel. Married to Randy Bickley, Cantrell is a graduate of Mercer University and Georgia College and State University. She and Randy have two daughters and three grandchildren.